MICHAEL ANTHONY was born in Mayaro, Trinidad, in 1930. He attended Mayaro R.C. School and then the Junior Technical School in San Fernando, the second town of the island. He went on to work in an iron foundry at the Pointe-à-Pierre oil refinery. He left Trinidad for England in 1954 with the dream of being a writer. During the time that he was working in factories in London he had several short stories accepted for the BBC programme 'Caribbean Voices'. He published his first novel, *The Games were Coming*, in 1963. Two more novels followed shortly afterwards, *The Year in San Fernando* (1965) and *Green Days by the River* (1967). In 1968 he left England to live in Brazil. He stayed in Brazil only two years, although he considers it the most fascinating country he has ever known. Returning to Trinidad in 1970, he continued his writing career with the works of fiction *Cricket in the Road* (1974), *Streets of Conflict* (1976), *Folktales and Fantasies* (1977), *King of the Masquerade* (1977), *Bright Road to El Dorado* (1981), *All that Glitters* (1982), and *The Chieftain's Carnival* (1993), as well as producing a number of books on the history of Trinidad and Tobago.

Michael Anthony is married and has four children.

MICHAEL ANTHONY

IN THE HEAT
OF THE DAY

Heinemann

Heinemann Educational Publishers
A Division of Heinemann Publishers (Oxford) Ltd
Halley Court, Jordan Hill, Oxford OX2 8EJ

Heinemann: A Division of Reed Publishing (USA) Inc.
361 Hanover Street, Portsmouth, NH 03801-3912, USA

Heinemann Educational Books (Nigeria) Ltd
PMB 5205, Ibadan

Heinemann Educational Botswana Publishers (Pty) Ltd
PO Box 10103, Village Post Office, Gaborone, Botswana

FLORENCE PRAGUE PARIS MADRID
ATHENS MELBOURNE JOHANNESBURG
AUCKLAND SINGAPORE TOKYO
CHICAGO SÃO PAULO

First published by Heinemann Educational Publishers in 1996

British Library Cataloguing in Publication Data
A catalogue record for this book is available from the British Library.

ISBN 0 435 989448

Cover design by Touchpaper
Cover illustration by Jane Human

Phototypeset by
Wilmaset Ltd, Birkenhead, Wirral
Printed and bound in Great Britain by
Cox & Wyman Ltd, Reading, Berkshire

96 97 98 99 8 7 6 5 4 3 2 1

*To little Amber and her mummy, Jennifer;
to Marie Ann and Julien, and their daddy, Keith;
and to Yvette, Carlos and Sandrinia*

The characters and events in this novel are based on the characters and events in the Water Riots, which took place in Port-of-Spain on 23 March 1903.

1

Eva and Clement sat without saying anything to each other. It was Friday evening before the great waterworks debate and they were both thinking of what might happen on Monday. Because the masses in Port-of-Spain were angry and nervous about the waterworks bill. For if the bill was to pass and become law, few of them would be able to pay for the water they normally used. Because meters were going to be put wherever there were taps with running water. The people were almost in open rebellion against Walsh Wrightson, the Director of Public Works.

And yet in a way Eva was glad for the waterworks bill.

The mottled sky outside the window was a dome of light and heavy clouds, with wells of blue spaces between, and to Eva's troubled mind this was just like what life was like. Only that hers did not have that many blue spaces. She had grown very anxious about what was developing, and thanks to Captain Walter Darwent, she had got a vivid picture of what the Englishmen intended to do in respect to Trinidad. Nothing. Yes, this was their plan. Live it up and do nothing – and rule. In other words, although she did not have any children yet, she could safely say that her children, and grandchildren, and even great-grandchildren would see the same sort of Trinidad that she was experiencing now. Strangely, this had not worried her before – she had never thought about it – but since she began working for Darwent, the fire brigade chief, she had become very concerned.

For her uncle, Mzumbo Lazare, had been labouring under a big illusion. As a leader, he believed in grandeur and growth, and change, and he was spreading the message that in time the people of Trinidad would be able to aspire to the highest posts in the land. That an inspector of police, for example, or the police chief himself, or for that matter the very Governor, could be a man born right here in Trinidad. Why not? Wasn't it right? Why did such an official have to be sent from England? In fact, when she thought of it, such a person could be her own son! But the fact was, she

1

told herself, not a damn thing would happen unless it was made to happen. Unless there was action. She looked at the date ticked off on the calendar, Monday, March 16, 1903, and her heart raced a little. She could hardly wait for the debate. She wanted the coming show of anger, and Darwent, for whom she washed, starched and ironed, felt very strongly that the public should not keep quiet. This was a very unusual stance for an Englishman, and a captain on top of that, and she often wondered if his feelings were genuine. But she had seen nothing to cause any doubt.

What it was that started Darwent off, she did not know. Sometimes she liked to think that it was she – because of his feelings towards her – but really she could not be sure. What she was sure of was that Darwent had lit something inside her – something like a fire of caring for this country. Because she knew that now she was seeing the future clearly. There must be change, once people stood up for themselves. It was high time. She knew it would be a struggle but there was hope in the valley. What hurt her most of all was that the labouring classes were living in misery and squalor while some of these foreigners were strutting about like peacocks. Some of them were so arrogant that they treated you like the foreigner in your own land. Thanks to Darwent for opening her eyes.

As she turned her face from the window she suddenly became aware of Clement looking at her. She turned to him but said nothing. He said, 'Whenever we begin talking about this your mood get so bitter. I think things will change, Eva. But we have to push, that's all.'

She maintained her silence. Clement saying things would change was just like saying nothing. Things would never change unless they themselves made them change. But she knew that what Clement really wanted to talk about with her was their own future, about when she would move in with him and settle down, and things like that. But he had only just got to know her and did not realise what fire was raging inside her. There could be no settling down until that first big issue, the waterworks debate. She could not relax until that, at least, was resolved.

She said, 'You think we would succeed in that thing we was talking about? That thing with Uncle?'

'You mean about coaxing him away?'

'Aha.'

'Don't know. Let's see what will happen Monday.'

'I saying this because something have to happen on Monday. Something

2

drastic. Otherwise it will be the same old story, Clem. You'll have the big water debate Monday, but whatever the outcome, in the end the Government will still pass the stupid bill.' She turned round and faced him fully. 'The point is, you'll agree it wouldn't make any difference whatsoever if they pass the bill or not. Maybe these barrackyard people really wasting water and deserve these water meters. I don't know. But for all I'm concerned, and I speaking for me, Eva Carvalho, I saying they could bring them in or they could throw them in the sea – for all I care. But Clem, I mean the real issue – you get what the real issue is?'

'Yes. And I always agree with you on that. It's the principle.'

'This is 1903. They can't get away with the nonsense they getting on with. Things have to change. Apart from principle, this is something to fight those ruffians on.'

She looked at him, expecting him to say something. It was clear that the fire raging inside her was not raging inside him. He stopped a little while and then he said, 'But you know, with all we was saying, I like Mzumbo.'

'Well, Uncle is all right. He know his beans. When it come to this sort of thing he know all the finer points and he could beat them on their own finer points. But Clem, you can't see? Uncle is much too much of a gentleman for these bold-faced bas—' She stopped, then she said, 'For these vagabonds.' She continued, 'Look, when he's giving his speech he is always talking about what is proper for us to do, and what is right, and everything must be constitutional. I say to hell with "constitutional". When this ruling clique doing what they please, and when they please, you think they think about constitutional? Since when it's constitutional to bar people like me and you from places where they live? And that is only one thing. One out of a thousand things. And our own poor people, especially those backward barrackyard people, they don't even know the word "constitutional", let alone how to spell it. And they'll never get educated because Governor Maloney and company don't want that. They prefer to keep them like the damn cattle in the field. You see, Clem, these overlords have to keep us in ignorance in order to rule, you get me point? We mustn't get too wise.'

He watched her and tried to look interested. In spite of the obsession she had, he felt so strongly attracted to her that he did not want to lose her. And at the same time he could not help getting the impression that what she was saying was only right. He said, 'Sometimes I wonder where you get all these ideas from. You really sounding great.'

'But these ideas didn't come from heaven!' She leaned forward to him. 'These ideas there all the time. See what I mean? They say who have eyes to see let them see, that's all. Most of us sufferers don't even have time to see nothing. We have time to mind one another's business, and we busy fighting each other, while the Englishman busy dividing us. The Englishman laughing.'

He looked at her small bony frame. 'Girl, you small but you know you is a power house?'

'Oh please, Clem, I ain't no power house. But this is my country and I have a right to get vexed. I know you ain't feeling like me. You ain't feeling to fight. The other day Edgar Maresse-Smith said: *He that is not with me is against me*. From the Bible or something. I ain't believe it have to be so. Sometimes Edgar's a little rash. But look at this. You met me just about two weeks ago at one of Mzumbo's meetings. And okay, well we like each other, and you hot and sweaty to settle down with me. Okay, you ain't feeling exactly like I feeling, but I know you ain't against me. But if you stop and look at things you may feel worse than me. More bitter. You see, the thing is, Clem, okay, me question: if we get together in a house you'll be content to have children to catch hell and be under these people's boot-heels? No, just tell me. I want you to tell me. You want to have a daughter who will end up in the Englishman's kitchen, or doing like me, washing, starching, and ironing? To hell with that – excuse the language. At least my boss always talking with me like a human being, but our daughter will have to be lucky. Look, Darwent is one in five hundred thousand, if not five hundred million. Although he is big fire brigade chief he ain't too big to talk to me.'

'I would like to know this Darwent.' Clement tried to smile. He was sure the rumours that were flying about were not true. Not Eva. He believed in Eva.

'You'll know him one of these good days.'

'He is the man who giving you these ideas?'

'Not really. I don't talk to him all that much. Only sometimes. But let's face it, he knows what going on is wrong, and he ain't 'fraid to say so although he's one of them. That's why they don't like him and they treating him like a leper. But Captain Darwent is a man for justice. Come on, Clem, let's face it. This is not slavery, this is 1903.'

'You right,' Clement said. He tried to be enthusiastic but he looked a little vacant.

'What's the matter, boy? You looking as if you have something else on you mind. You want to go home now?'

'I really have to go out, I didn't tell you? It must be about six o'clock now. Let me go and look at the sun.'

When he came back in he said, 'It's about half-past six because the sun low low over the gulf. Almost touching the water.' Eva laughed. Clement said, 'No, you laughing but it's true. The sun could tell you the exact time. And it look as if some sort of rain will fall. I don't know, Eva, I suppose it's not the best time to talk to you about anything. Because you ain't with me—'

'But I ain't against you.'

He laughed. Then he said, 'Perhaps after Monday you'll be calmer.'

She laughed again. 'Poor Clement! Clem, you know, apart from this debate business for Monday, boy, you have any idea what sort of relationship I just came out of? I ain't making any excuses but living with a man like that Sergeant Holder is hell. Thomas Holder. Nice name but Holder more evil than Satan. I suppose that's what opened me eyes too, because apart from Holder being a tyrant and a bully, he's such a blasted stooge for these people. You could never know, let me tell you. I don't even want to think about it. But I know you just want to get together with me because you say you in love. Just let's wait just a little little bit – I ain't rejecting you. In fact, I think we'll do well together. I ain't fooling you, I really like you, and I want something good in my life. It's time, because I touching twenty-eight years.'

She looked at him and smiled with tenderness. She seemed a different person. She said, 'You believe me, boy? I really like you. And I know you feel the same.'

'No, I ain't feel the same. You say you really like me, and I saying I really love you. That's not the same thing.'

'Oh God, Clement. Patience. Me mind not at ease. You see with this water bill coming up? I feel like a fish out of water. I'll do anything to see these bleddy people on their knees.'

5

'I know, but you think we could win the battle now for now? You think we could change Trinidad in one day?'

'No, but we have to start doing something, else we'll never change a damn thing. And these parasites will live happily ever after. Look, let me tell you this: I know in my lifetime my son or nephew or niece or me friend son won't be running Trinidad. But he has to be far better off than me and going forward. Mzumbo was saying in the meeting the other night how in England people could vote. They could vote for who they want to put to run England. And you know what Uncle Mzumbo is? He ain't talking through his bowler hat, like Colonel Brake like to say. I mean, you know Uncle was in England in 1897, the Diamond Jubilee, and oh God, Queen Victoria admired this man. She said, "Please, officer, what is your name? What part of the Empire have you come from?" And these fellers here can't stand it. They don't even like to see him in his bowler hat, because they think he playing Englishman. They still hate him, those jealous bastards. Rooks went to England too, you know, leading this hoi-polloi contingent – planters and merchants or what you call it. Elite. And Queen Victoria didn't so much as spit on them. Oh Lord, that hurt them. But we talking about voting now. The ordinary people voting in England, mind you, and here these devils don't want to give us the vote. Yes, we want it, and we have to get it.' She thumped the table. 'We want it and by Christ we don't have to wait a thousand years.'

She looked up at him, 'To make it short, Clem, I blasted fed up. That's why I want to see a big turn-out for the debate.'

She paused a little, and there was silence. She said calmly, 'To come back to you, big-boy. Mzumbo Lazare is always talking about patience. Sometimes patience is good, sometimes it's bad. I think if you have patience with me it's a good thing. Because I like you, but I can't really focus on you now. This debate's on me mind.'

She looked at him softly but her face hardened again. 'You see, these people so arrogant, you know, wrong and strong, and I think we must show them something. At least we could show them who born here. Mzumbo Lazare won't agree with me. No. You think me uncle will agree with me? Never. He's too much of a gentleman. Clem, I know I have you confused. Just have a little patience with me, me boy. I really like you so much, and I could learn to love you. You see me point?'

He said, 'Sometimes you say such nice things.' He paused. Then he got

6

up from the chair. He said, 'Anyway, Eva, I think I have to go now. Look at the dusk outside. Time to light up, girl. See you. I have to meet somebody from San Juan.' He moved towards the door.

'A lovely girl? Tell me. A little sweetie?' Eva teased.

'I have only one little sweetie.'

'Oh yes? Where she is, boy? Where she living?'

'I suppose you know the place. Right in this house.'

Eva laughed, but at the same time she felt suddenly relieved. Because for a moment she had thought there was really somebody else. She looked at him now. 'Oh yes? In this house? I never knew that.' She got up and held his hand, and said seriously, 'Look, big-boy. Let's see this debate through. Okay? I don't know what will happen, but we can't let them ride roughshod over us. Monday, what we want to see is hundreds of people in the public gallery. The public gallery in the chamber. The Ratepayers' Association looking after this, and we have one of the best speakers in the Legislative Council. That's Henry.'

Clement turned around, enthusiastic. 'You talking about good stuff, girl. They can't match Henry Alcazar. Henry? They can't touch him, although Edgar could sway a lot of people.'

'But Edgar isn't in the Legislative Council. I talking now about the Legislative Council. Because we fighting on two fronts, like in that war what finished last year. The Boer War. We fighting on two fronts: one side to press the Government, and the other side to rouse up the people. And by Christ we'll have to rouse up the people because I know the Government wouldn't budge one damn inch – excuse me language. So that's a waste of time. So you right, Edgar Maresse-Smith is more important to this cause because he could get the masses together. I shouldn't say the masses, I should say the mob, like Colonel Brake and those English people always calling us.'

She laughed ironically. 'We'll show them mob! I have to move with people like Lolotte Borde, the sweetbread lady. You know Lolotte Borde, the lady who selling sweetbread and paymie and pone under Harriman Store? That fat lady who made three months for throwing stones and—'

'But who don't know Lolotte Borde?' he interrupted.

'Right. I have to get in league with Lolotte. But okay, big-boy, we'll be making it together soon. By the grace of God. Just have a little patience with me, I'm just a little confused. Let's see the debate through. Okay? I

7

don't know what will happen Monday. But I'll tell you, if we have a big crowd in the public gallery and making noise, that bound to frighten them. They have to know we ain't 'fraid. This will be the first time in history the public taking an active part in the Gov—'

'But the part they taking is only in making noise, Eva!'

'This is the only thing we could do for now. The ruffians have the guns, you can't see?'

She had sat down again but she got up at this point. He was looking outside and as he was talking he was observing how the dusk was falling fast. Eva had lit the lamp and almost all the dwellings around already had their lamps lit. He turned to her and put his hand under her chin. He said, 'I have to go now. If I have patience with you, you will have patience with me too?'

'But of course – how you mean! I like you so much. I want to go round with you.'

'And I love you. And I don't only want to go round with you, I want to live in a house with you.'

She smiled. He squeezed her hand and left.

2

The bell rang three times, each time sharp and short, and Darwent hurried downstairs. As he was going he looked at the clock: 6.40 p.m. It was not quite dark but the gloom was heavy, and there were lights everywhere. He came right under the house beside the store-room. He had closed back the upstairs door to the stairway so that if he heard the door open he would know his wife was coming. When he saw the figure beside him he said, 'I was looking out for you earlier.'

'I couldn't come. Somebody was home and I couldn't. I just came to bring the clothes and I can't stay. You gave me the money already.'

'You could never stay.'

'Captain Walter Darwent, you know what Monday is? I don't want to argue with you. I just want to thank you for all the encouragement you give me. I don't know what will happen on Monday.'

'What do you expect will happen?'

'Don't know.'

'Well I can tell you. Nothing at all will happen. You don't know us,' he laughed. 'You don't know us Englishmen.'

'So, Captain Walter Darwent, you agree something drastic have to happen? To make them see the light?'

He did not answer for a little while. Then he said, 'You always put me in a funny position. I don't want to talk of anarchy and insurrection. You get that?'

'What is anarchy?'

'And the next thing you'll ask me is what is insurrection.'

She just looked at him. All the while he was talking to her he was listening to hear where the footsteps upstairs were going, and when he wasn't hearing the footsteps he listened even more intently. At the moment he knew from the sound of the footsteps that his wife was in the kitchen. He said, 'Eva, let's put it this way. What we the British are doing, and I'm British – I mean English – let's face it, what we—'

9

She put up her hand. 'They don't even regard you as English.'

'Oh yes, they do. They don't regard me as having been born in England because I wasn't born in England.'

'And so what? What's that?'

'*You* ask them. I would like to know what is the answer. But I know it's important to them.'

'So that's why they treat you so awful? Eh? That's why they treat you so off-hand?'

'Let's face it, I treat them off-hand too. I told them frankly what I felt about this whole water business. That it's wrong. And why have one law for the bigwigs and one law for the black masses. It was from then on they began treating me as if I have the plague – I've told you all this already. But I won't compromise my principle. Now don't ask me what is "compromise", please. Or what is "principle".'

She smiled in the gloom. She said, 'I happen to know that. Captain Walter Darwent, you very well know that my uncle is Mzumbo Lazare. And you know that all these Englishmen in Trinidad, it could be the Rooks, it could be the Brakes, it could be the Maloneys. When it comes to the English language, well, you know what Queen Victoria said about me uncle?'

'I heard it a thousand times.'

'Anyway, I can't stay long. You was saying—'

'Okay, I'll be brief. These are the clothes here? Right. Thank you. Don't expect too much change coming from that debate. The debate is just a formality. They will give that bill the third reading and pass it, but that might not happen this coming Monday. But the real change we were talking about, to give the people an opportunity to vote. Mzumbo Lazare and Maresse-Smith are good on that subject. I have heard them. Very, very good. But two things: they are not in the Legislative Council, and even if they were, it would make not a scrap of difference. Because the nominateds and official members are the Governor's voice. It's as plain as that. But on the other hand, I don't want to tell you the masses should riot and destroy. But do you know something? It is the only thing to frighten these people. Both the Government here and the Colonial Office in London. It is the only thing to shake them from their complacency and bring change. But how do I feel saying go out and riot! And then what will happen is, lives will be lost. And it could be lots of lives. Do you think I want you to get killed? Look at you, a lovely lit—'

'Captain Walter Darwent!'

'People say I criticised Wrightson and condemned the waterworks bill just because of you.'

'I know that. But that isn't true. It's true?'

'Life is strange. I suppose there is a connection. From the time I was small I liked fair play. We the English people here have never been fair to you—' He stopped.

'To you natives. I could finish it for you.'

'You object to the word "natives"? I am a native. I was born here.'

Eva didn't say anything. She did not want to argue. She was beginning to feel it was time she should be going.

Darwent said, 'We have not been fair.'

'And you ain't think I know that?'

'Well, I told them frankly what I thought about the waterworks bill. They had been discussing it since about 1900. Mzumbo was all hot under the collar about it. Do you know it was by accident I found out last Christmas, you know when I asked Mzumbo about a washerwoman and he said he had a niece—'

'Captain Walter, sorry to interrupt you. But I always feel so terrible to hear this. Me own uncle. He recommend me to wash, starch and iron for you. You think I could feel proud about that? Me uncle is a councillor, a member of the Board of Health, a man who led a contingent to England in 1897. For the Jubilee. You think I proud to do this washerwoman work? This work is menial work, but I can't do nothing else. But I feel shame because it's menial work, but I can't do nothing else and I glad I have the job. It sound silly, ain't it, what I'm trying to say. I happy I have the job, but here is me own uncle, fighting to give we black people a chance, fighting to give us dignity so we wouldn't do menial work, yet recommending his niece to do the same menial work he is condemning. I know I sound confused but you know what I mean.'

He wasn't hearing footsteps at all now. But he had not heard the upstairs door open either so he knew it was all right.

'Eva, I know what you mean. You think I like to see you doing menial work? You think I like you to do this sort of work for me? The whole question here is education. Education of the masses. I talked with Mzumbo

11

about this one day. Frankly, we the English don't want to educate colonials. Because it's not in our interest – by that I mean it's not in *their* interest, the British. I know I'm sounding a little confused too. We don't want to educate colonials. Keep them daft, and there it is. Easier to rule. Tell them about Victoria, how victorious, and they are proud. They don't want to rule themselves. The fact that Victoria died, when? The fact that she died something like two years ago, yes, January 1901. Yes. The fact that Victoria kicked the bucket two years ago wouldn't make any difference. I can't keep talking to you down here because you know, upstairs, she'll come down. I've always told you, Eva, that I like you. But you never believed me.'

She said softly but bitingly, 'Look, it's not a matter of not believing you, but you could live with me in Trinidad? Your people will kill you.'

'One has to sacrifice something, Eva. People have to risk something.'

'Sacrifice your life? Then what is the point! I don't want a dead man.'

He himself had to laugh. Then he said, 'That's a great point there. But we are two human beings. We can't give in to the world. And even if they – no, I wouldn't use the word "ostracise" to you because you wouldn't know what that means. But even if they shun me. Why, they're shunning me already.'

She said nothing. She was a little upset because she felt sorry for him.

He said, 'The debate itself, law and order, pomp and ceremony, all those things will change nothing. The reality is there. You'll continue to be good colonials. My God, the other day for the coronation the schoolchildren were singing "Land of Hope and Glory, Mother of the Free". Well, then, if it is like this what more do you want? You probably think I'm mad.'

'To be honest, Captain Walter, I think you is a good man.' She was thinking a lot of things which she couldn't tell him. Then she said, 'People so wicked. I ain't saying this for me, but to think one could ostracise somebody—'

He interrupted her, 'You know that word?'

'No. I ain't know "shun" either. I ain't nothing to Mzumbo Lazare. Look, Captain Walter, I'll go now. To free you, and for you to free me. I have to go and pray and think about Monday. When I said I couldn't come earlier, it was because me boyfriend was there.'

His face changed.

She noticed it and she said, 'He so love me. You know what he said? He said he want to live in a house with me.'

12

'Well, why don't you go and live with him?'

'I might go. After the debate when me head clear, who knows, I might do that. So what? The man love me. I asked him to have patience.'

'Well, go and live with him. You didn't have enough of Sergeant Holder, go with this one.'

'Every man is like Holder? This feller is very nice and very gentle. You know how often he reminds me of you?'

He looked at her. He was jealous but he felt good.

She said, 'I happen to mention this voting question, and he want to know if it's you who giving me those ideas. I didn't want to talk about you too much. You know what men give.'

Darwent didn't say anything.

'I happen to say – now don't come near to me, Captain, but I happen to say you is one in a million.'

'Me?'

'Well, okay. It's my mistake. Anybody could make a mistake. Captain Walter Darwent, I'm going. So much policemen about, but it getting dark. They'll hardly make me out. I hope I don't bounce up with me ex. You know what I talking about? By the way, your wife was born here or in England?'

'In England.'

'And now you want a Trinidadian wife – not wife, woman.'

'Eva, I don't want any and every Trinidadian wife. I told you several times I just want you.'

'But Captain Walter. Okay, forget my case, but let's say you wanted to marry another woman. What would you do with *her*?' She gestured with her chin, indicating upstairs.

'I honestly don't know. But I'm ready to send her to England on a holiday.'

'But they saying so already. They saying she in England. Look, Captain Walter, you think you smart but you ain't smart enough. Right now inside me is the debate. I just want you to be with us in spirit. Thank you for all your good feelings, Captain. I'll walk out through that pathway. Captain, I gone.'

As she said that, she walked out of the yard to get into Abercromby Street.

3

No sooner had Eva arrived home and opened the door than she decided she had to go back out again. In fact, in walking up Richmond Street to her home she had made about three attempts to turn back, but somehow she did not want to go to Clement's place. But eventually she came to the decision to go. She told herself she just had to go. This was already Friday night and if she wanted action by next week Monday, she would have to move right now.

She locked her door again and was out in the street. Instead of walking down Richmond Street she walked due east along Duke Street, heading for Belmont. It was the first time she was going to Clement's home and she hated it. Because his family did not like her very much. Clement was much younger than she was, and they had wanted him to get a young girl not an experienced woman. Not only that but they knew her and knew she had been living with Holder, and – apart from the fact that they hated Holder, and so hated her – they were fearful Holder would kill Clement in cold blood for going around with her.

She decided that when she got to 17 Chenette Alley she would not go in but call Clement outside. She did not know if that would work but she would try it. She wished she did not have to see him tonight but she had to. She hoped he was in.

◆

It was so dark in Chenette Alley that Eva could hardly see the numbers on the houses, but having found number 1, which was not too far from the lamplight in Oxford Street, she stumbled her way to number 17. And fortunately Clement was home.

When she called and he hurried down she said, 'Sorry I had to come but it's something serious.'

'Like what? Trouble?'

'Look, no and yes. We'll be only wasting time to bother about that debate—'

'Come in. Let's talk in the gallery.'

'I don't want to. You know that. I'll talk for five minutes only.'

'I could come to your place tomorrow morning.'

'That's too late. If we have to do anything is now, if possible.'

'What it is? What happen?'

'I went to take clothes for Darwent. He said nothing will change with the debate. In other words we can't win. He said something about nominated officials and their voice is the Governor's voice and if they read the bill three times they could pass it.'

'But you didn't know that before? Oh cracky, Mzumbo saying that all the time.'

'This is the first time it really sink in. Because if they could pass the bill when they want this is a bleddy waste of time. Darwent said what I always tell you. This "constitutional means" that Mzumbo always talking about will never do anything. You know what we have to do? To hell with me uncle. We'll have to make them see the light.'

'How?'

'We'll have to do something drastic. I have something in mind but I can't talk yet. Not even to you. But that will make them see the light in a real real way. But what I want you to do, Clem. What I want you to do for me. And do it quick, quick, because Darwent said they wouldn't be able to pass the bill next Monday because they have to read it three times.'

'But you don't listen to your uncle? You know how often Mzumbo saying that?'

'Yes, but one day Edgar said they could just read it three times one after the other and pass it. Anyway, Clem, you know what we have to do? My uncle stands for law and order but I know we'll get no place unless we make a big bacchanal and show these people something. As you know, I couldn't care less about the water bill itself, but we have to frighten them. You know what I was thinking when I was walking back home from the fire brigade station? I was thinking of the same old thing we mentioned. This thing about getting Uncle to—'

'You mean the same old thing *you* mentioned,' he interrupted, 'not *we* mentioned.' He said this in a half-jovial sort of way.

'You know what I talking about?'

'Yes. Trying to get Mzumbo Lazare to Mayaro.'

'Well, I thought when I mentioned it you was in full agreement.'

He put his hand on her shoulder. 'I was and I am.' Secretly, he did not wish anything like intrigue, but he also did not wish to offend her.

She said, 'Uncle's best friend is in Mayaro – I already told you about Dick, Robert Alexander Dick. It ain't have nobody Dick like and admire more than Mzumbo. And I don't know if I mentioned Ivy. That's Dick's wife.'

'You more than mentioned Ivy.'

Eva laughed. She said, 'I talk too damn much. I was so glad when Dick got transferred to Mayaro, because something was bound to happen, and Dick was bound to find out. Goodness me, those two, Mzumbo and Ivy! Anyway, I hear Mayaro is a nice quiet place, with sea, and fish, and coconut water, and chip-chip, and peace. What more Uncle want? Clem, if Monday pass and not much happen, and when I say not much, I mean not much of a muchness. If nothing happen Monday, I want you to go up to Mayaro for me. And I'll tell you what to do to get the Dicks to press him to come down. For a little rest. Because Uncle wouldn't go just like that. Not with the debate pending.' She paused. After a brief silence, she said, 'So I could depend on you to go to Mayaro? This is really why I come here. I want to know.'

'Yes, of course. Yes.' Clement said.

'Okay, that's great. I feel relieved now. I could sleep tonight. You see, sweet-boy, if Mzumbo stay in Port-of-Spain nothing will happen and in the next reading they'll pass the bill. Nothing will happen because Mzumbo want everything to be nice and legal. And even though he's saying we must make noise on Monday, he still don't want too much noise. Mzumbo is a gentleman but as I always say, he's too bloody gentlemanly for those Englishmen. That's why they love him. You see how so much of them went to his New Year's Eve ball? Rooks, who called him agitator, he was most present. You see, they know he is a fighter for rights but decent, in bowler hat, a man who could only deal in law and order. Now tell me, how could you fight in a bowler hat! And waistcoat to boot. You can't even bend, let alone fight. But they want to keep him just like that. Bark but don't bite. Make a lot of noise but no action. Big-boy, I only wanted to know that you prepared to go to Mayaro for me. That is all.'

He tried to be enthusiastic because the longer she stood there it was the more he felt he wanted her and no one else. But he also sensed that this was crucial not only to her but to the future she wanted. For although he did not want chaos he realised that law and order and 'constitutional means' was not really going to produce anything, and maybe in doing this for her he would be helping to bring about a new day. But the main thing for him was not so much the new day but the new life for him and Eva in a house. If he could bring off this feat, get Mzumbo to Mayaro for the second debate, his future was assured. He began feeling a little excited. He turned to her.

'Well, if I have to go up to Mayaro you'll tell me what you want me to do.'

'Now? You want me to tell you now? You don't want to wait to see what will happen Monday?'

'I was thinking about the coastal steamer. We don't know how they sailing. With me, I could always beat up my way to Mayaro any how. I could get the train to Sangre Grande and hop any old cart to Mayaro, though that is umpteen miles. I don't mind. I could sleep on the way, I could get wet. But if Mzumbo have to go to Mayaro he'll have to sail. We have to find out how the steamers moving and we really have to be busy busy.'

Yes. That was true. That was a point. The question of how the steamers were sailing was very important. It was crucial to find that out and quick. And on the other hand it was almost certain that nothing substantial was going to happen on Monday. She was wondering how to move. She wanted a little time to think about it. She said, 'Sugar-plum, tomorrow is Saturday. I could see you early? Around 8 o'clock? Yes? Okay. Then let me sleep tonight and think about it and work things out, and when I see you tomorrow I'll know what we doing.'

◆

When Eva heard the early-morning knock and opened the door she cried, 'What is this? Big-boy, you more hurry than me! So when you want to go to Mayaro?'

'I want to leave now. But me mind telling me wait till Monday, in case anything happen to you.'

'Oh my darling, you so sweet. Nothing will happen to me.'

17

'Nobody knows. I ain't sure what to do. I passed to see how the coastal steamer sailing and it ain't have nothing until Wednesday. But I could go to Sangre Grande by train and chance me luck. They might have some cart or buggy going Mayaro.'

'And the next steamer going to Mayaro is when? I thinking of Mzumbo now.'

'Could be Wednesday. They ain't fix that up yet. Look outside. Rain drizzling. Look over there over the gulf. The horizon white with mist.'

She smiled.

He looked at her and said, 'You believe it's a sign?'

'Yes. It's a sign that rain falling. And it's a sign that we have to move fast. You going to Mayaro today or you waiting?'

He looked at her, trying to make up his mind.

She said, 'I really want you to do it. In any case we'll have to move quick. Clem, you realise something? This whole island depending on what we doing now. I sure, sure. What you about to do for me, Clem, you about to do for your own self. And you doing it for everybody who born here. Every native. And we might be dead and gone when you'll find the ordinary Trinidadian could stand up and say, yes, this is my country, I is boss here. You ain't excited?'

Her blood was pumping fast. 'Because I telling you now that what I thinking of will frighten them, and they'll see the light. In the true sense of the word. And then Mzumbo himself, and Edgar, and Henry Alcazar, they will take things forward. They will take things from there. This is for your children and mine, big-boy, and if you succeed at all, whether you go to Mayaro now or you stay till Monday, if you succeed, Sweetie, your children and mine will be the same children, if you see what I mean!'

She looked at him with smiling eyes. His heart thumped. He was truly excited.

'When you want me to go to Mayaro?'

'I want you to go to Mayaro tomorrow, but tomorrow ain't have no steamer.'

'Don't bother about steamer. I'll reach there. It have train to Sangre Grande, and I'll have to catch some cart or something but I'll get to Mayaro.'

'Great, Clem. You talking like a hero. Tonight I'll think out exact details of what I want you to tell them. And tomorrow morning I could meet you by the railway station on South Quay. What time you leaving tomorrow?'

'It have a 6.05 train to Sangre Grande. I could take that.'

She paused. She said, 'Clement, I'm a little confused. I feel as if we rushing it. I feel I want a little more chance to see if I can't make Uncle go on his own. I really like your keenness but let me see just one little time more if I can't bring this off. And I'll tell you tomorrow. Okay?'

4

Although the valley of Diego Martin was bathed with early morning sunshine, as it grew to mid-morning dark grey clouds floated over it. Mzumbo leaned over the banister at Lazdale and began getting a little anxious. He looked over to Crystal Stream Estate, which seemed to occupy much of the low ground in the distance, then his gaze shifted to the northwards where the blue skies over Diamond Estate had turned to black.

He was feeling a little depressed. These days everything seemed to be working against him. He was anxious to hold his lawyers' meeting this morning in preparation for the council debate on Monday, but now with the skies overcast it might soon rain, and in that case nobody would be able to come to Lazdale for the meeting. He stood up there, shifting from one foot to the other, until he heard a voice behind him: 'What happen, Manuel, why you so uneasy?'

Without turning round he said, 'Just look at that sky. This morning you yourself was saying what a nice day. You see what's happening now?'

It was only as he spoke that she remembered the meeting. He had talked about this at length yesterday but she never bothered too much. Because she knew that Manuel would never be easy and contented. The more influence he had it was the more he was striving. He had a wonderful little estate right there around Lazdale, and he had a flourishing legal practice. But no, that was not enough. He had to be in the centre of the storm. He was now making a big issue about Wrightson and the waterworks bill, and all his so-called friends were egging him on. All in the name of what he called 'Government by the People'. She just stood up beside him and said, 'Well, I said it was a nice day, but I ain't in charge of the weather. So if the weather change, don't blame me.'

He turned around and said testily, 'Am I blaming you? Marie, you see how you want to irritate me this morning?'

'Me? You on edge because it looking like rain and you want to take it out on me. Look, I didn't fix your meeting for this morning you know!

20

You getting all worked up but take it out on Mr Walsh Wrightson, not on me.'

He was so vexed he did not even trust himself to speak. That was all she could say: take it out on Walsh Wrightson. She didn't understand a damn thing. Marie was always like that. To her democracy meant nothing. She just looked on the waterworks bill as a joke, and on the Ratepayers' Association as a joke. It was only when Jerningham abolished the Borough Council she was different. As a rule it was no use his having any serious talk with Mammie Marie. It was a complete waste of effort to try to explain to her that without agitation people like herself and him would be relegated to second-class citizens for ever. It was no use even trying to have a discussion with her on anything like voting. On this she was a complete idiot. Even little Hilda was more aware of what was happening than she. As Hilda passed through his mind he turned around and said, 'Oh, I nearly forgot. I can't take Hilda to music lessons this morning, eh?'

'Of course you can't take her to music lessons. Because you have your friends coming and you have your big meeting?'

'Marie, please! Oh God. Don't spoil me Saturday morning. You know what Monday is? Okay, you don't care to know, but you have to realise that the fate of this country is at stake. Please try to understand. Even Ivy Dick said this is a just cause. You think this situation is so simple? You think water is all we have in mind?'

'Ivy will say anything to make you feel nice. Ivy will never tell you that you wrong. Just cause, my foot! Work out your soul-case for the rabble! They could run any country? Good, chase out the English and put those fellers from the barrackyards in the Legislative Council. Mannie, you'll never understand until you bring yourself to ruin. Look at what you have. You have this big house, Lazdale, you have all these green acres round it, all these fruit trees, you are a solicitor, you are this, you are that. You are on this board, you are on that board. All that come through hard work. Now you want to throw it away with this nonsense about democracy, and "Government by the People". You too damn happy!'

Mzumbo ground his teeth but did not say anything.

She said, 'For instance, that report in the *Port-of-Spain Gazette* about the meeting last Saturday on the Savannah. How the crowd cheered when you called the Legislative Council "this pernicious system, this diabolical plot by the Secretary of State". How come the system suddenly get so pernicious? This is not the same system where you got all you have? You are one of the few black men in Trinidad to make the grade. They all respect you. Even Governor Maloney was at your New Year's Eve ball. And by the way I notice you didn't invite your stone-throwing friends. Your jailbird friends. Hold, wait, let me finish this. Don't flare up yet.'

He had turned to her, bristling. She continued, 'Spare me this because if you insult me I'll leave your house today. I just want to remind you that what made you achieve what you achieve is hard work and seriousness, and now all those good-for-nothing idlers want to break you down. But you can't see that.'

He changed his mind about flaring up because firstly he had lived with her too long to part now, or to have any scandal whatsoever – he could not cope with that; and secondly, there was a grain of truth in a lot of the things she was saying. For example, if he was just starting out, he would not have been able to give so much of his time to the pursuit of democracy. Never. For he would not have been able to have a roof over his head. Also, he knew that most of his support, which came from the barrackyards and from the shanty towns of Port-of-Spain, were composed of thieves and cut-throats, prostitutes and paid killers. He knew that. But there were a number of poor honest people who were crying out under the yoke of the system. And there was more against them than the mere system. He did not know how in the name of heaven he had made it and was so respected. For these overlords did not favour black people. He had vowed to fight to give black people a place in the sun.

He listened her out and then he said, 'If my people want help and are crying out, I mustn't help? It's people like me to help; people like me who are in a little better position. We have to try to give them a place in the sun.'

'Yes, try and give them a place in the hot sun, where they could do some labour for a change. They deserve a place in the sun. The hotter the sun the better.'

He turned to her with shock. 'Marie, how could you be so waspish, and wicked and unfeeling! Anyway, with all you say I will never turn my back on them.'

She smiled derisively, 'No, don't turn your back on them. Fight for them. Even spend money on them. When they break the law defend them for nothing, like Edgar. Back the mob with your last penny. But I'll tell you something, when in a few years' time you ain't have nothing, you see that big barrackyard in St Vincent Street where most of those vagabonds and troublemakers live? That Jablotin? Go and get a room there. But I telling you, you going alone. I ain't going with you, you know. Long before you ready to go there, I'm gone.'

He didn't feel that he could explain to Marie that whatever happened he could not stop; that he had set off on a mission and there was no turning back. It was either you were a warrior in the field or you were not. History was there to show. Nothing succeeded unless there were men and women prepared to go out and fight and sacrifice. Of course Marie did not believe that Representative Government, or Government by the People, was worth fighting for. That much was clear, and here was where they differed fundamentally. Even the people who were with him did not know the significance of democracy or representative government. That was why he had to seize the opportunity to fight the Government over the waterworks bill and had to keep on talking about water. And all the poor and ordinary people had rallied to him because they needed water every day. The authorities had made two bad moves and they would be sorry for them. Sooner or later they would be made to pay. He would make them pay dearly for abolishing the Borough Council in 1899, and he would make them pay equally dearly for having drafted a waterworks bill.

She was looking at him as he stared across the wide valley, his eyes no doubt seeing nothing. She knew he was thinking hard and she knew she had upset him. It would be so good if she had made him see the folly of what he was doing. As her eyes followed his across the valley she could not help comparing the view now with what it had been like when they had just got married and had come here to build this house. That was in 1892. At that time, looking over to Diamond Estate, and further to the north to River Estate, one couldn't see anything but trees and labourers' barracks. Now the scene was so different. Dotted across the valley were labourers' villages. Even here where they were, in the centre of a beautiful green expanse, with fruit trees, cocoa, coffee and sugar-cane, even here was at that time abandoned highwoods. And Mzumbo had rolled up his sleeves and had said: 'Mammie Marie, I have plenty work.' And it was like this now, all because of Mzumbo. That was why she would never leave him. She would warn him and even threaten him, but she would never walk out. Walk out to go where, anyway? And would he suffer? She well knew he would be snapped up very easily. Even Ivy, yes Ivy, her good friend, Ivy would snap him up without blinking. Whether he would go to Ivy, she was not sure, but she was sure, the way Ivy liked him, that she would throw herself on him body and soul. She watched Mzumbo still looking across the valley, then she turned her head to look at their vast herd of cattle grazing on the southern side of the hill. There were more than a hundred head of cattle and oxen and she was grateful for the way he had built himself up, and fearful lest he should throw it all away now by his present madness.

She got a little worked up, for it was easy just to look around her and see what a great job Mzumbo had done. And he was ingenious with his hands, too. She thought, 'Look how he brought down water from the top of that mountain behind us right down to the house in pipes!' This was ironic because that was what he was now beating up himself about – water. Simply because Walsh Wrightson was about to put the brake on those water-wasters, he was going crazy. He, Mzumbo, had running water in his house, and he didn't have to pay a penny in water-rates – unless he had to pay it to the green hills – yet he was worried about Walsh Wrightson's waterworks bill.

She looked at him and softened a little. She left where she was and came up behind him. He did not seem to notice. She said, 'Manuel?' He did not answer. She laughed. She said, 'Mr Emmanuel Mzumbo Lazare.'

'Marie, leave me alone, eh!' he said. Then he turned round. 'You want to tell me poor people suffering for water and this whole thing ain't mean a damn thing to you – thing to cry and you laughing?'

'Thing to cry? Oh no, Mr Emmanuel. Wrightson drafted the bill because he said too much water was wasting. It's not true? The ladies and gentlemen of the barrackyards don't leave the taps open night and day? The water inspectors telling lies on them? I don't have to be there to see, but I have me opinion, because I know these ladies and gentle—'

'Go on, laugh at them.'

'I ain't laughing at them. In fact it is they who laughing at me. And more so at you. Because you have what you have by the sweat of your brow. You burn you eye with pitch-oil lamp smoke to wrestle with books and become a solicitor. You study agriculture, and the sciences of politics and government. Good heavens, Mannie, the other day you talked about Lolotte Borde and Greasy Pole at your meeting as if *they* were the distinguished figures, and not you and Edgar. Those people care about things like self-rule and democracy? To me the key syllable in their kind of democracy is *mock*.'

'Yes, mock them. At least they care about water.'

'Yes, because that is one thing they have to use every day, and in fact they just damn well wasting it.'

He looked at her, shocked. 'So you for Wrightson and against me? You for the Government?'

'I ain't for Wrightson, and I ain't for the Government, and honest to God I won't say anything like this when your friends come here. Especially Edgar, because he is more of a fanatic than you. But Manuel, let's face it. Our poor people here is just a waste of time. They don't care about anybody. When you talk and they go wild, you think it's because they love you so much? It's because you giving the Government hell – that's why. They make a big thing about you because they like the bacchanal. You think they really care about you?'

He just stared at her without saying anything.

'I'm just telling you the truth. It's just you and I alone here and Hilda in the back. She is a child, she doesn't understand nothing. Sorry to say it but what the people like is Carnival and bacchanal. And blaming the Government for everything. You remember last Carnival? It was just last month, February 23rd and 24th. You was the one who told me you weren't taking Hilda because you didn't want her to see the vulgarity. And who making the vulgarity? It's the people you spending so much time on. You own business suffering because of this famous debate. Just you wait and see what they want. Wait and see if it's liberty they want or democracy, or if it's not just chaos and ... and catastrophe.'

Mzumbo had turned to look eastward to see if any carriages were coming, but now he turned back and just looked at her and shook his head.

She said, 'Okay. Just wait. You'll find out.'

He retorted: 'That's what you want but we'll make you think again. That's what they say all the time – Brake, Rooks, all of them. And they never say "crowd". Their word is "mob". That's what they waiting for – to see us bite the dust. But I am a soldier, Mammie Marie. You know that. I am Captain of the Light Horse. You, my wife, will associate me with chaos and disorder?'

'Me? I never said that. You could never be chaotic even if you try. And if you were that way you wouldn't find me here. I wasn't talking about you, I was talking about your ladies and gentlemen of the barrackyards. I suppose you seeing them as just ready for Sunday school.'

He laughed for the first time that morning. Then he looked up at the sky again. It was slate grey now and the sun was completely shut out. His face hung. He said, 'Rain will fall. You could believe it? And it might fall tomorrow too and Monday.' Then he said, 'If it falls tomorrow I wonder if they'll still call tomorrow *Sun* day?'

He looked at her. He wanted her to laugh. But she was not in that sort of mood. She said, 'I'll tell you point-blank I wish the rain could tumble down from now till tomorrow and Monday to give the place a nice cooling down.' She was leaning to look towards the south, without thinking of anything but possible confusion at the Red House and the ever-present police threat to her husband. But just then her eye spotted a carriage. She went on talking. 'If we have some water tomorrow, then those layabouts wouldn't turn out in their thousands, as you all calling for. And it wouldn't put any pressure on you. By the way, you so hot and sweaty about the debate, you in the debate?'

'But how could I be in the debate? Am I in the Legislative Council?'

'But you will be most present in the chamber, I heard you saying that.'

'In the public gallery. We have to go. We have to make noise there and outside. We have to stop this Government.'

'Yes. Go and disturb the peace. Holder just waiting for your tail to pitch you in jail.'

The carriage was drawing near up but Mzumbo had not seen it yet. And there was even another one behind, far away. The storm clouds were gathering fast and a cold wind was beginning to whip in over the hills. Marie said, 'If it's water you all fighting for, some good bucketfuls of water will soon be on the way from upstairs.'

Mzumbo said nothing. When Marie, in looking round, spotted a fourth carriage she said to herself, 'Look, I'd better go back inside. Let them hold their meeting, and talk their nonsense about bringing down the Government. You see how the sky looking? They want water, they'll get it. I was head and head with Manuel when the British cut out the Borough Council in 1899, but what he get now he'll have to take, because he looking for it.'

And as an afterthought she said, 'But in the end I'll have to stand up with him. What to do – I love him.'

26

5

Eva and Clement were sitting on the concrete battlements of the old fort, just beside the harbour-master's office. They were sitting facing Railway Headquarters and to the right of them, just on the edge of the sea, was the lighthouse. Over the sea itself it was blindingly bright, although quite misty, and now fleecy clouds were beginning to skid across the sky. When Eva and Clement had arrived at the steamer's department, around 9 o'clock – not even an hour ago – the weather was very warm, but now the atmosphere felt cool and bracing, and there was a little breeze fanning in from the sea. The water was growing choppy though, and grey, and as the small boats off the jetty danced to the whims of the waves the mistiness was tending to obscure them.

Eva looked at Clement's big body beside her, and for a moment she felt so happy and strange and different. She could not remember the last time she had done anything like this: sit down and relax and be happy to be close to her companion. Certainly, she had never done it with Holder. She turned towards Clement.

'Big-boy, you know sometimes somebody could feel so free? Although we came down to check on those round-island steamers, you know I nearly forgot that? This town ain't bad, you know, to look at. By this part, anyway. I can't even remember looking at the lighthouse. I hear everybody saying it leaning and you know this is the first time I noticing that?'

He laughed. She had her hand holding his shoulder. He did not seem to be wearing a vest and she could feel his rugged muscles under the shirt.

He said, 'The lighthouse was always leaning.'

She said, 'It's so great sitting down here. I feeling so good and so free.'

'That's nice.'

She was not feeling completely free, although she wanted to believe so. Deep below the surface of her mind was the present upheaval, but she did not want to think of it. Yet it kept her mood subdued. What was not very subdued in her mind as she had her hand on Clement's shoulder was the thought: 'Suppose it so happened that Holder wandered down here!'

She kept telling herself it was so unlikely, but even though it might have seemed so, who could tell what oddities could lead to Holder just finding himself by the old Fort San Andrés? And anything could happen on the Saturday before the big debate. She also kept telling herself that Holder did not own her, but she herself replied: 'Could anybody stop that madman from pulling the trigger?'

She winced when this came to mind and she drove it from her head. She said, 'Boy, you know how long I ain't enjoy something like this?' She looked at him. 'Something on your mind, Clem?'

'No, good gracious. I enjoying myself. I just like the sea. And I so glad we came down here. I know you feel bad that the boat ain't sailing till Saturday but don't fret about that. You know something, Eva? After this debate business we must come back down here one Sunday evening or something and just relax and enjoy it. But now have too much tension. Gosh, it nice here.'

He smiled. In spite of the smile, though, his mind was not free either. He, too, had been thinking of Holder. Holder was always hovering around the Red House – especially these days – and the Red House was not far from here. A few moments ago when she had put her hand on his shoulder he was going to throw his arm around her waist, or at least around her neck, but he had refrained because of this thought. He looked at her now and gave her a big smile.

She said, 'I'm not so worried the next steamer is till next Saturday morning, but what I was saying was if we did know that yesterday when we was talking, you coulda gone this morning. What's the schedule again? 6.20? All now so you'd be near Cedros. Because it must be about 10 o'clock now. But in that case I wouldn't be sitting down here with you now and thinking of those lovely things. So in a sense I'm glad we didn't know. Although you may have some hardship Tuesday morning—'

'Why hardship?'

'You know as we sitting down here, every time I hear a train come in I thinking about you going up.'

'I too. But that's no trouble. I'll catch the 6.05 easy, easy, and make me way. From Sangre Grande I should be lucky to get something.'

'You sure it's okay, my darling?' She smiled, showing all her teeth. He was still reluctant to embrace her and she sensed it.

He said, 'It's much better for me to go up Tuesday instead of tomorrow. We have time.'

'Not a lot, but it's okay. You said you want to stay for Monday in case anything happen to me. I don't think nothing will happen but it will be still nice to know that you around. Monday I might just want to see you.' She looked at him.

He wanted to say, 'I want to see you every day of the week, not only Monday.' But he did not say it. He said, 'Eva, the time ain't so tight, you know. Between Tuesday and—' He stopped, working things out.

She took her hand from his shoulder and eased round to turn to face him. She took his right hand in both of hers. She said, 'Look, Tuesday morning you off to Mayaro, and you should get there in the evening. I really hope you get something from Sangre Grande to carry you as it ain't have no train from there. Okay, you'll stay with Ivy and Robert overnight and you leaving to come back Wednesday morning. If we lucky and get that letter, you back Wednesday evening and if things work out, Mzumbo catching that Saturday boat.'

Clement chuckled, then laughed.

'You laughing? Sometimes Uncle himself say: "Thing to cry and you laughing?" You just pray to God that things go to plan.'

'Well, tell me, what you want me to say when I reach?'

A rider passed on horseback going down South Quay and this reminded Eva of Darwent. It distracted her and she looked at the galloping horseman and at the same time she took the opportunity to glance to the St Vincent Street side of South Quay to see if there was any policeman like Holder around. Then a bare-backed labourer with three-quarter shorts came rolling a rum-keg out of Railway Headquarters to a cart on the other side of the street, and this caught her attention. Then she turned to Clement and said, 'Well, what I was saying was this, talk to Ivy more than to Robert, because she is the main one. Robert is Mzumbo's good friend. This man admire Uncle so much. But it's Ivy who's mad about Uncle. She'll go crazy just to hear Mzumbo want to come. So this is the one to attack.'

Clement chuckled.

'I mean, you know what we trying to achieve.' She looked round to make sure nobody was near, but she still kept her voice low. 'Two points you have to stress. Now yesterday I already told Uncle that Robert had a touch of malaria.'

Clement rocked with laughter and at the same time he looked up and down South Quay but Holder was definitely not about. Clement said, 'You told him that? What he said?'

Eva was laughing. She said, 'He was shocked. He said, "Malaria is a killer." But instead of saying "I'm going up to see him," he said, "You think we'll get some more news next week?" I mean, if he want news why he don't go up? So then I thought, "Clement will fix you up. Clement will have to go to Mayaro".'

'Me?' Clement burst out laughing. 'I'll go up to Mayaro for you, but it's *you* who fixing him up.'

'Ah, Clement, you ain't part of this? I want to feel you with me.' She threw her arm round his waist briefly.

'I'm with you,' he said. 'I was just making a joke.'

She could see that in this matter he was moving towards being one with her.

She regained her enthusiasm and she said, 'But this thing about malaria really hit Mzumbo hard. And of course we just found out he was enquiring about the steamer.'

'Oh, it was he? That's what the clerk was saying? By the way the clerk know you is his niece.'

'Oh yes. That's Joel. Joel Asnel. He is always at Mzumbo's meetings. He knows me well, but we didn't have time to talk this morning.' Then she said, 'Look, what I want you to tell Ivy — by herself, mind you — what I want you to tell Ivy is this: that I told Mzumbo that Robert has a touch of malaria. But say this was just to get him up there for a rest, because he badly needs a rest, and this debate business will kill him dead. Tell her he's so obsessed with this Legislative Council debate that he wouldn't leave on his own accord. He's stubborn. Ivy know that. Say he's working hard, meetings, meetings, meetings all over the place and he's tired, he isn't looking good at all. Don't worry if—' she laughed. 'Don't worry if when she see him he's looking in the best of form, because she could put that down to the sea-breeze. It will be too late anyway. In any case she'll be so thrilled she wouldn't think about anything. But look, tell her — don't laugh — tell her if she get him to come she must keep him there. Because when he see Robert's okay, ha boy! But she has to get him to leave town for Mayaro, that's the main thing. I already set the scene with malaria and she could round it off. After all, malaria is a killer. Please don't laugh, Clem, but she could tell him to expect a funeral. We'll run for cover afterwards.'

Clement nearly fell off the wall, for laughing.

Eva said, 'And look, I nearly forget this. This is important. Tell her the authorities planning to seize him and jail him before this big debate next week Monday. The 23rd. Between you and me, Clem, at first I made up this story, but you know now I hearing a rumour saying just that? But whether it's true or not, tell her Holder said they'll lock up all the agitators before the debate, and that he said Mzumbo is number one. So tell her she *must* get him to come to Mayaro. That's about all.'

They had been sitting there about an hour and now there seemed to be a lot more people about. It must be after 11 o'clock, Eva was thinking. She was beginning to feel a little uneasy but it was only when she saw a police uniform in the direction of the St Vincent Street wharf that her heart slammed. It was not Holder, but she did not want to know. She got up. Clement said, 'Eva, before you go you want us to just go across to the Ice House?'

The Ice House was at the corner of Abercromby Street and King Street, and this was just the place where Holder was likely to be. At first Eva thought Clement was making fun, but as he kept a straight face, she said, 'Ice House? Why?' And she said in her mind, 'You crazy?' She said again, 'Why?'

He said, 'I just wanted to buy you an ice-cream.'

She chuckled and said, 'You so sweet.' Then she added, 'You know another way of spelling ice-cream is I - S-c-r-e-a-m? Well, I don't want to scream and I don't want you to scream. So let's go home.'

'What you mean?'

'Go home and think about it.' She stared at him. Then she relaxed and said, 'No, my darling, I don't want any ice-cream. Big-boy, you could just go across and catch you train for Barataria. Give me a quick kiss and let me scram. I have a few things to do.'

He embraced and kissed her lightly and she turned and walked hurriedly away.

31

That afternoon torrential showers swamped Port-of-Spain. But although the downpour had lasted just about two and a half hours, and the sun had come out bright and hot again, Lolotte, from where she sat, could see water still cascading down the gutters of Abercromby Street and Chacon Street. Although it was Saturday evening, and, especially so, Saturday evening before the important Legislative Council debate, there was no din anywhere on King Street, nor on Marine Square, nor even on Frederick Street nor Abercromby Street. And there was just a small group on the pavement outside Jablotin, close to the junction of St Vincent Street and King Street. But most surprising of all there were only about twenty people inside Brunswick Square. However, with the sun having come out brightly and blindingly once more, the place seemed to be waking to life, and by the same token the police seemed to be waking to life too.

Lolotte Borde could not contain her laughter. Her friend, standing right there beside her, well-dressed in jacket and tie, and chatting but looking all around him to take in the whole scene, said: 'Oh, you laughing? Me friend Zumbo always say this is thing to cry not laugh. No, I like your caramel. Make me a pot of hot caramel for Monday. When your boy Wrightson bend to sign, I'll give him it in his—'

Lolotte Borde laughed so convulsively that her whole body shook. The stool upon which she sat, and over which her huge body seemed to sprawl, creaked as though it were going to break. Sitting there at the corner of Lower Chacon Street and Marine Square, her bosom hung so far over the pavement that breaking into patois Edgar Maresse-Smith referred to her as *Tototte* Borde, which made her hurriedly clasp her arms over her bosom, while appearing to collapse with laughter. Now she looked up from her tray of paymie, pone, buns, drops, flannel-pants cake and caramels, and still laughing uncontrollably she managed to say, 'Edgar, you know you wicked!'

'That's exactly what Mrs Wrightson told me. I went there to see Walsh

Wrightson to give him a final warning. He wouldn't answer the bell and the maid came down and told me quietly he was supposed to be ill. But the maid already give me the tip. She already put me up. So I put on this English accent and I said, "Oh dear, Mrs Wrightson, I understand your husband is a little indisposed. I came to see what I could do. Could I recommend a little bush medicine – a little *chado benie*, or perhaps a little democracy?" '

Lolotte Borde erupted into laughter again, then she cried out, 'Oh Lord, well yes. Well, well, well.' Then she said, 'Edgar – I mean Mr Maresse-Smith. You don't mind?'

As he answered her, keeping his eyes on her fat, pleated, shining face, he stretched his hands and took up a caramel. He said, 'Lolotte. You could call me anything but don't call me too early in the morning because I ain't wake up yet. But look, this is serious. Monday morning don't play the fool, you know. Don't play up in your, in your caramels, you know. Lolotte, you laughing, you can't stop laughing, you know what today is?'

She tried to get serious and fix her face. 'Mr Maresse-Smith – I mean Edgar – Edgar, is you who making me laugh!'

'Anyway, bear in mind what I told you to do for Monday morning. And I want me pot of hot caramel.'

'You see!' she almost shrieked out with laughter. 'You see it's you who can't talk serious!'

'Look, Lolotte,' he said, and it was as if he needed eyes all around him. He swivelled round, glancing in all directions, and then he said to her, 'It's me, Edgar, talking to you, keep it under your hat.' She chuckled because she never wore any hat. He put his hand on her head. He said, tugging at her plaits, 'Keep it *here*, if you see what I mean. This is Saturday evening and Monday morning it's – you see what happened today? Thunder and lightning? So much depend on you and Greasy Pole. Look, I know you have rock cake in your tray but when I say you must pelt rock I don't mean to pelt rock cake you know.'

She burst out in laughter again. He said, 'Look, listen to this.' His gaze was all around. He bent down to her and whispered something. She burst out laughing and looked at him surprised. He said, 'Everything depends on you. We looking out for that.'

◆

Standing at the corner of Chacon Street and King Street, and pressing hard against the wall of 'The Don', was Sergeant Holder. He was keeping most of his body behind the white-and-blue wall of 'The Don', and he was holding his cap in his hand and glancing across the street, in a slanting direction, but pretending he wasn't looking at anything in particular. There were few people about in Chacon Street and so it was easy for Sergeant Holder. Although when anybody drew near he began fidgeting innocently and smiling sweetly at the person, everybody knew the sergeant for what he was, and everybody feared him. Maybe it was the very fact that he was in Chacon Street that made the street so sparse of people.

He stood right up against the wall now and seeing nobody in view around him, he leaned again and glanced between the trees at the corner of Marine Square and Lower Chacon Street. For weeks now he had been keeping Lolotte Borde under observation and he could hardly believe his luck to see her chatting with Edgar Maresse-Smith. But to him the word was not chatting, it was plotting.

He said to himself, 'Sarge, you born lucky or what!'

In fact he had rubbed his eyes to make sure he had seen right. Nobody could mistake Lolotte Borde, even if one did not know which was the regular spot she sold on. It was clear that if you could not miss a big tram-car in the street, or a motor omnibus, or the Red House, then you could not miss Lolotte Borde.

He had smiled. So that was it. He had heard little rumours that Maresse-Smith, as well as Lazare, and even Alcazar, were fraternising with Lolotte Borde and Greasy Pole and other underworld characters, in an effort to bring out the mob for the reading of the waterworks bill, but this was his first real proof.

He thought, 'Just fancy.' He remembered how at the riot in 1898, the same bread riots at Rapsey's, when he had broken Lumpress's ribs, how Lolotte had thrown stones and smashed up the glass case. Maresse-Smith knew very well because he was her lawyer then. And in spite of all the rantings and ravings he, Holder, had given evidence and the magistrate had sent her down – rather up, because it was up Clarence Street to the Royal Jail. She had made three months, but he could see she wasn't tamed yet. Incidents of November last were there to show.

Let them plot, he thought. If he met them up anywhere round the Red House on Monday the Lord be with them!

He stiffened against the wall again and after a few moments he looked and they were still there. He withdrew a little. Passing on the other side along King Street was the tall fisherman from Corbeau Town and he had to smile because when he glimpsed him at first his heart jumped and he thought, 'Look, Greasy Pole.' But it wasn't Greasy Pole, it was Mr Saul, who minded his own business. Or seemed to. He didn't even attend those so-called ratepayers' meetings. But not Greasy Pole. The last time he saw Greasy Pole was last Saturday afternoon when Mzumbo Lazare was talking to the mob on the Savannah. In fact he, Tom Holder, had not even known that Greasy Pole was out of jail, and straightaway he went down to check to see if Greasy Pole had broken jail as usual, and—'

He heard a noise and looked. It was a cart that nearly skidded into the wall on the other side. He looked at the time. Five-thirty. After such a horrible midday and early afternoon, it was so nice and bright and clear now, yet although there were a good many people about, the crowds of this morning had not come back. In a way he did not know if he should feel sorry or glad. The Inspector-General of Police was always excited about getting crowds away, driving them away from near the Red House. But he, Holder, always welcomed them. The more they were seething in fury the better. Because he always wanted a challenge and he felt so nice when the rabble was threatening and rumbling and boiling over, just like a volcano ready to erupt, for on those occasions, with police support behind him, he could plunge into the middle of the volcano, pluck out the most heated lava of a ruffian, rain down cable-whip lashes on his head and across his back, then take him just opposite the Red House to Police Headquarters and shove him in a cell.

The evening was placid and beautiful, almost golden, as he stood on the pavement beside 'The Don'. Under the sign, 'The Don', were the words, 'Bespoke Tailors', and it was to him a coincidence that it was Maresse-Smith who was across the road talking with Lolotte. For wherever this scoundrel was to be seen he was always with jacket and tie and stiffly starched white shirt, sometimes candy-striped trousers, and there was always the pointed kerchief flashing from his left breast pocket. He made a quick peep again and he ground his teeth. He pulled a little away from the corner because it appeared that Maresse-Smith had suddenly glanced his way. He looked towards the other end of Chacon Street and up at the junction he could see a few people going into the yard of Trinity

Cathedral. As he looked, his mind still on Maresse-Smith, he said to himself, 'Ten to one he ain't see nothing, but if he spot anything he just spot a police uniform. He ain't know who it is.'

Suddenly he became aware of a man walking along Queen Street who turned down Chacon Street. He straightened up and kept his eyes on the man. As he looked at the figure walking down on the other side he could not help admiring the man's bravery. This was Stamford Lord, who he had beaten up at the ratepayers' meeting on the Savannah only last Saturday. He was a young boy, only about eighteen, but big. The last information he had of him was that he was in hospital, and he could not help feeling now what a determined vagabond this youth was, not only to be out in the town looking for trouble, but to walk down the street in spite of seeing that he, Holder, was there. As Lord walked down on the other side, at times looking across at him, he did not know whether he should let him pass or whether he should accost him: stop him, call him over, and search him. Then it suddenly came to him that he'd be better off watching the movements of this scamp and see if by any chance he was going over to join Lolotte and Maresse-Smith. However, in an unconcerned way Stamford Lord reached the corner of Chacon Street and King Street, and stood up, looking up and down. Then he turned back and walked up again to Queen Street corner. Sergeant Holder, on the other side of the street, walked up too. Lord stopped at Queen Street corner and exchanged a few words with somebody he saw in Trinity churchyard, but Holder had not walked up fast enough to hear what he said. Then Lord, without crossing Queen Street, turned back and walked down Chacon Street again, and at this time he was acting as if Holder was not there at all. He stopped at the corner of Chacon Street and King Street and then crossed King Street and turned east, as if he was going to the Roman Catholic cathedral.

Sergeant Holder looked at him. He thought, 'The swine ain't get enough. He was expecting the mob to be circulating. I hope it ain't going to have no rain Monday so they could come out because so help me God I'll teach them a lesson.'

He eased back to the corner to have another glimpse of Maresse-Smith and Lolotte Borde in conference. And it was as if his heart suddenly went wild. Neither of them was there.

◆

As Lolotte sat in her ramshackle two-roomed house on Clifton Hill with the pitch-oil lamp flickering in her face, she said, 'Oh God, I hope this rain ain't coming down again because what will happen if this thing continue right into Monday? Get up and close the window, please.'

'God is good,' Mzumbo Lazare said, as he pulled the window shut. 'He'll keep Monday nice for us.'

Edgar Maresse-Smith laughed. 'So God like bacchanal?'

Mzumbo said, 'They say, *Blessed are they who struggle in justice's name for theirs is the kingdom of Heaven.*'

Maresse-Smith turned to him, 'That's not the quotation. You can't tell me about the Bible.'

Mzumbo did not reply. Lolotte said, 'Edgar, you don't have to be loud. You don't know who could be around.'

Mzumbo looked at her. 'Are you all afraid? Fear is the great enemy. Look, we have a cause. Monday the 16th is a crucial day. I can bet you they will rush through this thing in the council to reach the third reading and sign this into law...'

'They can't do that. You mad?' Lolotte said. 'And we'll stop there and see that? In any case Henry waiting for them. They can't play with Henry Alcazar, you know. In any case Henry already said that's unconstitutional.'

Lolotte Borde had no idea what 'unconstitutional' meant.

Mzumbo Lazare was talking to them but he had a heavy heart. He did not want to tell them anything but he was depressed and confused and he did not know what to do. He hoped everything would be concluded on Monday and that they would find success. He said, 'With all respect to Henry and Edgar, I am not so sure. I'm talking of the question as to whether it's constitutional or not. The British have a way of bringing in Law and Order to override anything. But in any case, you think you could stop the British when they are out to get you? Look how they abolished the Borough Council in 1899 just because we wouldn't do their dirty work. That was constitutional? Of course, let me make this quite clear, this was not necessarily the British, as such; this was the Secretary of State and Governor Jerningham. Joseph Chamberlain did what he pleased. That's all. As a whole the British respect the constitution.'

Maresse-Smith did not speak and Mzumbo said, 'Look, this is going to be a busy night for all of us so let's leave Lolotte in peace.'

Lolotte cried, 'But Edgar already bring me here. I just started to sell after the heavy showers. I ain't even make any money. He tell me you coming here for the final chat and made me bring back everything.'

Maresse-Smith said something in patois which sent her into hysterical laughter, and Mzumbo, who didn't understand patois, said, 'You two laughing as if what we are preparing for is some silly tea party. You remember what we said at the meeting? Edgar, on Monday we can't be making fun, and I want to ask Lolotte again – I don't want to go over the details – but work just as we told you. Organise. They all know you. Every man-jack knows you. Because—'

'Because I so big and fat.'

'Good heavens!' Maresse-Smith stood up. 'You? You will look at you and call yourself big and fat?'

'No. *You* will look at me and call me big and fat.'

There was such a cackle of laughter that Mzumbo said, 'Edgar, what do you think we came here for? What was the purpose? If you and Lolotte want to laugh and get on maybe I shouldn't be here.' His heart, which was already pained, became more troubled. His thoughts were on the urgent issue here, and yet his thoughts were on a place a good many miles from here, under some coconut palms. Those bitter-sweet thoughts racked his heart. He thought of a dear and beautiful presence. But what could he do?

Maresse-Smith and Lolotte Borde were talking and Mzumbo heard Maresse-Smith say, 'Lolotte, Mzumbo really serious? He ready to quarrel and yet he dreaming away. *Ca ou ka fait, garcon?*'

Lolotte laughed. They both knew Mzumbo did not speak patois – or pretended not to speak it. Mzumbo said, 'I'm not dreaming away. I'm just thinking of something. Lolotte, I already talked to you. I related you the whole thing and I told you, confidentially, what happened at the meeting this morning. Edgar knows what I'm driving at. We have some bigwigs behind us. Real bigwigs. Bigwigs who say they believe, who swear "I believe", but they'll never come here to Laventille. They will never come up here to Clifton Hill, to this shanty town – I beg your pardon if I offend you. But those bigwigs, even if they see you in the middle of a serene Port-of-Spain on a fine day they'll never say good morning to you. But they are with us in this water business and in reform. Mainly reform. Edgar already explained why. They want representative government too because they already have the money. Then they'll have the vote and control everything.

But don't dislike them because, considering everything, they are very nice men. Really big men and they have their money behind us. Even if they also have their axe to grind. Really fine men. Men like Goodwille, he and Wilson who have that big store near to where you sell. Men like Mole who publish the *Mirror*. Men like Papa Bodu, but he would come up here, of course, Papa Bodu. We have the key people, people who are powerful, but you know what? People who could do nothing if we don't have people like you in front.'

Edgar said, 'And all of them bristling and waiting. And Lolotte, you already know Alcazar is a firebrand and he'll be on the floor first thing Monday. All of them was at the meeting this morning.'

'Cyrus was there?'

Edgar said, 'You mean Cyrus David? But how you could ask if Cyrus was there, *Cocotte*? That is one of the most faithful.'

Lolotte looked quickly at Mzumbo and chuckled. Then she said, 'I like that man too bad.'

Edgar said, 'You like him because he buys out your toloom,' and he finished the sentence in patois, sending Lolotte almost crashing to the floor with laughter. Then he looked anxiously at Mzumbo and said, 'I'm finished. This is it.'

Mzumbo looked at him fixedly but said nothing. The light was not flickering so much now because the window was closed. Lolotte, with tears of laughter streaming down her face, said, 'Edgar, I really hope you finish now, because I ain't able with you. You see how Mr Mzumbo vex?'

Mzumbo Lazare said, 'Lolotte Borde, you already know the situation, and you know what you have to do. If you see Greasy Pole early in the morning you could tell him. Pick and choose the place to talk. See who's around you. Don't broadcast anything, please. I really hope everything go well on Monday.'

'Yes, Mr Mzumbo.'

'Edgar, don't forget that special meeting for the lawyers tomorrow morning. We have to look at the constitution. Don't forget.'

'How could I forget?'

Looking at Lolotte Borde, Mzumbo said, 'And I hope everything comes to a satisfactory conclusion, and we win. I hope it doesn't go over to next week Monday for a third reading because we can't risk this confusion twice. And although on Monday I said we are making noise, you remember I told them at the public meeting we have to watch it. We can't have chaos. In any case if we have chaos and the police start shooting we don't know who will be here for next week Monday.'

Lolotte Borde did not like to hear that and she covered her face in her hands. Maresse-Smith looked at Mzumbo. He told him, 'Listen, old boy, in a confrontation like this one, none of us might be here. Who knows? It wouldn't take much for the police to shoot, anyway. Must we be chicken-hearted?' He wasn't making fun now. He said, 'Mzumbo, you yourself said fear is the greatest enemy. All we have to have is courage, and of course we have right on our side. And come what may.'

Mzumbo was not sure he agreed but he preferred not to reply. He simply said, 'Monday morning I myself will be out early. I'll be in my chambers from about seven, and I'll be in Brunswick Square as soon as people begin to gather, because I want to talk to them. We have the advertisement in the *Port-of-Spain Gazette* but we have three Indian town criers with carts and they'll be going up and down. And look – you see Monday? I don't feel rain should stop anybody. You hear me?'

'It can't stop me, Mr Mzumbo, not me. I don't know what time I'll be out there but Mr Mzumbo, I can't sleep from tonight and I could tell you I'll be in the square Monday by the break of dawn.'

Edgar Maresse-Smith said, 'That is the way to talk.'

As they were talking the rain was drizzling heavily and seemed to be playing a tune on the galvanised roof. So much so that when Mzumbo got up to go, Lolotte said, 'Mr Mzumbo you going? You ain't hearing?'

'But of course. But Lolotte Borde, I'll tell you this: people who want change just can't sit and wait for rain to cease, you know.'

She chuckled.

He said, 'While ago you said Monday morning—'

'That's different, Mr Mzumbo. Monday is a different day.'

He did not listen her out. He went on: 'While the poor and down-trodden are cringing, sheltering from rain, and the wind blowing too cold so they can't do anything, the oppressors are taking night to make day to keep them under heel. This was just a little illustration. I have to go now because I have work to do tonight, and in any case the carriage is under the big tree down the hill by Madame Monereau's spring. When I was coming here Holder was on South Quay as if he was looking for somebody. Perhaps he has already tracked me down.'

Lolotte Borde said silently, 'That's why I was telling Edgar to talk soft.'

Edgar Maresse-Smith touched Mzumbo and said, 'Could be he was looking for me and Lolotte. I didn't tell Lolotte anything but when we were talking by the corner – you know the corner where Lolotte is?'

'Harriman's corner.'

'No. Lolotte's corner.'

Amidst Lolotte's laughter, Mzumbo said, 'Edgar, you can't be serious for a single minute?'

'But I was telling you. When I was talking to Lolotte, Holder was standing up by the corner close up against the wall by the bespoke tailors and peeping at us talking.'

Lolotte opened her eyes in awe. 'Holder was there?'

'Look, even if the whole of Port-of-Spain scared of Holder, Maresse-Smith is one man who ain't scared.'

Mzumbo said, 'Maresse-Smith and Lazare.'

'Amen,' Edgar said. He got up too.

Lolotte Borde said, 'But you fellers ain't hearing the rain? It coming heavier.'

Mzumbo said, 'Edgar could stay, you know. I didn't ask him to come. I said I was going.'

Edgar Maresse-Smith hardly heard. He said in his mind: 'Showers of blessings. This was the omen I was looking for.'

Lolotte said, 'Edgar I ain't even have any umbrella to give you boys to go down the hill. You staying till the rain pass? Because you'll get wet. You ain't have your carriage, Edgar?'

'No, but I have Mzumbo's carriage. I'm going home with him. In any case what will I be staying for? My name is Cyrus David?'

Lolotte Borde was still laughing when the two men stepped out into the rainy night.

7

Colonel Brake and Walsh Wrightson were standing together on the steps of Police Headquarters, when the colonel saw Sergeant Holder coming around the Hart Street corner of the Red House. When he hailed out to him, Holder ran along the pavement a little way up St Vincent Street and when he was opposite to Police Headquarters he ran across the road. He saluted the colonel.

Colonel Brake said, 'Just the man I was looking for. The Honourable Wrightson wants to go to the Union Club and he was going to walk down, but I refuse to let him go unescorted—'

Holder was appalled, and interrupted the colonel. 'What, Sir? The Honourable Wrightson wanted to walk down? Without escort? Those hooligans will take his head, Sir. You want at least four policemen to walk down with him.'

'Right. You are the man for me. I could have got Empson or Superintending Sergeant Peake, but I called you. Not because I saw you. I thought about you.'

Holder felt proud. He said, 'I will join the escort meself, Sir.'

'I knew that. I'm sure you wouldn't let any harm—'

'Harm, Colonel?' Holder was standing erect. His face was a mixture of pride and courage twisted with pained anguish that an Englishman had to be escorted and could not walk free in Trinidad. 'Harm, Sir?' he said again, as Wrightson was going to talk. He declared, 'I'll protect the Honourable Walsh Wrightson with me life.'

'Why, thank you!' Walsh Wrightson said.

Colonel Brake, who could not always stand Holder, said, 'Well, good, Sergeant. I'll leave him to you. What's on the cards for tomorrow? Anything suspicious afoot?'

'A lot of things will be on foot if you let them. I have to pounce on everything. Sir, I'm telling you again, we might have to take Maresse-Smith. From the little things I'm seeing and hearing Maresse-Smith wants open rebellion. He isn't saying so at the big meetings because it have police there. But from what I hearing this man should be taken in for sedition.'

All the time he was talking Colonel Brake was laughing. What could Maresse-Smith do? There were guns all over the place. All the crack policemen had guns, and Rooks's soldiers, thirty-five of them, all had guns, and all the officers, including Walsh Wrightson, had revolvers. In fact Wrightson did not need any escort to go down the road, Colonel Brake thought. He was too damned cowardly. If he wasn't a coward he would have just walked to the Union Club, he wouldn't have to come to tell him he was walking down to the Union Club. So if it was an escort he wanted, let him have it. Colonel Brake listened to Holder saying Edgar Maresse-Smith should be taken in for sedition, and he said, 'Very well. But look, if I don't get moving, with all the confusion around me, I, Hubert Brake, will be tried for sedition, and hanged and quartered.' He smiled, and Wrightson and Holder laughed. 'Of course,' the colonel said. 'Because it will mean I'm conspiring with the enemy. By the way, you mentioned Maresse-Smith, what about Lazare?'

Holder said, 'Lazare want some good beating over the head. Some good batons over the head for saying what he saying about the British. But he ain't dangerous, Sir.'

Brake was laughing. Holder continued, 'He ain't dangerous. He want peace. He telling people to demonstrate, and he keep talking about rights and rights, but he telling them about law and order too. Lazare ain't want any riot.'

Colonel Brake said, 'Lazare is a soldier. He's adjutant in the Light Horse. In spite of all the hoo-ha, he knows the value of law and order. But you know something?' Before continuing he turned to Wrightson and said quickly, 'I know you're hungry, old boy, I'll let Holder go now.' He resumed, 'You know something, the man I'll be charged for conspiring with is an Englishman like you and me. And like Holder, too, because Holder's more Englishman than a lot of them.'

Holder felt exceedingly proud.

'The man I'll be charged for conspiring with—'

Even before he finished, Wrightson said, 'Is Darwent.'

Holder's face crinkled up like an addled egg.

Colonel Brake told him, 'Take the Honourable Wrightson to the Union Club. Get four other escorts.' And he turned to hurry inside. As he looked

43

back to watch Wrightson step into the street, he saw the revolver bulging in his pocket. He said to himself, 'Honourable Coward!'

◆

It was a good thing Colonel Brake had sent an escort to accompany Wrightson, and it was a good thing too that Sergeant Holder had decided on five, not four – five of the best and most courageous armed policemen, including himself – otherwise they would not have succeeded in passing the Red Star barrackyard.

As they crossed Queen Street to the pavement of the Carlisle Hotel they heard someone scream, 'Look, Wrightson!' and within a few seconds a number of people were rushing on to the pavement from the barrackyard with stones and sticks and pieces of iron, broken bottles, and all sorts of weapons. It happened so suddenly that Wrightson himself forgot he had a revolver in his back pocket and began to tremble. Holder screamed, 'Stop!' his rifle pointing at the crowd.

His blood rushed to his head. It was a good thing this mob was on the other side of the road else he would have killed somebody. Sure thing. But he had enough sense to know that with the situation as it was, and with the crowd on the barrackyard side, he'd better not fire because he and his escort certainly would not be able to come out of it alive. And at the moment they had no backing. He and his five escorts stood up with the barrels of their guns pointing to the crowd and he was astonished that what he thought of as whores and hooligans and seasoned criminals did not break and run. There was a lot of noise and confusion and some of the voices were crying, 'Shoot me! Shoot me!' But the majority were clamouring for Wrightson and eager to get their hands on him, though there was no movement forward from them. It was because they knew Holder. In fact they must have been surprised he didn't shoot yet.

Somebody shouted, 'Maresse-Smith say it's once to die!' and part of the crowd that had walked a little way up St Vincent Street now made to dash across Queen Street, and Holder shouted, 'Not a man move!' He gave orders to two of the escorts to cover that part of the mob, and when he saw there was still movement in front of the gate and by the Queen Street junction he gave a command to his men, and as with one action they all lifted the barrels of their guns and fired into the air. The mob on the

44

pavement scattered back into the barrackyard and there were hellish cries of 'Oh God,' and some were running pell-mell up St Vincent Street. Every one of those was being arrested, for the police were now aware of the commotion after the thunderous clatter of the rifles. About a dozen armed men from Police Headquarters came running down to join Holder's men.

The guests in the Carlisle Hotel had all been looking and had been obviously frightened. One of them said loud enough for people in the street to hear, 'If we didn't have Holder what would become of us!'

The manager of the Carlisle, who had been looking over the banister too, did not say anything. He watched the five escorts and Wrightson walk down the road. He said silently, 'Let him go. Let him go and eat in the Union Club.'

◆

Colonel Brake ordered more armed men for the debate. He wanted Major Rooks to have sixty men on call from St James's Barracks, and he wanted Inspector Norman to be at the ready with thirty armed men – that was in addition to what was already on the alert.

It was about 7.30 p.m. and he sat down with them in his office, with a plan of the Red House area. Everybody was grave. Colonel Brake relaxed a little and he said, 'The Director of Public Works looks spent; I expect it was rather scary.'

Wrightson said nothing.

Colonel Brake added, 'You'll have to realise that being in the colonies isn't exactly like being in England. These outbreaks occur, and that's what we are here for – to quell them. We have to be able to contend, and be firm, and command respect. Why not? We are British. So don't let the experience shake you unduly. What? That's not the problem? That's what you're saying? Well, you have no problem. Things were scary, but you were in the hands of a brave man.'

He looked towards Holder. Holder's chest swelled with pride. But it was not pride that was uppermost in his mind. He was hearing again and again, as if it was right there in his presence, the voice that had shouted, 'Maresse-Smith said it's once to die.' He had already told Colonel Brake about it but the colonel did not make much comment. In fact he had just laughed, because he knew it would not be easy finding the man who could die twice. Now Colonel Brake, simply having referred to Sergeant Holder as brave, and simply having tried to be cordial, emboldened Holder. The sergeant said to him abruptly, 'Sir, what we doing about Edgar Maresse-Smith?'

'Why are you all afraid of Maresse-Smith? He's a bag of hot air.'

Holder said, 'The Honourable Wrightson could ah lose his life, Sir. I and me escorts, they could ah beat us to death. Nobody could—'

Brake interrupted, 'Come on, Sergeant. I know there was really a little riot. But do you think it's because Maresse-Smith told them it's once to die? Did they not know that before? They thought it was twice, Sergeant?'

'Colonel, they didn't have the guts to behave so before. This is the first first time a crowd rushed me.'

'They're excited. I suppose it's because they had all this big talk pumped into them.'

Holder turned around quickly. 'Thanks, Colonel Brake. Thanks for saying that, because when I said it you didn't seem to want to hear me.'

'You didn't say that, did you?' Colonel Brake was a little confused. He said, 'Tomorrow when they come to the Red House they'll know where barley grows. Relax, Sergeant.'

'Today I nearly knows where barley grows.'

The colonel turned away and laughed heartily.

'Sir, you laughing? That Maresse-Smith is dangerous.'

The colonel tried hard to look serious. He said: 'Well, Holder, what do you want of me?'

'We should hold him.'

Colonel Brake was still amused. He said, well under his breath, 'He's as mad as an Alpine chaser.' He said to the sergeant, 'I know you are a holder, Sergeant Holder, but you cannot hold everything, you know. Let us see how tomorrow goes. Honourable Walsh Wrightson, you are laughing at my feeble joke. Actually the situation is very grave, and while there is no real threat it wouldn't help us to hold popular people. If things get tight and threatening, then for the next debate we'll hold every one of the individuals who pose a danger to peace. But don't stir up a hornets' nest because we don't want to use firearms. You understand me, Holder?'

Sergeant Holder looked at him with a forced smile. Outside was now pitch-black. The time was almost half-past eight and the colonel was asking himself what would tomorrow bring. He was nervous and talking lightly because he was so unsure. But he was not afraid. Wrightson wanted to remain close to him, but Holder went quickly back out to patrol the streets.

46

8

It was eleven o'clock on Sunday night and the town was quiet. Colonel Brake knew that the town was quiet and that there was nothing extraordinary going on because about half an hour ago his most reliable policeman on the beat had come in and reported to him. But he was not fully content because he had a load on his mind. It was very strange what happened today and he began to wonder if the rumour he had heard was true. He had heard it weeks ago and he had laughed it off but today he heard it again, and even more strongly.

As Major Rooks was speaking Colonel Brake was wondering if he should break off the discussion and raise the issue. He thought not. He looked round at the other four officers sitting in a sort of semi-circle in front of his desk. He was giving only half of his attention to Major Rooks and now his mind drifted off completely.

Major Rooks stopped and said, 'Colonel, you asked for my opinion but to be honest I don't know if you really want it. I don't know if you're attending to me.'

Colonel Brake roused himself then looked sharply at the major. 'What is it, Major Rooks? Please don't get jittery. Of course I am listening to you.'

Inspector of Police, Charles Norman, looked towards Major Rooks and smiled quietly. His deputy beside him looked away. The other two, Sergeant-Major Lewsey and Superintending Sergeant Robert Taitt, just looked gravely in front of them.

Colonel Brake said, 'This is a tense night for you officers – for everybody – and I understand. I might have been looking vague, because that last part of what you said, well, I'm not sure I understood it.'

Inspector Norman said, 'It was the very thing you suggested, Colonel. The very first thing you said and we all agreed with you. Putting an armed force in the Red House.'

'But not for tomorrow. Tomorrow is only the first reading of the bill. We'll put—'

Major Rooks was trying to attract the colonel's attention, and the colonel looked at him and said, 'Will you hear me out, Major?' Then he said, 'Very well. What is it?'

Major Rooks said, 'There was a misunderstanding, Colonel. I did not say anything about tomorrow. In any case it's now gone eleven o'clock. Nearly midnight. We could not put any armed men in there now for tomorrow. I think the fatigue is getting hold of all of us.'

Colonel Brake said, 'It's the fatigue, the stress, the strain, and all this blasted confusion going on in Trinidad. Look, do you know, we are supposed to be Englishmen, but one of our own – I'd better not talk about that now. But just that this is incredible. Could you believe, for instance, rumours you heard weeks ago, that—' Colonel Brake stopped short.

'That what, Sir?' Sergeant-Major Lewsey said. As the colonel turned to look at the sergeant-major he was aware that all the other eyes were on him.

Colonel Brake said, 'That what? Every one of you knows. And not only that – anyway, I think I'd better shelve this subject until the storm passes. We are sitting here tonight to discuss what measures to adopt for tomorrow, and I think you could say we are agreed on all the essential steps to be taken. You two, Superintending Sergeant Taitt and Sergeant-Major Lewsey, I think everything centres on you for the St Vincent Street side. That's your charge, and we already settled this whole question of the deployment of police in the town. Unless, of course, anybody wants to say anything.'

They were all silent. Colonel Brake went on: 'You know this matter is crucial because there'll be a lot of troublemakers when that bill gets through the first reading. By the way, Inspector Norman, remember you are covering Knox Street, with an eye on Abercromby, and Holder will control Abercromby and Hart. No, no, no, Inspector. Holder has to control something. I wouldn't say this if he were here but he would die for us. What's that? Yes, yes. Well I know he's no Englishman but he likes to feel he is. Oh really? That's far-fetched. Contrary to what you say I don't think the population will respect us less. Very well, these are my orders. Are we agreed? Now, officers, I want you to know and remember this. They call me Commandant of Local Forces and Inspector-General of Police, but with all these big titles I am nothing without your support.'

Major Rooks said in his mind, 'Oh, you know that? Now that we have a crisis you're getting wise!'

Colonel Brake continued speaking. 'Now there is the question of the Red House itself, especially the council chamber, and we have to protect everybody. Collectively and individually. We can't make fun with this one because with the expected mob round the Red House things could just happen like that.' He snapped his fingers. 'That's why in fact I thought of putting armed men inside the chamber. That is the best course of action. Of course I didn't think of it for tomorrow because it's too late. And in any case tomorrow is not the flash point, the flash point will come the following Monday, when our Government rushes through the second reading and completes the third.' He looked around at his officers. 'I am depending on you. We have to protect everybody, even those stupid members like Hall and Alcazar who are only inciting people. Is that clear?'

Sergeant-Major Lewsey was talking to Inspector Norman. He kept his voice low: 'I'm making no apologies. I feel bloody strongly about that.'

Colonel Brake heard the murmuring, and said, 'You were saying something, Sergeant-Major?'

Inspector Norman said, 'He said he feels strongly about having to protect the agitators.'

'Don't we all. But it's the law, Sergeant-Major. And we are British. We have to be concerned about protecting every member of the Legislative Council.'

There was silence.

'We are servants of the Crown, officers. All of us. Do you think we can do what we like? Do you think we can be guided by our hearts? No, by God! We all have instructions and let's put our heads to them. Don't you think I know those crazy people like Hall and Newbold, and Wainwright, and Henry Alcazar – they are trying their damnedest to undermine the Government, and to undermine law and order? I heard Alcazar the other day and I can tell you that man should be banished. But that is for the Government to do. The police have to maintain law and order.'

Sergeant-Major Lewsey got up, went out and looked up and down St Vincent Street, then came back and sat down. He said, 'Colonel Brake, I really liked what you said. You never spoke more truly as when you said that man should be banished.'

The colonel chuckled. Then he pulled out a watch from his fob pocket.

He said, 'Sergeant-Major, you see the watch on this chain? This watch is showing 11.30 p.m. It is only a few hours to what might be a most harassing day. What we are meeting here tonight to talk about is strategy. Not to banish people. The deployment of policemen is taken care of and I'm pleased about that. In the Red House itself we have to ear-mark some people for strong protection. But we have to protect everybody. All the legislators. But you know who is the number one man we have to guard? Perish it, but do you officers realise who is the number one target? We can't afford a slip-up.'

Everybody knew but nobody said anything. Sergeant-Major Lewsey, who was sitting close to Inspector Norman, nudged him in the back. Superintending Sergeant Taitt looked towards Deputy Inspector Owen. They all knew that regardless of what happened that was the one man the colonel wanted to protect.

Colonel Brake said, 'So I suggest to you to keep it in mind at every instant. In order to protect him properly it seems to me we ought to have five armed policemen close up and guarding the Director of Public Works *all* the time. The Honourable Walsh Wrightson will be moving mainly around the chamber. And that's throughout these debate sessions. And Governor Maloney, too, mind you. Intense measures, please. Because that wild speech which Lazare made in the Savannah last Saturday, and which Holder reported verbatim, that is clearly inciting the people against the Governor.'

Major Rooks said, 'Colonel, that's what we've been saying from beginning to end. Lazare is full of influence and his words can lead to trouble. Can we not arrest Lazare and at least detain him if we don't have enough grounds for laying a charge?'

'We don't want to tamper with that. The Ratepayers' Association has too many legal men for us to risk a chance and lose. Especially so as Alcazar is their legal adviser. You see, one is not sure yet that Lazare broke the law. But tomorrow,' he looked at the five of them. 'We've already worked out what's happening tomorrow and all we have to do is to implement it. By the way, what we talked about this morning, that is the key thing. Entry by tickets. This will really cut down the crowd. Nobody's getting into the chamber except by tickets. Is that clear?'

Everybody said yes. They'd take the crowd by surprise then and the chamber would be only half full. That would be a great breathing space, and for the following Monday they could have the armed men locked up in the chamber waiting for trouble.

Major Rooks wanted to talk but Colonel Brake was making a point. Colonel Brake said, 'Tomorrow morning I'll be at the door myself. And there will be notices posted saying: *No entry except by tickets.* There'll be a shock and a lot of opposition and I expect Lazare and Maresse-Smith to be in league with the crowd, trying to blast us out of existence. Now, your men have staves – we'll use firearms only when the worst comes to the very worst. I hope to God this doesn't happen. Of course I'm talking to you, Inspector, and Sergeant-Major and Superintending Sergeant. By the way, that's why, Inspector, that's why I want you to keep those sixty-four men under your orders, not for tomorrow but next week. But you can handpick them from now.'

Major Rooks said, 'That's what I wanted to know. Are we sure Monday week will be the crucial day, and in fact we wouldn't rush through the bill tomorrow?'

'The Honourable Director of Public Works assured me the bill cannot be rushed through by tomorrow – and this is no device to give me a breathing space, it just cannot be done. The main reason is that the Honourable Wrightson has to introduce the bill at length, with all the proposals, estimates, suggestions, and other measures. Then we have the opponents, and in the end the Honourable Wrightson has to reply, before the vote is taken. It is impossible to do that in just one session. Look, do you know what we have to confront tomorrow? Alcazar is going to talk for at least three hours, just to parade himself like a peacock before the public gallery. And if it comes to it Hall will speak, certainly Wainwright, Newbold. Do you think they'll sit down and see us rush the bill through?'

Major Rooks said, 'When you say "us", Colonel, we are not in the Government you know, and—'

'Exactly,' Colonel Brake interrupted. 'Glad you pointed it out. It's my slip-up. The police are absolutely impartial, that's why I keep saying we have to protect everybody. Of course if it happens at any time that we are partial, then we have to be partial on the side of right. We cannot give in to the mob. These half-wit people can't challenge the Government.'

'I know, Colonel, when it boils down to it we have a duty to defend what is right. I agree with you.'

'But I must point out, Major Rooks, that although this is true, and there is no doubt that the Government is right, we are constrained at all times to be objective. That is British law. So you were exactly right when you said "us" is not the word.' He was thinking, 'Didn't he himself say "we" a while ago?'

'And you said you are confident it will come to a conclusion Monday week – the debate?'

'I'm sure. The Honourable Wrightson said it can't be finished tomorrow. That's why we'll need to prepare ourselves for the following Monday. When we have armed police in the Red House we could control the crowd who might want to storm the chamber on that Monday. That's, let's see, the 23rd. So the debate will not even have the interruption that the one tomorrow might have. So according to Wrightson the bill will reach third reading by Monday week and pass into law. We certainly don't want a further Monday.' He noticed that except Major Rooks, the officers did not seem to be paying attention now, and some were slumping in their chairs. He shook his head.

He himself was tired. It had been a hectic week, with tension such as he had never seen here before, a tension seeming to rise suddenly, thanks to the frenzy whipped up by Lazare and Maresse-Smith. He had to appear unbiased, especially in front of his men, but what would he not give to see a bullet lodged in the throats of Lazare and Maresse-Smith, even if he had to put it there himself! Or a bayonet in each of their bellies! But he had to be careful. He had often thought of the faithful Sergeant Holder, but he had to be careful. He looked round at his men and even Major Rooks looked tired now. It was getting on towards midnight. No one wanted to talk any more. Everybody was thinking of limiting himself to a three- or four-hour rest and getting up at the crack of dawn. A few eyes were closed, but nobody was really sleeping. They were all sitting erect, only with head bowed, and – strange to believe, but true – they were still alert. They were all in khaki, including Colonel Brake, and in a strange sort of way they looked like brothers. Noticing this, the colonel said, 'Now then. You'll be just five minutes more with me. You know we are just like brothers?'

Inspector Norman smiled. 'Oh yes?' The rest opened their eyes and had their heads up.

'But why "Oh yes"? Why are you saying it like that? What do you think we are? We are all Englishmen. And even if we are here to uphold the law and to uphold it impartially, you chaps won't be able to help feeling a little more deeply for your own kith and kin. It's natural. But I am calling upon you for the objectivity which the British are known for.'

Most of them nodded their heads. Sergeant-Major Lewsey said, 'Of course, Colonel Brake. But I agree with you that such feeling is natural.'

'Though you won't always think so with the rumours you are hearing.'

Major Rooks looked towards the colonel. He said, 'I told you who told me about it. I am by no means sure. It's Holder who told me and you know how hasty that sergeant is. Perhaps it's better to put it aside unless you have grounds.'

The others looked alert. They were a little confused at first and then they realised what the talk was about. Colonel Brake said, 'You are quite right about putting it aside because it is so incredible. I wasn't thinking about it but I went over to the Union Club today and I met the captain himself. Fire brigade. Do you know what he was saying?'

'The captain himself. Captain Walter Darwent?' Major Rooks turned to the colonel.

'There is only one captain in the fire brigade – thank God.'

They were all eager to hear what Walter Darwent had been saying.

'It's downright ridiculous,' the colonel said, his face reddening into a rage. 'It is scandalous that one of us should speak like this. Just fancy, the captain was saying to me – I really don't like to call his name – we were in the veranda looking down on Marine Square, I eased up on purpose to the rascal, not looking his way. Do you know what he said? He said, "Colonel, these suffering people, they are really up against it. We have to look at both sides of the story." Both sides of the story! Could you believe that?'

Superintending Sergeant Taitt said, 'Yes, Colonel, I could believe that, with what I have been hearing. There are rumours, everybody's hearing rumours. Most of the men under me know a thing or two. But as you always say, Colonel, one can't encourage rumours. Whether they are true or not. One has to scotch them. And let's face it, we all see it as a disgrace for us Englishmen. And the worst thing of all is, the worst thing of all is this – I understand it's a washerwoman – his washerwoman.'

A gasp went round the room. Everybody was wide awake now and sitting up. Most of them, if not all of them, had heard of the relationship between Darwent and his washerwoman, yet to hear it being confirmed made it sound really sensational. Major Rooks said, 'But, Colonel, tell me, has anybody actually seen anything?'

'I do not know.'

'Well that's it,' said Superintending Sergeant Taitt. 'That's it. I myself haven't met anyone who said he has. At least we, the officers, it's just a matter of hearing. Though there's no smoke without fire. But even to talk about it. It's downright disgraceful.'

The colonel cried, 'Disgraceful? A bloody shame. When everything passes off well tomorrow, and then next Monday, and the bill's already signed into law, and everything's calmed down again, we'll—'

Charles Lewsey, the Sergeant-Major of Police, interrupted with a chuckle. He said, 'You really think this, Colonel? I mean, saying when things get quiet again. You think things will ever get quiet again?'

Inspector Norman shook his head, 'Things will never calm down now.' His eyes found the colonel, who was looking at him. He said, 'I have to agree with the sergeant-major. Things won't calm down. You see, the mistake we made is showing respect for law, as in England, and giving these agitators a free rein. I am sorry to say this, Colonel, but by your leave I want to feel this is where we went wrong. If we had put them behind bars from the very start, at least when Governor Jerningham abolished the Borough Council in 1899 and they kicked up hell, if we had thrown at least Lazare and Maresse-Smith in jail and at least detained Alcazar for a while, things wouldn't have reached so far.'

The others agreed but Colonel Brake just looked at them and said nothing. He said in his mind, 'These chaps are excellent police officers, and you can call Major Rooks an experienced soldier, but what do these officers know about the law? And in any case they could say any damn thing because they don't have responsibility. I wasn't here in 1899, I only came last year, but I'm not so stupid to rush and arrest Lazare and Maresse-Smith. Though if these two break the law, by God! But they are both solicitors. And they have Alcazar there, that misguided fool.'

He looked around and said, 'Officers, I won't tell you the time. But you need to be alert tomorrow morning. I'm not going to say another word. I just want you to go to your quarters and get a little snooze, because you have to be out at the crack of dawn. Promise me one thing: you'll be firm but you won't lose your nerve. Let's hope reason prevails with that mob and we don't have to use firearms. Officers, dismiss.'

The men got up. They each saluted the colonel and went out.

9

There was no relief in the blackness over Petit Valley. Nothing could be discerned, not a shadow. Not even the crest of the massive mountains. Although it was well past two o'clock in the morning it could be called neither the crack of dawn, nor the peep of dawn. But as Lolotte Borde would have said, it was a different day.

Mammie Marie was supposed to be in bed but she was huddled right up against the wall, trying to hear what the two men were saying in the veranda. Her husband was right up to the corner, on the other side of the bedroom door, and the steps leading downstairs just dipped beside them, not too far away.

The voice was saying, 'So I thought I'd come and clear this up. I know rumours are flying around. I just wanted you to know what is the real situation. And what is my position.'

'I appreciate it,' said Mzumbo. 'This is a really unique situation. But when it comes to rumours, yes I heard a thing or two. But I have no time for rumours, honestly. For me, Captain Walter, these are most trying times. These are serious times and one has to fight it with all seriousness. I'm saying this in all honesty: the devil is abroad in the land. I'm not pinpointing any particular devil or of any particular hue. I'm not even saying it's Wrightson, or Brake, or even Governor Maloney. I'm just saying the devil is abroad. The poor are under pressure. Lazare's not fighting for himself. Lazare's offering himself in a struggle. In a cause. Therefore, Captain, I really appreciate this. I can't tell you enough how I feel about your coming tonight.'

'And I can't tell you how I feel about coming. It's been real hell. You know what my clique gives. It's been right royal pressure. As I told you, this whole thing for me began in 1899 when Jerningham made that awful mess and suspended the Port-of-Spain Borough Council.'

Lazare said, 'But in the end it's really Joseph Chamberlain. He is the boss. He is Secretary of State for the Colonies, not Jerningham.'

Darwent felt odd to hear Lazare defending Jerningham. He said, 'Jerningham is the man who recommended it. It's nice of you to forgive him, because I remember in the debates he was harsh—'

'They are all like that. They are taking instructions and they can't see anything else. It's like your horse outside with the bridle. He can only see straight ahead of him and nowhere else. Not on the side or what's around him. Captain Walter, the really unique thing for me is that you have no bridle and you can see. Because you have a clear conscience. I'm really impressed. Thanks for coming.'

Captain Walter Darwent did not know if the 'thanks for coming' meant good-night or not, but it was time to go. Just that he was in the mood for pouring out his heart to Mzumbo Lazare. He was feeling awful. It must be nearly morning although he could not see any easing in the blackness ahead of him. He had spoken truly when, on Mzumbo Lazare opening the door, he had said, 'I have wanted to come for a long time now. From the time these rumours started. In any case I didn't ever want you to feel that it's only because of this girl I'm taking that line, I was always like this. That is my nature. I never liked the injustice – you want me to be frank? I never liked the injustice we the British are inflicting over people of your race. I was proud how Queen Victoria admired you for the jubilee in 1897. But it was 1899 that hurt me. When Jerningham abolished the Borough Council.'

Now that they had exchanged a few words and Mzumbo had said, 'Thanks for coming,' he said hastily, 'Mr Lazare, let me say this. I'll try to be brief. I know you were surprised to see me here. But I had to come because tomorrow might be a tough day and I don't want you to blame all Englishmen. Because I have withdrawn myself from my own people, in justice's name. I withdrew – I'm sure you heard that. The other reason why I came to you is because Eva must have already told you, and you are hearing rumours but you don't know. I don't know how much you know. The main thing I want to say though is that I am with the people of Port-of-Spain. I tried to reason with Wrightson but that's impossible. I know the waterworks bill will pass in the house, not tomorrow, but next Monday, but there can be no doubt it will pass. So I thought I had to come and tell you how I feel. And I already explained why I came at this ghastly hour. I already explained that I just don't know who's looking at me – who's tracking me down.'

56

Mzumbo nearly said, 'Holder's tracking you down!' but he managed to hold his peace.

Captain Darwent said, 'I'll make my way back now. Thank you for giving me a hearing.'

'A pleasure. Thanks for coming.'

'I hope you will be all right tomorrow. Don't be disheartened if the—'

Mzumbo was chuckling. Captain Darwent said, 'Did I say something funny?'

'You keep saying 'tomorrow'. You know what time you knocked on this door? When you knocked on the door I looked at the dial and it was 2 a.m. It is about 2.45 now. Now is today. Today is when we have the fire and brimstone. Tomorrow is . . .' his mind went to Lolotte Borde. He said, 'Tomorrow is a different day.'

'I hope we don't have fire and brimstone. I don't know why we can't live in peace.'

'Because Walsh Wrightson does not want peace. Because Governor Maloney does not want peace. If we don't have the real fire and brimstone today then we'll surely have it next Monday. Because the masses do not want the bill to pass.'

The two men could not see each other clearly in the dark. Mzumbo continued, 'Wrightson prefers to have blood and riot. You know how many times I tried talking to this Director of Public Works? I almost beseeched him on behalf of the good people of Port-of-Spain. He doesn't want to hear me. Captain, it's not a matter of peace with Wrightson, he does not want it. And I am forced to say it's either peace or pieces.'

'Don't be so dramatic.'

'What can I do? Wrightson is not the only stubborn one. What about Hubert Brake, your own police chief? You yourself know that Brake is a warrior. Since Christmas, when this crisis really broke out, Brake is preparing for war. He recruited new policemen as reinforcement. He got soldiers to come down from St James under Major Rooks. I see he brought Inspector Norman right under his wing. And look how close he is with Wrightson? Colonel Brake is no politician and the best thing for him to be is neutral. But is Brake neutral? In any case all those damned—' He stopped. He had almost forgotten that Darwent was British too. He did not want to cast aspersions. He continued, 'All those blighters in the police and the army are just ready to beat up and arrest. And those politicians want to have their way. It's as though they are telling us: "You either submit to the Crown or else!" Nobody to speak up for the people.'

He was worked up but Darwent was thinking it was time to go. He had spotted a little glint of grey above the Fort George hills and there was a puff of what he called 'the morning breeze'.

He said, 'Mr Lazare, good-night. I am not cutting your talk short but please know you are preaching to the converted. I dare to be different, the only such Englishman here – although I wasn't born in England. I won't be seen tomorrow but I'm asking you to take things calmly. The other day I overheard you when you were talking in the square. You told the people something like this: 'Wrightson could try to keep water away from the poor but he can't keep freedom and justice away. The time is bound to come when you'll have your Borough Council again. The day is bound to come when you'll have a voice in the affairs of your country.' I heard you saying that. I think that this is what matters. No matter what happens tomorrow, that is what you have to fight for. Because that is justice and justice will prevail. Goodnight, Mr Lazare.'

'Good-night.'

Captain Darwent disappeared down the steps, and then he was just a dark shadow in the yard.

◆

Mzumbo watched him for just a few minutes. Darwent's carriage had a dull, flickering lantern. It seemed to be moving away fast, and Mzumbo remembered that Darwent always used two horses in tandem. He watched him just a while and then the darkness dissolved everything and he hurried into the bedroom.

His wife was lying on the bed covered up, and he was surprised. He said, 'Mammie Marie, you sleeping and I told you to listen to the conversation? When I opened the door and saw it was Darwent I pretended I was just coming for me night-robe and I told you to go to the corner door and listen. That's why I was standing up in the recess by the stairs.'

She said sleepily, 'I was listening for a little bit.'

He pulled the sheet off her. 'What's wrong with you, girl? You ain't seeing that me tactics working? It's working. With Darwent in the doghouse we opened a wide breach in their ranks. We need that. We have to split their unity. We playing them at their own game: divide and rule.' He shook her again, 'You still sleeping or you wake up!'

She rolled over. 'Manuel, you don't realise it's nearly morning. Good grief, I know tomorrow is a big day but—'

'You making that mistake too? Tomorrow is a big day? It's not tomorrow, it's today. Today is Monday 16th March. Tomorrow – tomorrow is a different day.' He put back the cover on her.

She lay motionless. Her only action was to pull the cover better over her.

He shook her. 'Wake up, sleepy head.'

Marie was furious. She turned over. 'God, what manner of man is this! I worked so hard today but this man has no reason. I'm trying hard to get some sleep to send him off early and look how he's persecuting me!'

'I'm not depending on you to send me off. It's so late already that I ain't even going to risk lying down – in case I oversleep.'

'So because you won't risk lying down you don't want me to lie down?' She was sitting up on the bed now, one hand holding on to the bed-head. She was fuming. 'What's wrong, Mannie? God of Mercy!' She stared angrily for a few moments and then she lay down again.

She had been overjoyed when she had seen it was Walter Darwent who had knocked on the door, but she had been so tired that when she had come back to bed she sank into a heavy sleep, and it was only now she was regaining full possession of her thoughts. She said in a gentler voice, 'Darwent left a long time?'

'He just left. He just just left.'

'You didn't invite him inside and offer him a drink or something?'

'No. I didn't know he was going to stay any time.'

'It seems to me a hell of a long time that I came in to bed. Just imagine you standing up talking at the door. You who's so famous for entertaining. What will Darwent think of us?'

'You worried about that?'

'No, but I want them to know we have class too.'

'Darwent was so damn worried about the situation.'

'What he said? This thing about Eva is true?'

'But you know it's true. We didn't talk about that.'

'So why he really came here?'

'But didn't you say you listened a little bit?'

'But I didn't hear too much.'

'He mentioned Eva just once. He said he knows we know about it, and rumours are flying about.'

She turned over, sat up, pushed herself back, and leaned up on the bed-head rails. 'Eva told him she told us?'

'Well that's it. But he didn't seem ashamed about it at all. I mean let's face it. Englishmen don't own up to that sort of thing in Trinidad. You have to hand it to Darwent. All those big boys know what's going on. He said he has withdrawn from his own people.'

'You mean *they* withdrew from him.'

'That's it. That could be so. But you know he said he's with the people of Port-of-Spain.'

She sat up straight. 'That's because of Eva.'

'I knew you would say that right away. I meself don't know if there's something there. Something genuine. I know I wanted Eva to get that job bad because she's so clever and intelligent she could be like a spy for the Ratepayers, and then knowing that Darwent was at odds with the clique I wanted her to try and drive a bigger wedge between them. But I wasn't catering for what the rumours saying now. In any case I don't know if it's true. I think he started off with some sympathy for her because of our cause.'

Mammie Marie had leaned back again. All the while Mzumbo was talking to her he had been standing, but now he sat down on the bed. Through the jalousies on the side looking towards Maraval they could see the dawn coming.

Mammie Marie said calmly, 'You know I like to hear you talk! So a man has to feel sympathy for a cause to make a move on a woman? Look, Eva was washing for this man and he just tried something. That's it. And you know people. Rumours start to fly. I meself wouldn't put my hand in fire for your niece, but knowing Eva as I do I know she'll never let down Clement.'

Mzumbo said nothing. Mammie Marie smiled and said, 'You ain't answering because you want to believe it's just the cause of what you calling freedom and justice and all that sort of thing. I suppose that as Eva's your niece you believe everything. Because you want to believe everything. Anyway things could be happening. She is a woman and he is a man. But I don't think your so-called "cause" has anything to to with it. And I don't need to tell you that just because she is your niece. Eva is poor but she is no woman of easy virtue.'

'Thank you for saying that,' Mzumbo said. 'I could assure you that the cause also has a part to play – on Eva's side. You know what she told me? She said something to this effect: "Uncle he seems to like me but I'm fighting for our rights and if I could use him I'll use him." '

'She said so?'

'Yes.'

'Well, blow me down! I wasn't expecting that.'

There was silence. Mammie Marie was looking up at the ceiling a little perplexed, and Mzumbo was looking at her, but hearing a chorus of parakeets he turned to look outside. He exclaimed, 'Marie, look! In these few minutes look it's clear morning outside already, let me go and see me dial, eh! I might have to hurry up for the Red House.'

She watched him getting excited and busying himself about, looking like the proverbial fish out of water. For a moment she thought she understood the passion that moved him, his love for the people. But it was a foolish love, a wasted passion. That was not the way, she said to herself. Eva, too, was moved by this unreasonable love, she thought. Instead of those people in the barrackyards and shanty-towns organising themselves to make noise, throw stones, and fight the establishment, why didn't they use that energy in a productive way; to lift themselves above the gutter, to educate and elevate themselves and so give the Englishman something to think about? Then she would have backed them with her whole heart and soul. But there would have hardly been any need to back them then for they would have won already!

She said, 'Oh you have to leave in a jiffy. Let me get up and light the fireplace.' She got down from the bed and unlatched the window to the west, and pushed it open. As she looked out the bright light of dawn hit her full in the face, and surprised, she cried, 'Oh my God!' She was genuinely taken aback. She looked round for Mzumbo and not seeing him, she called, 'Manuel, what's the time?' She threw on her house robe. Mzumbo, who was at the front downstairs in the bathroom taking a bath, called back to her that it was five minutes to six. She said, 'When you coming up bring up some firewood. Okay, sweetheart, doodoo?'

'You trying to sweeten me?'

'I'm not trying to sweeten you, but I don't like you by that Red House today.'

'So what you want me to do, stay home? Are you crazy?'

'If I had the courage I'd come right there with you. But not me!'

10

The heavily built woman walked gingerly down Clifton Hill heading for the town. It was very early in the morning – so early that nothing else seemed to be stirring on Clifton Hill. She was dressed in white with a white head-tie, and she was carrying a heavy hand-basket. After reaching the bottom of the hill and taking the Old St Joseph Road, she crossed the turnpike at Madam Monereau's spring and was now beside Columbus Square, and then there were the giant dark trees of Tamarind Square. From there she could see the heavily shrouded shadow of the building and as she walked towards it she made the sign of the cross. She came to the junction of Rue l'Eglise where the signboard said Duncan Street. She crossed the street and walked into the cathedral, which was open. She put down her hand-basket and made the sign of the cross before moving into a seat, but no sooner had she sat down than someone eased up into the seat and said, 'Lolotte!'

She jumped. She said in a loud whisper, 'Who is that? Who is the person?'

'It's me. You mightn't know me. It's Eva.'

Lolotte's heart started to thump. She did not know Eva to talk to but if it was *that* Eva she knew all about her. Almost the whole town must have heard about her because of the Darwent affair, and to be frank that was the reason she did not strain to meet her before. Because those Englishmen were all the same. She, Lolotte, was one who nobody could catch with that talk that Darwent was really against the waterworks bill, or that he loved Eva. Of course he had his differences with his brother-overlords, and that was why he was putting the waterworks bill as an excuse. She was thinking all this as she looked at Eva and moved round a little to let her sit, although there was nobody else in the long empty pew. The gloom inside the church was lighter than the gloom outside because there was the 'eternal light' burning on the altar. There was also light from two massive candles which had almost spent themselves out. Lolotte wanted to talk but she could not talk in the church. She whispered, 'What you doing here this hour?'

Eva whispered, 'We'll chat afterwards. Let me pass me *chaplet*. Me rosary. Move round a little more and we'll pray together.'

The two women prayed in silence. Lolotte had no rosary but in any case all she intended to do was to say one 'Our Father', one 'Hail Mary', and one 'I Confess'. She was not going to have any long conversation with God this morning. All she wanted to do this morning was to acknowledge herself to God and to ask a special protection. And she wanted to remind God that this was a war, and that everything was in his hands. It was not going to be a fair war, because there had to be a lot of underhand things. The rich people were using all kinds of dirty means to have their way, and the poor had to do just the same. Because it wasn't an equal war. The authorities had force because they had arms and if the poor people had to use stones as ammunition it was the only way they could fight. Her hand-basket of little boulders was on the other side of her but she was not thinking of it so much. When she was finished saying the little prayers she began thinking of this slip of a girl beside her, the girl who they said had the fire brigade man going out of his head. She could not see much of what the girl looked like because it was not light enough, but she wondered what really was going on. For one thing, she did not believe that Darwent was going out of his head. But he had his differences with his people all right. And what were the differences? The other night Mzumbo hit the nail on the head when he simply said Darwent wasn't born in England. Although she never talked with Mzumbo on the subject of the rumours, for the reason that she knew Eva was his niece, she understood that Mzumbo felt there was true love there. True love, my hat! she said to herself. And she grunted 'Hm!'

Eva heard the sound and turned to look. Lolotte whispered, 'No, I didn't say nothing, young lady.'

Eva seemed to be a very young woman, Lolotte did not expect her to be so young. And she was extremely thin. Skin and bone, as they said. Lolotte had expected that for a washerwoman this person would have had more size. And a little more weight. Not of course, big and fat like a Lolotte Borde! She chuckled. At first she used to hate herself for being fat. Now she accepted herself, simply because the town accepted her and respected her. The other day Maresse-Smith said, 'There's only one Lolotte Borde!' She fretted, but she liked that.

She glanced at Eva. As she waited for Eva to finish passing her *chaplet*, her thoughts shifted from Edgar Maresse-Smith to what this day might be like, and she began thinking of the crowds who would be gathering by daylight, and of how policemen would be swarming the place like ants, and she began thinking of the debate and the confusion, and maybe the worst would really come to the worst and the police would use their batons, but if that happened at all, if that happened, Oh God have mercy, but stones would have to fly. Yes, stones would fly. She suddenly became worried because the few stones which were covered over in her basket were not enough, and she began wondering wildly where she could get more. Then her thoughts slipped to Greasy Pole who said he would beat up Wrightson, and what she hoped would be the wildness and the fury of the people began to grow vivid in her thoughts, and she became anxious to go. In fact, where she had thought of going at first, when she had left home, was to Trinity Cathedral, because it was so near to the Red House, just a stone's throw. She smiled but she did not like that kind of humour so early in the morning. But since Trinity Cathedral was just facing Brunswick Square, that was the place to be – not in the Cathedral of the Immaculate Conception. It was true that God was everywhere, but leaving God aside for the moment, if she had been in Trinity Church now she would have been able to stay right there and have a good peep at what was happening, and afterwards join the crowds when the crowds came out. But she was where she was because the impulse had come over her. Being Catholic she felt she could not pass the Catholic cathedral to go to pray in the Anglican cathedral. She was annoyed with herself because it was only the priests who made that sort of fuss. She told herself again that God was everywhere, and again she put God aside, and tied her head-tie tighter. She looked towards Eva who seemed to have nearly finished her chaplet. What Lolotte thought she would do now would be to ease out on the side with Eva, when Eva was finished praying – ease out on the side between the cathedral and King Street, by the wrought-iron railing, mainly to see what the girl looked like, although she did not have to make it look obvious. And she had to find out what side Eva was really on, although she felt heartened because it looked clear-cut; and she had to see how the girl would fit in with her plans to— She jumped.

Eva had whispered, 'You ready?'

Lolotte said, 'I was waiting on you all the time.'

'Where you going now?'

'First, let's go outside here by the wall. Let's see what's happening on King Street. We could stand up by the wall and look down the road.'

Even before they got out into the space between the cathedral and King Street, Lolotte had already assessed Eva. Eva was very small and slender, and Lolotte supposed if Darwent wanted his head to be turned he was welcome to it. In any case, being a woman herself she was no judge of the attraction of women, but she had lived long enough and had seen enough to know that men loved these very insubstantial ladies and did not turn much of an eye to full-bodied women like herself. She felt a little badly, as she held the rails and looked up King Street. Men were stupid anyway, she thought, as she watched. There were quite a few people in the street, mainly down at the crossing of Abercromby Street and King Street, stretching as far as Marine Square. Overhead the sky was much brighter than the atmosphere around but it was growing light very fast. In fact, when Lolotte had arrived at church she would not have been able to see anything down King Street. Her eyes were at the moment looking much nearer than the corner of King Street and Abercromby Street. In fact they were looking towards the other side of the road around the junction of King and George streets. There was nothing there but if there was anything at all it would come from there. Eva roused her from her thoughts. 'Lolotte, what really brought you out here this unholy hour?'

'How you mean? What about you – you ain't here? Talking about me, well I couldn't sleep, that's why. This is the big day. Something have to happen today. Tell me, you is Eva? I mean you is the real Eva?'

Eva chuckled. 'Yes, I'm real all right.' She was in an old print dress and she thought maybe that was why Lolotte asked if she was the real Eva. She didn't know what people expected. So much was being said about her, she was well aware of it. Sometimes it made her laugh and sometimes it made her angry, and at other times she just had to shake her head. Looking at Lolotte she had found it so odd that this large woman should be dressed in white – a white dress with white head-tie – to go into what was bound to be a seething, sweating, unruly mass. White already made one stand out so much. She, Eva, had dressed very lightly in a sort of washed-out blue all-in-one print dress that used to have hibiscus flowers and humming birds.

No flowers and birds were there now, though. The flowers had faded and the birds had flown away. She smiled tiredly. She looked at Lolotte, 'I suppose I have to say I is the real Eva. Because I feeling real vexed this morning.'

'Vexed? Why?'

'Because people shouldn't have to do this. People shouldn't have to be up early in the morning to fight for what should be theirs already. By birthright.'

'You could tell the Englishmen that for me.'

Eva just looked at her but said nothing, and Lolotte said again, 'But you know something? We'll win, you know. We bound to win in the end. But I don't know when the end is. That's all. But I hope what will happen this time will teach them a lesson.'

This jolted Eva. 'What will happen?'

'I don't know meself, but something have to make today different. In fact, just the people turning out in numbers mean we ain't 'fraid them and we ain't 'fraid the guns they toting. You heard what happen yesterday evening? They nearly beat up Wrightson when he was going down to Union Club. Four or five police had to fire off in the air. Holder was there. You didn't know about that?'

'I was in Red Star barrackyard at the time.'

Lolotte was taken aback. 'Good God! True?' She had not heard Eva was living there. She was not sure. She said, 'Careful, girl, those police could raid that place anytime. You ain't living there though? You living there? Where you living?'

'Oh, not there. I ain't living there. Where I living? Duke and Richmond. Corner house. But you know Greasy Pole living in Red Star. And he's a key man in this business.' She didn't elaborate further.

Lolotte was just looking at her. She did not put her thoughts into words but she was thinking: 'You small but you brave.'

The day had cleared up quite brightly while they were talking. The cathedral clock was showing five minutes to six but they could not see it. Lolotte said, 'Look, in those few minutes I get to know you I feel I could ask you this. Tell me, you is the same Eva they talking about with Captain Darwent?'

'Yes, it's me.'

67

'I ain't going to ask you if you involved with him or not because that is your business. But tell me, you getting any special protection?'

Eva looked at Lolotte as if Lolotte was crazy. She said, 'Darwent ain't getting special protection, let alone me.'

'They against him so bad? He really against the waterworks bill, or they hate him because of you?'

'He was against the waterworks bill even before I went to wash for him.'

'Oh, I see. I hear he wasn't born in Trinidad.'

'Well, that's another point why they don't make such a fuss about him. But I don't see why not. These people crazy.'

'You seem to think a lot of him.'

Eva chuckled. She knew very well what Lolotte wanted to find out. She had known Lolotte a long time by sight, but they had never spoken. In fact only last Saturday she had seen Lolotte on the Queen's Park Savannah poised to throw a stone. But in any case, who did not know Lolotte Borde, the fat lady who sold caramels and tolooms, paymie, and pone, at the corner of Marine Square and Chacon Street? On Harriman's pavement? Lolotte was one of the most ardent supporters in what she, Eva, saw as the main struggle, and she really admired her. That was why she came up and talked to her this morning. But she was always slightly amused about Lolotte because from what she could see, policemen were afraid to tackle her. She seemed to lead a charmed life simply because her size could make two or three of the average policeman.

Eva wanted to change the subject of Darwent and she said, 'Look down King Street. Look at the crowds swarming down there, I don't know if God will help us this morning and we could get those police bastards to back off.'

The word almost made Lolotte back off, so surprised she was.

Eva said, 'People just have to fight. They just can't sit down and take everything.'

'But I . . . I can't see how—' Lolotte paused.

'How what?'

'Well Mzumbo, who is me good friend, and Edgar, and Greasy Pole, they think you doing a really good job. But I'll tell you frankoment, I did never believe in you. Because I tell Edgar if you is friends with the fire brigade you can't really be our friend.'

Eva laughed. And then her mouth twisted slightly. She was looking down King Street while she was talking and all of a sudden she was sure one of the policemen she could see standing at the corner of the Ice House was Sergeant Holder. She always felt a little uneasy when she saw Holder. She said to Lolotte, 'You feel like making a move now?'

'But my move is for Trinity.'

'Yes. That's fine with me.'

'We could stay in Trinity and see what's going on by the Red House grounds before joining the crowd. At least I'm speaking for me. I'm known to the police so I have to keep scarce.'

Eva smiled. She said, 'And I have to keep just a little more scarce. You see who's down there, by the Ice House?'

Lolotte looked. Then she said, 'You mean the police on the pavement? As if he leaning on the wall?'

'You know who is that?'

'That look like Holder.'

'Yes. You right. I should know. I used to live with him.'

'You used to live with that beast?'

'Once upon a time.'

Lolotte said nothing.

Eva said, 'I don't trust that so-and-so. First he used to beg me back every day. Every time he met me. I told him I'll never go back with him. Never. He used to still beg me to come back. Now he stopped begging. You know what he told me last week? He said he'll blow me blasted head off.'

'Oh God of mercy!'

'You going now? Let's make a move. Jesu! Look at the people in the street already. Come, Lolotte, let's pass up George Street and make for Trinity.'

Lolotte hesitated, 'So much police up George Street. I hope they don't check me basket.'

'It have police everywhere,' Eva said. She looked up and down the street then she glanced at Lolotte's hand-basket. It was covered over delicately with gauze as if what she had in the basket were coconut tarts and sugar cake. She chuckled ever so slightly. She said, 'That ain't looking like what's really in there. But if you 'fraid, leave it in this church for the time being.'

Lolotte looked up and down. There were so many people walking along the street, on the pavement, and crossing the road, that the policemen seemed to have the time of their lives to keep their eyes on everybody. She said, 'You ready? Let's go. I'll take me chance. Look, just one second.' She was gazing at the sky.

In the space between the buildings at the junction of George Street and King Street there seemed to be a beam of silver light streaming between some heavy clouds. For an instant it seemed so bright compared with the sky over the street that Lolotte was over-awed. Her heart thumped. She said inside of her, 'Father, this is a sign? Speak to me heart, Lord. O God, hallelujah.'

She looked towards Eva who was again watching up and down King Street. Lolotte looked up at the sky again, but winds had blown clouds over the bright part and made the whole dome appear grey again.

Lolotte said, 'That's funny. That patch of light done gone. In a split second! I feel that was a sign.'

Eva looked up but saw nothing. 'Sign?' she said. 'I ain't seeing nothing but, yes, perhaps it was a sign for me.' Then she said to herself, 'I hate that crazy Thomas Holder. He said he'd be looking for me to blow me head off. I know he can't do me a damn thing if the crowd there. And I could sure sure make me getaway.'

Lolotte was looking at Eva. She said, 'Buck up, this is not a time to daydream. You said that was a sign for you? What sign is that? You looking for a sign?'

'Just a joke,' she said. 'I was thinking of this church. Immaculate Conception. The Archbishop here is not Flood? Vincent Flood? You never see these people in a time of crisis. In a moment of glory, yes. But not in crisis. The church people so powerful but they don't cry stop. They let people like Wrightson and Colonel Brake ride roughshod over us.'

Lolotte just looked at her.

'That's true. You ain't notice? And if it have any tragedy, like when people get killed, you'll hear them with "*Blessed are they that mourn, for they shall be comforted.*" That's all we have to do: mourn. I don't want to mourn and I don't want to be comforted, and I don't want to hear any damn nonsense from these people,' she said angrily.

Lolotte put a hand on Eva's shoulder. 'Don't let them get you hysterical,' she whispered. 'You okay? Take it easy.'

Eva had turned away but now she glanced at Lolotte: 'You ready to go?'

'Ah, yes,' she said distantly. Lolotte was very deeply moved by what Eva had said. Sometimes this was exactly how she felt. She made a move to go.

Eva was suddenly staring about and looking towards various points. She said, 'But it drizzling a little bit.'

Lolotte had felt the light wetness but had not even remarked on it. On a day like today she was ready to withstand anything. She said now, 'Showers of blessing. This ain't rain. Let's go. This is only a passing cloud.'

Eva said, 'No. Come here. Come, let's go back inside and pray a little.'

'But we ain't pray already?'

'Come. Come here. I want to tell you something.'

'*You* can't come? You stick-up against the wall or something?'

When Lolotte drew near Eva said, 'Lolotte, look, you brave but for Christ sake, be real. You was asking if I is the real Eva. You is the real Lolotte Borde? Who everybody know? Well, I'll tell you something, the real Lolotte is a lot – I ain't laughing at you. But as you know, everybody know you. And the police will be vicious, vicious today. I mean, if you was in the crowd it would be different. You displaying yourself in the open so much. I was just noticing! Be real, the police know you is a ring-leader. If even *I* know that, you ain't think the police bound to know? Clement said the police have a few people well marked. He mentioned me uncle Mzumbo, Edgar Maresse-Smith, you ... '

Lolotte jumped. She said, 'Who is Clement?'

'Me chum.'

'How you mean "chum"?'

'Well. A sort of boyfriend.'

'He is police?'

'No.'

'And how come he know that the police marked me?'

'I can't tell you everything. There's some things you can't talk. All I could tell you is don't push yourself in the firing line. They'll cut you down now for now. It's better to go back inside the church. Too much police and some looking our way. You see how it getting bright and the drizzle passing? Let's wait for the crowd. So far as me uncle said, by half past six it will be a jam session round Brunswick Square.'

'That's where we should be,' Lolotte said. 'That's where we should be, in Trinity Cathedral, near Brunswick Square. But anyway, what I want you to know is this: Lolotte Borde might be big and fat but she ain't 'fraid nobody—'

'But it doesn't mean you have to expose yourself to get cut down. In any case so much depend on you. Me uncle said you could rally the crowd, and I meself saw you on the Queen's Park Savannah. I never knew you could talk so. You see this morning by the Red House? We want you.'

'But if you 'fraid the police, how you'll get there?' Lolotte laughed. She looked around. The drizzle was coming a little heavier. She said, 'It's almost daylight, let's go back inside the church, since you want to go inside the church.'

They went back inside the church and Eva was most relieved. But although she was so relieved it did not mean that she was less brave than Lolotte Borde. It was only that the number of grey and black tunics had upset her. Also, Holder was not too far away and she knew what he was capable of. She had noticed of course what effect the bit of flattery had had on Lolotte – telling her she never knew she could talk so.

In fact she had never heard Lolotte speak. On Saturday at the Savannah Lolotte had spoken but she, Eva, had reached late. The truth was she was never very much in the heat of what she called 'confusion', and maybe it had to do with her having lived with Holder. The sergeant, knowing she was Mzumbo's niece, and seeing Mzumbo as the chief troublemaker, was always following Eva to see if he could find her in the crowd. In fact, she, her uncle, and Maresse-Smith, were really people marked by Holder. Maybe Lolotte Borde too, but she was not sure about it. But Standish, the informer, did mention Lolotte's name to Clement, this was no lie. She kneeled down on the hard knee-rest and eyed Lolotte Borde from the side. The church was light now and the bowed head, the white dress, and the white head-tie did not fail to make an impression on her. She looked around and she was surprised because there were quite a few more people in the church. It was nearly six and the priest was bound to come to say mass. He said mass at six every day in the cathedral and if he did not say mass today it would be clear he was not with the people. But did he not say only yesterday morning, Sunday morning, did he not say he would be with them until the end of the world? She wished Holder had heard that. What would Holder have done if he had heard that, she could not guess. Holder was more for the Government, more for the British, than the British themselves. For instance, if Wrightson had heard Father Martin say that, he might have hung his head in shame and might have said, 'Bless me, Father, for I have sinned.' But not Sergeant Holder. He would have caught a fit.

She looked at Lolotte beside her and then she turned in front and bowed her head as if she was praying. But she was thinking. She was thinking of the great clash today in the council Chamber, with Alcazar against Wrightson, and with the uproar in the public gallery – for she had no doubt that people would get in without tickets. And then she thought of how she was forced to lead on Walter Darwent, a really good man. Not lead on, really, because she had grown to like him. But her passion was for Change, and her own heated desire was to see the down-trodden triumph. And that desire was in her blood, it was not put into her by her uncle. Even before the water crisis began, in fact even before the Borough Council was abolished in 1899, she had burned with quiet fury to see how the foreigners wielded their power, lorded it over everybody, and had things their own way.

She began breathing a little quicker but she did not raise her head. She did not hate Darwent at all. He was a true gentleman, tender and kind, and – she was ashamed to say this – more likeable than any man she had ever met. More likeable than Clement? Her heart was saying yes, but she found it hard to admit this.

◆

'Um!' She started. A hand had shaken her shoulder. She felt as if her blood ran cold, and then she realised it was Lolotte.

'You sleeping or praying? You look as though you was having a doze.'
'Me? Oh no.'
'You saw when the priest came in?'
'The priest here?' She raised her eyes to the altar, concerned.
Lolotte laughed softly. Eva looked around and saw the church almost full. Lolotte said, 'You wanted to be in the crowd. When this mass finish we'll follow this crowd to Brunswick Square.'

Eva rubbed her eyes, and she looked up at the altar. Her heart thumped. That was not the priest, that was the archbishop. He was in purple and he had both of his arms outstretched. She was overwhelmed. Her voice trembled as she murmured, 'Your Grace, you are here, and I said harsh words. Bless me, Father, for I have sinned.'

11

Colonel Brake and the Honourable Walsh Wrightson stood quietly in the little tower of the Red House and watched the scene in and around Brunswick Square. It was six in the morning and although on the ground itself it was quite bright it was still dark in the leaves of the trees. But yet, from this early hour, people were assembling from different points of the town and drifting aimlessly around the square. There was a fair number inside the square, already, and in the centre of the square, close to the small fountain, a cluster of young men had collected. There were a few carts, and these were seeming to come up Abercromby Street and turn into Hart Street, and at times into Knox Street. The two officers glanced every now and again into the yard of Trinity Cathedral. There was a mass in the cathedral and when the mass was over it would be a good indication as to what would happen, because as far as was reported, people had been going into the church all through the early hours of the morning. Colonel Brake and Walsh Wrightson watched in silence. At least they could see Trinity Cathedral beneath them at the southern end of the square; but they could see nothing at all of what was happening at the northern end of the square owing to the denseness of the trees.

To the north of the square was Knox Street and as it ran alongside the square, just around its middle on the opposite side was Pembroke Street, running north, right up to the Queen's Park Savannah. Colonel Brake always had at least three policemen at that junction because the northern gate of the square faced Pembroke Street, and if there was any trouble in the square people would surely try to escape out of that gate and up Pembroke Street.

For another reason, that was also a strategic gate in the thoughts of Colonel Brake. On one side of the very junction lived Dr Pollonais, who always described himself as a humanist, and on the other corner was the new public library. The new library was exactly on the spot where the Town Commissioner's office had been, there being no Borough Council.

The colonel stared towards that junction as if he could see through the leaves. It always riled him to think of the doctor. The fact that Pollonais was well known for his sympathy for the rabble, together with the fact that what was called 'Town Commissioner's corner' was a rallying point for mischief-makers, made that junction a very dangerous one indeed. The Government had demolished the old building and built the public library in 1901, but that corner still attracted violence. Colonel Brake was still thinking about this and wondering if he should not reinforce that part, when Wrightson nudged him on the shoulder and pointed down Abercromby Street.

As Colonel Brake saw the buggy he said, 'The villain!'

There was silence for a while. They both looked towards the buggy. Wrightson said, 'I knew he'd be out early.'

The colonel said, 'He was up to something last evening, I forgot to tell you. Don't know what it was. We saw him pass down St Vincent Street in his carriage. I can't tell where you were. We saw him pass, and Holder, who was on Abercromby Street, came in with other news. I told the stupid Holder that Lazare just passed down in his carriage and to track him. He ran outside and dashed down the street like a madman. Just to come in about two hours later to tell me he spotted Maresse-Smith talking to Lolotte Borde ... '

'Lolotte—?'

'That is the big fat spy. We had her in for a little time last November. Stone-throwing. Don't you remember? She sits at the corner of Chacon Street and King Street. Usually with a tray, pretending she's selling. Holder wants to arrest her again, but she is so clever that — look, look, Lazare's turning into Hart Street.'

The two men strained to see where he was going. The carriage stopped briefly in front of Trinity Cathedral and three people got out and went into the pathway. The carriage went off again but was soon obscured by the trees.

Colonel Brake said, 'Holder is so zealous that sometimes I think he's unbalanced. He detests Mzumbo, and yet, fancy this, yet he lets this man slip out of sight because of Lolotte Borde and Maresse-Smith!'

'But Maresse-Smith is dangerous too. Don't trust Edgar Maresse-Smith!'

'He's a blow-hard, but popular. And that's why he's a blow-hard. Because people are impressed with words. Hot air, but nothing behind it.

Mzumbo Lazare is the man, not Maresse-Smith. Lazare's dangerous. The only good thing about him, and that's why I don't want him in yet, the only good thing about him is that he talks about law and order. And believe me, Mr Wrightson, that's the key. If we don't have law and order, the guns will have to speak, and I don't want blood.'

There was silence.

The colonel spoke again: 'Else, how can we say we are ruling in harmony, and about the great love for the British throne? But the trouble is, Holder badly wants Maresse-Smith.'

'Who is the boss – Holder or you?'

'Good question. Sometimes it's better to let Holder feel he's the boss. You get so much more out of him then. He could be a vicious tiger to his own people.'

'At least they're terrified of him. You heard the rumour of his common-law wife?'

Colonel Brake listened and immediately fell into silence. He was not going to talk about that this morning. Although it was very remiss of Holder to let Mzumbo get out of sight yesterday, the sergeant more than made up for it by his usual zeal. He, Colonel Brake, did feel a little embarrassed and guilty that afterwards, to make amends, Holder had attempted to snatch Maresse-Smith from his carriage on some false charge, and that he, the colonel, had to intervene, but when you were operating in this sort of atmosphere – what did they say? *All is fair in love and war.* The blunt fact was that Holder, as one man, had the whole town scared. Nobody knew what he would do next. People were more scared of Holder than they were scared of Rooks with his thirty-five crack marksmen. And then Holder, having sprung from the masses himself, knew the criminals; he knew their vices, and he knew every nook and cranny where one could find them. So why not make him feel he was boss sometimes? This was in the best interest of the British flag.

Wrightson said several things that the colonel did not hear well, and to which he would not have cared to reply anyway, and now Wrightson was speaking again. He said: '...So I grunted, "Aye, aye, Captain". You see, Colonel? You see what I mean? Now about – is it Charlotte? I know nothing about Charlotte Borde, and I can't say much, but I can tell you, Colonel, that man Maresse-Smith detests me because of the water bill. Of course you know that. He attacks me everywhere he speaks. He says all sorts of unfounded things about me.'

Colonel Brake listened. Then he said, 'Let's be honest, Mr Wrightson, they all hate you. In any case, although it is not right to say this, the bill has flaws.'

The two men were close together. They were both in full uniform, and Wrightson's cork hat was so white it was beginning to gleam in the morning air. Colonel Brake, in the uniform of Commandant, had his khaki-covered cork hat in his hand. He was looking at the Director of Public Works to see his reaction.

Wrightson did not speak, and Colonel Brake said, 'You didn't imagine you were one of the dearly beloveds, did you?'

Wrightson snapped, 'I did not come here to be loved. I came here to do my work. What I want to know is if you think I deserve being hated. What I am doing—'

'I know what you are doing, Honourable Director. I was just making a point.'

'Well since everybody hates me, as you say—'

'I never said that. I said, "They all hate you." If *everybody* hated you, I wouldn't be here now.'

The Public Works Director asked himself, 'Doesn't *all* mean everybody?' But he said nothing. The colonel put a hand on his shoulder. 'I know you are nervous and tired. Who wouldn't be! Anyway, this might be just the day you have to be strong and tough. So bear up. Oh, look!' he pointed down at the cathedral yard.

Wrightson looked and said in his mind, 'God!' It was quite light and they could see scores of people pouring from the church. He said, 'I wonder how many of that scum's already here.'

'But can't you see?' The colonel looked at him. 'Scores. Scores of those bloody idlers are already present. Looks like hundreds. They are still pouring out of the church.'

In the churchyard, beneath them on the left across the Hart Street junction, it looked as if several hundreds of people were already outside and there was still a stream coming out of the northern and eastern doors. Very few of them seemed regular church goers, and as they emerged into the morning light they seemed to be uneasy and looking round as if waiting for something to happen. Colonel Brake felt very pessimistic but he did not want to speak to cause any further upset. The Director of Public Works stood back a little from the trellis of the tower-balcony. He muttered, 'Hundreds of them already.'

'Don't forget it's morning mass. There's mass every morning.'

'But you don't get hundreds going to morning mass, do you?'

'How do you know, Sir? Have you ever come out to look before? You are directing public works and I am directing the police, and I can tell you there are lots of things you don't know.'

'You can't convince me these people came to mass. Do they look to you as if they came to mass? If you look at them well you'll see they came to battle. Look at the clothes. But I could see your policemen are well on the alert.'

Colonel Brake just smiled quietly. He had noticed his policemen a long time before. It was reassuring that he did not need to pass down any fresh orders this morning. Policemen were sprinkled at various points, and in fact about fifteen minutes before, five of them had walked up Abercromby Street with Inspector Norman. Now on the pavement on the far side of Hart Street, almost on Frederick Street, he was noticing Sergeant Holder. He wondered if Sergeant Holder would tell the people in Trinity churchyard to get a move on. Perhaps at this point the sergeant did not even know the service was over because the crowd had not come out on to the pavement at all. Not on Hart Street. But as the colonel looked down Abercromby Street he could see a few people walking down the road, and it seemed as if a few roughs were walking up from the junction at Queen Street.

The Honourable Wrightson was correct: what most of them had come out for was to do battle. A few of them were in torn-up clothes, which the colonel saw as 'battledress'. To the north of him people were already approaching the square. He heard the ringing of a bell almost beneath him in the street and he knew at once it was one of those carts with the criers calling on people to come to the square. He turned to Wrightson. 'Let's get out of here. I'm ready to go outside and watch what's going on. Please just go to the council chamber. I'll send some coffee to you.'

They both withdrew from the tower.

◆

It was now bright daylight, at least a quarter to seven, but only a small part of the crowd had moved from the yard of Trinity church. But there were already a lot of people in Hart Street, both on the side towards Brunswick Square, and on the other side by the fire brigade station. There were groups walking up and down St Vincent Street too, and Colonel Brake was getting regular reports about what was happening on that side. He was standing on the southern side of the Red House, facing the square across Abercromby Street, and he was standing still, and at ease, smart in his khaki uniform, with short trousers and sash, short sleeves, and his hands holding his baton behind his back. Now he did not think of himself as colonel. He was standing there as Commandant of Local Forces and Inspector-General of Police.

Although he seemed perfectly still it was as if he had eyes at all points of his head, for he seemed to be seeing everything. He saw when Sergeant Holder sent a group scampering into the square from the Hart Street side, and he saw when Lance-Corporal Leon Alexander turned back a cart which was coming down Abercromby Street. From where he was now, he could see Dr Pollonais's house clearly from between the trunks of the trees in the square, and when he saw Dr Pollonais come outside to the front of the house the inspector-general pulled out his timepiece which was on a gold chain.

He breathed hard and he said to himself, 'Five past seven and the blasted doctor doesn't have anything better to do than to come outside. He wants the crowd to see they have his support. I'll break him if it's the last thing I do. He doesn't know how easy it is to be behind bars!'

The inspector-general continued to stand up there, his face seemingly in a straight line with the monument in the centre of Brunswick Square. In a sense he was just like one of those figures of the monument, for he was motionless, his face veering to neither right nor left. Yet he noticed when Darwent came out of the fire brigade building and spoke to a policeman, and then spoke to somebody in the crowd. And he saw when Alcazar and John Wainwright walked up the street in lively chatter. Wainwright was secretary of the Ratepayers' Association. He simply had to see those two because they passed just in front of him. Yet although the buggy of Mzumbo Lazare was not passing in front of him, but on the distant side of the square, he spotted it. It was on the far side of Frederick Street, and the foliage of the trees on the other side of the square was like a thick green curtain, but in spite of this Colonel Brake glimpsed Lazare's buggy between the south-western edge of the square and the meat merchants, Messrs Eric Grell. He had been standing there for just about fifteen minutes but in that time the crowd had swelled to about twice the number it had been before. He was still calm but he was beginning to grow concerned.

Now he moved. Instinctively he looked around for his key policemen. He could not see Holder and this puzzled him. Holder was outside the Trinity Cathedral gates only a moment ago. He had seen most things but he had not noticed when Holder had chased one of the youths into the church. He kept glancing around for Holder, mainly using his eyes, not turning his head.

◆

Sergeant Holder was kept from rushing into the cathedral by Bishop Hayes. Bishop Hayes had heard the commotion and he saw the crowd scatter and as he rushed down from the altar he saw the young man entering through the eastern door and before he himself could reach the door the sergeant was in front of him.

Bishop Hayes stretched out his hand, impeding entry. He cried, 'What is this, Sergeant?'

'The scamp broke the law. He is inside the church.'

Bishop Hayes said softly but firmly, 'This is a house of God, Sergeant. The youth who ran inside the church may have broken the law – the law of man – but this is a house of God. Please respect the church. Inside these walls God gives his people sanctuary.'

'He is God's people?' Sergeant Holder almost raised his voice. He was so fed up that it was only because Bishop Hayes was the Bishop of Trinidad that he did not push him down and enter. Because he could see the fugitive, the baker, one-armed Lumpress, pressing against a crowded pew with the whole congregation startled and staring towards the door. He was infuriated. The words 'sanctuary' and 'House of God' had no meaning for him now. He was bristling. He could not push down the bishop because not only would the crowd riot immediately, but the very people whose servant he was – Brake, Wrightson, Norman, Governor Maloney – they would squirm, and they would chase him out of the force and banish him, or even lock him up. He did not even want to glare at the bishop, for fear the bishop would communicate with Governor Maloney. And here again was irony at its highest. The bishop, like Dr Pollonais, like Croney of Ice House Hotel – like all the cronies, in fact, he smiled sourly – even people like Goodwille and Darwent, these people were nothing but snakes in the grass, and holding a knife to the throat of the very government who would jump to support them. And soft soap them. Especially Darwent.

As Holder stood there before the bishop, with the congregation looking on, Darwent flashed to his mind and his blood rose. He had been wondering whether Eva was somewhere in this church or over on Darwent's side. He never had real proof of what they were saying about Darwent and Eva but nevertheless he believed it, because he knew she was washing for Darwent, and anything could happen. If Darwent was of the same sort of people like himself he would have already found some excuse to shoot him down, but with these Englishmen, they always supported each other, and if he dared to be so rash he could easily find himself slung out of the job and tried and even hanged. This thought riled him. Because Darwent was out in open rebellion against the Government, but they would never lock *him* up. Darwent could stand neither Wrightson nor Brake, and just moments ago he, Darwent, had left the fire brigade office and walked over the road and had openly spoken to Thomas Meade Kelshall, a prominent member of the Ratepayers' Association, and one of the organisers of this din. All these thoughts flashed through the head of Sergeant Holder in one wild moment, and looking at the bishop he thought it would be better to remain calm just in order to get inside the church and take Lumpress away. And of course to look to see if Eva was there.

While he was thinking, the bishop was speaking to him and saying something about the beatitudes and the law of heaven and forgiveness – something of the sort, he wasn't even listening. Now, anxious to get inside the church to seize Lumpress, he said, 'Bishop, you see me? I'm just a servant of the law. I'm a servant of law and order. In other words, if the higher-ups do wrong I can't be held responsible, but that ragged young man glaring at me from over there...' he pointed, and if he had raised the gun he might have fired. He struggled to keep calm. He said, 'He already lost an arm. He ought to be put away behind bars. Bishop, we'll obey the laws of heaven when we get there, but now I want to obey the law of the land. Please let me take that boy. He ought to be put away. If we put him away he'll grow up proper.'

The bishop quietly said, 'It's some of the higher-ups who ought to be put away, believe me, Sergeant. You call him ragged. He's ragged because he is poor. Shame on you. That police uniform you are wearing is not your own – it was not bought by you, so you are not ragged. That boy is poor as is everyone else. Almost, everyone who came to my church this morning is shackled by poverty. But God loves the poor. Blessed are the poor in spirit for they shall see God.'

It was as if Sergeant Holder wanted to puke. He said, 'Bishop Hayes, Your Lordship, I just wanted to come inside to see if somebody's here.'

'Somebody else? In addition to the one-armed fellow? In any case, no. No.' He had put down his arms but now he stretched them out to their full width across the door. 'No, Sergeant, this is a house of God. I want no conflict. And Sergeant, you have interrupted my service. I am praying for all the poor and all the wretched. People like yourself. I am asking for God's grace. Within this church there is only peace, not conflict.'

Sergeant Holder felt so frustrated and angry he could hardly contain himself. 'Bishop Hayes, you saying now you ain't want conflict but all your sermons preaching against the Government. You taking the side of this wicked good-for-nothing rabble. That is what causing the conflict.'

Then, looking at the whole congregation, he turned again to the bishop, 'Look how everybody looking at me. And laughing at me. You making me feel shame.'

The bishop shook his head with pity. Sergeant Holder stood there, his face overwrought. He was feeling very embarrassed because it was the first time that people were seeing him stopped, but although his heart pained him he was trying not to look disrespectful. Yet with all his control there was a burning inside, and he felt very aggressive. The butt of his gun was resting on the concrete and he was supporting it by the barrel. He hoped this was saying something to the congregation. He 'broke' the barrel of the gun so that it wouldn't fire off by accident and shoot him. The bishop lowered his eyes to the gun. It looked immaculate and well-oiled. The bishop thought, 'What sort of day will this be, Father?' He felt as if his heart was weeping. It was useless to talk to Sergeant Holder. The bishop closed his eyes and murmured, 'Oh God, let thy divine counsel speak to the hearts of evil men.'

'What's that, Bishop?'

'Sergeant Holder, I did not speak. I simply prayed for you and for those you serve. Excuse me. I think I will close the church.'

Neither the bishop nor Sergeant Holder appeared conscious of the crowd of people looking at them from every side. From the church and from the churchyard. When the bishop said he would close the church the sergeant felt the atmosphere tense.

He said, 'How you will close the church if it's full of people?'

The bishop did not answer. His head was bowed and he was muttering something.

'While ago I think I heard you say the word "evil".'

'Evil is everywhere. You have a gun to kill. To kill for what reason? Water? The people want water to drink not to be killed for it. Is it blood you want, Sergeant? Excuse me, I will close the church.'

'The people want water to waste, not to drink. They don't want to pay for nothing. All they want is bacchanal, and they have big-time people encouraging them and—' He stopped suddenly. He did not want to go too far. These Englishmen, even when they were vexed with each other they stuck together.

The bishop's face showed pain. He said, 'Sergeant, will you excuse me? I want to close the church.'

The sergeant flared up again in spite of himself. But he controlled his voice: 'Close the church? With that man inside?'

Bishop Hayes said in his mind, 'Yes. To protect him from you.' He said to the sergeant, 'Excuse me, please.' He turned around to the people and he raised his hands. He turned to those outside and it was as though he was blessing them. They took it as if he was calling to them and as many as could cram inside the church, got in. For they were all frightened of Holder. All the doors were shut except the one at which the bishop and Holder were standing. Then it was as if someone inside shrieked, for the bishop left Holder standing there and went and blessed those who remained outside. Holder just turned round and looked to see what the bishop was doing. When Bishop Hayes came back Holder said, 'If I did want to I woulda run rampant in here when you went outside.'

Bishop Hayes said, 'There is a God above. I believe in him. Sergeant, I will see the inspector commandant to remind him that this is holy ground. I cannot have my prayers to God interrupted. And I will have to tell the inspector commandant that blessed are the meek for they will inherit the land. Will you withdraw, Sergeant?'

The sergeant was already scared. When he backed away the bishop shut the door.

12

Eva was not inside the church. When she and Lolotte Borde had got into the crowd they had soon lost each other, and when she got to Trinity Cathedral, although she had knelt down to pray she slipped out as soon as Sergeant Holder came to the door. When he was accosting the bishop she was retreating hastily through the back gate facing Chacon Street, and she had turned right on Queen Street, gone straight past the Carlisle Hotel, and had turned up Richmond Street for home. She did not stay home long. She left directly after changing her dress for she decided she had better go to the barrackyard, 'Red Star'. She had come mainly to collect the money she had put aside. She never liked even being around 'Red Star', and especially when she thought of it by its popular name: Jablotin. Most times the very word, Jablotin, made her squirm. For the patois word painted a picture of what it really was: a den of devils, a nest of intrigue. Usually she was ashamed to think of it and of what went on there. But sometimes she was glad of this place, for it took devils to stop devils. However, devils or no devils, this morning she just had to go there.

The truth about Jablotin was that these days it was like a nest of wasps. With the waterworks issue, the place was swarming with desperadoes bristling to attack, and expecting to be attacked at any moment. It was more tumultuous than ever. At the best of times few policemen could enter it alone – not even Holder, armed. Now policemen could not even pass on the street outside unless they were in groups. For with the big debate to take place at the Red House rumours had it that the police were set to raid Jablotin, and the people of Jablotin were nervous, and ready to strike first. For a lot of soldiers had come down from St James's barracks and were at headquarters. Nobody was seeing them on the streets, people were only seeing policemen, but everybody had seen when the army cart had brought the soldiers. And so overnight a lot of crooks and criminals had sneaked into Jablotin to defend it.

Eva knew all this because Greasy Pole had been keeping her informed.

And he should know because he lived there. She was sorry that when she was talking with Greasy Pole the night before last she had not stressed what she was going to him to discuss now, because although she had mentioned it, she had drawn back in horror. But now she was convinced that drawing back made no sense. She was convinced that this was the only thing to do.

◆

She walked straight down Richmond Street to King Street and turned left to get to St Vincent Street. All the way down she had been thinking of the crowd and the confusion that was going to be the Red House scene today. When she reached Lower Prince Street junction she stopped and looked east towards the Red House. The signboard said Sackville Street, but she could not get used to any of those new street names which they put up only last year. From here there was a clear view, for of course on this side Prince Street went straight through the middle of the Red House. On the other side was Brunswick Square and afterwards Prince Street resumed. Although it was not yet seven o'clock there seemed to be scores of people in the vicinity of St Vincent Street and she knew that trouble was on the boil. Her heart began to race. She thought of that man who had entered Trinity Cathedral and had accosted the bishop. What manner of beast was he? Did he have any respect for the divine? Was anything sacred to Holder? She only hoped she would have her way with Greasy Pole this morning. She did not know if he was getting up early to go to the square. She had her reasons for thinking he had not. Her thoughts raced and went back to Holder. She could not help feeling that it was a lucky thing she had slipped out of the cathedral when she did. For she was sure she was the one he was looking for. This made her anxious about the little transaction at Jablotin. Now that she was on St Vincent Street itself and about to enter the barrackyard she began to feel nervous and afraid.

When she turned into St Vincent Street she saw the huge crowd gathering in front of the Red House. Not too far up the street, and right in front of her, at Queen Street corner, there was already a knot of people collecting. There was a policeman there, walking busily up and down. In the brightening light she could see a few people looking down from the veranda of the Carlisle Hotel.

She quickly turned into the entrance and was in that sleazy, weird world of Jablotin. Strangely enough it was a silent world this morning. It would have been the best time for the police to raid it, for everybody seemed gone to the water debate. Only that the policemen were needed right there at the Red House for the water debate.

She wanted to move fast to get to the room she was seeking but she was not quite sure of the place. After turning into a few foul-smelling dark corridors, she noticed a blue pole with a gas-light and she remembered. She went to the door close in front of it and rapped.

The door was in two halves. Somebody came to it, quietly, and opened the top half just a little bit. It was darkish inside, but through the crease one could see the flickers of a pitch-oil lamp.

Eva said, 'You there? It's me.'

'Oh, is you?' Greasy Pole's voice came. He couldn't see her clearly but he caught her voice. He pushed open the top half of the door, then he unbolted the bottom half and said, 'Come in quick.'

'What happen? You so in a hurry? You expect police to come for you?'

He said, 'You could trust police?'

'Well, they have their hands full this morning.'

'Thank God.'

'Look, I was in church, and that beast – anyway, before I tell you about that. Listen! I was in church, Trinity, and I just tell meself I have to see you bad. I was—'

'Well sit down,' he interrupted. 'You keep standing up. Look, there. Sit down there.'

He showed her to an old cane chair. It was a very small room, and the fact that here was in the darkest recesses of Jablotin seemed to make it look even more dismal. There was a small corner table and upon it was an old pitch-oil lamp without a shade. There was no bed but what seemed to be an old torn-up fibre mattress on boxes. This had neither sheet nor pillow, and though the room was so gloomy, she could see across one box the words: 'Blue Soap', and on another, 'Green Pasture Butter'.

She looked at him. 'But how come you home this morning, and everybody out in the street, in the church – boy if you see people outside! People like peas. From early early. By the way I meet up with Lolotte in the Cath—'

'Lolotte Borde?'

'It have any other Lolotte? She was with me in the Catholic Cathedral. Immaculate Conception. And then we went to Trinity together, and – Oh God I can't talk about that.'

'You can't talk about what?'

'I can't talk about what happen. But that is part of the reason I come to see you.'

'That's part of the reason you come to see me and you can't talk about it!'

'Greasy Pole, give me a chance. I want to collect meself. But I so glad to find you home. I didn't expect to meet you home, you know. I hope they don't—' And she stopped short.

'You hope they don't what?' He raised his head towards her. She was looking towards the door which Greasy Pole had closed back. She was going to say it looked as if he was hiding and she hoped they were not on the point of taking him away again. The police. She half-suspected that he was inside because the police was looking for him.

As she had not answered him he said again, 'You hope they don't what, Eva?'

'Well we already talk a little night before last. And even before. In fact, some weeks ago when I was right here we mentioned it and—'

'*You* mentioned it.'

'Okay, I mentioned it and you said yes you'd do it, and you mentioned some money and I asked you if you sure and you said, "Yes man, oh God," and I even said, "You ain't 'fraid," and you said you is Greasy Pole.'

He was looking at her. 'So what's all that for?'

'That's why I asked you that question.'

'Which question? We didn't talk our business orready?'

'Yes, but I just want to make sure so I asking you again.'

'What you asking me?'

'Oh, I didn't ask you yet. I was saying I only hope – let me talk frankoment, I was saying I only hope the police don't pick you up again.'

Greasy Pole looked at her as if she was crazy, then he looked away again. Then he turned back to her and leaned towards her. He had squeaky eyes and they were blinking all the time. He said, 'Eva, even if I break jail a million times it doesn't mean I ain't a man to me word. It have something you want me to do. Okay? I promise you because I want to see that happen as much as you want to see it happen, so I'll do it. I bound to do it. I swear to God. You talk about money the other night and I ain't shame to say, yes, I'll do it for that money. I tell you I'll do it. If I tell you I'll do it, I'll do it. I'll do it for the money, when I get the money.'

She whispered, 'I only have part of it now. Today is only the first reading of the bill and Mzumbo said they can't get through the second and third reading today. So before next week Monday I'll bring the rest.' She opened a little leather purse which was in her hand. 'This here is half.' She handed it to him.

He said nothing. He counted it silently.

She said, 'Before next Monday I'll bring the rest,' and she trailed off with, 'That is if...' He did not hear her. She looked at him and said boldly, 'That is if you still outside.'

She watched him still counting. She wanted to tell him that it was what happened this morning that made her go for the money for him because, oh God, she was so ashamed to say it but she went for the money for him now to do that job because she wanted him to do something else afterwards. To do something else if not that same day soon soon afterwards because it had to be done, if not she could not live in peace, ever. Perhaps she would not even be able to live. She wanted to say she didn't know how much he would charge her for this next terrible job, and that she could not pay now, but he knew she was washing and starching and ironing for Darwent and with the Darwent money – God bless Darwent – with the Darwent money she would pay him every cent, sure sure.

But she said nothing. When he was finished counting he put the money under a bottle and she could see he was pleased. More light had flooded into the room and even though he had put out the lamp she could see his twisted smile. And she could also see the musty vest he was wearing and the mildewed pair of brown trousers. She was sure he had slept in them. As she was thinking of that, he said, 'So you was in Trinity Cathedral with Lolotte this—'

'Wait, I didn't say I was in Trinity with Lolotte. We was in Immaculate Conception because we is Catholic but we wanted to be in Trinity Church to be near Brunswick Square. Because we knew the crowd coming out early. It had police like flies and when we was walking over from

Immaculate Conception, Lolotte was keeping scarce because you know they could pounce on you for nothing when you already known to the police and something brewing, and when we reached Trinity, boy, I didn't see Lolotte at all, but then such a scary thing happened!' She opened her eyes large and she expected Greasy Pole to shrink back. But Greasy Pole, who never shrank back from scary things, leaned forward and said, 'What happened?'

And it was only then she decided to make it a little more scary than it had been. She said, 'The brute came inside the church and roughed up Bishop Hayes.'

'He did what? He roughed up who? You crazy?' Greasy Pole's face was crinkled up in a grimace. He couldn't believe it.

'He roughed up Bishop Hayes. He came in with the gun and stopped the service.'

'And what those blasted Englishmen did?'

'They don't even know. None of them was there. In any case you think they'll bawl at Holder? You think they'll chase him away? You'll never see that. Not on a day like today. Today with that water debate and with thousands of people milling round, and with things building up and they getting frightened and panicky, they'll back that butcher to the hilt. They'll back him against Hayes anytime.'

Greasy Pole looked at her, appalled, his mouth open.

'Look, I telling you that and you could believe it. Although Hayes is one of them and he's an Englishman and he's Bishop of Trinidad I could tell you they'll back that stooge against Hayes any damn day.'

In the room the gloominess and murkiness seemed to have completely lifted. Which meant that out in the street the sun was probably up. Looking at the horror on Greasy Pole's face, Eva said, 'I didn't know you was a man of God.'

'Hayes is a man of God, not me. I is a jailbird.'

Eva laughed.

Greasy Pole said, 'Hayes is the only white man I like. Because I always remember that sermon he preached. That Saturday when he come out in the square when Wrightson was so vexed. Remember what Hayes tell the people who Wrightson was calling vagabonds? Hayes said he'd pray for them and would stand beside them till the bitter end. He said, "Let not your heart be troubled. For I shall always be with you." That is man.'

90

'He was only quoting. It's Christ who said that, something like that, not Hayes. But I was telling you, this bastard had his gun bright and shining, and when he saw me in the church you know he picked up the gun?'

It was now that Greasy Pole shrank back. 'What?'

'First I make sure I duck, then I pushed people out of the way and bolt outside the church. I went straight up home, Duke and Richmond. I changed the dress because just in case he looking for me he'd be looking for a blue dress and I in yellow. I pick up that money and I say "Let me go and give Greasy Pole this for the first job. Because he'll have to do a second job. If I have to live at all, Greasy Pole is me friend and he'd have to do that second job." '

Greasy Pole looked at her questioningly. He said, 'What second job is that, Eva?'

'You know.'

'Yes, but you have to know that ain't my line.'

That jolted her. She said hotly, 'And that's why you'll always be in jail. You proud they calling you Greasy Pole because you could slip out from anywhere they put you. But I'll tell you something, Mr Greasy Pole. They'll slam that door on you so hard one day that you wouldn't be able to slip away. And who is the cause of it? Holder. For the past seven or eight times who put you behind bars? Not Holder? Even from the time I was living with Holder I realised he didn't like you. You know what that girl told me? What's her name again? I could never remember this girl's name. Anyway she said Holder say you could be as slippery as you want, you could run but you can't hide. Holder told her if he can't bend you he'll break you, and since he's the younger man he'll watch you rot in jail.'

'Holder said that? Which girl told you that?'

'The name on the tip of me tongue but it wouldn't come.'

'As soon as you remember it just tell me.'

'But I thought you knew all that. I thought that's why you was inside for the day.'

'I didn't know that. But I know they watching me. And I trying to keep real safe. You give me a job and if I ain't outside I can't do it. That's why I trying to keep safe. Just that.'

'Yes, you have to keep safe. But you have to deal with Holder too, because if you make a slip, you behind bars. And if you don't want to do what I'm telling you, you'll always be behind bars.'

'You gave me one job, that isn't enough?'

'Do that one job first,' Eva said boldly. 'Then you'll think of the next one because I rewarding you rich. That's why I run up home to get the money to come and talk to you.'

'That money is for the first job. And this is only half.'

'I know. I tell you you'll get the next half next week.'

'Well, I'll do the job next week!' Greasy Pole said defiantly.

'That's all right.' Eva smiled. It was a sort of glamorous smile and she was showing her white teeth. Greasy Pole had never seen her smile like that, and he vaguely thought of Darwent, and he said to himself, 'Ay, ay, I wonder what Eva's up to. She trying to sweeten me!' But he did not let her put him off. He said seriously, 'I'll do that job, because I want to see that happen. So help me God me soul will be glad when that brightness—. Look, Eva, I'll do the job. I don't want to say more. But I ain't doing nothing until I get all the money.'

'But I have told you already,' she said firmly. And she said in her mind, 'Sometimes they make me talk like Darwent.' She said, 'Listen to me, Greasy Pole, I done tell you you'll get it next week.' She was looking towards him but Greasy Pole's eyes were staring at the floor. She went on: 'Listen. You listening? Me uncle say the debate wouldn't end today, anyway. Darwent said so too. It will have to come to the third reading. Darwent said they'll pass that bill next week Monday. But God forbid, we have to frighten them off. Let's see what will happen. The people set like Jack Spaniards. Today we have to go in the public gallery and make noise, and get on bad to make them see we ain't 'fraid and we mean business and we have to make sure the bill don't pass at all. The bill mustn't pass either now or next Monday. I don't know what will happen if it pass. If they pass that bill, fire and brimstone in Port-of-Spain.'

Greasy Pole said nothing because he was thinking of a number of things: of the money and of the thousands of people that must be out on St Vincent Street now, and by the Carlisle, and in Brunswick Square. And he was thinking of that job. The *first* one. He was thinking of it and how he would do it, and then he became excited, and then he let himself grow cool again. And he and Eva chatted for a while before Eva got up. She could see a shaft of sunlight between the crease of the door and she knew it was at least half-past eight. She looked back and said, 'I still can't believe you ain't going nowhere today. Look, what we talked about, don't forget, I'm dead serious. And what I say I'll pay you, I'll pay you. Now, concentrate on that first job first, eh?'

'Aha.'

She said, 'You know what just hitting me?'

'No.'

'The quietness of this place. Hear! Nothing. Nothing at all. Not a sound. You know something? You is the only man in here.' Then she said, 'Look, just a minute. You hearing? If you listen good you'll hear the roar coming from the Red House.'

He listened and nodded his head. He had a deep craving to be there at the square.

She said, 'So I going. If those people was thinking we scared, they make a big mistake. I feel good to see everybody come out. This morning people like sand, boy. Anyway, let me go. I have to get inside that public gallery. We have to show them something. They feel they could get away with murder, but we'll show them what's coming for them.'

'They already get way with plenty murder. You don't listen to you uncle? Mzumbo Lazare could tell you.'

'Sometimes I feel – although he's me uncle – sometimes I feel he's too, how to say it ... Let me use Darwent word: he's too *moderate*. That mean he's too "soft".'

'I'll tell you straight, I prefer Edgar Maresse-Smith.'

She was going to say, 'I too,' but she did not. Blood was thicker than water. On that sort of subject it was only Clement she could be open with. And Darwent. She looked around and listened and heard nothing. She said, 'You know what I was thinking? Two things. First I was remembering how we met up in that band. You and me. That Jour Ouvert band. That was just – let me see – that was just three weeks back. You is a brave man because you didn't have on no mask. And the police know you so good.'

He chuckled. Then he nodded his head. Then he shook his head and said, 'Ayayai, girl.'

She said, 'And you so tall and ... and—' She stopped. She was going to say 'tall and greasy', but she went on, 'You so tall and handsome.'

Greasy Pole straightened up from the blue-soap box. He was puzzled. He did not know what was going on. He said, 'Eva, what you really want? You want me, or you anxious for me to do the job?'

'Both,' she said playfully, and laughed. Then she said seriously, 'But a woman could say that. She could say you handsome, it ain't mean she want nothing. So what! Greasy Pole, even before I saw you I liked you. You know why I liked you? Because you always giving the police hell. And you always harassing the Government—'

'Don't forget you was living with a policeman.'

'Yes, but Holder wasn't always so stupid. And I wasn't always so – well, I don't know what to call it. I ain't have any patience with these blasted people. I remember when I was staying by me uncle and I used to hear him talking and talking and ranting and raving about this and that and the other, and about these people in the Government, and foreigners, and what they doing to poor people, and people like us, I used to ask meself what's wrong with him! Because we was living good, so I couldn't see nothing. And then he used to hold his famous Old Year's Night ball, and the same bigwigs would come and dance, the men in coat-and-tails, the ladies in their lovely gowns – we liked them, Mammie Marie and me! We couldn't understand how Uncle was raving so and still entertaining them. I still can't understand it. To this day. Mzumbo used to be talking about the Government, and colonials, and what is democracy and what is not democracy, and to be honest me and me auntie couldn't stand it. Mammie Marie even threatened to leave him. But then when I left to go and live with Holder it slowly dawned on me what's happening. I mean, that was when I start to see what poverty and ignorance really is. And on top of that it just happen that I had to live with a stupid ruffian like Holder. You hearing? Because Holder was getting more and more stupid and the fool couldn't see that these people riding him as a jackass and didn't care a damn about him. I was seeing it plain then. And then we was living in a leaking house and hardly having food to eat and you mean to tell me you'll sweat and beat up yourself so for these bleeding barbarians?'

'They was bleeding?'

'Don't bother with me and me crazy self. Greasy Pole, it's because I so vexed. You see, from then on I began to ask meself – I say to meself, wait, what sort of devils we have with us, boy – you could tell me? And I saw the plan. In me mind it was as clear as day. And I said to meself, all right, Governor Maloney it's a fight you want? It's a fight you looking for, man to man. Because I was born here – you understand that Greasy Pole? And you want to tell me people will come from England and from oheeoho and order me about and insulting me and calling the tune? As if this place is theirs? Never. But I like your style, you feel just like me.'

As she talked she had been watching his face, and she saw how the anger had tightened it and how the veins had risen up in his neck. She said, 'I like your style. But we have to take it easy and fight the good fight.' She sat up. 'You know something? Half the people out there now, round the Red House, they don't even know what we really fighting for. They don't know what they fighting for. They think it's water. But even so, you think they really care about water? They waste it all the time. They let it run in the drain. That's what Wrightson saying, and it's true. What they care about is bacchanal. They want confusion. But you know what really changed me, Greasy Pole? What really scared me and got me vexed? That thing in 1899, when Jerningham abolished the Borough Council. Putting Trinidad men out of office so they could rule free. Because that is what it really mean. Alcazar talked till he was sick. He said, "It's not the mayoral chain I'm losing." He was Mayor then, remember? He said, "It's not the mayoral chain I'm losing. It's the big political chain of slavery you are putting around our legs." That man could talk, boy. I remember Mr Rapsey crying like a child. Maresse-Smith and me uncle – they didn't know what to do.

'What these people think we is, Greasy Pole? That was the time the break between me and Holder started. Mind you, I'd already had enough of the cuffs and kicks. No, I could speak to you frank. Holder is not only a stooge he is a beast to live with. He don't know how to treat a woman! I could talk to you like this because I want to be open to you so you would know what's going on. I seeing hell, but I don't want me uncle to help me, but all I could do is servant work, and that is because of these damn people. Because they don't intend to give the so-called natives any blasted education so that our people always have to stay there and never be able to do anything except servant work. And with all this me uncle keep saying one day we'll take charge! How the hell we'll take charge!'

She was feeling tense and worked up. She realised she had worked him up, too. She saw the fire in his eyes.

She said again, 'I know you feel something. You is one in a hundred. You size up the situation and you know. And you feel it.'

'How you know that?'

'Well I could see that. And me uncle noticed certain things about you but it's really Lolotte Borde who said that.'

'Lolotte could make good caramel and toloom.'

'What the france! You want to tell me that is why you and Lolotte is friends?'

'The thing you want me to do, you ain't gone gossiping with Lol—'

'Me?' she interrupted. 'I ain't breathe a word to nobody. You crazy? I hope you yourself ain't—'

'Oh no. Me? Never. And you think I'll change me mind? Never. Although if they ketch me is years in jail.'

'But you know they can't hold you in jail.'

He did not smile now. He was looking tensely into space. She could see he meant business. She herself knew that if they caught him it would not be the Royal Jail on Frederick Street, but Carrera, the island prison. The island prison off Chaguaramas, surrounded by hungry sharks. It churned up her belly just to think of this. If Greasy Pole was sent there and tried to escape he'd never see the light of day again. She shook that out of her mind. Outside now the day was very light. Bright, one might say. She went to the window and glanced up through the crease, trying to see the sky, but it was impossible in this grimy, gloomy, closed-up, uncomfortable place. It made her feel uneasy just being here. Even as she talked she did not breathe freely because of the sickening smells in the air.

She thought of Bishop Hayes's favourite theme: 'Blessed are the poor in spirit for they shall see God; blessed are the meek for they shall inherit the land.' She loved the bishop for having the courage to be on the side of the poor, but were these people stark, staring mad? She did not want any poverty. She wanted luxury. Often she thought of Bishop Hayes as a good man but wasn't this the thing that was keeping the British in power in Trinidad? Making people feel they couldn't get to heaven unless they were poor? So they wouldn't want education, they wouldn't want money and luxury? Wasn't it – as had come across her mind often – wasn't it a quiet conspiracy by the church?

She threw this off her mind for the moment because it was so confusing. And so depressing if it was true. And also she did not want to stay in this hell-hole too long.

She looked again between the crease and had a glimpse of bright sunlight on the ground. It must be at least a quarter to nine and she had to be in the public gallery for the debate beginning at nine. As she moved to get up she said, 'I still can't believe you ain't going nowhere today. Look — what we talked about, don't forget, I'm dead serious. And what I say I'll pay you, I'll pay you. But please concentrate on that first job first, right?'

'It's only the first job ah concentrating on.'

She stood up and glared at him without saying anything. She pretended she was serious. She liked the way he was staring back at her with his squeaky-looking, reddish eyeballs, and his small shining face. She knew when she was ready she could talk him into the second job.

'Whatever you do, Greasy Pole, take good care of yourself and avoid the police. Keep yourself safe for next week. You hear me?'

'Yes, General Eva.'

She chuckled as she moved towards the door. Greasy Pole got up to open it to let her out. She stopped and said, 'You know what I was thinking? Funny, eh? We'd never know this, because we might be in the grave twenty-five, fifty years. But you know if we succeed in this business — ha, boy — you know we could be responsible for really shaking up Trinidad?'

'You make me feel sorry, because I didn't want to be in the grave, I wanted to see.'

She laughed. 'I, too. The worse thing is nobody will know about us.'

He nodded his head, sadly. After a while, he said, 'Eva, don't forget. Try and get the rest of the money and you could say you job done.'

She felt thrilled. She said, 'When you do it I'll call you a hero. Okay, thanks, I think I just *have* to go now.'

He opened the door for her. Before she slid out she said, smilingly, 'Don't forget to close back the door, eh? Nice and tight. Okay? You'll do the job? Hm? You want me to blow you a kiss so you won't forget?' She blew a kiss and flashed the same sort of smile as she had done earlier, and for the first time a smile broke on his lips.

With his long body leaning over the closed half of the door he stretched and looked to both sides of the yard then he said, 'No point in talking about forgetting. I could never forget that. Because if I forget that I forget meself.'

She was thrilled.

'But you wouldn't forget the rest of the money by next Monday though. Eh?'

'Of course not, tall-boy.'

He watched her hurry away and out of sight.

13

It was not even half-past eight yet but people were beginning to cluster before the council chamber. From the Red House grounds the crowd was already spilling on to Abercromby Street, and even across the street the crowd jammed the railings of Brunswick Square.

The door of the chamber was not even opened yet but Inspector-General of Police, Colonel Brake, was already standing up before it, because he wanted to be there when people began going into the public gallery. As he stood there a number of members of the Legislative Council came up and passed to go in. Every one of them who came so far was of the rebels – of the other side – the set he called the 'instigators'. They were furious with the Government and of course with the police, and when they came up they said absolutely nothing to him but called on the clerk to open the door and they just went inside.

That suited him. He was in no mood to say anything to them either, not even 'good morning'. Because if things got out of hand it would not be a very good morning for any of them. He relaxed his hold on the baton with his left hand and felt his pocket, but he had already passed the tickets on to the clerk. Whether people liked it or not, entry would have to be by ticket this morning. Because he did not want the rabble in the public gallery. This was just the first reading of the bill, not the crucial reading, and if the people were being excited to the extent that the streets outside the Red House were jammed already, then it was a lucky thing he had thought of tickets in the nick of time and even luckier that Thomas Thompson was able to print them yesterday itself and deliver last night.

But was not that the way with Englishmen? he thought proudly. And then his heart fell. For close to him, in fact, on his right hand, were two of the men who by their actions were tearing down the British flag. He did not look towards Trinity Cathedral but he was thinking of Thomas Hayes. He refused to think 'Bishop Hayes', for by his actions this was no bishop. Trinity Cathedral was now a den for the wicked, for the bishop was encouraging the mob inside and telling them that what they were fighting for was just, and that God was with them. And that God was giving them sanctuary. He really did not want even to think about Thomas Hayes this morning, nor to look to the west of Trinity Cathedral towards the fire brigade station. He did not even want to see that building. For it was not only anger that welled up in him when he thought of Walter Darwent, but shame; shame so intense that he could not vouch for what he would do if he came upon those two together – Darwent and his washerwoman. But was it true?

As he looked before him and saw the crowd swell, he was asking himself that question. For he had not really seen anything, just that rumours were all around him. As he was thinking his eyes caught a knot of idlers in front of the new library building, opposite Dr Pollonais. There was a little commotion there and he was seeing it through the trees. But Sergeant-Superintendent Empson was there with his detachment of policemen and he knew it would be controlled because from here he could see that Empson wasn't even agitated. But while he was looking over to where Empson was standing beside the new library, there was a burst of cheering in the street right in front of him.

It was a crowd led by two men with a banner. He knew this was further incitement, and although he would have stopped it right away, he did not have the powers. Governor Sir Alfred Maloney had warned him about that, because these bright men around knew the state of the law, and he had to be careful about trying to crush lawful demonstrations and freedom of speech. He glanced up the street as if he did not really glance, and in a flash he saw that Deputy Inspector Owen had the detachment from St James's Barracks, the detachment specially trained for riot. He was pleased and yet he wasn't satisfied, for these men should not be on display. They should have been waiting in Police Headquarters and unleashed only if trouble broke out. He did not want them on show at this point. But he was relieved they were here. And he felt relieved too to see a number of the regular policemen around the square. Earlier he had seen Sergeant Holder cross the square by the diagonal road and speak to Owen, and the sergeant was now back on Hart Street. The men with the banner coming up Abercromby Street were close up now and the noise of their followers was almost a din. An Indian boy was ringing a bell and crying 'Come out in your thousands,' and the words kept ringing and burning in Brake's mind.

In that quick time between when he first heard the noise and now, the place seemed to be swarming. Now as he looked out into the road at the banner passing, his heart shook inside him. It was as if it went voom! voom! It was Mzumbo Lazare holding one end of the banner.

He said in his mind, 'You crook, even if I have to frame you, I'll bring you in. They are scared of Maresse-Smith, but he's nothing but a blowhard. It's you.' And then he called to mind what Holder had told him this morning. He had heard it before but he did not believe it: that the washerwoman whom everybody was talking about – Darwent's washerwoman – was Mzumbo's niece. He thought, 'Scheming blighter. I wouldn't be surprised if it was you who put her up to it.'

He remembered that at a ratepayers' meeting on the Grand Savannah towards Christmas he had seen someone like this girl talking to Lazare. Someone like this washerwoman. That had seemed to him strange. Although all sorts of people of the lower classes were always talking to Lazare, it had seemed to him odd that a servant of the fire brigade chief should be talking to the enemy. Of course he had not known then that, to Lazare, Darwent was not the enemy, and when he had mentioned it to Darwent the next day the fire brigade chief was not in the least upset.

Recalling all these things now made him feel the rumours were true.

As it was approaching nine o'clock more people shifted from the road and eased towards the council chamber. He did not know where people were coming from but they seemed to be multiplying before his very eyes. Although his policemen were keeping them moving the crowd grew thickly by the minute.

He glanced at his watch. There were twenty minutes to go. As he was putting the watch back into his pocket he saw Inspector Norman passing and he hailed out to him. As Norman came towards him a few people moved with Norman, and Brake called on some recruits to move the crowd back. He said to Norman under his breath, 'What's happening on Knox Street?'

'Beginning to sizzle, Sir.'

'As I said last night, if we need more assistance from St James...'

'No concerns yet, Sir. I was going across to Darwent. He's the only—'

'Just this minute,' Colonel Brake interrupted, 'Just this minute I spotted Major Rooks going there.'

'Major Rooks is just going to make observations from the fire brigade tower. To see what's happening in Brunswick Square.'

'Oh.'

'I was saying Darwent is the only one of us not out.'

'I thought of it. But do we need him? We don't have a fire.'

'No, but if the Honourable Wrightson – well, I don't know.'

'Why should we need him if anyone tries to attack Walsh Wrightson? What did we give out guns for? Inspector, what's the matter?'

Inspector Norman did not speak. The colonel said, 'You know of course Wrightson is inside the Red House.'

'Yes, I know. But I must be frank. I just feel Darwent should be out.'

'And so do I. After this bill is read into law we'll deal with Darwent. Buck up – look, Alcazar and Hall are coming. It's getting close to the debate. Look at how this blasted crowd is swelling.'

Norman saluted. He said, 'Going back.'

Colonel Brake touched his forehead with his baton, but even during that gesture he saw many members of the Legislative Council coming in. Then behind them he saw a crowd of followers. Bursts of cheering were going up for Newbold, and for Wainwright, and there was the warmest shower of cheers for Alcazar. At that moment he glimpsed Maresse-Smith coming over from Brunswick Square but he promptly lost him in the throng. Alcazar came to him looking somewhat agitated. Alcazar said, 'You are Commandant of the Local Forces and Inspector-General of Police?'

'That is true, Mr Alcazar, as you know.'

'There is an infringement of the people's right. The right to go into the public gallery of the Legislative Council and attend the sitting.'

Now there was a humming of the crowd on either side of Colonel Brake and even across the street.

Brake turned and pointed to the sign. 'Nobody is stopping anybody. If they have tickets they will get in.'

Alcazar was fuming. He said, 'Inspector-General, I am going to the Governor.'

◆

Henry Alcazar did not go to the Governor. He went inside the council chamber. Just before he went in he saw Maresse-Smith at the Brunswick

Square gate, and he signalled him over. They were on the pavement with the crowd passing and he kept his voice very low. He said, 'Edgar, I think with the debate going on you have to be very careful. They'll put you away easily on the slightest charge. I know why I'm telling you this. I heard something.'

'Yes. Thanks for telling me. And they already tried. But when they coming they have to come very good, because my profession is law.' He nodded his head, looking at Alcazar.

'Just be careful with these people,' Alcazar said.

'You call them people too? I call them oppressors. The crowd is with me, and even if they jail me and throw away the keys, these people will in the end throw them out and inherit this land. Tell them that. Let them put it in their pipe and smoke it.'

Alcazar said, as if to himself, 'Edgar Maresse-Smith. The burning spear. He is so impatient and impetuous and without tact. But his tongue is so sweet.'

Maresse-Smith said, 'Me? But look who is talking! Henry, I want to hear you this morning. Badly, badly. Because I'm learning from you, the way you put things over. I hate to praise anybody to his face, but you are a master of words. I don't want to keep you back, and please don't keep me. I want to give a little pep-talk in the square. Take it easy, Henry.'

Alcazar went into the council chamber and put down his books and papers. He had already completely forgotten Edgar Maresse-Smith. He found himself very flustered and uneasy. The inspector-general had sprung a trick on him and frustrated the chief plan. For the chief plan was public response to his speech, and with noise which should come from the public gallery he was hoping that this session, and all other sessions, would be interrupted and therefore postpone the passing of the bill for as long as possible. He had been ready for his debate and he had worked up himself for it and had counted on a lively public gallery. But now the scheming Government had acted to reduce the participation in the public gallery. They could not simply ban people from the gallery because they knew that would be against the law, but saying entry was by ticket meant they had played a very smart card. What made it smarter was the fact that they had played it now, this morning, and not before. The Government had not given them time to think. So far as he could see there was nothing that could be done about it. The prime opponents of the bill in the Legislative

Council and the members of the Ratepayers' Association would just have to suffer it to be so. He just could not think, he did not know what to think. If he had had a quick consultation with a bright man like Mzumbo Lazare, for instance, he would have known right away if there were any avenues. As it was, he would just have to leave it and take a more direct stance in his debate. He felt a little confused. They had tried a fast one and had wrecked his plans. But he would raise hell in this debate. He would refer to the underhand blow dealt, not against him, nor against the Ratepayers' Association, but against the people of Trinidad and Tobago. As he collected his papers in front of him and thought of his speech, he could hear other members of the Legislative Council coming in, and he could hear the buzz of the crowd outside the chamber. He settled down to rethink how he would couch his speech. For now he could not play to the public gallery. He had to give a hard-hitting and incisive speech on constitutional rights.

◆

Meanwhile, as a result of what Alcazar had said, Colonel Brake had sent a note to the Acting Attorney General to make sure that entry into the chamber by ticket was not illegal. He was sure it was not illegal, until the reply came back. The reply simply said, 'Legality not certain, await advice from Colonial Office as move will possibly infringe British constitutional law.' Colonel Brake said nothing but folded the note and put it into his pocket. He stood outside the door as people for the public gallery poured in. They never questioned him about tickets and he in turn did not ask them for any. For it appeared the riff-raff had their rights too. So although he had been belligerent over the issue, and he had a sign up, he wasn't going to ask for any tickets.

◆

It was precisely at nine that the debate began. Just before then thousands of people were milling round the Red House and many more thousands were in Brunswick Square, where both Lazare and Edgar Maresse-Smith had been holding pep meetings. And Maresse-Smith, in particular, had had a field day, for he had whipped up the crowd to a frenzy and had some of the women crying. But when the debate was about to begin he was one of the first to leave the square. He rushed over to Abercromby Street, skipped across it and rushed up the flight of stairs to the council chamber door, and just as he was about to lunge inside to get a seat Colonel Brake, standing in the doorway, extended both arms and stopped him suddenly. He was shocked. He said, 'What's the matter, officer?'

Colonel Brake gave a wry smile. He said, 'I know in your haste to get in you do not recognise me. Although I would have hoped you would recognise my uniform. My name is Brake. Colonel Hubert Brake, Inspector Commandant of Police.'

'Yes, Inspector Commandant,' Maresse-Smith said, a little breathlessly. 'Thank you. I am heading for the public gallery.' He forced a smile.

'I am afraid all the seats are taken.'

'But they could not be. The debate has just begun.'

'The seats are all taken, Mr Edgar Maresse-Smith. I am standing in front of the door to prevent overcrowding. I am sorry.'

Edgar Maresse-Smith looked round. In the few moments since he was stopped there was already a knot of people behind him all the way down the flight of stairs. He looked at them, and his face was almost deformed with anger and hurt and impatience. He said to those behind him, 'The seats are all taken.'

A burst of cursing and exclamations of anger ripped through the crowd, and hardly was this let loose than a contingent of policemen elbowed their way through the crowd roughly, with batons in the air. They cried 'Ey! Ey! Order here.' And a few batons crashed on some people. There was no fight back, and Edgar Maresse-Smith, joining his hands in mock prayer said, 'Blessed are the meek for they shall inherit the land.'

Colonel Brake, who was right close to him with his arms across the doorway, said, 'A fine example, Mr Edgar Maresse-Smith. You always set a fine example. You were just declaiming to them there in the square and now you are inciting to riot.'

Edgar Maresse-Smith looked a bit surprised. 'Because I am praising their meekness I am inciting to riot? They were very calm in the face of brutality and I call them blessed because I feel they were truly meek and submissive and the scriptures give them hope to possess this very land which is their own.' He looked around and there was a roar of approval, and then cheers, and a thin female voice cried, 'Talk, boy!' Colonel Brake beckoned to two police guards to stand in front of the door. Then he said, 'Mr Maresse-Smith, I am warning you against inflammatory words.'

'Me? Inflammatory words? It is Christ who taught "blessed are the meek for they shall possess the land", not me.'

There were more cheers right there on the steps, and Holder was now squeezing past and hurrying up the steps to join the colonel. A voice from below shouted, 'Touch him! That's what we want. That's what we waiting for. Touch him and you'll see.' Holder stopped and looked back down the step, and there was a little tumbling, and pushing, and running outside. But the man who had spoken did not run. Holder was not sure who it was but he saw a face looking up at him and he felt he had recognised the voice. So he just made a note in his mind, 'Lodrick John', and he continued climbing the steps. When he reached Maresse-Smith he made a sign to Colonel Brake, who waved back 'no' with his baton. At this time there was a great burst of cheering in the public gallery, and somebody said, 'Alcazar's on the floor.' Maresse-Smith was so anxious to hear him that he was on the point of losing his nerve. But he took hold of himself. Then he turned to Colonel Brake and said, 'I commend these people. It is hard to be meek when doors are slammed in your face. Or when doors are open before you but you may not enter. The forces you represent, Sir, are crushing the people. There is democracy in England, ask Lazare, he was there in 1897. He was there for the coronation of Queen Victoria and Queen Victoria stretched out her hand to him. But in Trinidad in this 1903 the policy of you and your policemen is stifling to life, Sir. In Rome, even if you don't agree with Caesar, you are allowed to hear him and even heckle him. In England, even if you don't agree with the English Queen she will stretch out her hand to you, but in Trinidad, great God, you cannot go into the public gallery and listen to words of justice.'

Just as he was finishing, a shower of cheering came from inside and that had to do with what Henry Alcazar was saying about the waterworks bill. But what also went up now from the steps was as vibrant a cheer for Maresse-Smith. Colonel Brake was glaring at him. As Maresse-Smith ended the sentence he turned to go, and Brake looked quickly towards Holder. When their eyes faced each other Brake winked. His wink was as quick as lightning and few saw it, and those who saw could not see any significance in it. But Holder was relieved because he knew this was the signal he had been waiting for all the time. He stepped lightly behind Maresse-Smith.

◆

When Edgar Maresse-Smith left, a good part of the crowd turned around to leave, but not Eva. She had left home with the intention of getting into the public gallery, and now she was waiting and looking. When she turned back, she saw that although a good many had left with Maresse-Smith many more had come up. She saw a familiar figure far back on the lower steps but as much as she waved Lolotte could not see. Then Mzumbo came to mind and she looked around carefully. She had not seen her uncle at all since she came back from Brunswick Square and she wondered if he was already in the public gallery. He usually left his carriage at Dr Pollonais's, and she thought of just going outside and looking across to see if it was there, but then she decided she did not want to have to fight her way through this crowd and then afterwards try and get back here. She said to herself, 'Better forget Mzumbo for now.' Although when Maresse-Smith had spoken she had screamed: 'Talk, boy!' and had joined in the cheering, she thought he had been too brave and too rash this morning.

Usually she preferred Maresse-Smith to her uncle, because although her uncle was more substantial and more knowledgeable, she found him too accommodating with the Englishmen. And last Old Year's Night was ample proof of that. Because with all his agitation one never saw so many English people together in one place anywhere in Trinidad as at Mzumbo's ball. Why? It was because they knew he was their best friend in causing people to refrain from violence. It was because they the English knew he was military and would never compromise with law and order. And that made them feel safe.

She liked Maresse-Smith's style. Show them, show them, show them we ain't 'fraid nobody! Let them know this is our land and we going hell hard to possess it – come what may. But as much as she supported that, she realised he could have shown them something else this morning. She realised he could have shown them and the crowd a good bleeding head and broken ribs for being so outspoken and rash. For although the crowd was angry and like a raging sea, she could not see it defending Edgar with so many policemen around. And with almost all of the policemen carrying guns. She liked Maresse-Smith but it was foolish to provoke your enemies when they were so strong. If you could catch them unawares, yes – give it to them.

She looked around her impatiently. She wanted to get into the public gallery to help cheer Alcazar, and after Alcazar there would probably be Wainwright, and perhaps Goodwille – although none was as forceful and sweet as Henry Alcazar. Maybe the only man who could edge him out was Maresse-Smith. Not *maybe*. But Maresse-Smith was not in the Legislative Council. She listened to the cheering and she began feeling frustrated about not being inside. Brake was not leaving the door. The Legislative Council session was going up to two o'clock and since Alcazar was still speaking it was clear the debate would not finish today. So why didn't Alcazar give Wainwright a chance? Everybody should be heard. She was a little irritated. Sometimes although you were sweet you still had to know when to shut up. Her mind now quickly drifted and she was thinking and planning for the following Monday. It was not enough to cheer in the public gallery. Something must be done. Something had to be done. Something dramatic. And then she suddenly remembered her own carefully laid out plan, and in her mind she exclaimed 'Oh God, yes, that's it. And while it happening they will be so panicky and scared, they wouldn't know what they doing, and we could push down and break up everything.'

As she was there waiting and thinking, the crowd was building up fast below her on the stairs and now in the din she heard a woman scream. There was a scuffle with a policeman and Colonel Brake turned to rush down the steps. As soon as he moved Eva slid past the door and into the council chamber.

◆

After Colonel Brake had broken up the scuffle he went out into the street and called Inspector Norman and after a while a lot of the policemen who were under Inspector Norman came up and lined the steps thickly so that nobody else could come up. Brake himself missed the little woman in the yellow dress. He had known this was the woman who was working for Darwent, and he said to himself, almost without thinking, 'Where's Darwent's harlot?' He had noticed how quietly aggressive she was and he had been keeping his eyes on her, just as he was keeping his eyes on the lady below – whom he thought of as the big blubber and stone-thrower. And there were a few other people he was watching such as Lumpress, and Lodrick John, and about two or three whose names he did not know. He was quietly amused about the stone-thrower and he was thinking she was either reformed or she was trying something. He was sure it was something she was trying and in fact he felt it rather odd that Holder did not recommend that this stone-thrower be thrown into jail for safe keeping. Before this debate was concluded he wanted to get all the potential troublemakers off the scene. Without moving his eyes too much he was covering every face in the crowd, and every now and again he looked at the powerful stone-thrower to see if he could read any signs of imminent mischief on her face. He had at first taken her for one of the Shouter Baptists who were always running away from the law. He had thought so particularly when he saw the white head-tie. He had come to Trinidad to take up this post only last year but he had already gained enough experience not to be fooled by anyone. Just imagine, an agitator and stone-thrower dressed in white. He chuckled. White for the pure in heart.

As he was standing there at the door he glimpsed a sudden commotion down the stairs, and when he looked again and he saw the carriage he was suddenly panic-stricken. He tried to rush down through the crowd but the stairway was packed with people, and the funniest thing was he was even pushing aside his own policemen to get a gangway. People laughed convulsively as they looked at him fighting his way down. He wanted to get downstairs and out into the courtyard in the quickest possible time. For there was so much in his head this morning he had completely forgotten the Governor had not come yet. He didn't know how he could have forgotten that and he certainly could not tell the Governor that. By the time he got downstairs and managed to hastily assemble a guard of honour and escorted Sir Alfred Maloney into the chamber with due ceremony, he was astonished to see how the crowd in the public gallery had swelled. It had swelled to about twice the size it was when he had first spotted the Governor's carriage. He escorted Sir Alfred to his seat, and all the time, although he was trying to be gracious, he was in a raging temper. His temper grew even worse when his eyes fell on the woman in yellow. He felt tricked. After escorting Sir

Alfred to his seat he saluted and did all the ceremonies while planning for what he called 'these nitwits and hooligans'. He hurried back to the chamber door.

14

Inspector Norman was standing with Colonel Brake at the chamber door when they heard a little commotion and applause and looked and saw that it was Darwent crossing the street. Colonel Brake felt riled and scandalised but said nothing. After a moment he said, 'Take charge here for me. If things get out of hand get Rooks to move all the men back into Brunswick Square. Not the thirty-five in the Colonial Secretary's office, you know. I'm talking about the volunteers who just arrived from St James's Barracks. Don't shift from here. If you want Rooks, signal to Holder to get him. I'll be back directly.'

He went into the council chamber and although the debate was in full flow he walked right up to the southern side. As he came in there was a heightened buzz in the public gallery and the eyes of all the legislators were on him. Alcazar had at last finished and the speaker now was Wainwright, who, because he was momentarily distracted, got vexed, but still carried on. Wainwright, a famous opponent of the waterworks bill, had just been speaking of police repression and the rights of the people when Colonel Brake stepped in. Now he was bitter and fiery and wanted to show that even this act of Brake's was evidence of police repression. But Wainwright also, while he was speaking and raising his arms like a martyr, was wondering what brought Brake to the chamber. He saw Brake go right up to the Governor.

The Governor himself was concerned as the police chief walked up to him. As Colonel Brake reached up and bent to him, he whispered, 'Trouble?'

'No, Your Excellency. Everything's under control.' He was whispering softly but now he whispered even softer. 'Darwent just came out of the station in civilian clothes.'

The Governor smiled inwardly. He thought, 'So what?' He knew what they all felt about Darwent. He said, 'He came out in his civilian clothes and did what?'

'He came over to this side of the Red House. The crowd applauded him. The roughs were rejoicing and out of hand.'

The Governor did not like that. He did not see anything wrong with Darwent coming over to the Red House in civilian clothes, but he did not like to hear that the crowd was applauding Darwent. Darwent was entitled to his opinions and the Governor knew Darwent felt Wrightson's bill was wrong, but he could not approve of Darwent ridiculing the Government in public. Or of causing the Government to be ridiculed in public. He put it that way because he realised of course that Darwent himself had not done anything and if it was that the colonel wanted him to give an order for Darwent's arrest, it was out of the question. In any case, arrest an Englishman in public? No, no. Brake could not possibly be wanting that. He knew Brake. Brake would never want that. Nor would he, himself.

He whispered to the colonel, 'Did he say anything to make the crowd applaud him?'

'No, Your Excellency. When they saw him they just applauded. Because they know he's against us. And as he came out in civilian clothes, you know—'

'Know what, Inspector-General? What do I know?'

'Well, the mob knows he's for them. They know he's for lawlessness, and for everything that's against us. When he comes out like that he's saying, "Don't blame me. I'm not with them. I have nothing to do with the waterworks bill." '

The Governor agreed, but he did not say anything.

'The crowd likes him,' Brake said. 'And it cuts against our morale.'

'What do you want me to do, Inspector-General?'

'I just thought I'd inform you, Your Excellency.'

'I thank you.'

Something else quickly came to Brake's mind. 'I came mainly to inform you because my men are thin-skinned. The locals. They can't take provocation. If there is any taunting—'

Colonel Brake stopped. Governor Maloney just looked at him, then turned his head again to Wainwright who was still on his feet. As he turned back his head, Colonel Brake said, 'We just had to take Maresse-Smith for provocation because—'

He stopped when the Governor turned to him fiercely. The Governor said, 'What's that? Please do not aggravate the situation, Colonel. Whatever you do, please don't arrest popular figures like Maresse-Smith. At least not now. Please, Colonel.' The Governor's voice was soft and biting and he wanted to be firm without being imperious. But he just was not going to bargain for trouble. Not now.

Colonel Brake stood to attention, saluted, and hastened to see Sergeant Holder.

◆

The Governor knew Brake was hurt. They were both hurt. The Governor looked towards Wainwright, who was still continuing, then he looked towards Walsh Wrightson who, he realised, was constantly eying him. The Governor's glance was quick and as he caught Wrightson's eye he flicked his brow and smiled a little as if to reassure 'all's well'. He did that because he knew Wrightson realised that all the anger, all the commotion, all the heat and all the hate was because of his bill; all the fury was directed at him.

The Governor took out his gold watch and saw the time was creeping up to 12 o'clock and he was relieved. But yet he felt concerned because it was clear now that the bill could not pass through all its stages today and become law. He had not expected such a passage but he would have welcomed it – just to get the tumult behind him. But he was sure the strategy of Alcazar, Wainwright, and company, was to prevent just that. It passed through his mind that it was ridiculous there was no regulation in the rule-book limiting the speaker's time. Alcazar had spoken twice as long as he should have, and now Wainwright was going on interminably. What time would Wrightson have to make a proper reply? He glanced at the strain on Walsh Wrightson's face and then looked away. He said to himself, 'Sir Alfred, I wonder if this tumult is worth all this trouble. As Superintending Sergeant Peake said to me, if the people waste the water then when they don't have it that's their bloody problem. Makes sense to me. I wonder if the candle is not costing more than the funeral!'

He kept a stony face and continued looking fixedly at Wainwright.

Wainwright rambled on, sometimes thumping the desk, sometimes punching the air, whipping up what was certainly false wrath. But he knew he had been talking long, and even Alcazar was fed up. For despite

Wainwright's actions he was no longer forceful nor sweet. What distracted him most of all now was the way Governor Maloney kept staring at him. He glanced at the clock and realised that Wrightson did not now have the time to reply fully and to enable a vote to be taken, and so he decided to stop. Looking at the Governor from the corners of his eyes, he said, 'And Honourable Members, since it is not desired that I should continue to speak in defence of a defenceless people, I say no more but leave all to the judgement of God.'

A great buzz of dissatisfaction rose from the people in the public gallery, but this was nothing to what occurred when the Honourable Walsh Wrightson rose to reply. When Wrightson rose, a storm of booing shook the chamber. Colonel Brake rushed into the chamber. He was stunned. He looked back to call for reinforcements but armed soldiers had already rushed past him and surrounded Wrightson and Governor Sir Alfred Maloney. When he saw this he hurried towards the Governor, relieved. He had never heard such thunderous booing in a council chamber in his whole life, and even the Governor sat staring, appalled. Neither of them seemed afraid, but the colonel was certainly startled by the turn of events. He did not know what to do. He turned around. There was only one thing to do, but he did not want to do it right away. However the noise increased as Wrightson spoke, and Wrightson was forced to stop. Colonel Brake was going to speak to the Governor, but first he wondered how were the policemen deployed outside. He wondered about Empson, and Norman and Peake, how they had deployed their men. They had not discussed this eventuality and he hoped these high-ranking officers were on the alert and ready to deploy their men in strategic places. He couldn't guess where Holder was, nor whether he was with any armed men. He walked towards the near window. The rest of Rooks's men were in a nearby office and he knew order could be imposed inside the building. Anyway there was little time. He dashed to the Governor's chair.

'Your Excellency, we may have to suspend the sitting.'

'Very well.'

Brake rushed to Wrightson's podium. All around him were policemen, and Sergeant-Major Lewsey, with Major Rooks, stood behind him. The colonel said in a loud voice, 'In the name of public safety I am asking the Governor to suspend this sitting. I am asking the police to clear the public gallery. God save the King.'

Although hell seemed to break loose inside the chamber, the police were everywhere and were well in control.

◆

The Red House was cleared and there seemed to be thousands of people everywhere. In the little passage leading from Abercromby Street there was a little scuffle. Lumpress, who had been walking round and round the Red House with a signboard, had been stopped, and this caused the crowd to converge. Holder had not only stopped him but had hit him across the shoulder and was arresting him, and that brought out all the venom in the stout woman. Shoved out of the council chamber, she had been trying to keep cool, but now she dashed up to the corner of Knox Street and Abercromby Street and she cried, 'Inspector Norman, I want to see you.'

Inspector Norman did not even look towards her. She cried, 'Officer, you is Inspector Norman? You don't want to answer me? When you people get a lot of big stick in Port-of-Spain then you'll answer. It's a riot you looking for. But you'll be sorry.'

He looked at the woman. She was all in white with a white head-tie. Vaguely he thought he had seen her somewhere before. As she spoke of riot his blood rose and the fingers of his right hand gripped the baton instinctively. A few people drew near to see what was going to happen.

He looked at her fiercely. 'What did you say?'

'You is Inspector Norman?'

'Yes. Why?'

'You ain't see what just happen down there?'

'What happened? In any case, who are you?'

As Inspector Norman spoke to her he was angry and bristling but when she spoke about 'down there' and he looked towards the far entrance near Hart Street he noticed there was some sort of commotion. His heart pumped a little faster, but although he was a little flustered he did not look at her less severely. When he had said, 'Who are you?' Lolotte Borde wanted to say: 'A human being,' so riled she was. She thought, 'These blasted English overlords!' She did not answer him and he asked again, 'Who are you?'

'Jane Baptiste.' There was laughter, and at the same time a murmur ran through the crowd which surrounded them. It was not a big group for the commotion at the far end was growing and people were running towards it.

He said, 'What happened down there? You said something happened down there.'

He really wanted to know. Most people around him did not even wait for Lolotte Borde to talk. There was a general jumble of comments as a way of information to the inspector, and as a way of protest. Much of it was in patois, and the general thread, which the inspector did not understand, was about how Lumpress was walking with his signboard, and how Holder, with baton, grabbed him, and beat him – but the inspector wasn't even listening, because he could not understand.

Lolotte tried to calm herself. She just said, 'The man was walking with a signboard since morning. Walking round the Red House. That's his civil rights.'

The inspector got hot with anger. He did not know where this woman had got those words from: 'civil rights'. But that was what agitators did. Here was this silly, daft woman talking about civil rights. That came from Lazare or Maresse-Smith or in any case from one of those hotheads. He was looking at her stiffly. He let her go on.

Lolotte Borde said, 'The man is Lumpress. He ain't hurting nobody. All he was doing was walking round with a sign.'

'What did the sign say?'

'All the sign say was "We Want Water". Just that, and that is what we want. Holder just stop him just a while ago, and arrest him, and I hear he beat him too but I didn't see.'

'And why did you come to tell me? Why are you wanting to interfere with the police? You want me to arrest you?'

Lolotte Borde could hardly believe her ears. She felt as if her heart gave a big bang. Only there was no noise, she just felt it. She had come with anger and rage, a little crowd behind her, but now she suddenly felt fear and she had to look out for herself. She suddenly realised she could be arrested and thrown into jail without any redress whatsoever because these people could do what they wanted. She was bewildered as she stepped back. The commotion here had grown but in no comparison with what was happening at the chamber entrance. She did not see that, nor did she see how the sky had become grey. She was suddenly frightened about the threat. She did not want to be thrown into jail for nothing. Lazare and

Maresse-Smith always talked about their willingness to suffer jail, but somehow at this moment she did not want any part of it. She crossed the road and walked on the side of the railings of Brunswick Square and when she came to the first gate she turned into the square. She was so hurt and humiliated she wanted to cry. But she did not cry. She said, 'Oh, that is how they want it?' She felt a chill wind rushing through the square. Without looking up she said, 'Oh God, don't let rain fall. If rain don't fall they might still get what they looking for. Then I could make a jail for something.' She sat down and she could hear the noise of the commotion that was in front of the Red House chamber.

◆

Meanwhile the crowd in front of the main entrance of the chamber was so threatening that Colonel Brake called out the reserves in case there was going to be trouble. He had conferred hastily with Rooks, and after the Governor had suspended the sitting and he had got Sir Alfred and the legislators safely out of the milling crowd, he had had a few quick words with Sir Alfred inside the carriage. Wrightson was sent to his carriage too, of course, and there seemed to be more protection for Wrightson than for the Governor. After Brake had conferred he decided he was not going to make any arrests today, because it could turn out into a nasty riot, and he had neither planned nor prepared for that. In any case the jail would be too full. The reserves from St James's Barracks were now spread out at every point and pretended they were ready to shoot, but he had no intention of ordering the Riot Act read because he was not prepared for that either. The first thing he wanted to do was to keep the crowd under control.

Despite the reserves the angry crowd was not moving and more than once the reserves raised their guns to fire. But Brake had warned them not to fire without the reading of the Riot Act. There was a great deal of tension and angry words and the very feeling and atmosphere stirred Lolotte Borde, and her mind ran on her basket of stones.

Lolotte looked but she could not see what was happening. In the midst of the unrest in front of the chamber door Sergeant Holder was holding Lumpress, trying to lead him away. Lumpress's only arm was pressed behind his back. Holder was trying to hustle him away, but a big section of the crowd was trying to block him. Holder had tried to pass through the chamber, and up the low flight of stairs and then left through the door that would take him to St Vincent Street, but when he had got there and had seen the raging mass of people that were waiting out there he had come back. Now he tried to get gangway because several reservists were there. He pushed Lumpress in front of him, and he tried to move along, passing close to the bared bayonets of some of the reserves. Yet, despite the presence of the armed reserves someone swung a blow at Sergeant Holder, and as he let go one hand to parry the blow, Lumpress slipped from his grasp.

A cry went up, then cheering, then a few rough volunteers elbowed and pushed their way through the crowd to try and hold Lumpress. After that moment the fury of the crowd broke out. Hardly anybody noticed that a drizzle was coming down. There were scuffles all over the Red House grounds as the drizzle, which at first was like powder blown about, started getting heavier. Suddenly came one stone, then another. Three shots were fired into the air and Colonel Brake was rushing all over the place to find a justice of the peace to read the Riot Act. Coming down the stairs now he saw a man trying to enter the Registrar-General's Office. He pulled out his revolver and pinned the man to the wall. The man kicked and the colonel pounded the butt of his revolver on to the man's head and the man slumped to the ground. As Brake bent to push him down the stairs the man suddenly sprang to life and surprised him: he threw his right arm round Brake's neck, tried to wring the revolver hand and pin it at the elbow, and then went down and tried to hold the colonel in a scissors clinch.

Meanwhile Colonel Brake still had his hand on his gun and the man was struggling to wrest it away. Brake suddenly said, 'Stop, or I'll shoot.' But the gun was turned the wrong way. The barrel was turned towards Brake's belly, but the intruder did not know. Brake prised the hand away from his neck, and freed himself, and with surprising agility he skipped to his feet and again hit his assailant full on the head with the steel butt. When the man slid to the floor Brake rushed down to the hall to get police reinforcements to take the man away. But when he came back the man was gone.

Disregarding the disappearance of the man, he rushed outside to see if the riot had quietened, but instead found that it was at the point of danger. He remembered seeing Sydney Bowen, the warden, on the St Vincent

Street side but now any justice of the peace would do to read the Riot Act. As he made towards the corridor to get to the chamber, there seemed to be a loud roar outside, and as he burst out through the chamber door he met a storm of torrential rain. There were still a great number of people on the grounds and in the street but not half as many as there were just a short time ago, and he could see a number of people fleeing from the rains. There was so much steam rising from the hot pitch, and so much mist, he could hardly see the square across the street. He did not go out into the rain, and he knew the danger of a riot was past. He sighed, 'God is good.'

◆

Close to the fountain, under the big samaan tree in Brunswick Square, a lady in white was standing. She was dripping with water and not too far from her was a man standing under the rain. She said, 'Why you don't come across here, Greasy Pole? Don't stand up there in the open. You think Brake finish with you?'

Greasy Pole did not answer. He did not care where he stood. The rain was pouring over his head but he was not more soaked than Lolotte who was under the samaan tree. He just wanted to see what was happening at the Red House. He did not care now if he died because he had come so close to dying. Just that he did not want to die before he did that certain job. This seemed the wrong day for it, there could hardly be a worse day. But he had promised Eva, and he had promised himself too, and he wanted to do it. He really felt it should be done, regardless of pay. His heart was hurting him. Maybe he could say his heart was hurting him even more than his head, although the butt of Brake's gun had almost made him unconscious. His heart was hurting him because he wanted to do the job, not just for Eva, nor for himself, nor for Lolotte, but for justice's sake, and for revenge – revenge, especially so now, after what had happened a while ago with Brake. It was a miracle how he did not pass out. He wanted to do the job not only because Eva had paid him. He remembered Holder now, how he cracked that baton over Lumpress's shoulder. Eva would appreciate that. She used to get more than that from Holder in the house. He almost jumped, as Lolotte's voice came again. 'What happen, Greasy Pole? You in a trance?'

'Me? I just looking across there.'

'I thought you was in a trance because I was just talking to you and you wouldn't answer.'

'You was talking to me? What you said?'

'No, I was just saying the rain look as if it passing.'

Greasy Pole did not notice. His clothes were soaked and dripping. It made little difference now.

She said, 'Well, this was a bad day. They suspend the debate and we ain't get anywhere. When things was really squaring up for a fight the rain come down. I thought God was good. I thought he was a Christian.'

'Lolotte, what you talking about?'

'He didn't stand up for us. After all the pain and suffering, when we should give them what coming to them He send rain.'

'Lolotte, stop. You know me, I ain't no church type, but you getting me vex. Look at you, you dressed all in white, this morning. Who you did that for? I know you. It's only because you disappointed you talking stupidness.'

'Stupidness? Look at that place. Almost everybody gone. The police in their glory. We wasted our damn time.'

Greasy Pole looked at her angrily. Inside her she was making no fun. She said, 'You could be as vexed as you want, you don't know how I planned for this morning. Yesterday I went to Edgar's house, I went to Mzumbo, Mzumbo and Edgar came up by me. I prayed and prayed. This morning I wake up early and went to church. I even met Eva in church.'

'Eva? She was by me this morning.'

'Oh yes, but I didn't see her in the crowd.'

'I glimpsed her. But I didn't so want her to see me. She didn't so want me to come because she scared the police would take me.'

'But why? Just like that? She's your protector now? Anyway I don't get it. She was with me this morning. We was in church.'

Greasy Pole said nothing. The rain was only drizzling hard now. Over the Red House and slightly to the west, there was a tinge of blue. The dark grey of the sky shaded into a lighter grey towards the sea.

Greasy Pole said, 'Maybe she didn't want to stay around too much. She was saying something about Holder this morning. I think she scared like hell. You know she left Holder?'

'I didn't even know she used to live with Holder — not until this morning. She's with a young boy now. That's what I hear, don't say I say.'

'I ain't even see Mzumbo, and even in all this bacchanal I ain't seeing Edgar at all.'

'Well I glimpsed Edgar, but afterwards I didn't know where he melt to.'

◆

As they were talking they were both looking towards the Red House, and they were both thinking the same thing. Because anybody could see that today was a failure. The place was almost empty now, save for the policemen, and the volunteers. The policemen and the volunteers seemed to be swarming about now that the people were gone. Some of the policemen were in long black cloaks, but the volunteers were in khaki. Looking at the policemen seemed to bruise the sight of Lolotte. With her clothes wet and dripping and clinging to her she began to feel more and more dejected.

Greasy Pole was looking and it was as if he was thinking of a thousand things at once. He said to Lolotte, 'This bloody excuse about suspending the sitting. They only playing for time. Wrightson only playing for time. Then they'll just suddenly pass that bill. You'll read it in the papers.'

'They can't pass that bill. What? Not now. You see how much people was here today? We'll make so much noise outside they wouldn't even hear what they saying.'

Greasy Pole gave an ironic chuckle as she talked. When she was finished he said, 'They'll hold that debate you wouldn't even know when.'

She suddenly looked scared.

He said, 'They suppose to suspend the sitting till next week Monday. That's what they said. Till Monday. Because of the noise in the public gallery. But they could just meet on Wednesday and pass the bill.'

'Mzumbo wouldn't allow that. Edgar would never stand for that. And don't forget Henry Alcazar. Alcazar waiting for them.'

'These people could do anything, Lolotte. They have guns. We'll have to teach them a lesson.' Then looking towards Pembroke Street his heart shook, for he saw Inspector Norman, Superintending Sergeant Peake, and Sergeant Holder looking towards him. He said, 'Lolotte, I ain't staying here no more. I better go. I have a job to do and I have to be outside, not in jail. And I have to be alive. Just look up there by that new library.'

When Lolotte saw the three men looking towards them her heart raced.

121

She instinctively moved away. She said, 'Greasy Pole, let's get away from here.'

He turned with her towards the Frederick Street side. She said, 'No point in staying in Brunswick Square anyway. We done lose today. I was staying there because I so vexed. I was dead vexed.'

Greasy Pole said, 'I making the rounds and going to Jablotin and staying inside. Because I have a job to do and I have to be alive and outside to do it. And don't forget I on the run, what they say, fugitive from justice? But I know the police don't know I in Jablotin. Or they 'fraid to come inside there. I wasn't even planning to come here this morning, but after Eva left, I say hell, I have to be there too. I'll risk it.'

Lolotte looked at him somewhat amazed. Because of the overpowering events of the day she had somehow forgotten Greasy Pole had broken jail and was on the run. Silently she wondered if the policemen at the library corner had recognised him. She thought not.

She turned to him. 'Greasy Pole, if not for my sake or for your sake but for heaven's holy sake, you could do me a favour by avoiding the police and trying to get inside Jablotin? And please, to help me, take that red cap from your head and put it in your pocket? For kindness you could do me this favour please?' She had to grind her teeth when she said so because it gave her great pain to see how careless and foolish this man was. It was unbelievable. A well-known fugitive standing up in the square and tempting the police. And at the same time advertising himself by wearing a stupid red cap. She shook her head ever so slightly.

Greasy Pole grinned. 'Don't mind me cap. It was in me pocket when I was fighting so they didn't mark me. You better go home too, Lolotte, because these crazy people could shoot. And shooting at you, I mean, they can't miss.'

She realised he was referring to her size but she did not know if he was joking or not. She did not smile. She could not smile. She just was not feeling in the mood, what with the day being so terrible and hurtful and Greasy Pole capping it off by being so silly. 'Capping' was just the word, she thought.

When Greasy Pole left, her anger rose like a river breaking its banks. The depth of her feeling against the Government, against Walsh Wrightson, Brake and Holder, and especially against Inspector Norman, came back with full force. It was like a tornado. She walked back to the overhang of Grell and Company – on the Frederick Street side – and just stood up and stared bitterly at the Red House. People passed to and fro, including policemen. Lolotte just stood motionlessly and stared at the Red House. Outwardly she was calm. But she was angry and hurt and she could not have felt more deeply offended. She was so offended that a few teardrops glistened on her face.

15

Before the suspension of the debate, while Wainwright had been talking and the tension had been increasing, Major Rooks had slipped away to climb the fire brigade tower quickly. This was to look around and see if any serious threat had been building up. But when the rain had begun to drizzle heavily he had come down again, and as he turned to leave the building by way of the side gate Darwent straightened up against the wall and Eva stiffened with fear.

'Oh God!' she thought. It was a good thing she was well into the recess beside the narrow concrete stairway.

Both their hearts were thumping so loudly one could almost hear the beats. After a few moments Darwent made a soft 'Whew!' He said, 'That was a close one.'

'We shouldn't even be here.'

Darwent glanced at her, surprised. Where she was, in the deep gloom underneath the stairway, he could hardly see her. He said, 'It was you who wanted to be here. I wanted to go in the stables.'

'I prefer here because of the side gate and in any case I was just going to stay a few minutes. That's what I talking about. When I say we shouldn't be here I mean we shouldn't be here still. All I come to do is to tell you what I come to tell you. If that man did see us, oh God, it woulda be hell.'

'No, it wouldn't have been hell.'

'How you mean?'

'Well, he would have just shot us.'

'Good Jesus, Saviour!' She nearly fainted to hear that.

Darwent's instinct was to move from there as fast as possible. Because he did not know if Rooks would be coming back. This was just before the suspension of the Legislative Council debate, and from the roar and din coming from the Red House he felt enough was happening there to keep Major Rooks. He could hear the various noises of anger and discontent, some scuffles that may have been taking place in Abercromby Street, and frequent bursts of cheering from the public gallery. He was listening intently and at the same time he was thinking of Rooks coming back. Luckily, from where he was he could see clearly over to the little gate and if Rooks came back, all he, Darwent, had to do was to shift in beside Eva and keep quiet. He did not want to make Eva panic by talking about this. He tried to rest his arm on her shoulder, and he said, 'You're all right?'

'But that question is stupidness. Anybody could be all right here?'

'No need to be so nervous.' His heart was still thumping.

'Nervous? You didn't say the man woulda shoot us?'

'I'm afraid so. Yes, if he had seen us. Yes, if I know him at all, he'd have done that.'

She said, 'Good Christ. I mean I ain't 'fraid to die but to think of somebody shooting us here, at point-blank range, and everybody coming and seeing the two bodies lying down here. A white man and a black woman. Not that this mean anything to me and you but that is how this stupid world is! And not just a white man but Captain Walter Darwent. And not just a black woman but his washerwoman. You could imagine the scandal?' She looked towards him.

He did not want to try to imagine the scandal nor did he even want to think about it. His wife and two children were upstairs at the other end of the building. He did not want to imagine the scene that Rooks could have created. Not just the rabble jam-packing the fire brigade precincts by the front entrance and the Abercromby Street entrance to come and watch the bodies; and not only his fellow officers coming to look, but his dear wife and children. His dear wife and children whom people said he had sent to England so he could be free with his washerwoman. He did not want to think of what Rooks could have done. At least it would have confirmed the rumours as true – the rumours that were sweeping the place.

He said, 'Eva, this is still a new year, although we are in March. You have always been saying we should stop this nonsense. You think we should stop now for good?'

She looked swiftly at him. 'I ready to stop it now. If I get away from this place without nobody seeing me, I ain't coming here again for the rest of my life, and I ain't seeing you again. Just one question I asked you – one thing I want you to do for me and you ain't answering me. I'm telling you Brake will suspend that debate and I left and rushed here just to ask you this. But you wouldn't answer me.'

'That is a hard thing. Tough. You really don't want to come here again and to see me again. Because after that, well – none of my fellow officers would want to see me again.'

'Well, you could play sick or do something. You is a man who say you love me!'

'Yes, but if I even hold your hand you pull it away.'

She did not speak but she said in her heart, 'I didn't tell you *I* love you.'

For a moment he kept quiet, listening, and to him the din at the Red House was getting greater. There was a lot of booing and he felt it was a matter of time before the police opened fire. He did not feel safe here. At the moment he didn't expect Rooks to come back but he still felt he should get out of there.

He said, 'That was a bad time to come here.'

She said, 'When I saw the debate looking as if it will stop, I was sure then that something big had to happen next Monday. And I just want to know if you would do us this favour. I just want to sleep good.'

'That is tough. That is the most painful thing you ever asked me.'

Just then they heard a hammering and they did not know where it was coming from. She said, 'Look – let me go.' She looked towards Abercromby Street.

He said, 'So you want to go out to Abercromby Street?'

'How it looking?'

'From what I can see it looks clear. Everything is clear.'

'And what about—? You know what I mean. That man with the gun.'

'Oh no. Don't think about him. He wouldn't come back here.'

'But somehow I don't think he woulda shoot, you know. At least not you. I mean, two Englishmen? Englishman to Englishman? No. Not that. Me, yes, perhaps he woulda shoot me. But seeing me with you—'

Darwent said, 'That's why he would have shot us even quicker. You don't know that man. Don't forget I am one of them. I live with them. Of all these scamps he is the – I don't know what to call him.'

'You said his name was – what again? – I can't remember, but it was some name like Crook.'

Darwent laughed. 'Rooks. Rooks. Not crook. But you're right. He is a crook. And he's not an Englishman, you know. Not in the true sense. He was born here, like me. But he is worse than all of them put together.'

She was only listening to him lightly. She was still trying to imagine

126

what could have happened if Rooks had seen them, and when in her mind she saw the two bodies lying there, with blood all over the ground and pieces of flesh all over the concrete, she felt faint, and she cried softly, 'Oh God, don't make anything like that happen to us!'

'What's that?'

'Captain Walter, you could imagine if that man did see us? You could imagine that kind of death, without even preparing you soul?'

He said nothing for a while. Above what seemed more bursts of applause, sheer din, high-pitched threats and the crash of stones on wood, he said, 'We'd be better to get out of here. Take it easy, people seem to be running up the road.' He stopped talking and listened. Eva was trembling. Walter Darwent took her by the shoulder. He said, 'Look, Eva. We'd have to meet later. '

She said, 'Captain, if the worst come to the worst, you'll do that for us? Please. I going now. I making a dash for it.'

He said, 'Listen, Eva, when you dash out of here don't run directly into the road. Stop by the hedge first and look. I'll creep over to the stable and try to get upstairs.'

'Okay.'

'Don't run directly out into the road, please. Else you really mightn't have time to prepare your soul!'

He looked at her fixedly. She moved out from where she was. He said, 'You all right?'

'Don't hold me, please. Before this thing is over you know what to do. You know what to do to make me all right!'

He did not answer. As she dashed out to the hedge she felt the heavy drizzle that was coming down.

◆

Darwent slid quietly through the corridor. He passed the pump-room, he passed the warehouse area where all the equipment was kept, then he dashed across the courtyard and went up to his quarters. He had put on his uniform just in case any of the officers spotted him, but he was firm in his resolve not to show himself again today. When he got upstairs his two children were playing on the floor and he saw his wife at the northern window as if she were trying to see what was happening in St Vincent Street. She swung round when she heard his footsteps.

'Walter, where were you? When I didn't see you for some time I was worried. What's happening out there, darling?'

'Well, the crowd's out there in force. And it looks like trouble. You didn't hear the booing. I think that was Wrightson trying to speak. There was a shot a while ago, but I don't know if it was in the air. Listen! I don't like what's going on and please keep inside.'

'You are telling me to keep inside? I want to tell *you* to keep inside. This is very scary.'

'Take it easy, nothing will happen to us. I just came from the council chamber. There are police and armed soldiers all over the place. Maloney and Brake are inside.'

'I didn't expect them to be outside. But what I want to know is this: I thought you said you weren't going over there at all. Change of heart?'

'Look, Gwen, I still feel the same way. I went out to show myself because, after all, you know what my position is. But a wrong could never be a right. After all, I resent what is going on. You yourself said a man must have to have courage to do what I do. They are wrong, rather *we* are wrong. I mean I wouldn't go as far as Lazare to say they are grinding the people into the dust, but good God, Wrightson and that set, they are really ridiculous.'

She was silent for a while. Then she said, 'When I said a man has to have courage, I mean – well I don't know. You have principle. That's good. But you also have a wife and two children. I really don't know. You see if they kick you out of the fire brigade—'

She stopped. He was looking at her. He just shook his head and smiled.

She said, 'You have to look at that, you know, Walter. Because Walsh Wrightson could go back to England and get some big job—'

'I like that. Walsh could go back to England and get a big job? Well, for your information Walsh is a blasted dunce.'

She had put up her hand. She said now, 'Listen to what I'm saying, Walter. While Walsh, and Norman, and Owen, and Lewsey – all those police officers. Well, Walsh is Public Works, but while all of them could go back to England and find something good, you can't go. You aren't an Englishman.'

'That's what you always say! For what it matters. I am surprised because you did not think it mattered before and now you are talking like them. I wasn't born in England but I feel I'm worth half-a-dozen of those fellows put together. I hate their bloody guts. In any case, look at the work my father did for this country. I believe I told you he's the one who found petroleum for them. And now they so damn cocky.'

'It's not "they so damn cocky". It's "they *are* so damn cocky". You are beginning to talk just like your washerwoman. I don't always correct you but I hear you sometimes. Anyway, about the petroleum, at least Randolph Rust acknowledges it.'

'Because he knows. And he knows the hard work that goes into drilling. In any case Rust is Canadian. But look, sometimes you yourself say that I want to be English. I'll tell you this, Gwen, I don't want to be anything special. I'm a man, aren't I? I belong to Trinidad, and here is where I want to stay. And here is where I want to see justice.'

'Yes, like that madman Mzumbo Lazare. And Maresse-Smith!' she said, fuming.

'Are you calling them mad? Do you know anything about them?'

'But Walter, do *you* know anything about them? It's only lately you started calling their names here.' Then she put her hands on her hips and looked at him and said, 'You know, I wouldn't be surprised if that rumour Susan Norman told me about is true. No, I'm honest, I wouldn't be surprised if you and that little washerwoman are having some affair. Yes, well, don't blow up, but I speak my mind. Please, Walter, don't explode. Darling, I didn't expect you to be in fire brigade uniform this morning.'

He turned from the room. 'You and Susan Norman and the fire brigade could go to hell!'

She swung round and followed him. 'Well, you don't have to get vexed because I say what I say. In any case Susan just repeated a rumour which everybody's saying. You think she's the only one who told me that? But I know why they're all trying to sink you. They want to sink you just because you oppose them, and in fact you must be the only white man in Trinidad who's opposing Wrightson, opposing the Government, and siding with the masses. I don't mind that. If that is your passion for justice, I'll stand with you. A wrong could never make a right, no matter from what angle you look at it. No matter—'

The noise from another roar of booing was coming through the window, and then applause, and then it was as if there was the clash of stone on galvanised roof, and violent scuffling. She stopped and went to look through the window. They were in their bedroom now and the two small children were playing on the floor. She took up the smaller one and turning back towards her husband she said, 'I hope for your sake there won't be any trouble. I know the crowd wouldn't touch us, because they know where you stand and they like you. But I trust this damn waterworks bill will get settled one way or the other. Where are you going, Walter? You have to go out? I have to confess that – that I'm scared.'

The sound of unrest outside had grown more severe and Darwent took off his uniform and was changing hurriedly into one of the suits he went out in. He went to look through the window although he knew that with buildings in the way no window you looked from would give you a view of the Red House or the streets around it. The very fire brigade building was blocking the view of Abercromby Street in front of the Red House. He said, 'I'm going to see what's happening.'

'Mind, you know, Walter. You know none of these officers care for you. Mind! Although Susan is my friend, you think I'll trust Charles? I won't trust any of them so far as you are concerned. All of them dislike us because you aren't supporting the waterworks bill. The only one of them who talks to me nicely is Rooks.'

'Rooks is a crook.' Walter Darwent stopped abruptly at the door as he was about to go down the stairs. His face had a terrible frown and he looked furious.

Gwen was taken aback. 'Oh God, Walter. What's he done to you?'

'He was the one who started this rumour.'

'Didn't you say he never liked you? Susan was saying he told Charles he saw you with the washerwoman. Well, all right, you know they are all out to get you. If I were you I wouldn't say anything to oppose anything. It doesn't mean you are backing off. But you can't stop those boys, can you? You just can't win, and they feel you are embarrassing the clan. That's all. You are the fire brigade chief. The Government's paying you to fight fire. Okay. I suppose it's the same like the other day when Kathleen told me what Charles said. I suppose Charles was right. You remember that story about when they were talking about you in the Union Club and when Charles said, "Let Darwent fight his fire and keep his mouth shut"?'

'Well, you didn't tell me that.'

'Well, that was what Kathleen said.'

'Oh I see. Oh, that's what. You just told me he said my job was to fight fire.'

'Don't take them on. Calm down. Don't go out there.'

'What?' He laughed an ironic laugh. 'You think I'm scared of those fellows?'

'Perhaps the officers won't do anything. But you know there are some mad policemen. You yourself said how some of them are so vexed with you. For instance, does Holder talk to you?'

'He is such a damn stooge and reptile. I'll give him a piece of me bloody mind.'

'What?' She was shocked. 'Do no such thing, please. If you don't care about yourself, fine, but for my sake, and for the sake of these two little children, do no such thing. Take it easy. Because whatever you tell Holder will reach Brake, and from Brake to Wrightson, and one of them will tell Governor Maloney.'

'To hell with Wrightson, and to hell with Maloney, and to hell with the bloody lot of them.'

She almost couldn't hear him now for there seemed a steady roar coming from the streets.

She said, 'You really have to go out? If I were you I wouldn't go out in the street. Stay by the pump carriage. God, I'm not feeling so safe in here. You know what I feel, Walter? I feel you ought to take me up to the Queen's Park Hotel and let us stay there for a while. Far from this madness.'

'Gwen. Now I have to tell you to take it easy, for God's sake. Those fellows won't do anything to this house.'

'I know.' She was listening intently.

'But if the worst ever comes to the worst I'll do just that. I'll take you up there. But they aren't shooting. Those cracks of gunshot were in the air.'

She did not say anything. As she saw him moving towards the door she said, 'Walter, do you have to go outside? I would prefer it if you don't.'

'I have to go and see. So what! My family is here and I'll be in the house and not know what's happening?'

He disappeared down the stairs. As he opened the downstairs door he realised that the loud roar he had been hearing was of torrential rain. The deluge went on for about an hour before it began to drizzle off.

16

The rain stopped completely and when the sun came out again a lot of people drifted back to the area of the Red House. There was not such a strong police presence now because the Government knew it had won. Clement was among those who came back to the square. He had been in the public gallery when the debate was suspended and since then he had been looking for Eva. He even went under the rain and looked in Independence Square but he did not see her. There had been a lot of people sheltering in Croney's Ice House Hotel, but she was not there. He had no idea where Eva was. When Colonel Brake had had to go for the Governor, he, Clement, had been on the lower steps leading to the council chamber, and although he had not meant to 'storm' the council chamber he had been swept in with the scores of people who surged into the public gallery when Colonel Brake left the door. And in the confusion which followed the booing of Wrightson, when armed policemen rushed into the chamber, the feeling he had that the police would run amok and massacre people had made him desperate. He had been thinking wildly of Eva, and could not guess whether she was on the stairs, or in the very chamber, or in Brunswick Square, or on any of the streets outside. He just did not know.

The armed police had come into the chamber mainly to escort the Governor out, and to protect Walsh Wrightson, and some had remained to see that some of the members of the Legislative Council got to their carriages safely. And afterwards the people were cursing and pushing and quarrelling, but the police had got behind them and had shoved them out of the Red House in the rain. He had not even known rain was falling. Since he was pushed out into Abercromby Street he had run wildly about, soaking wet, trying to find Eva. And when the rain had passed he had gone all around looking. And afterwards, seeing the light of the sun, and the crowds wandering back to Brunswick Square, he had come back, hoping against hope that she would be one of the crowd that drifted back.

For he felt sure no tragedy had taken place and she was alive and well.

He walked across Abercromby Street into Brunswick Square but the police, who seemed also to have returned in force, were calling on people to 'move on' all the time, and even in Brunswick Square the police had been signalling him to move on. But there were so many people they could not do much. Everybody seemed to have come back. Some were still wet from the rains but most looked dry, and there were quite a few umbrellas. A few groups started singing and soon the square and all around it were filled with song. The chorus which resounded now was: 'How Long , O Lord!' This seemed to irritate the police but when some of them resorted to using their batons freely he heard Colonel Brake screaming to them not to beat but simply to disperse the crowd.

Now, standing on the Abercromby Street side of the square, he was looking around frantically to see if he could spot Eva so that they could clear out of this place. She had been so busy these days he had not seen her. He had gone to her place yesterday but she was out, and now he was really worried. At one instant he saw a woman in yellow pass in front of the fountain in Brunswick Square and the gait was so much like Eva's that he had dashed off towards the fountain to verify it, but by the time he had made a few steps it was hopeless. She was lost in the crowd. He walked up to Knox Street, but here the police looked too threatening and in any case if Eva was here at all she would be around the Red House. So he walked back to Abercromby Street, going in the direction of Trinity Cathedral. There was a knot of people on that side and some were on the side of the fire brigade station. He stood up a little by the western gate of Brunswick Square, facing the entrance to the council chamber. Where he was standing there was a little knot of people who had come from the square. He saw two policemen approaching them and he knew they were going to be moved on so he started walking again towards Trinity Cathedral. Just then he spotted a familiar face across the road. Clement hailed out but the lady did not hear. He looked up and down, then edging between a cart and a group of people he crossed the road and tapped her on the shoulder.

The fat woman said, 'Ay, boy, is you? So how? I ain't see you it must be a week.'

'It's about a week. Lolotte, tell me, you see Eva at all?'

Lolotte hesitated. It could not be *that* Eva he was talking about. But there was no other Eva. There was no other Eva in this dangerous affair. She said, 'Oh, you mean Eva, the girl who—'

'Yes, Eva. Eva Carvalho.' And he was going to add, 'The girl I living with.' But he wasn't living with her yet. She had only promised they would live together. He said, 'Me girlfriend, you know.'

She was taken aback. Lolotte Borde who knew most things of that sort did not really know this. Yet she knew Clement so well by seeing him around, that she realised he was under the impression she was aware of this. She was a bit confounded, but in a lively way she said softly, 'Oh, Eva? We was together. Early this morning we was together in the Catholic church. But I ain't see her since I come here.'

'So you don't know if she's here, or if she was here and gone?'

'Well yes. She should be here. Perhaps she went after the heavy rain. That was a sudden rain, eh? Maybe she didn't come back. Not everybody come back, you know. For instance I was going home.'

'I only came back to look for Eva.'

'Maybe she was sheltering from the rain somewhere. That was a heavy shower, eh? Look how wet the road still is. And look at the water in the drains! Maybe she was sheltering from the rain? We couldn't shelter in the Red House. They shoved us out of the Red House. But it's your sweat and mine what build that!' She said angrily.

'You so right.'

'And everything against the poor and downtrodden although people keep saying God loves the poor. When they suspend the debate and everybody was furious and ready to give them what coming to them, stones started to pelt already, you know that is the time when God will send rain?'

Clement felt very disturbed to hear Lolotte say that. Because in the little time he knew her he could see how much faith she had. Her white dress and white head-tie were soaked and crumpled but they were all evidence of how she felt. He was disturbed about her but it might have been because he was already troubled. Where in the name of heaven was Eva? Should he go up to the corner of Duke and Richmond again and see if she was there now? He said to Lolotte, 'I think I going back and see if she's home.'

'That's the best thing. You must be worried. I think you said she's your girl?'

'Yes. You didn't know? I can't tell where she disappeared to. You said she was in church with you this morning? What colour dress she had on?'

'It was blue, with fady red flowers.'

'Oh I saw a yellow—'

'No, it's blue.'

'I so worried I don't know why.'

'Because you love bad, that's why.'

For a moment Lolotte wondered whether he knew Eva was fooling around with Captain Darwent, for what came to her mind now was: 'She must be in Darwent house!' But she wasn't going to say that. In any case, how could she say a thing like that? True, she had heard that Darwent had sent his wife to England for the sake of really playing the fool with his washerwoman, but if the person who should know did not know, why shouldn't she keep her mouth shut? However, the Eva she saw this morning was no walkover. She could tell that. She had to confess to herself she did not know what was happening. There were lots of rumours. All she knew was that she wasn't going to mention anything about the fire brigade chief. In any case, since the whole of Port-of-Spain knew of the scandal, Clement was bound to know.

She said, 'To tell you the honest truth, me boy, I meself would like to see Eva. As you see, the case really grim, and now that they suspend the sitting for next Monday then next Monday something have to happen. They can't keep us on tenterhooks and go on installing those blasted meters, and go on trampling us down—'

'They begin to install them?' Clement's voice cut across hers.

'That's what I hear. But you think I care about meters, really? They could keep all the meters, they could even install them in me earhole. Just give me the right to run this island. Me and you. These foreigners living off the fat of the land too long, and we ain't putting up with it no more! It's Mzumbo Lazare who opened me eyes.'

'Yes, Mr Mzumbo opened everybody eyes. He and Mr Edgar Maresse-Smith.'

'And you know I can't stand them when they try to cover this up with all this pomp and foolishness. When I was on the steps this morning. And the police chief rush down to meet Maloney. That's Brake. When he rushed down to meet Maloney, I coulda laugh me head off. That fool. And escorting the Governor in state, mind you, and Maloney coming with all this pompousness, with all these sashes and tassles and this tall hat, looking like a lion—'

'A lion? You ever see a lion?'

'But look Grell right there. Grell have a big one for their bread cart.'

'But that's a donkey.'

'In other words an ass. Well yes, that's what ah mean.'

Clement burst out laughing. But he was still very worried. In fact he had only been half listening to Lolotte Borde. He was taken up with glancing around to see if he could spot Eva, and at the same time he did not like the look of the policemen. For although most of them were armed only with batons, they seemed extremely aggressive. He was amazed at how the sun had come out so bright and hot again. All the more reason why Lolotte was so peeved, he thought. The rains had come just at the right moment to save the foreigners. He looked around at the police and he was feeling a tinge of fear. He wanted to clear out of the area to be safe but he could not leave without seeing Eva. He was thinking of going over to the Frederick Street side to see if he could find her and at the same time this would at least get him away from this side where the police were most active. In fact, right before his eyes at this instant he could see a policeman beating someone with a baton, in the midst of a little crowd.

He cried, 'What's that? God! Look at that? Look over there, just opposite the fire brigade station.'

Lolotte looked to where he was pointing and she winced. She said, 'Unless somebody cripple Holder he'll never stop.'

They watched in silence and horror. Lolotte added, 'That feller is Lodrick. You know Lodrick John? He challenged Holder when he was on the stairs. Holder's so wicked. Now he ketch up with him and he's letting him have it!'

Clement was sickened. He did not know Lodrick John but he felt outrage. He just said, 'Going over to the Frederick Street side to see if I find Eva. You walking this way?' He threw another glance at where the commotion was going on and he saw Lodrick John on the ground. Around Lodrick was the redness of blood. But Lodrick was not dead. He was trying to get up. Clement turned away and pointed to the overhang of Grell and Company at the corner of Frederick Street and Brunswick Square. He said, 'You going so?'

'Yes. In fact, I was standing up there for a long time. Greasy Pole was with me in the square then he went home, and I was so fed-up with this debate business that I came back and just stood up there wet, staring down the Red House and wanting to slaughter Walsh Wrightson. Walsh

Wrightson and especially Inspector Norman. You see how the sun come out hot? I completely dry again and me blood still tingling. But nothing ain't happening. At least we can't fight them today. Today they win.'

She sounded depressed. She thought of her basket of stones in the hedge by the deanery, and of course she did not dare go for it now. She said, 'I think I going home. We can't do nothing today. Today is theirs. Anyway, if you see you girlfriend tell her how Brake give Greasy Pole a good beating.'

'Oh yes? How come? What Greasy Pole did?'

'I don't rightly know. They was fighting. Greasy Pole went in the Red House during the rain. Maybe he went to shelter. You see behind his head, here?' She touched the back of her head, on the left side. 'Brake let him have it here with the butt of the gun. It swelled up as big as a mango.'

'It was a good thing it was with the butt of the gun and he didn't pull the trigger.'

'Yes. Anyway, tell her that,' Lolotte said. 'I going. Today is *their* day.'

Clement didn't know what to say. He looked at Lolotte. She was so much like Eva in her talk. The things she said, the way she felt. They didn't look alike. Not at all. Her bulk could make three or four times that of Eva's, but their anxiety for change was the same. But although, because of Eva, he was beginning to see himself as a radical too, he was going to be nothing but a silent radical. Because he could not see how they could fight guns. He wanted to cheer up Lolotte, so he said, 'Girl, you all in white. And even white head-tie to go. Caramba! You looking nice. White is purity.'

'They say blessed are the pure in spirit. I have faith in God. He wouldn't see us fall.'

Clement teased, 'But you was just saying he sent rain to save Wrightson. And you was just talking about fight. That's the point. Warrior talk. Now you holy? You was just talking warrior talk and now you saying: *Blessed are the pure in spirit.*'

'Of course ah saying that. So you can't be holy and be a warrior? What about Michael the Archangel – he didn't kick Satan from upstairs?'

Clement laughed. All the time his mind was on Eva and now as he reached Grell's corner he said to Lolotte, ''Scuse me,' and he stood up and looked up and down Frederick Street, and turned around and was looking all over the place.

Lolotte said, 'She ain't there. But don't worry, nothing happen to her. Out here dangerous and she have to look out for Holder.' She quickly bit her lips. She did not know if Clement knew Eva used to live with Holder. She said hastily, 'It's no use, she done gone. Better to get away from all these rifles. Maybe she gone to start planning for next week Monday. Because next Monday something bound to happen. As sure as there is a God above.'

'I just have to find her. In any case I might be travelling tomorrow. I have to go to Mayaro.'

'Mayaro? For long? Boy, you'll be getting the fresh breeze and chip-chip water. And peace perfect peace. I hear it's a great place, but far.'

Clement was wondering how much he should tell Lolotte. He did not know how much Eva wanted her to know and he thought he'd better keep his mouth shut. For since he was going to prepare the way for Mzumbo's temporary exit, Lolotte Borde might become alarmed. In any case, did Eva give him the authority to talk?

He said, 'I love the ozone in Mayaro and I have to go for a rest. It have plenty coconut water there, and chip-chip is me middle name. Don't know when I'll come back.'

Lolotte was smiling graciously. But she was saying in her mind, 'Don't come back. Stay. Stay drinking coconut water in Mayaro while you little woman fighting, and dodging baton and bullets and taking on this corrupt scum that say it come from England.'

Turning to him, she beamed and said, 'Okay, me boy, you be careful. I going home to me little shack on the hill. Me little ranch on the range.' She looked around, and there was a furrowing of her forehead, showing concern. She said, 'I ain't so sure you should stay round here looking for Eva. You realise how dangerous it is? I know you worried about your girl, but I sure she's safe. And perhaps she done gone, anyway.'

◆

It wasn't long after Lolotte went home that the area again seemed deserted and quiet. In spite of what Lolotte had said, Clement stayed around, hunting for Eva, but now, as the big clock in front of Decle's store showed two p.m., he decided there was nothing else to do but leave. He was sure Eva was not at home and he felt that instead of walking up to the corner of

Richmond and Duke, then walking back to the motor-bus station, he, too, had better go home and rest. For he had got up very early this morning, and if he was really to go to Mayaro he would have to rise very, very early.

The motor omnibuses were doing brisk business with people going back out of town, and no sooner did Clement reach Marine Square than a bus was ready to leave. But before he could board the bus he heard a shrill voice, 'Clement!' When he turned around, there in front of him was the woman in yellow.

'Eva,' he cried. 'Goodness me. Oh God, I so glad!'

17

It rained again on Monday night but as it drew towards morning the sky was light and starry. Mzumbo's heart lifted. He had not expected it and in a way he had never seen anything like it. The whole view of the valley and up to the hill at North Post, and towards Cocorite due west of him – the whole view seemed bright and shining as though washed clean by the rains. This must be a good omen, he thought, and then he laughed at himself. For he had always considered himself an island in a sea of superstition. A hard, practical man. Yet he was really surprised at the sharp cleanness of the dawn.

Dawn?

He got up and looked at the clock, then he chuckled and went back into bed. It was just three o'clock. Maybe five minutes past. It could hardly be called dawn but the scene was great and inspiring. He almost did not know how to describe it. It was more a feeling. It was the way the sky was and the way the morning was. Maybe it was inspired by the strange glow of what people called *fore-day morning*, which was the very brink of the dawn; as well as by the coolness of the atmosphere, the valley being without any mist, and the sky mottled, but clean and beautifully well-defined. Even the darkness did not look like night, although it certainly was not day.

He was feeling good. He had gone to bed quite upset and feeling defeated, but his heart was lifted by a serene dream, with a voice saying to him *Let not your heart be troubled*, and he had woken up to this fine morning, and he was sure it was a sign that there were good things in store.

Sign?

He tried not to think that way. He could not sleep and he got up from the bed and went into the veranda. As he stole out of the room and closed the door behind him, Mammie Marie raised her head from the bedsheet to see what he was up to.

◆

Mzumbo was out in the veranda and the air fanning him was bracing. The night seemed darker, but the sky was alive with stars. From where he was he could not see the morning star. Before him the valley was quiet and sleeping. He said, half aloud, 'Oh God, they think they win. They think they win but something will happen, I don't know what. Me and Edgar have to meet first thing. Then maybe I'll pass by the Caledonian Store to see if I could see Goodwille. George will have to help with some of the banners. Me niece say she want to see me bad but I hope I wouldn't have to tangle with Holder.'

The memory of Holder roughing up Lumpress, cracking down the baton across his back, almost changed his mood. But he remembered that when Maloney was going into the carriage Maloney had spotted him, and there was no hostile look. He did not know what to make of Maloney's face at the moment when their eyes had met but the look was not hostile. And this was the Governor! The Governor respecting an adversary. The Governor respecting Mzumbo's commitment to the people. The Governor probably sensing that right will have to prevail in the end. Mzumbo laughed to himself. He remembered the hymn 'Fight the Good Fight'. He smiled. He simply had to fight the good fight, he couldn't help it. When he remembered the number of men and women who were devoted to him and to the cause, and who despite all the odds were prepared to fight the good fight, and even die, water came to his eyes. He said aloud, 'Today is Tuesday. I don't know what this day will bring. But this is a crucial week. I have to see a lot of people today. We have to avoid trouble, but we have to win.'

Beside him his wife said, 'You have to—'

He jumped. 'Good God,' he said. His heart heaved.

'What happened? Good God, what?'

'I didn't know you were there, Marie.'

'I know you didn't know I was there. But I live here. I living with you but you ain't living with me. You living for the people. You came in late

141

last night. You keep tossing, you can't sleep. Now you out here talking to yourself saying you have to win.'

He kept silent. She looked like a ghost standing there in her white night-gown and her head tied in white. In fact she reminded him of his good friend whom he had glimpsed by the western side of Brunswick Square, just after Holder had held Lumpress. Just a vague recollection, and the two persons were not truly similar. Because his friend was fat and Marie was so slim. It was just a flash of memory, but as he thought of Holder he said: 'Marie, you know Holder is really a beast. Holder—'

She put up her hand to stop him. She said, 'Mzumbo, look, I tired hearing about Holder. What I getting concerned about is you, not Holder. I don't know what's happening down the road. You know, since you left early early yesterday morning, this is the first time I seeing you to talk to? You left saying you going to this big debate. Before that, Edgar was here, I think even Eva came, everybody taking up your time and you taken up with everybody and with this so-called debate. Early, early this morning – yesterday morning – this Mr Mzumbo left here, the groom didn't even come yet to give the horse water even, but the buggy gone. You came back late last night and not even one word about the debate, but now you telling me—'

He stopped her. 'Because you was sleeping! Oh, Marie. Good grief.'

'Yes, I was sleeping. I know. But if it was something like when they locked up Papa Bodu, you woulda wake me up. Don't think I care about the debate, you know. But I only telling you.'

He turned to her, swiftly. He said, 'Darling, that is just it. You don't care a damn about the debate. So I didn't wake you up. There are lots of people out there in Port-of-Spain who – well, let me say this. I didn't wake you up because you don't care about the debate.'

'I know what you was going to say, you know.'

'Marie, don't let us quarrel. The morning too nice to quarrel.'

'When you get sick, when you fall down here on me and get a stroke or something, I'll see if those hundreds of friends will come to see you. All those people out there in Port-of-Spain.'

He put his hands round her neck. 'You quarrelling?'

'I mean I like Edgar. And fellers like Cyrus David, Papa Bodu, and the others, they seem sincere. But you all ain't going to change those Englishmen. Those rulers. And sometimes they right about these damn people wasting water. It's a fact that they waste water. They don't care. Eddie is only a groom, he isn't in politics, but he was telling me how those barrackyard people leaving the tap open for spite.'

At first Mzumbo was going to snap, 'Who's worried about water!' But when he heard what Eddie had said, that chastened him. He did not say anything. He simply said, 'It might be true, because most of those barrackyard people are as illiterate as those cattle of ours. But it's the principle, Marie. When they abolished the Borough Council they thought—'

'Why you don't say it's the Borough Council you worried about! But you always say "It's the principle". When you drop dead I'll see "principle". Even you niece, Eva – you know what Eva told me once? She said, "Tantie, you think it's the water I care about? It's men like me uncle who fighting to get us to take over, it's that I care about." And she said, "Tantie, you think we have any rights here? We ain't have no rights here. The foreigners lording it over us and they ain't think we have no right to have rights." Well, Mzumbo, I smiled, because I know that sounds just like you and it's you it came from. Then Eva said, "Just fancy men like Wrightson and Rooks and Brake ordering me uncle about." Something like that she said. So I said, "Child, you think you could change things? You only wasting your time." '

Mzumbo had not heard about this conversation before, but it showed how devoted to him Eva really was, and that was precisely why he liked her. Of all his sister's children she was the one who cared about what he did. She was the one who felt for him and felt like him, and watched with him. And she was the one who cared about the destiny of this country in which she was born. Marie went on talking but he wasn't even listening. He was reviewing his thoughts and he didn't like saying Eva 'watched' with him. He was not Jesus. The fact was that he liked Eva because of all his sister's children she was the one who loved him, and not only loved him but felt exactly like he did. He had never pumped anything into her head. She was like that. And the action of Holder and the rest of the police force, as well as the action of the Government, had made her make up her own mind. As he was talking to himself he was looking up at the sky to see if the day was really going to be good, or if rain clouds were lurking still. Although the atmosphere was sparkling, the dawn was still so grey that he couldn't be sure of what the sky said. As he turned to talk to Marie, he found she was gone.

He went back into the bedroom sheepishly. He just lay down in his place at the front of the bed and he did not say anything. Mammie Marie turned on the sheet so he knew she was not asleep. After a few moments she turned again. Then she said, 'If it's one thing I can't stand is talking to people but they too big to answer you.'

Mzumbo said nothing. There was silence for a while and then he said, 'What time you said Eva came here?'

There was silence.

'Eh, Marie?'

'Oh, you want me to answer you? And you had me there in the gallery talking to you and not a sound?'

'Girl, I'm so sorry. I didn't hear. Things tight.'

'Things tight? What's that!'

'The case is blood.'

'Blood?' She rose to a sitting position and looked at Mzumbo.

'That's just a figure of speech, but it might well come to that.'

'Mzumbo, for God sake.'

'It's not my fault. The hardship whipping up the people. And they can't take no more. And those – hm! You hear me? Those so-called gentlemen from England, those dense officers, they are so arrogant they'll get anybody furious. They don't know how to handle people. Things nearly got out of hand today – I mean, yesterday.'

Marie did not say anything.

'And it's not as if I'm not playing my part. I'm begging people to have patience. But not to sit idle in the vineyard, as Lolotte said Saturday last. Not to sit idle but to have patience and to have respect for law and order. Mind you, Lolotte doesn't like this part. And Edgar neither, as you well know. I made the mistake to agree with Edgar that something drastic has to happen, because this Government is so stubborn. Something drastic but without violence – and so I agreed that they should make noise in the public gallery. They love it and today we had a din like hell itself. That strategy about making noise in the public gallery is disrespectful but I dare not go back on it. I dare not back-back. I mean, how can you drown out a speaker's voice? That's bad. Well, they did that to Wrightson. It was awful. But at the same time you know what's happening? The police are infuriating the people. Both the police and the Government. As I was telling you, yesterday thing; nearly got out of hand.'

Marie still did not say anything but she could not help feeling that the rabble did not care for anything respectful anyway and didn't know and would never know how to accept good treatment, even if you served it on a silver platter. In any case she simply had no confidence in the locals to rule themselves; she felt she had seen enough, and in her heart she always said, 'Heaven help us if they get home rule.' She never liked expressing any of those sentiments to Mzumbo or even to Eva, but with all Mzumbo was doing in that field she never ever showed the slightest interest, because so far as she was concerned it was a dead loss. He spoke of things nearly getting out of hand yesterday and she supposed he wanted her to ask him what happened. But she did not really care. Since Carnival these unruly people had begun creating chaos over the water bill, and she felt they were looking for just what they got. What right had thousands of people to go to the Red House and interrupt proceedings while the Honourable Members were debating a bill? What were things coming to?

She listened to Mzumbo talking and she wondered why the hell these things were allowed to go on; why was the mob, that is, the masses, why were they being allowed to endanger life without let or hindrance? In a vague way she was glad they were allowed to, because had they not been, Mzumbo might have been taken by the police a long time ago. She had long resigned herself to the fact that she could not change Mzumbo. The only good thing he did, and in which she gave full support, was that elegant Old Year's Night ball. Nothing else he did, especially in politics, had the slightest importance to her. Of course he was a good farmer and agriculturist, and he was even a good solicitor. But his main action was in politics, and there was where he made her feel ashamed, backing that band of thieves and vagabonds called the masses. And pumping into their heads the notion that they could run this country. There was not one good mark for him in this awful exercise. Which was a pity because he was really such a fine person, who had a wonderful heart. He was wasting his talent and energy on these backward people. That was fair neither to her nor to the island.

His voice interrupted her thoughts. 'What time you said Eva came?'

'I never said any time but it was about four.'

'I didn't see her today. Such a crowd. I didn't see her anywhere near the Red House. You know that ex-husband of hers is a beast?'

'Please don't tell me anymore about Holder.'

'He got me so sick today. Today crowned it all. He's so wicked and hostile. Cruel son of a so-and-so. And on the other hand you have Darwent. The fire brigade man. Darwent showing them frankoment he wants nothing to do with repression.'

Marie turned around swiftly, 'Darwent has his axe to grind. Eva was telling me something today.'

'But even so. Even if he's doing it for Eva – and I don't know about that. But even if it is so we have to admit that this man has more guts than a calabash.'

'Until Holder finish him off or finish Eva off, or finish off both of them.'

Mzumbo did not hear that. As he turned he had suddenly spotted the sky through the slate window at the side of him, and he jumped up. 'It's raining, girl? The sky so grey.'

'If you look through slate what colour you expect to see the sky?'

'Oh cracky! For the moment I didn't realise.' He laughed at himself.

'Because this damn waterworks business getting you off your mind. And you have those silly people with nothing to do just going to the Red House to cause sensation. You see me? You see how cool I am? Any time you see Mammie Marie leave Diego Martin you could be sure it's for some lawful business. But Mr Emmanuel, Mr Emmanuel Mzumbo, you are my husband and I have to appeal to you. If you don't cut it out you'll be in jail very soon now. Take it from me. You'll either be in jail or dead.'

He did not answer her. He got up from the bed and went into the veranda. From there he could still hear her mumbling.

He said to himself, 'Marie will never stop niggling. I mean, at this point who could change me?' He looked around. 'It ain't raining, thank God. Only the sky a little misty, and that could mean sun like fire. Today, I just have to see Edgar and Papa Bodu. And I don't know if I could talk to Edgar. But I want to pass at Eva, too. I wonder what brought her up here! I wonder if Lolotte will be out at the corner today. Look, this morning I have to move early. We have a lot of things to do before next week Monday.'

◆

146

It was only half-past eight when Lolotte Borde saw the red-and-black carriage coming up Chacon Street from South Quay. She was just laying out the things in her tray when she saw it, and she put everything down and put her hands to her hips. She said, 'Bless me soul! Mzumbo out already? I was so wanting to see this man.'

There were few people in the street. When the carriage came up she said, 'Mzumbo, I have to say it's God not Man who do that.'

'Who do what?' He pulled up the horse so effortlessly it was as if the horse knew he wanted to talk to Lolotte Borde. 'What's that? You mean yesterday? That disaster?' He pulled the reins very gently to the left and the horse eased close to the pavement.

Lolotte Borde said, 'I ain't talking about yesterday. I talking about now. I was wondering about you, and God send you! I was so worried about you. Especially this morning. Because yesterday I just glimpsed you in front the chamber. I think it was you. Just saw you head. But all that ruction and confusion I never saw you again. Oh God. And all those policemen we couldn't do nothing.'

'We couldn't do anything because nothing happens before its time. And I didn't want any trouble because I am a man of peace. You see how it rained Monday and up to last night? And Sunday it rained in the valley. I don't believe in signs because I'm not superstitious. But early this morning at home when I glanced through the window, for a moment, for a brief moment, the sky was so deep and lovely, and it was as if I was seeing the promise of wonderful things.'

'Oh yes?' Lolotte said. She was remembering how that same sign had fooled her when she had left church early yesterday morning.

Mzumbo said, 'Don't ask me to explain anything but that was the way I felt inside. Today promises to be a very beautiful day—'

'It's yesterday which shoulda be the very beautiful day.'

'Nothing happens except in good season. In the fullness of time.' He looked at her calmly. He continued, 'When I talk about the fullness of time I don't mean in the distant future. Not at all. If yesterday was a bright, sunny day you know what would have happened? We might have been burying people all now. God knows what he did.'

Lolotte said nothing. She was almost convinced by what Mzumbo said, although just momentarily. Mzumbo spoke again. 'I was saying this day promises to be lovely. And why not? Because this is March. Monday coming should be nice. This is the hot season, if you see what I mean.'

Lolotte stared him in the face, almost with shock. 'Thanks, Mzumbo,' she said excitedly. And she said to herself, 'He finally coming round. He's a man of peace but he planning some hot action for Monday.'

Mzumbo said again, 'It should be hot and nice and our efforts should bear fruit. But don't thank me, thank God. And don't say thanks before anything happens. But mind you, Lolotte, there could be thunder and lightning too, you know.'

Lolotte could have cried. Her heart sang out, 'We'll give them thunder and lightning!'

Mzumbo said again, 'Nothing happens before its time.' He said it to please Lolotte because this was one of her favourite phrases. Whenever he heard her with: 'Nothing never happen before the time', it always irritated him because he felt it was high time a lot of things happened. How long would it be before the Borough Charter was restored? How long would it be before elected Government was introduced? Could he dare to even hope to live to see it? He shook it off his mind and mentioned some platitude about her point of vantage. He said he liked the view through the tree-trunks of Marine Square because one could see the crucial streets. And one could see those bigwigs that came and went from the Union Club. She would know where she stood, then, he told her. And she quipped that she was not standing but sitting. Mzumbo grinned. He got out of the carriage and she stopped laying out the things on her tray and she said, 'As I was telling you, Mzumbo. Oh God. It's God who send you this morning, not mankind. I was so confused this morning. You know why I'm out here? I just keen to know what we doing for Monday. We can't stop, you know. We have to plan for those – for those—'

She didn't say the word and he just smiled. He was happy. He said, 'You said we can't stop? I thought you was saying nothing happen before the—'

'It's you who said that this time. It's you who said nothing happen before the time.'

'But that's your favourite.'

'Because God is good. He always make things happen when they ready.' Then she said quickly, 'Look now, for instance. You was in me mind last night. And this whole business yesterday, it had me so mashed up. But with all that I made a few things to sell today because I say I have to go out and sit down there. I have to be out here. I have to be out here to see what's happening and just to satisfy meself that the people still vexed. And when I reach here me mind went on you and I'm so shocked because when I look again, you carriage come.'

Mzumbo said, 'And when you look again me carriage gone. Because I have to go. Today is a busy day. But you know what? I just passed here to see you.'

'To see me?'

'But are you surprised? I just wanted to see that you are there and that you are well. By that I mean, not injured. Not injured from police brutality. And I wanted to see that you have not lost courage. I haven't met with Edgar yet or with anybody. We have to talk and plan but it will be more or less along the same lines.'

He didn't say then that it would be necessary to cut out the booing. He continued: 'We have the same objective, and we want everybody to have the same spirit. What happened yesterday was nothing.'

Lolotte cut in, 'But you yourself said it was a disaster.'

'I just said so because I realised everybody was disappointed. I was disappointed too. It was a disaster because nothing was achieved. But I know in the end we are bound to win.'

'You feel so?' She was excited and her fat, anxious face broke into a smile.

'Yes, I feel so. And it isn't just feeling so. I *know* so. But nothing—'

'But nothing does be happening before the time?' she looked at him sideways.

'Amen.' He smiled. Then putting his foot on the carriage board, to hop in, he stopped and said, 'Look, Lolotte, I have to go, but just one point. We may have to call a public meeting, so as you sell, pass the word. I have to round up a few people today. "Just the main characters", like Cyrus like to say.'

Then he thought quickly, 'Good God, I wonder if Cyrus David is here or down in the country.' And thinking of country he could have hardly avoided remembering his friend, Robert Alexander Dick. He said now, 'Anyway, look, the main thing is the public gallery Monday next. Because the Government will say again all entry must be by ticket, but nobody's going in with any damn ticket. They had said that for yesterday too, but retreated, but perhaps now they know they stand on firm ground. If it is so

I have to see Alcazar and discuss what constitutional means we could adopt. Then we'll have to let the people know what to do so we might have to hold a public meeting either Saturday or Sunday. On the Savannah. But I don't know yet at what time.' He got into the carriage. 'We can't lose this time round. We mustn't lose this time.'

She did not come to grips with everything he had said, but she was excited by those last words: 'We mustn't lose this time.' She declared, 'We'll never lose. God is good. Look, Mzumbo, I nearly forget. Take this, I made this paymie especially for you.'

He stretched his hand. 'Paymie is me favourite,' he cried.

It wasn't just to make her feel good that he said this. He loved paymie, especially the way Lolotte made it, and served it with a little dipping of coconut milk and cinnamon. But this was not the morning to think about paymie. For Lolotte's sake he unwrapped the sweetmeat right there and took a bite. Lolotte was delighted. He was going to put his hand in his pocket but he knew she would be offended and would refuse any money. While munching the paymie he held the reins with one hand and turned to her. 'Lolotte, if I don't see you I'll send somebody to talk to you. Keep it up, eh. Thank you for all you are doing. Keep on the alert.'

'Yes, Mr Mzumbo.'

'If you have any message, urgent, and you want me you know how to get me.'

'Yes, Mr Mzumbo Lazare.'

18

When the red-and-black carriage reached the corner of Richmond Street and Duke Street and stopped, it took Eva by surprise. She said, 'What you doing here, Uncle?'

'You don't want to see me?'

'What? You saying that so easy? How you mean? I went home by you and couldn't find you. Come in and sit down.'

It passed through her mind that with his carriage by the side of the road the people around would know Mzumbo was there and would be on the alert to find out what plans he had for next week Monday.

As he walked into the room she said, 'Here, Uncle, sit down.' She was showing him the good morris chair. In fact, the morris chair was the only good chair. She never had any furniture which she regarded as worthy of Mzumbo Lazare. This was about the fourth time he looked her up and she always felt self-conscious because his furniture was so luxurious and his home, Lazdale, was such a palace to this 'rat-hole'.

She said, 'First thing I want to tell you. Because I feel you should know. That's what I went down to Lazdale to tell you. Mr Walter Darwent told me you ain't safe.'

'What's that? What you mean?'

'Well, when I went to take his clothes – the clothes I washed and ironed – he asked me if I heard the rumour. I said, "What rumour?" He said, "About Mzumbo." I said, "Oh yes, but it couldn't be true." '

Mzumbo Lazare said, 'What rumour is that?'

'Some silly rumour was going round that the police planning to take you. Holder told somebody on Monday they'll seize you any time this week because it's you who's stirring up the people. Who said what, Uncle? Who said Holder said they'll seize you? Let me see – Oh yes, Greasy Pole told me Lumpress said that when Holder was beating him he said so.'

Mzumbo was silent. The thought of Holder having beaten Lumpress angered him. He was there and he saw the cruelty. His blood boiled up now. But he suppressed the feeling enough to give a false laugh. He said, 'Take who! Seize who!'

'I meself didn't believe. Not until Captain Walter Darwent said so yesterday.'

'But if that was so, shouldn't Darwent have told me personally? But listen, you could tell Holder and even Walter Darwent and all the so-called authorities, that nothing will stop me. That even if the raging storm was to kick up, I'm going through. But I know that is not the problem. They wouldn't touch me, because they know. They only trying to start up rumours to shut me up.'

'Well, I could tell you for one thing, Walter Darwent ain't want to stop you from doing nothing. And you know that too, Uncle. Because you know he don't want no part of these oppressors – as Edgar Maresse-Smith call them. In fact he told me he was going to warn you and I said leave it to me. Because I did hear the talk but at first I didn't believe it, because, well they even have rumours about me. But when he said that I took a little fright. So that's why I wanted to see you so badly to tell you. That's why I went to your place yesterday. But I didn't want to scare nobody so I didn't tell Mammie Marie anything.'

'They can't scare me.'

'Uncle, you have to listen to us. This thing, this movement. Ratepayers or no ratepayers. This thing, however you want to call it. Freedom Movement if you want – whatever they want to call it, but this thing have to go on. So we can't afford to have you in jail.'

He looked at her. 'So what you want me to do?'

'Clement was saying—' She stopped.

'Yes, go on. What was Clement saying?'

'Uncle, we can't afford for you to be in jail,' she said. 'These people out to get you. You have your best friend out there in the country. The man who admire you so much. Somebody said he had a touch of malaria, but I don't know. In any case, I told you this already. Sure he'll be still glad to see you.'

Mzumbo laughed, but inside the news of the malaria frightened him. He did not know what to think, nor what to do. It would be hard to get off the scene now. When he realised she was staring at him, he said, 'Wait, what you talking about? Talk plain. In any case you started to say "Clement was saying". Saying what?'

152

She was muddled for a while because she was not sure what to do. She wanted to see if she could get him to leave for Mayaro on his own accord. However, if that failed, Clement would have to travel to Mayaro tomorrow and try something. But even so, she could not quite get into words what she wanted to tell him. She had begun well and almost convinced herself that Darwent had really made such a disclosure, and it was not all a fabrication. But it was just that she couldn't go on from here. She never had the patience to shape things slowly, and convincingly, and to come to the point in a gradual way. She was cool up to a certain degree, and could often maintain her calm, and could even act coldly and viciously if she wanted to. But when matters like this came up she could not think of the best way to be subtle and to express herself. So she said, 'Clement was saying you should go to Mayaro.'

'What!' Mzumbo exclaimed. He himself looked round, startled, so loudly his voice came.

'It would be better for us, Uncle. All of us.'

'Never!'

She said, 'Monday coming we must have the public gallery full. And we have to make noise because the waterworks bill mustn't pass. God forbid, Uncle. It mustn't pass. But I could tell you, with the first bit of jostling and pushing and scuffling, with the first bit of upset, Brake will seize you. In fact, the police will start to provoke, and with the first scuffle, even before anybody get in the public gallery, they'll seize you. That is, if they don't do it long before Monday.'

Mzumbo Lazare just looked at her. She did not want to give him a chance to say anything. She said quickly, putting her hand on his shoulder, 'I ain't saying "arrest", you know. It's "seize". Kidnap. They'll trap you and take you so easily. They'll surround you, and even before you know where you is, you'll be on the ground. Rooks and his special riots brigade – what you think that is? And what you think they have in their hands? It's guns! I'm telling you, Uncle, I know the whole plan. You see, I didn't want to go into it and tell you a little more. You think I'll just rush up to Lazdale if it was just empty smoke? There's no smoke without fire anyway. Trust me. Trust me and Clement. I'm you own niece. And you could even trust Mr Walter Darwent. I mean, *Captain* Walter Darwent. Uncle, you see Edgar yet?'

'No, I haven't seen Edgar but I'm hoping to see him this morning. It's crucial. As you mentioned Darwent, I have to tell you again: do you realise the whole town is talking about you and Walter Darwent?'

She chuckled. Then she said, sweetly, 'What I could say? I washing for him. From the time people see me talking to him you know people would talk. But you know your niece. And you know people. But Uncle, this is 1903, and we have so much to do and so much of these devils to deal with, that when I hear people talking this nonsense I just shake me head. I take it with a smile. I already tell you the situation, and I know you trust me. If the man love me I can't help it. But we have a big cause. And if I could use him, so who is me? Uncle, you see me point?'

'I was never really doubting you.'

'No? For a little while I thought you was. Anyway, just think of what we have to achieve. Because we have to win.'

'We *must* win. If there is any justice in this world!'

'In fact, I shouldn't say "have" to win. We bound to win. Uncle, you see Edgar yet? Oh, I ask you already.'

'Why, what happen to Edgar?'

She did not want to alarm her uncle. But she had vaguely wondered what had happened after the confrontation between Edgar Maresse-Smith and Colonel Brake on the stairway. For after she had cried 'Talk, boy!' and Edgar had spoken again and Brake had warned him she had noticed Holder tripping nimbly behind as Edgar descended the stairs. But she was sure nothing had happened, for Holder would not have dared to touch Edgar in that crowd. Holder was wicked but not stupid. But the fact remained she had not seen Edgar since. She said, 'You ask what happen to Edgar? Nothing. I was just thinking he must be disappointed bad. I just find it odd that I just glimpsed him once yesterday and I ain't see him since. You bet it's because he's so disappointed!'

'But who isn't? I mean, amongst us, who isn't? You think anybody more badly disappointed than me? And now you asking me to—'

'Uncle, it's for your own good,' she interrupted. 'And look, let me tell you this. It's not only for your own good, it's for the good of all of us. And for the good of this place. This island.'

He looked up at her. The way she said this touched him. He was not afraid of the fight and he did not want to run away. But what she said touched him. True, these people could plot anything. He didn't put it beyond them. He knew for one that Empson wanted his head badly. And for a long time. And as a matter of fact there was nobody among that set who liked him. With the exception of Darwent. You could put them all together: Brake, Rooks, Empson, Wrightson, Courtney Knollys, Lewsey, Alfred Owen, Charles Norman – not one of them cared for him. They all saw him as a troublemaker. Only last year, Ladysmith Day, when everybody was so happy and celebrating that Boer War victory, that time when the British broke the siege. Their war, mind you. Their victory. And he was on King Street, parading with his contingent, the Light Horse Brigade. Could one imagine he overheard Rooks calling him a dirty agitator? Right now the scene was alive before him: there it was, Marine Square and King Street, gaily decorated. The pavement lined thickly with cheering people. And there were the plumed horses and officers in full regalia. The cathedral bells tolling. Flags everywhere. And the parade. And—

'But Uncle, I talking but you mind's far away.'

'Oh – ah, yes. No I ain't see him. Maybe Edgar is home. I stayed so long here, I'm thinking—'

She smiled. She was sure Mzumbo was thinking about strategy. She was sure he was planning something for next Monday. And then she suddenly got serious because she did not want him to plan anything for next Monday, she wanted to get him out to Mayaro. She had never been to Mayaro herself but she had heard Robert Dick talk about it when he was here last month for the Carnival. From the sound of it that was the ideal place for Mzumbo. Sand, sea, and chip-chip. Beautiful piano music from Ivy. Coconut palms, coconut water, sun and shadow, books, cultivated chatter from Robert Alexander Dick. That was the sort of thing Mzumbo liked. Let him enjoy all those things. Let him go and enjoy the sweet Mayaro sea-breeze while – she thought of a phrase but she didn't quite know where the phrase came from, it may have been from her uncle himself, but it came: 'while flames lick the air'.

As she shook off the thoughts and came back to the moment she was a little surprised to see how bright it was outside. The sun was out hotly. She looked at her uncle. She did not want to press the issue too much because if he wasn't keen to go she would send Clement to Mayaro tomorrow morning, and she did not want to arouse any suspicion. Earlier, when she had said Robert was not too well she had said that for a purpose. She thought she would make a last attempt. She said now: 'Uncle, you is a busy man and it getting late. I just want to say this. You is a key man in this struggle. People seeing your carriage outside there and their heart beating. Because you is the key man, I ain't sweetening you up. But we just don't want you in jail. If they put you in jail, all's lost.'

'Ah, come on, Eva. Pipe it! All's lost? What's the matter with you. Talking about key man. Ah, pipe it! Mzumbo Lazare is here now, waging war for the people. Because things look serious. But if he isn't there, another leader will come up. And perhaps a better leader. Oh come on, pipe it!'

He seemed genuinely irritated to hear her say he was the key man, and Eva said to herself, 'That's exactly why he is the key man.'

Mzumbo said, 'I'd better go. I was thinking of going across and having a talk with Alcazar before I look up Edgar.'

'Incidentally, I told you Robert's very ill? This is just by the way because I don't even know if it's true.'

'You said he wasn't well, a touch of— Anyway I haven't heard from him. Since he went back for Carnival he didn't write.'

'Because he's sick. That's why. It's one of Ivy's friends who I met in town. She knew I knew Dick and she said Dick's wife wrote her. She said Dick's very poorly. Perhaps Ivy will drop you a line.'

'Oh, so that's why you trying to get me to go to Mayaro! It's to see Robert, and you telling me about kidnap?'

'No, Uncle. I really heard they have that plan. A secret plan.'

'Edgar knows about it?'

'First of all I only glimpsed Edgar yesterday,' she said. 'And Darwent only told me on Sunday. It's a secret plan. And Uncle, you think I'm so crazy to tell Edgar anything even if I see him? Edgar is a hot-head.'

Mzumbo made to get up from the chair but he was so tired he sat down heavily again. He just chuckled and said, 'But if I was to be so silly as to go to Mayaro in this crucial time, wouldn't he be looking all over town for me?'

'Oh God, Uncle, I mean to say—'

'You mean to say what?' he turned and stared at her.

'When Edgar start to look for you he'll just have to go to Mammie Marie. And she'll tell him. Because you wouldn't have time to go round trying to find everybody. And people so busy with this – I don't know what to call it. Uncle, we'll have to leave everything to you, whether you want to go to Mayaro or not. Ivy's friend said in the letter Ivy asked about Mannie — but of course the friend wouldn't know who that is.' She chuckled. 'Uncle, you don't have to let those things confuse you. Ivy and Robert is your buddies but you have enough to see about.'

He was looking at her as if lost. He said, 'I wonder when we'll get more news. You think we'll hear something next week?'

It was exactly the question he had asked that first time. This made her decide. Clement would have to leave for Mayaro first thing in the morning. Having already convinced Mzumbo that Robert was ill, it shouldn't be too difficult at this stage to pull off the final trick. This was Tuesday and she had to have Mzumbo away from here by next Monday. She was embarrassed about this kind of intrigue but the candle might be worth the funeral. She was suddenly taken aback, and had to cough to suppress a laugh. She asked herself silently, 'Did I say "funeral"?'

As she turned to speak, Mzumbo said, 'What amused you?'

'It's just the way Ivy is. Her friend said throughout the whole letter she's only talking about eating chip-chip and playing piano.' And she laughed again. Then she said, 'Uncle, I'll leave you to think about this Mayaro business. I could see you want to get on with things because you have so much to do today.'

He was standing up. Eva continued, 'Give Mammie Marie my regards. Poor Ivy. I hope Robert Dick gets over the malaria.'

'I wonder if this malaria is real. Malaria is no joke you know,' Mzumbo cried. 'That's a killer, girl.'

'Yes, but we don't know what could happen. If Robert Alexander Dick gets over the malaria he wouldn't be the first.'

19

Ivy could not believe what she was hearing. She said, 'Wait. Young man, you said you come from Mr Mzumbo Lazare?'

'Yes, Madam. I'm now from town. His niece sent me to see Mr Robert Alexander Dick. I asked over there and they told me this is the schoolmaster's house.'

Ivy was excited. 'Of course this is the schoolmaster's house. But tell me again, you said you come from Mr Mzumbo Lazare? And his niece sent you? What's her name?'

'Eva.'

The lady broke into nervous laughter. She was sure now that he was talking the truth. She said, 'Come in, come in. How is Eva?'

It was Mzumbo Lazare that was topmost in her mind and she really wanted to hear about him first of all. But she did not want to ask about him yet. She led Clement into the drawing room, which was full of cushioned easy chairs, and rocking chairs, and in which there was a polished grand piano. The room was as elegant as Mrs Ivy Dick was pretty. Outside of the window there were coconut palms everywhere, and the breeze, puffing and blowing up the curtains in the windows, gave him a glimpse of blue sea, and a broad wide beach. He sat in an easy chair and the extraordinary Mrs Dick sat opposite to him, her legs stylishly crossed. She was clearly nervous. She smiled excitedly, showing a row of white teeth.

'How is Mr Mzumbo Lazare?'

'He is the same thing, only worse.'

She was puzzled. *The same thing only worse!* What was the same thing? The trouble was that when she had asked about Eva she had not listened to hear what the answer was.

She said, 'The same thing? I don't get it.'

'Well, I said Eva's all keyed up with the Wrightson confusion and working hard. And Mr Mzumbo? Well, this thing have him giddy. He's busy, holding meetings, going from place to place, organising, he have so much pressure I can't even tell you. In fact that's why they sent me. No, no, it ain't have no trouble. Mr Dick's not in?' He asked this, forgetting Eva's instruction to speak to Ivy more than to Robert.

'Yes. Let me see.' She got up to look at a big clock in the dining room. When she sat down again she said, 'The time is half-past three. He'll soon be here. The school is just at the back. But tell me, how did you come? I didn't see any steamer? At least, I don't think—' She went to the window and bent to look at the sea.

'I didn't come by steamer, Madam, because the steamer this week is till Saturday. And we wanted to see you and Mr Dick before that.'

She stared at him with the sort of look which said she wondered why. She was still standing at the window and she looked towards the school as if anxious for Dick to come home. She said, 'Your name is?'

'Clement Lovou.'

'So, Mr Lovou, how did you come?'

'I left Port-of-Spain by the first train for Sangre Grande because they said sometimes you could take a chance and you might get an estate cart going to Mayaro.'

'*They* said? Who is they?' She was chuckling.

'People. In talking I heard that. I didn't know where Mayaro was.'

She broke into a fit of laughter. She cried, 'Tell my husband that!' And then she said, 'Young man, it is very interesting that people should say you could take a chance and get something to come to Mayaro, because in fact people do not come to Mayaro – so far as we know. And when anyone comes it is by steamer. The landing place is just there, on the beach opposite the Catholic church. You saw the church? This place is Radix. In Mayaro, of course. The coastal steamer lands people here. So you came by train to Sangre Grande and you took a chance and you were lucky and you got something?'

She did not seem to be able to stop smiling, and she appeared always to be on the point of breaking into laughter. Clement said, 'As soon as the train reached Sangre Grande I saw a cart. That was Mr Reid, and he had come to bring some bags of cocoa to send down by the train. I didn't even know him before. I was stranded in Sangre Grande and somebody pointed him out to me and said he was going to Mayaro and I could ask him for a ride. When he said yes, I was so glad.'

159

'And I guess he was so glad too. Old Reid! I understand it is a very lonely road from Sangre Grande.'

All the while she was talking she kept peeping out of the window at the school. She said, 'I can't even see a little child so I could send a message to Dick.' She seemed anxious although it was now only about ten minutes to four o'clock and he would be coming home then. She asked a few questions about Mzumbo Lazare, if he was still so worried about that silly waterworks bill, and why, and whether Clement knew Mzumbo was not only a solicitor, but a planter, and a farmer with more than two hundred head of cattle, and not only that, but also an engineer who brought water into his own house from the mountaintop, and did Clement know Mzumbo built Lazdale single-handedly? And when Clement said he had never seen Lazdale she laughed heartily again. She asked, 'Did you see Mzumbo Lazare in 1897, with the big red sash, when he was leading the contingent to England? And the crowds came on the wharf to see them sail and he drilled his soldiers in full regalia right there on the wharf?'

'I only heard about it.'

She laughed. 'Mr Lovou, you missed so much. That's only a little more than five years ago. You haven't seen a lot, have you? Did you hear about how Queen Victoria picked him out from all the soldiers on her Diamond Jubilee parade in London and she asked one of his men, "Please, who is that officer? I must have him presented to me," and the soldier said, "But Your Majesty, he have somebody orready. We can't make a present.' And Ivy broke into hysterical laughter. Clement was laughing too. Before she revived to give Clement another anecdote the bell to dismiss school rang out.

'He'll be coming in a jiffy,' she said, still chuckling. 'It's four o'clock.'

◆

As soon as Robert Alexander Dick came in Ivy said, 'Come here in the drawing room, boy. Somebody to see you.'

'Somebody to see me? Who is that?' He hurried up the few steps.

She was standing in front of the drawing-room door. She said laughingly, looking back at Clement, 'I think it's a man from the secret service. Because he wouldn't disclose to me what he came for.'

When Dick walked into the drawing room and saw Clement he was a

160

little puzzled. He said, 'You came to me? I think I've seen this face before. But where? How are you?'

'I'm well, Mr Dick, but a good friend of yours is not so well.'

Dick looked puzzled. He said, 'Wait. Where did I meet you recently? Don't tell me. Was it at Beaumont Estate? Where?'

The schoolmaster was intrigued. His wife was smiling but saying nothing.

Clement said, 'Carnival. In Jour Ouvert.'

'Oh yes, yes,' said Dick, a little embarrassed. He was disguised as a woman then, and a little tipsy, and making merry in the band. He hoped the young man would not elaborate. He sat down in one of the easy chairs and said, 'Oh yes. That's when I was in Port-of-Spain for Carnival. I was staying at Lazdale with Mannie.'

'And we hoping that Mannie will be staying a little bit at Mayaro with you.'

'What's that?' Dick said. Ivy was excited. She could hardly believe her ears. The only question in her mind was: why was it necessary for this strange young man to come if it was just that? And why did he want to hide it from her? The best thing in the world for her was for Mannie to come to spend some time there. He didn't even have to ask. All he had to do was to come.

When Dick had asked, 'What's that?' Ivy had said, 'He said Mannie wants to come.'

'But why Mannie doesn't come? He has to send somebody to sound us out? What's really going on!'

That was exactly what Ivy wanted to find out. She said to Clement, 'Look, tell us. Is Mannie all right? We'd like to know. We'd be delighted if Mannie was to come to spend some time here. By the way, that's Mzumbo Lazare. We call him Mannie.'

Robert Alexander Dick was listening to his wife. Her voice had taken on a brighter tone, her eyes had taken on a new glow. Mzumbo Lazare was his good friend, his great friend, and although Lazare was a trustworthy friend too, Robert Dick was not entirely happy. Because there was nothing in the world that Ivy liked better than Mzumbo Lazare. Lately, Ivy had been harassing him to allow her to go to spend a little time with her mother in New Grant and it seemed to him that now was the best time to let her go to New Grant for a while and let Mannie come in the meantime.

161

While Robert was thinking, Clement was explaining certain things to Ivy at Ivy's request. He was telling Ivy of the great water debate and what a great toll it was taking on Mzumbo Lazare. That Lazare was all right, although extremely weak, almost stumbling. She was horrified. Clement said Mannie was so tired he could hardly keep his eyes open and they were afraid he would drive his buggy in front of a tram-car. She almost screamed.

Clement said, 'We can't get him to stop and take a rest. Once he's in Port-of-Spain he won't rest.' And looking at Robert Alexander Dick, he said, 'I don't want to say it, Mr Dick, but Mannie's a little stubborn...'

Dick said, 'Mannie was always stubborn.'

'Robert!'

'But you yourself said this so many times. When Chamberlain abolished the Borough Council on them weren't you saying that? We were living in Diego Martin then and he was a like a fish out of water. Remember how you used to be saying, "Forget it, Mannie. Politics is not the world?"'

'That is hardly the point, Robert. Right now the man is weak and tired and— Young fellow, what's your name?'

'Just call me Clement.'

'And Clement is saying because the debate is on, Mannie doesn't want to come.'

Clement said, 'That is why they sent me. In secret. Eva said—'

'Just one point. Mammie Marie sent you too, because—' Dick stopped.

Clement thought quickly. Mammie Marie had no idea of what was happening. But whether she had or not, the cause was greater than the confusion could ever be. Afterwards he and Eva could always run for cover! He said, 'Mammie Marie was the chief one. She and Eva.'

Ivy said, 'And they sent you. You are related?'

'I am Eva's – er – let me see.' He scratched his head. 'I am Eva's gentleman.'

Ivy laughed heartily. Robert looked surprised. He asked, 'She isn't with that sergeant fellow now? The fierce fellow?'

'She left him long time. You mean Holder? She left him.'

Ivy said, 'Obviously.'

Dick asked, 'And the debate was when?'

'We had a debate last Monday and the next one is this coming Monday and they say the strain will kill him. So they want—'

162

Ivy looked at him, 'Who is *they*?' She was on the point of laughing.

'Mammie Marie and Eva. They send me here to ask you if you could write him a note and invite him. They want him to come right away to keep him from the strain. It's killing him. Yesterday he nearly fainted.'

Ivy gasped, 'Oh God!'

Robert Alexander Dick was more angry than in sympathy. He said, 'He's bound to faint. It's because Mannie is so stubborn!'

'Ah, Robert,' Ivy said. She got up from where she was sitting and went over to his chair. She said, 'Dearie, before you criticise why don't you write him a note asking him to come immediately?'

'Immediately?'

'If not sooner.'

Clement laughed. Ivy grinned at the young man and said, 'Clement, when are you going back?'

'Well, I'd like to stay till tomorrow morning. If it's all right with you all. And tomorrow morning first thing I gone.'

Ivy laughed at the way he talked. But she also laughed because she was in a good spirit, and of course Robert Alexander Dick realised that. He was thinking very hard. Ivy was going to ask Clement what he meant by 'if it's all right', did he think they would put him out, but she did not bother. She said to Dick, 'Darling, look, before you have dinner' – she was smelling the frying fish and chip-chip accra that the maid was preparing in the kitchen – 'Before dinner, I want you to write that note to Mannie—'

'You think he'll ever come, with that debate fixed for Monday?'

She said, 'Well I could tell you candidly that if you don't write a note and you don't invite him, he'll never come. And you could lose a friend.'

This was when Clement ventured something he had wanted to say, mainly in order to help them out. For he himself knew that unless the note was compelling, Mzumbo Lazare would never come. He said, looking at Ivy, 'Eva already tried to convince him to come here. She tried to force him. She knew if he didn't come here Mr Dick would lose him, so she tried to scare him by telling him he's about to lose Mr Dick.' And when Ivy raised her brow, puzzled, Clement whispered, 'She told him Mr Dick dying with malaria.'

'What?' Robert exclaimed. Ivy had such a bout of hysterical laughter that she almost fell to the floor.

When Ivy recovered she said, 'Well, write the note saying you have gotten worse, you don't have to say you died.' And she rolled with laughter again. Clement laughed and turned his head towards the sea.

Ivy said, 'Robert, write the note saying you are critically ill.'

Robert said, 'Could a man who is critically ill write any note?'

Clement looked at Ivy. He wanted to change Robert's sentence slightly. He wanted to say: 'Could a dead man write any note?' He realised that Ivy was very sympathetic to the cause, and he had something to suggest to Ivy, but not yet.

Ivy said, 'Robert, Bobby. Why don't you see what you could do for Mannie. If you don't want to do it now, maybe you could have your dinner first and do it later on. Clement's going in the morning.'

'I can write the note,' Dick said, 'But I cannot tell a lie and say I am sick.'

'No, don't tell any lies. Just invite him to come. Invite him to come on the weekend coming up.'

Clement just nodded his head. His eyes were on the coconut trees.

Robert said to his wife: 'How's your mother doing?'

'Fine. Why?'

'I was thinking that if I could invite Mannie here why can't I send my own wife to see her mother. And you've been clamouring to go.'

Ivy did some quick thinking. 'I'd have been so glad to go if Ma was in New Grant.'

Robert was surprised. 'She isn't there?'

'You don't listen when I'm talking to you,' she said, 'Ma's in San Fernando by me brother. You go and have that supper now and afterwards write that note. We'll be depending on it.'

Ivy secretly hoped that Dick would have no opportunity to discover that her mother was safely in New Grant because she, Ivy, was not going to New Grant nor anywhere while there was a chance that Mzumbo would come here. If Mannie was coming nothing could get her to budge from this house.

During supper, although Ivy was laughing and talking and had changed the subject, the subject was very much in her mind. Clement did not say much but he, too, was very concerned. He didn't have the feeling that Dick's note would be strong enough to make Lazare come, and somehow he got the impression that, although Mzumbo and Dick were good friends, Dick was not so exceptionally keen to see his beloved 'Mannie'. He looked towards Ivy and he was eager to make a suggestion, but not now when Robert was with them. Because it had to be private. Maybe he would get a chance later. He looked towards her and said, 'Glad I'm in Mayaro. They talk so much about it. By *they*, I mean, people.'

She laughed. 'Don't bother about people. They only talk, they don't come.'

'But they know about the fish and chip-chip and coconut water.'

'But Mayaro is more than that,' she said. 'When Bob goes to write the letter I'll take you around a little and show you. As I told you, this little part here is Radix. It's the main part. The school's in the back there, then the Anglican church is over in front, then the Catholic church which you saw, that's over there,' she pointed north, 'and these exquisite little houses under the palms. And I will take you on the beach and you'll see the two beautiful headlands. When you are finished eating?'

'I'm ready,' Clement said.

'You want to go now? Robert, since he's going first thing in the morning I'll show him around a little. You go and write your note. Do a nice note for Mannie.'

Dick said, 'Young man, how did you come? You couldn't have come by steamer.'

Ivy said, 'Baba Reid gave him a lift from Sangre Grande.'

'And you walked down from Reid's when you got to Mayaro.'

'Yes, Mr Dick.'

'Well, Ivy, Clement has already seen all the coconut trees and the blue sea and the headlands.'

'Who's saying no? So if he had come by sea he wouldn't have seen it? All I want to do is to show him what this little part of Mayaro looks like.'

'Oh.'

'Go and write that note, darling, and write a nice note.'

She put her hand on his head and rocked his head playfully. Then she kissed him on his cheeks. But as she smiled softly at him, she said in her mind, 'I could understand you don't want Mannie to come because you jealous, but, after all, you'll jealous Clement too?'

◆

When Ivy was finished showing Clement the village and they were going back to the house, she said. 'Mammie Marie and Eva and yourself really want Mannie to come here?'

'Yes, Mrs Dick.'

'Okay, but now it's not Mrs Dick talking to you, it's just Ivy. When you want him to come?'

'Well the steamer is Saturday.'

'Oh, I see. Oh, yes. And Eva told Mannie that Robert is badly ill with malaria?'

'Yes, I don't know why.'

'It does not matter why. She wants him to come for a rest. She loves him. We love him too, and bad, and we want him here, bad, bad. The means justify the end. You ever heard that phrase?'

'No Mrs— Oh, sorry. No, Ivy. Mzumbo is stubborn and the important debate coming up next Monday. He wouldn't want to leave. You think Mr Dick will write a note strong enough?' He wanted to make his suggestion but he had lost courage.

'Don't think about that. Tomorrow morning when you are leaving I'll be up. I will keep the note that my husband is writing and tear it up, and throw it in with the rubbish. And I am going to write one myself tonight. My own strong note. When you get to Port-of-Spain have the note delivered to his house. Get somebody on the wharf to do it, like a schooner captain. Pay him something. Let him deliver it and let him say it's from the captain of the Mayaro boat. You yourself don't say a word to Mammie Marie. Tell her you weren't able to reach Mayaro, you couldn't get nothing from Sangre Grande. But don't hide anything from Eva. In fact I'll send her a note too. Mzumbo will be here by weekend.'

Clement was thrilled. He cried, 'Okay, Ivy. Thank you very much.'

'You thanking me?' She said. There was no laughter now. 'You thanking me? Don't thank me. You think it's you alone who love him? We here love him bad.'

They came in from the beach to enter the house.

20

Clement arrived in Port-of-Spain by the four o'clock train, and as the train came to a stop he hopped off nimbly and made his way across South Quay. But before he actually crossed the road he spotted a railway guard he knew and went to him.

'Anything unusual, Leo? You know what I mean.'

'Oh, the water business? Everything the same way. You was out in the country?'

'Yes, I had to go to— I had to go out in the country. Okay then.'

One had to be so careful. Even Leo he would not tell he went to Mayaro. He didn't know exactly why, but still, you could never guess who was who. It was only yesterday morning he left Port-of-Spain, yet everything looked new and strange, it felt a much longer time. Maybe it was because Mayaro was such a different scene. So sleepy and peaceful; no sense of crisis whatsoever.

As he left South Quay and went up Almond Walk towards Marine Square, he could see policemen all over the place. He was back in Port-of-Spain all right. As he swung left into Marine Square he heard a short, melodious whistle, as of a bird, and looking around he saw that it was Lodrick John. Lodrick was standing under the awnings of La Favorita store at the corner of King Street and Frederick Street, and he was waving Clement over. Clement pretended he did not see. He wanted to be extra careful and to avoid being picked up. Not before Monday, oh heavens! Although he was not at all known to the police, if he wanted to be picked up, stopping and talking to Lodrick John was one of the finest ways to start. For Lodrick could be described by the police as a veteran rioter and stone-thrower, a man who, like Greasy Pole, had stayed several times as a guest at the queen's big house on Clarence Street – now Upper Frederick Street. He crossed the road before he got to the Chacon Street intersection and walked among the trees in Marine Square and as he quickly crossed Chacon Street to head for Abercromby Street he walked fast, just glancing to see if Lolotte Borde was under Harriman's as usual. She was there and he waved hastily, without even looking to see if she waved back because he did not want her to call out to him.

When he reached Abercromby Street he just walked up to the corner of King Street and turned left in the direction of St Vincent Street. He was walking in this zigzag way for two reasons. These days the police were suspicious of everyone and he did not want to be easily followed. Secondly, Sergeant Holder was always keeping duty somewhere around the Red House. Either at the corner of Chacon Street and King Street, or Abercromby Street and Queen Street. The honest truth was that he was not sure if Holder knew him, because he had only just taken up with Eva. But he was not trusting. In any case if he had to deal with Holder some time then it was better Holder did not see very much of him.

He did not go up St Vincent Street but as he passed Jablotin he remembered Greasy Pole, and in spite of himself he was hoping that Greasy Pole would not put in an appearance on Monday. He admired Greasy Pole as one of the mad dogs of this struggle. But Greasy Pole was also known to the police and it was easy for them to pinpoint him and watch him and cause Eva's plan to fail. In any case, wasn't Greasy Pole a fugitive on the run? He took a chance last Monday but did he think a silly red cap would keep disguising him? And to be honest, the chore was very simple. Anyone, not known to the police...

The thoughts crowding his mind made him walk even faster and he was soon in Edward Street. He hoped Eva was home. As he walked up his heart began to pound.

◆

Eva heard the knock and when she opened the door she cried, 'Oh it's you? You come back so quick? I was worried about you. How things went?'

'Why you was worrying?'

'Well, I'm always worried about you.'

'Why?'

'Oh shut up, Clement. I know what you want me to say. I'm anxious to know what happened in Mayaro.'

'What's happening here – anything? Any changes?'

168

'It's just as you left. Don't forget you only left yesterday. Tell me about Mayaro.'

'You seem a bit disturbed. What happen?'

'Sorry. I just went by the Dry River to wash some clothes and—'

He interrupted, 'You don't go to Santa Cruz again?'

'No – um – here's nearer.' She did not want to tell him that Darwent came there sometimes and she did not want to meet him. Not this week. Clement, for his part, was wondering how come it was only now she found out the Dry River was nearer.

He said, 'You was going to say something when I—'

'Oh, I was going to say that when I was going to the Dry River I saw those English soldiers doing their bayonet drill in Brunswick Square. It upset me so much I came right back home. How could those people be so bloody unfeeling? This is our country, ain't it?'

'Take it easy.'

'I can't take it easy. I can't relax until – until Greasy Pole do this damn job and let them see we mean business.'

'But Greasy Pole might be in the calaboose, Eva. They might have him well behind bars. How you so sure he'll be lucky again and break jail?'

'If so, then God will have to be with us to bring us some sort of justice.'

'You think God care about Greasy Pole? You could forget that. I say already he's a marked man. In any case it will have police like peas on Monday. Police like lice. They'll see him when he's trying to enter. They know him. Nobody ain't know me—'

She drew in a sharp breath and her eyes flashed fire. She said, 'Look, Clement, look! Don't get me raving mad now. I already tell you, keep out of this. Completely. You know what my luck is! Nothing never work out for me. I was living with that brute Holder, and suffered so much, quite apart from the fact that he's such a damn stooge and idiot. All me life I catching hell, from the time I leave home. All me life, although me uncle is Mzumbo Lazare. He could help me but I want to help myself. But let me tell you this now: you is the only thing in my life that I really want and I can't do without. Don't try to be no hero, please. Keep out of trouble for God sake. Use your coconut,' she pointed to her head. 'I don't want you in that place up Frederick Street. Greasy Pole is a jail bird already and a desperado. You stay out of this and keep safe for Christ sake.'

He looked at her and said nothing. She looked straight at him and then she couldn't help chuckling quietly inside her. There was not much of her, she was so thin nobody would be surprised if a strong wind blew her away. Yet she could talk to big strapping Clement how she liked and he wouldn't say a word, let alone slap her – like most men would be inclined to do. That was part of the reason she liked him so much. Most men would have howled at her for raising her voice. Holder would have kicked her. That was part of the reason she wanted to keep Clement at all cost.

She said, 'Come on. Tell me how things went in Mayaro, big-boy.'

He told her in a few words just what had happened. First he told her quickly how pretty the place was, about the coconut trees, and lagoons, about the broad beach and blue-green sea. He told her about the giant breakers pounding when the wind rose. And then he talked about Robert, and about how charming Ivy was – he was afraid to say pretty. And then he came down to business. He described how he approached the subject, and about how Ivy was overjoyed at the prospect of 'Mannie' coming, but how he himself felt that Robert, although liking Mzumbo, had his secret fear that there was too much friendship between Ivy and 'Mannie' and so he was not too keen, but how Robert gave him a note for Mzumbo, which Ivy took from him graciously and afterwards destroyed, and how she wrote her own note and put it in an envelope and gave it to him as he was leaving this morning. He left even before the cocks crowed. He said he only just remembered Ivy had promised to send a special little note for her but Ivy forgot. He handed her the envelope he was holding in his hands as he spoke and he said Ivy said it was to be delivered to Lazdale as coming from the captain of the coastal steamer. Eva took the envelope and looked at it on all sides. It was addressed to Mr Emmanuel Mzumbo Lazare, and she looked at the way it was sealed. She said, 'You don't know what Ivy put in it?'

'No idea.'

'Well, we can't deliver it without opening it. Suppose she telling him "Have Eva and her boyfriend arrested!"' She laughed. She added, 'But in any case, as a matter of good sense, we have to open it. You object?'

'Not at all. That's what I was going to suggest. Steam it open.'

She lit her little pitch-oil stove and put on a kettle with water and when the water got hot and began to let off vapour she put the envelope over it and after a few seconds she opened the letter easily. It was not a very long note and it was scribbled in big handwriting. It said:

My dear Mannie,

      I am sending you this note to let you know that Robert is extremely sick – at death's door, really – and we would like you to come with all haste. He is so sick that he cannot write for himself, so I personally would like you to come, and come now. If when you come he is up from bed let us thank God. But please come with all haste because he has something to tell you and I would not like something to happen to cause you not to see him again. You know how malaria is! It is easy to find us because we are just beside the Government School and when you land at Radix you wouldn't have any trouble to find the house. When you land you'll be facing the RC church and Radix is the little cluster of houses on the left. We hope you could catch the Saturday morning coastal steamer which leaves Port-of-Spain at 6.20 a.m. and should land you here on Sunday.

                                 Yours, Ivy.

      PS I didn't want to tell you this, but the way Robert is looking I want to warn you to bring a black suit – just in case.

Eva was thrilled. She cried, 'Success! Success! He bound to go.'

Clement was looking at the letter. His heart became full. He never expected something as powerful as that.

She had passed the letter to Clement but now she took it back from him, placed it carefully back in its envelope, and tried to seal it down again. Her fingers were trembling, she was so excited. When she was finished she said: 'This letter bound to send him. Because he believe in Robert, and I'm sure he dying to see Ivy. Monday is ours. Edgar was supposed to be giving a talk this evening and he was to come here first but I ain't see him. He is the man we need although really it's me and Lolotte who's handling things. But nobody would be able to handle nothing when that debate start. So far Lolotte and me, we sound out almost the whole town and almost everybody will be there. Don't talk about Laventille at all, and up that hill. Clifton Hill. Only one thing I want you to do for me. The only little way you'll be involved and then no more. Just to make sure this letter is delivered, I want you to deliver it yourself. At the same time we'll keep to what Ivy recommend. Mzumbo knows you because he saw you here. But Mammie Marie never met you. Go to me friend Joel in the Steamer

Department and say I ask him please to lend you a captain's cap. Put it on and then go there to Lazdale, and watch out for Mzumbo carriage. If the red-and-black one's there then he's there and you can't do nothing. Bide your time because he's always going out. As soon as he slip out you slip in and hand this letter to his wife. Say you from coastal steamer *Alice* and the schoolmaster in Mayaro send this urgent letter to Mr Mzumbo Lazare. Okay?'

He was amazed and moved by her simple clear-headedness because he was worried about how to get someone to deliver the letter. He threw his arms around her. He said, 'Eva, you is such a smart person, I don't know why I love you so much.'

'I don't know either. Because I ain't pretty and there ain't much of me. Sometimes they call me skin-and-bone.'

She had thrown her arms around his waist. Now he squeezed her. 'Who tell you that you ain't pretty?'

'I ain't pretty like Ivy Dick.' She looked up at him.

'Who said that? Only you. You is me whole world, girl. There mightn't be much of you, that's true, because you really very small, but you is the biggest little honeybunch in the whole of Port-of-Spain. You so sweet.'

'Who gave you that speech?'

'That's me own. From me heart.'

He heard her chuckle. She was still holding on to him. She said, 'That's why I love you so much.'

21

Edgar Maresse-Smith leaned listlessly on his carriage, rested his hand on the horse's head, and asked Lolotte again, 'When you said this thing happened? Wednesday night?'

'This is what she was telling me. Late Wednesday night. She said perhaps it was even past midnight.'

It was Friday afternoon, nearly four o'clock. On his way home Edgar Maresse-Smith was paying a visit to the Harriman corner to see Lolotte Borde because he had some urgent news for her. At other times he would have been very alert, and forthright, and apt to get excited, and heated and annoyed, but now he had had too much. He was very tired and battle-weary, apart from a puzzle on his mind since yesterday, but now all those thoughts fled. He wasn't sure how to treat what he was hearing now. He said, 'But you said it happened just like that? You sure Greasy Pole didn't do anything?'

'Rosetta said he didn't do anything. She went to see him in the jail this morning and he said he didn't do nothing. But you know Rosetta. Rosetta was buying piece of me pone early this morning and she said they caught Greasy Pole inside the Red House and they lock him up.'

'Well, you see! Now what was he doing in the Red House? Those fools so nervous they bound to lock him up. What Eva said about that?'

'I don't even think Eva know yet. She was chatting with me yesterday about the same Greasy Pole and how he so wanted to be there on Monday he wasn't even going outside Jablotin. So she didn't even know he was at the Red House for the debate. Anyway, when I tell her she'll be so shocked! But I'll get the news to her, leave it to me. Rosetta and she, Eva, don't talk but I'll let Eva know in the morning. By the way, you know who Rosetta is — you remember the lady who used to live with Holder?'

Edgar Maresse-Smith was going to make a sharp reply but at the last moment he thought better of it. Just fancy Lolotte calling Rosetta 'lady'. Lolotte was ten times more of a lady than Rosetta. Lolotte made her pone, and her sugar-cakes, and her paymie, and day after day, rain or sunshine, she was at that Harriman corner. At least she was making an honest living, by the sweat of her brow. He said calmly, with an ironic smile on his face, 'Yes, I know the *lady*.'

'She thin like a whip.'

'The beast like them thin, so they can't fight back. Wasn't he living with Eva Carvalho too?' Edgar looked at her.

She said, 'Edgar, don't watch me size, please! Because I know I ain't thin like a whip.' She giggled.

But he was not thinking about anything like her size. He was quite upset. He looked towards the sea, then he looked at her again, then he turned to look in the direction of the Roman Catholic cathedral. In the direction of the cathedral, not *at* the cathedral, because he wasn't seeing anything in particular. He was rapt in thought. Then he began speaking, as if to himself.

'Greasy Pole was never going into any Red House. Why should he be going to the Red House? He has something inside there? That is only a smoke screen by Hubert Brake. They ready to pick up anybody who could organise anything or do anything to stop their dirty work. You bet they grabbed Greasy Pole right there in Jablotin – I mean, Red Star. Those criminals you calling police. Especially the English police inspectors – they are the real crooks and vagabonds! Yet me boy Mzumbo always talking about Englishmen being gentlemen. When will he learn, Lord? Always making big speech about loyalty to Queen Victoria – and now since she's gone it's Edward VII. You ever see thing so? It's either you go one way or you go the other. It's either you for the people or you bloody well against them. You can't be both. Ay, ay, what is this! Mzumbo is me friend, I like him, but since he went to England in 1897, that is what spoiled him. Nobody could tell me no. Always talking about freedom yet he want law and order – I ain't for chaos but how the hell you'll break the system without breaking the law? And Mzumbo crying out for democracy and justice but he can't see the English have him by the throat. As me leader I love him bad, but Lord, when will you remove the veil from his eyes? He is one of our finest sons. If it were not for the enemy inside him he could lead us to Zion. He and Henry Alcazar. But oh God, how long! Lord, you see how we are fighting against injustice and you wouldn't put a hand? Lord, how long must the wicked flourish?'

Lolotte was looking at him. He stopped talking but his lips were still moving. She did not want to interrupt him because she was sure he had had some sort of plan for Greasy Pole, and now he had simply to revise it. But when at length he turned to her, she cried, 'Edgar, what happen? You eyes red.'

'No, it's nothing.'

She laughed mildly. She said, 'Let me tell you this: you is a man with big talk, but you heart soft, but don't waste you tears on Greasy Pole. As you know he's always in there. Jail is like home to him.'

'Lolotte, you mustn't be so callous.'

'But that's the truth, me boy. If you had some plan for him naturally you'll miss him, because it ain't have nobody braver than Greasy Pole.'

'I didn't have plans for him, but in these times he is a good man to have outside. I know he's been to jail dozens of times. They joke and say he has his own room there. But Lolotte, what you have to remember is that almost every one of those crimes he committed was for us. In other words, for freedom — I hate to say that, it sounds so sickly. But from the time I know Greasy Pole he harassing the authorities. Like when he broke up those water-meters in Jablotin. But first of all, let me ask you this: you feel sure what Rosetta said is true?'

'Yes. About Greasy Pole in jail? Yes.'

'You remember what she is, I hope?'

'Everybody know she is a police informer but she ain't have reason to say they held him if they ain't.'

'Suppose she just want to spread confusion.'

'That's true. But the way she talked. And she said she went to see him. I don't know but I feel sure Greasy Pole up there.'

'I'll go up there now. If they put him on any charge I'll defend him in court.' He turned away.

'Greasy Pole ain't have no money to pay lawyer?'

He swung around to her. 'Lolotte Borde, you ain't out of your mind! Well, it's Edgar Maresse-Smith you speaking to. In all the hundreds of cases you ever know me to charge my people?'

'Well, I don't know.'

'When they had to put you inside for throwing stones, how much did I charge for you defence?'

'Well you didn't charge me nothing but you yourself said it was because of me potato pone.'

He smiled and shook his head. He looked at his horse. Then he made a few steps to his carriage door, and he said, 'Look, I'm going up to the jail house now. Today is Friday, listen out for if Mzumbo holding a meeting tonight, and whatever the situation please try and come. I like your spirit, Lolotte. They trying to grind us down but I could see that you really tough. Look, I better go up the road to see Greasy Pole.'

◆

At about six p.m., just before Lolotte Borde got up and put the tray on her head, she was surprised by Maresse-Smith's carriage coming again. He stopped, and said, 'Come in, Lolotte, move fast. I didn't expect you still here. I'll take you up to St Joseph Road. Come in.'

'Why? What happen, me boy?'

'Nothing. I just went up to see if I see Eva but she ain't there. But get the news to her in the morning, as I have to go out of town. I went up over there. Come on, girl, let me give you a lift quick. Because there isn't much time.'

'You'd give me a lift? You could lift me? Don't mind my little joke, I ain't so heavy.' She was only pretending to be cheerful. She was thinking about how disturbed Edgar was. She said, 'I ain't heavy, but I ain't no straw.'

Edgar Maresse-Smith was not listening to her. He said, 'I went to see him.'

'You went to see Greasy Pole?' She looked up at Edgar. 'You went up to the jail orready?'

'Yes. And I was talking to Greasy Pole for a long time.' He turned the carriage round in Marine Square and headed for the turnpike. When the carriage was clear of the Chacon Street corner Lolotte said, 'How he keeping up?'

'What you asking? Didn't you yourself say jail was home for Greasy Pole? He's keeping up very well for a man who they woke up from bed and handcuffed and slapped up and took into prison. When we get before the magistrate hell will roll. I always knew he didn't do anything.'

Lolotte did not speak. She thought to herself, well, if Greasy Pole didn't do anything that would be a nice change! Although she liked Edgar Maresse-Smith she always realised his heart was too soft to be a leader. And he was too easily taken in by rogues and scamps. It was true what he

176

had said, that it was good to have people like Greasy Pole outside in these uneasy times, but for her this was only because those English devils needed to contend with a character like that. She knew of no one so swift, so wicked, and so brave as Greasy Pole, and she was not in the least bit surprised to hear he was in jail. One of the things she liked about her slippery friend was that he was determined to hit the Englishmen and hit them hard. Anywhere, and with whatever means he had at his disposal. She often wondered if he really felt so deeply about the cause or if something else had happened. She had noticed—

'What's the matter, you don't want to answer me?' Maresse-Smith's voice almost startled her.

'Oh, sorry. What you said, Edgar?'

'I have some news that will shock you.'

'Oh yes? Let me hear it.' She leaned forward, concerned.

He did not speak. She guessed what he had to say was about Greasy Pole and she wondered if anything about Greasy Pole would shock her. She said, 'What happen to him? When is the case? You defending him?'

'You mean Greasy Pole? I told you this already. I must defend him. I'll defend anybody who's in the fight. And especially paupers like meself.'

He said so with a straight face, and Lolotte said to herself, 'You know I like to hear this Edgar? He's such a show-off so-and-so. A pauper does live in a big house, and have carriage? And have electric lights?' But she did not tell him anything.

He said, 'I wasn't talking about Greasy Pole a while ago. That is settled and naturally I am defending him. I'm saying I have a shock for you. In fact, it's a shock for all of us.'

'What's that?'

'Mzumbo. Lolotte, I'm so vexed I don't know what the hell to do.'

'What's wrong with Mzumbo?' Lolotte said hastily. Her eyes opened wide. Her breath was coming fast.

'You remember he had a friend here for Carnival. A house-guest from Mayaro? A schoolmaster?'

'Yes, that's Dick. You never knew Dick? Dick ain't from Mayaro. He's only teaching there. But what happen?'

'Apparently he died or is dying.'

'Bless me, Father!' She was shocked.

Maresse-Smith said, 'I'm not so sure what is the real situation. But they sent for Mzumbo.'

'Oh God. But he can't go. It's sad that Dick kicked the bucket but if he dead he's dead already. We'll have to have Mzumbo here for Monday.'

They had already passed the Roman Catholic cathedral. The carriage was heading for the turnpike, and just beyond that was Picton Street. That street was very narrow so Lolotte had to get out at the corner when they came to it.

'Well, that is what I thought. Mzumbo *must* be here for Monday. But he's leaving for Mayaro tomorrow morning.'

'You sure?'

'Yes.'

'How you mean, Edgar? You saw him?'

'When I left Greasy Pole this morning, I passed round at the top of Abercromby Street, because Papa Bodu always goes up home for lunch. I was lucky to meet him, but the way the talk went I thought I'd go straight to Diego Martin, straight to Lazdale, although I didn't expect to meet Mzumbo – he's the hardest thing to meet these days, as you know. Mammie Marie was so glad I came. When me carriage pulled up, she said, "Oh God, Edgar, come, come. This is a miracle because I didn't know how to get in touch with you. Mzumbo left you this. Come." She went inside and came back with a letter. I said, "A letter? Where's Mzumbo?" She said, "Well, read the letter." When I read the letter – well anyway the letter's right here, Lolotte. You could take a read.'

'You damn well know I can't read. Edgar, for heaven sake where Mzumbo gone at this time?'

'When I called there he had gone to town to get funeral wreaths. He's taking the coastal steamer for Mayaro tomorrow morning early. Mammie Marie said that. He wrote this note and left it for me in case I came. He said they sent for him urgent, he has to go, and for heaven sake could I take over.' He looked up from the letter. 'What's that? Oh, you want to know if Dick's dead? Well Mzumbo himself wasn't sure, but the wording of the letter looked as if Dick died or was sure to die before the *Alice* reached tomorrow. That's why he went to get wreaths. And Mammie Marie said it was lucky the boat leaving tomorrow morning because if the boat was leaving Monday or Wednesday, as is usual, he would have been sure to miss the funeral.'

178

'Yes. Lucky for him but unlucky for us – and for Trinidad!'

'You didn't just speak, you preached.'

'But what the hell happening to us, Edgar? You mean nothing could go good for poor people? Mayaro so blinking far, Mzumbo can't come back for Monday. So why he went? I know he and Dick was close, but when he get to Mayaro he could bring Dick back to life? He isn't Christ and so far as I know Dick isn't Lazarus. Blast it, man. Even the Bible say let the dead bury the dead.'

She was so annoyed and flustered that she did not even realise Maresse-Smith's carriage had stopped.

He said, 'We'll have to think. We'll have to put our heads together. I might not even sleep tonight. This is Friday.'

As he was saying that, she said to herself, 'Oh crimson, I reach.' She clambered out and Edgar Maresse-Smith helped her take out the tray. Her face was a picture of confusion. Yet she was able to put her thoughts together, and with the tray on her head she turned to Maresse-Smith.

'When you see Mzumbo do a thing like that, water more than flour. We don't know. All I could tell you is this: we can't go back. We mustn't go back. Because suppose something happen to Mzumbo – the world finish? Look, Edgar, don't tell nobody Mzumbo gone. And we have to put our heads together, it's true. But somebody have to takeover. A ship must have a captain. Somebody have to take over and that somebody is you.'

'Me?'

'Edgar, sometimes you get me so damn bombastic! It have anybody else better than you to take over? Alcazar forceful and he could talk but Alcazar has his damn head in the clouds. Look at the rest: Cyrus David, Wainwright, Papa Bodu, Thomas Mead Kelshall . . . They full of education but they don't have your touch. They don't have your ways with poor people. You know what I call you? The people's man. Anywhere you go you make us feel you is one of us. I always forget that you rich and—'

'Lolotte!'

'Look, this ain't no time to argue. Just see what you could do for us. Go home and plan. You is the man to take over and we ain't want to hear nothing else. The only thing I have to ask you is to be a little calm. You is a hothead. That's where Mzumbo Lazare beat you.'

And saying that, she set off for up the hill.

179

◆

It was about eleven o'clock that night when Lolotte heard a knock on her door.

At first she did not want to answer, then she said gruffly, 'Who is that?' She was tense. She always kept a length of iron nearby just in case it was Holder.

The voice said, 'Lolotte, it's me, Edgar. I wouldn't keep you long.'

Lolotte sprang up from the bed and opened the door. She had on her big pink nightgown but she forgot to change. As she opened the door she said, 'What happen, Edgar?'

He said, 'I lay down but I couldn't sleep. I was thinking of all sorts of things and I was thinking of what you said. I agree with you, a ship must have a captain. As Mzumbo isn't here, I think I'd better do something.'

'But that's the only thing, Edgar.'

'You and me and a few others have to plan. We don't have much time. We may have to get Alcazar, although Henry Alcazar's so damn proud.' He paused a little. His heart hurt him to think it, but he knew Alcazar would never sit down and plan with the likes of Lolotte Borde and he was trying to work out how it could be resolved. For one thing Alcazar didn't like Laventille, and for another he didn't really mix with poor people. True, he was fighting for poor people but he wouldn't live with them. They were too common for him. Although Alcazar was always talking about the rights of the poor man, you think he'd bunch with them? Maresse-Smith was already getting worked up, and maybe it was because he was so disturbed that Lazare was going to Mayaro.

He said, 'Lolotte, why I came to you is this: today being Friday already, I'll have to do a lot of running around tomorrow morning. But whatever it is, I want you to be with me. We mightn't be able to get much out of Henry Alcazar, nor the rest, but you and me, we'll have to see what we doing. No, I ain't coming in. I only decided when I got home that the ship, as you said, must have a captain, and I wanted to reassure you I'll stand in for Mzumbo. Because if Mzumbo dies, for instance, does it mean the cause is dead?'

She cried, 'Never!'

Edgar Maresse-Smith said, 'I would really have liked Henry to team up with us, because he has the brains. And the legal brains is very important. And this man could talk so well. But I know him.'

180

Although he said he was not coming inside, he came in nevertheless, since he did not want the door to remain open. He said, 'We'll have to do something, and I have to draft out me plan when I get home.'

'Edgar, you know how you is? No hot-headedness you know. We have to win. If it's to fight we'll fight. But even in fighting you have to keep your head on.'

'I know.'

'I don't know Henry Alcazar, except by seeing him, but I know he's not like you, friendly with everybody. But perhaps he's just the man to keep you in check.'

Maresse-Smith had sat on a chair and he was thinking hard. At length he said, 'I'll see Henry tomorrow morning first thing, and I'll also seek advice from Wainwright and Papa Bodu. But I want you as my right hand. I want you to put all your weight behind me.'

'Really?' Lolotte smiled.

He said, 'I didn't mean that weight. Oh God, no. You'll crush me!'

Lolotte laughed.

'Look, I came back just to tell you what I told you. Now let me go home and get a little sleep. Then I'll wake up early and plan for them. Look, girl, you could depend on me.'

'I know I could always depend on you.'

'The general isn't here but we have to fight with or without the general.'

'But you is a general, Edgar.'

'Me? I am the least of the apostles.'

'Edgar, you could get me so damn vexed! You like to show off eh? Everybody know you is a hero.'

'Me?'

She was hardly listening to him as he went on talking. He said, 'I will do what I could. Tomorrow morning early I might pass to see you. I'm seeing you first. Then I have to find Henry Alcazar and maybe Papa Bodu would be home or in the store, and if I could see Cyrus David. And then I have to run up to the prison to see Greasy Pole.' He shook his head and chuckled, 'I'm only one man. Heaven knows—' He stopped.

'Heaven knows what?'

'I'm a little confused and I ain't have the talent to—'

'Edgar, why you so damn overbearing – I beg you pardon, but you getting me peevish. It have anybody with more talent than you and Mr

Mzumbo? You have to run to see Papa Bodu, you have to see Mr Cyrus, You have to see Alcazar. Okay, they is great people, but without you and Mzumbo you think we'd ever see any sight of them? They is big shots. You think I could ever tell them they blasted so-and-so as I could tell you? Yet you is their master. So if you ain't see them tomorrow then you ain't see them, and that's that. Look, Edgar, the case is, how you say it – critical? What you saying? Critical? Okay, well it's like that, and we depending on you for Monday. Why you don't go and make you plans and then tell all of us what to do. Mind you, I ain't backing out of anything. If you want to plan with me I'll plan with you.'

Edgar just looked at her. The pitch-oil lamp on the table was burning weakly and the flame bent to one side then to the other at the whims of the little wind. He looked at it while thinking of Lolotte. What faith she had in him! The pitch-oil lamp was only a quarter full, and it was odd that the wake-song should come to his mind, *A little more oil in your lamp, keep it burning*. He thought he'd better leave now. The last time he was here that lamp had a shade, and it was reflecting on the wall of this shack the words 'Home Sweet Home'. The shade must have been broken.

He looked at Lolotte. She had seen that he was day-dreaming again and she had turned her eyes down the hill, and now he, too, looked down the hill.

He said, 'Lolotte I know you tired. I could see that. I'll leave you now. Dick died, he kicked the bucket, and we are rightfully upset. And we are upset because Mzumbo's going to Mayaro. But consider this, Lolotte.' His face was soft and mild and he was almost smiling. She said to herself, 'Yes, I feel rightfully upset.'

He himself was so tired he forgot what he was going to ask her to consider. He just said, 'I'll arrange tonight how we'll fix the meeting and for when. We could meet at my place. I have to see you first thing tomorrow morning and perhaps again on Sunday? We have to sleep with our eyes open.'

She smiled, and yawned. He got up.

She said, as if just remembering, 'By the way, you'll have to be careful. There was some talk about police picking up all the instigators before Monday. I don't know if it's true but don't take no chances. You know how Holder doesn't like you?'

'Who the hell is Holder!' he said sharply. 'That's why we have to get

182

Henry. I am a lawyer, but you think you could play the fool with a Queen's Counsel like Henry? Let Holder lay hands on me!'

'Well I'm only putting you on your guard.'

'I appreciate it.'

'Another thing. Those fellers could just look at you and shoot you down. As bright as Henry Alcazar is, with all his Queen's Counsel, he can't bring you back to life.'

Edgar Maresse-Smith chuckled. 'That's true too.'

'Mind you, nothing ain't stopping me from doing things, you know. For me, it's only once to die.'

His head jerked towards her. He was amazed. He said, 'Lolotte, you saying that?'

She said, 'So what? It's only once to die. Anybody could die twice?'

He said, 'Good grief, sometimes tough men scared to get involved, and now hear you saying that. Well, I never. Girl, you giving me so much courage. You know something? Even Lumpress last Monday, when Holder was raining baton on him he was bawling like a cow instead of planting butt on that stooge.'

'You think everybody brave like you.'

He was still looking at her with astonishment. He said, 'Lolotte, I'm so glad you talked like that. I always knew they can't scare you but you make me feel strong tonight. Look, I think I'd better get along. Tomorrow we'll meet first thing. It might be even before I see the others. Let me go home and get a little sleep and wake up and plan strategy.' He moved towards the door. 'So let's leave everything until tomorrow morning. Right? I'll see you first thing. Be good.'

'And you be careful.'

He went out of the door and then she heard his footsteps going down the hill.

◆

When Edgar Maresse-Smith got down to his carriage and made to get inside he noticed a figure standing beside it. He almost jumped.

The figure said, 'How do you do, Mr Maresse-Smith? You came from up the hill?' The voice was very pleasant but Maresse-Smith did not reply.

The person said, 'I don't know if you recognise the voice, but it's your

Sergeant Holder. I see you just came down from the hill? How is Lottie Borde?'

Maresse-Smith said, 'Sergeant, it's nice to see you. But it's almost midnight and I am tired. Sergeant, you think I could get away to go and have some rest?'

'Oh yes, sure, you'll get some rest. But it might not be at your home, Mr Edgar. I have two constables here and I want to ask you if you can give us a lift to Police Headquarters, and then we could have a little chat. Eh, Mr Edgar?' As he was talking two policemen moved up in the dark and hopped into the carriage. Then Sergeant Holder went in and sat beside Edgar Maresse-Smith.

22

Lolotte Borde went straight to the Lower Chacon Street corner, and as she rested down her tray besides Harriman and Company, she looked both up and down Chacon Street, and then along Marine Square. It was just about half-past seven in the morning and she could see the mist still thick on the Northern Range. She removed the cloth covering her tray and arranged the paymie and coconut sugarcake and benay sugarcake and potato pone and cassava pone, and she put the turnovers in the centre. It looked very attractive. But in spite of that she had done the exercise as a matter of habit. As a routine. She did that every morning and she did not even have to think about it. The truth was, this morning she was a little tense and anxious. She heard a sound and she looked down Marine Square then up Chacon Street, and she saw the papers-boy coming out of the *Port-of-Spain Gazette* office. She made a sign to call him. He did not see her but he was coming down the street anyway. When he got near she called him. She said, 'Sonny, you know Mr Edgar Maresse-Smith? You bound to know him.'

'I know him,' the boy said, 'But I didn't see him this morning.'

Lolotte said to herself, 'I wonder if he passed already.'

'Yesterday morning when I was coming—'

'Nobody ain't talking about yesterday, Sonnyboy.'

'I ain't see him, Ma Lolotte.'

'All right.' She wasn't even looking. The boy drifted away with his newspapers.

She said to herself, 'It's either he passed here early and didn't see me, or he ain't come yet. But if I know Edgar at all he already get up long time, he on the move, and he on the warpath.'

She was anxious to see him because there wasn't much time now and she wanted to know what he would like her to do and what plans he woke up with. For she was sure he wouldn't have slept well.

She shifted her massive body on the stool and looked around. She said quietly, 'Maybe when he woke up he realised he had to see Henry Alcazar first, and he went there.' And then she said, 'Or perhaps he had some new idea and he went up by the prison to see Greasy Pole.'

As she was talking she continued looking up and down Marine Square, and at last, from a distance she saw a staunch 'Ratepayers' man. He was walking up on the other side of the pavement, and he was coming from the direction of the Catholic cathedral. Every now and again she waved, trying to catch his eye. He was about to cross between the samaan trees just before he got to Chacon Street, and she got up hurriedly and whistled and called, 'Lodrick!' It was only then that he saw her, and he walked towards her. Lodrick John usually had a big grin, but the grin wasn't there this morning. Running across Marine Square to avoid the bicycles and carts, then crossing over to her side of Chacon Street, he said, 'Lolotte, how tricks? You know I didn't see you? I just come down here to see what's happening because I ain't hearing nothing. What they doing for Monday? That debate Monday. I ain't getting no news at all.'

He had bruises on the right side of his face and a bandage over his left eye. She was going to ask him if he was all right, but what was the point? But it didn't mean her heart wasn't riled. But she had Edgar on the top of her mind. She considered quickly and in that short space of time Lolotte had already decided what she would and would not tell Lodrick. She would not tell him about Mzumbo, nor even what was the latest. She said, 'Nobody ain't hearing nothing, but—'

'They giving up? They 'fraid?'

'Nobody ain't 'fraid. Whether we hear or ain't hear nothing we have to be at the Red House. Everybody.'

'But people have to know what's happening. I ain't seeing Mzumbo at all this morning and I ain't seeing Mr Edgar Maresse-Smith. Those fellers was never too busy before, but I say if they 'fraid because of what police do last Monday somebody have to take over. After last Monday we can't leave it so. If these leaders so busy or frighten, Lolotte, you may have to take over the damn thing. Today is Saturday—'

'What! Me? Me take over?' Then she said, 'I am the least of the apostles.'

Lodrick said, 'You see me? I getting jumpy. I don't like what's happening. We have to take things in our own hands. I ain't no lawyer and solicitor, or any Legislative Council man, or anything like that. I ain't no

Mr Wainwright, or Mr Cyrus, or Mr Maresse-Smith, let alone a Mzumbo Lazare. I could hardly write me own name. But I could throw a damn boulder, that's what I could do.'

'Lodrick! Take it easy please.'

'Take it easy when those crim—'

Lolotte stamped her massive legs and pounded her fist on her tray to show how furious she was. She said, 'Lodrick John, it have time to take it easy and time for action. I don't like to hear big talk. You see, if we have a meeting and you have a Mzumbo or a Edgar Maresse-Smith raising fire and brimstone I could listen, because me blood warm. But don't talk no big talk for me. And nobody ain't frighten. You know what I call you for? I call you because I want to ask you if you reaching up the road by Richmond Street. Richmond and Duke. I have to see Eva.'

'Eva Carvalho? Don't know if I reaching so far.'

'It's okay if you ain't going so far, but if you happen to see her—'

'If I happen to see her, tell her what?'

'Tell her it's urgent. I just have to see her. She must come down.'

Lodrick looked at Lolotte. Somehow the way Lolotte said that, and the way her face was, he could not help but suspect it had to do with the whole Red House business. Something was afoot. He said, 'I mightn't reach so far but if I happen to walk up Duke Street maybe I'll reach up there because I know where she living. Okay, Lolotte, I'll just go up the road, by Brunswick Square.'

'Right. Do what you could. This is a busy morning.'

Lodrick awaited a chance and ran across the road, and then walked away tamely as if he really had no zeal to go anywhere. But when he was out of sight he walked so briskly it was as if something crucial was about to happen. There were a lot of people and traffic about now because it seemed to be already past eight o'clock. Shops and stores were opening, people were all about in the streets, some carts were backing up to business places delivering goods, other carts and carriages were going up and down. The town seemed to have suddenly come to life. As Lodrick crossed Queen Street he turned left towards Abercromby Street then right, going up towards Brunswick Square. As he reached Hart Street, he looked well at the fire brigade station on his left, thinking about Walter Darwent. It was not that he was thinking Eva was there. He was sure she was not there but he was thinking of Darwent and the courage Darwent had in defying those ... those— His mind could not find the strength of the word he wanted.

When he crossed Hart Street the Red House was on his left and Brunswick Square on his right. He did not even slow down his speed because he had no intention of going to the square at the moment. At the top end of the square he looked right, and there, standing in front of the new building that was the public library, he spotted Sergeant Holder with a gun in his hand. He felt all riled up inside. This was the man who had beaten him so badly. Apart from the condition of his face, his neck and arms were still swollen and his back was raw. One day, one day, he would meet Holder without that gun!

He felt as if his belly boiled. But he passed on. He had seen policemen all over the town this morning. In fact, one had been glancing at him from King Street when he was talking to Lolotte Borde. That had amused him more than anything else. But now just the sight of Holder upset him. Holder was worse than Brake, Wrightson, Empson, Peake – he was worse than all the English inspectors put together, and as for cruelty, there was nobody at all he could compare Holder with. He crossed the street to walk on the left-hand pavement and of course the next street was Duke Street. When he got to Duke Street he turn left towards Richmond Street, and in a short while he was knocking on Eva's door.

23

Lolotte was struck with surprise when she saw Eva walking along the pavement towards her. Because of the number of people walking by on the pavement she had not noticed Eva until she came right up. When she saw Eva she cried, 'But what is this!'

'What happen?' Eva said. She meant it in two ways. One was because she was surprised that Lolotte was surprised, and the other and most important one was: Why did Lolotte send to call her?

Lolotte said, 'What happen? Just that I didn't expect to see anybody like you down here, I even send a message—'

'Yes, by Lodrick John.'

'Oh, you saw Lodrick already? He said he was going to Brunswick Square, but that if he saw you at all—'

'Lodrick came home. Lodrick was just home. He said it look important, that it's the Red House business but you didn't tell him.'

'You dead right I never tell Lodrick it's Red House business. The blighter want to know everything.' She looked around at the people passing and she whispered, 'Look, we can't talk here. I'll pack up me tray and let's go in the cathedral.'

Both cathedrals were nearby. Eva said, 'Which one? Trinity?'

Lolotte looked at Trinity in front of her. She wasn't so keen to go there although it was much nearer.

Eva herself preferred the Catholic cathedral but she could hardly wait to know why Lolotte wanted to see her. She jerked her chin towards the Catholic cathedral and said, 'That's only a stone's throw.'

Her saying that amused Lolotte, who stopped what she was doing with her tray and laughed. Then she said: 'It's only a stone's throw? Well not this morning. Not for me. This morning I ain't throwing no stones. At least not at the cathedral.' She laughed again and Eva, too, laughed at the joke. Lolotte, taking up her tray, said, 'Okay, let's go to Immaculate Conception. I feel safer in that one. You see, Catholic for Catholic.' She looked at Eva, 'And then you is Catholic too, because there's where I saw you last Monday.'

They had already moved off and were crossing the street beside them – Lower Chacon Street – to walk up Marine Square. Lolotte was as usual walking and balancing the tray on her head without holding it. She was in a blue drill dress this morning. Eva looked down at herself in her washed-out pink bodice and cream skirt. She was thin like a piece of wire, and felt even more so beside stout, strapping Lolotte Borde. She was a little nervous. She glanced at Lolotte and she said, 'I ain't hurrying you up but I mad to know. Once it ain't trouble, I okay.'

Lolotte paused. 'No, it's no trouble. No big trouble. No trouble at all. Look, we ain't have far now, the cathedral right there.' Then she lowered her voice. 'You see these days? Spies all over the place. True, Trinity nearer, but Trinity is not catholic.' They laughed at the slang. Then she said, 'Trinity's not safe. It's too near the Red House.'

'You sure right.'

Lolotte whispered, 'It ain't so safe being around there.'

Eva said to herself, 'Although you ain't no coward.'

The Cathedral of the Immaculate Conception was just in front of them now. They crossed Charlotte Street, and walked between the trees, then through the ornamental gates of the cathedral, then beneath the gothic arches.

◆

It felt eerie in the big silent cathedral. It was not completely empty; there must have been six other people in it. Lolotte and Eva walked up to just about the middle and then Lolotte eased towards the eastern wall. Eva was beside her. Lolotte's tray fitted snugly between the little aisle and the pews. When she rested it down she turned to Eva.

'Where's Greasy Pole?'

Eva was taken aback. Surely Lolotte did not make all that fuss and bring her to the Cathedral of the Immaculate Conception to ask her where Greasy Pole was?

Lolotte had spoken very softly. At first Eva was too shocked to answer, and after Lolotte opened her two big eyes and asked again, Eva said: 'Where's Greasy Pole? I don't know. He living in Jablotin, as you realise.

It's about – let me see – it's about ten o'clock now. I sure Greasy Pole there. He doesn't go out a lot these days. You see the police—'

'Yes,' Lolotte interrupted. 'That's it. The police. He isn't going out these days because he 'fraid the police. Well, the police done have him.'

Eva gasped. 'What's that? What you saying?'

'I saying that the police done have Greasy Pole. You friend come and buy a piece of pone from me this morning and she tell me that.'

'Who friend?'

'You bosom friend – Rosetta.'

'Lolotte this is a serious thing and you making joke? How Rosetta know about it? That is, if it's true.'

'How you mean *if* it's true? Course it's true. Rosetta is all over town and she have lots of police friends because she used to live with Holder.'

'I used to live with Holder too but I ain't have a single police friend. Anyway this thing is serious. Greasy Pole is one of our main men for Monday. Those police bastards realise this and put him in jail. You bet they went for him inside the barracks.'

'They ketch him inside the Red House.'

Eva was stunned. She stared into Lolotte's eyes as if she wasn't seeing anything, and in her heart she cried 'Oh God!' It was one thing to have such a key man as Greasy Pole in jail, especially at this crucial time when her uncle was away. It was bad enough to have Greasy Pole in jail but the urgent and desperate question was what did he tell them when they caught him in the Red House? Because if they caught him in the Red House he could only have gone there for one purpose. When they had caught him, did he confess? Did he tell them Eva Carvalho had sent him? Her heart pounded against her chest. She wondered if Lolotte Borde knew. She wondered if that was the reason why Lolotte Borde had sent a message to her. Yet if it was, Lolotte would never have walked her in the street in broad daylight to be a target for the police. Because if that was the case and Greasy Pole had involved her the police would be looking for her right now. And in any case Rosetta would have sent the police to her house, even if they did not know where she lived.

She said to Lolotte, 'I wonder what he was doing in the Red House.'

'I meself wondering. Girl, I wish he did burn it down.'

Eva's heart thumped so loudly she was afraid Lolotte would hear it. She could not tell Lolotte that this was exactly why Greasy Pole had gone there. He could not have gone there for any other reason. Why could he not wait for Monday, when there would be so much confusion that he could slip in and do the job? Maybe he was so broke he wanted to collect money from her right away!

Lolotte was speaking. 'I already tell Edgar about it because we have to help him. Sink or swim we have to do everything. Whether he get out for this Monday or the next one or the next one. Me only regret is he didn't burn down the blasted bungalow.'

As Lolotte said that, she looked at Eva defiantly. Eva reacted as if she was most offended to hear such a thing. She said, 'Why you saying that? You mustn't say these things.'

'I'll say it. I'll say it again and again – but not for the police to hear though. Eva, sometimes you like to play tough, but you really soft you know. In for a penny in for a pound. They putting pressure on us from noon till night, but as Mzumbo said, *Joy cometh in the morning*. You can't be soft with those Lucifers. They left England to come here and kick us about. If I had the money to pay somebody to burn the damn—'

'Lolotte, you in a church. Oh God.'

Lolotte wiped her brows. She looked towards the altar and said, 'Father, you'll pardon me. Me heart full. Father, I'm a good person, fighting for me daily bread. Father, have mercy on the Children of Zion. Deliver them.' She stopped suddenly.

Eva patted her back and said, 'Amen.'

After a moment Eva said, 'You said you talked to Edgar. He'll do anything for him?'

'Yes,' Lolotte said in a slightly broken voice.

'How Rosetta come to know about this?'

'Maybe police friends, I don't know. But she said as soon as she found out she went to see him.'

'What I'll do is this. What, it's about half-past ten now. I'll go right up to see him. Now. Then I'll come back home to cook some food for him. Then I'll come back down the road to see you later.'

'Yes.' Lolotte uncovered her tray and put a few coconut tarts and pieces of potato pone in a paper bag.

'Take this for him,' Lolotte said.

◆

Archbishop Vincent Flood was standing in the gloom beside the altar and looking ahead at the two women. He recognised the fat one, although he did not know what her name was. He knew only that she was one of those who had come to confession some weeks ago and had described her sin as 'pelting stones'. He pitied her then and he was pitying her now. He looked at the two women praying now, and although he did not know what was in their minds he told himself he would join them in a prayer for peace. He bowed his head and prayed with pain in his heart. When he raised his head they had already gone. He knew there was conflict all around and he knew that the debate in the Legislative Council on Monday would bring more confusion to the town. He opened out his arms and looking up he said, 'Lord, bring thy peace to this place and let love kindle the hearts of men.' He genuflected and came down from the altar. As he looked towards King Street he could see the sky silver blue, but a fleece of white clouds was floating high in the east. He went to the side door and looked out into the street, still thinking of the two women. There were many people in the street, some ill-dressed, and a few were begging, as usual. At the corner where George Street met King Street there was the police sergeant who everybody knew and feared. His name was Holder. The archbishop turned back into the cathedral. He said silently, 'Blessed are the poor in spirit for theirs is the Kingdom of Heaven.'

24

The guard opened the big grilled gate and led Eva in. He had a broad smile on his face. He led her to the visitor's cubicle, then opened a door and went to the back and shouted, and then he ambled back to the entrance gate.

After a few moments a tall figure appeared on the other side of the bars, and Eva said, 'How you do? What happen now?'

Greasy Pole was happy to see her although he found it difficult to look her in the eyes. And it was not only because his eyes were still burning him. He looked at the paper bag she held in her hand, and she gave it to him right away. 'A tart and piece of pone from Lolotte,' she said.

'Tell Lolotte thanks.'

In the first few moments she looked at him she cheered up a great deal, because he was not looking roughed up. Only that one of his eyes was red and part of his face was swollen. But he did not look downcast, and in fact, so far as his personal appearance was concerned, he looked better in the prison clothes. For at least they were clean. And the truth was they rather became him. But she could not tell him this. She said again, 'What happen?'

'Well, you see where they have me.'

She glanced around, but pretending she was not looking to see where the guard and the turnkey were. They had left the big gate open in order to watch.

She whispered, 'I heard they ketch you—' and she stopped.

'Yes. Rosie told you?'

'Who is Rosie?'

'Rosetta.'

She said hastily, 'You know I and this disgusting character don't talk.'

'I forget. She was the first to come to see me.'

'But how she got the news? Maybe she saw them carrying you up.'

'She didn't see nothing. When they bring me up here it was midnight.

That guard who talking to the turnkey there, he told her. She living with him now.'

Eva was taken aback. She said, 'That easy-going feller, who talk to me so nice? He living with Rosetta?' She couldn't think clearly now but she would have to think about it. Rosetta, her sworn enemy, was living with the prison guard. The prison guard looked pleasant enough, and had greeted her, but when Rosetta told him about her, would he greet her? But Rosetta was chummy with Greasy Pole, maybe that's why the guard was so nice to her. Her time must be almost up, she thought. She said, 'Oh, it nearly slipped me to tell you this. Lolotte said Edgar Maresse-Smith will—'

'Mr Edgar was here yesterday.'

Eva was shocked. 'Edgar was here already? Praise God! I feel sure Edgar will get you out.'

'But not for Monday!'

'Oh no.'

'But I want to be out for Monday.'

Eva said sharply, 'What's wrong with you, Greasy Pole? You realise where you is? I know you have fame for breaking jail, but if you try anything and they ketch you it's years, you know. Tell me – how those fellers ketch you in the Red House? Why you didn't wait for Monday?'

Greasy Pole, facing Eva, was also facing the turnkey and the guard. He could see those two were trying hard to listen, but he and Eva were talking just low enough to be private. Of course what Eva did not realise was that her being allowed to be alone talking with Greasy Pole was only a privilege. Because by law the guard should be standing right there beside them. Just that because of Rosetta, the guard was easy on Greasy Pole. And maybe the guard thought this woman was his wife.

Greasy Pole said to Eva, 'Why I didn't wait for Monday? I don't know. I was lying down there on me bed night before last – that wasn't Wednesday? – and some devil wake me up and say "Go and do the job. Now! Now, now!" Me eyes open wide and I seeing the Red House right in front ah me, but I ain't seeing the council chamber, I seeing the big door by the fountain, where the registrar office is. Plenty books and papers. The Devil said, "Go now! Go right now." I get right up and I put on me pants and I throw on this shirt, and I take up me little screwdriver and pliers, and me iron hook bar. And I have me box of matches and me cloth soaked in pitch-oil. Outside was quiet as Lapeyrouse Cemetery. When I get to the

195

corner by Queen Street, not a sound. Not even Holder. But I know up there it have a guard in front police headquarters. So I turn so, bam into Abercromby Street. I sneak up to the Red House and I ain't seeing any policeman so I feel to meself that Brake giving me a break. I looked round then I sneak up to the registry door. Night black like pitch. I use the screwdriver and me hook bar and in two twos I prise the door open. When I get inside, I ain't even take out me matchbox yet, guess what inside?'

'What?' Eva said.

'So help me God! You'll never believe. You'll never believe, girl. Jesus Christ!'

'Oh yes? Jesus Christ was there?'

'I talking serious and you just playing the fool.'

'But it's you, not me. I ask you what you see and you said Jesus Christ. Okay take it easy. Tell me what you saw. What was inside?'

Greasy Pole took a deep breath and shook his head.

'Come on, Greasy Pole, the time must be up already. They only give us ten minutes. What happened in the Red House? What you meet?'

'Really, is what meet me.'

'What met you?'

'Soldiers.'

'Oh God!'

'Soldiers inside the Red House. It's midnight and over one hundred soldiers inside the Red House. Soldiers with bayonets and guns.'

'Good God! What they doing there? What they was waiting on? You see how these devils planning for us?' As Eva said that she glanced back at the guard. He was looking towards her. She looked at him and said, 'We finishing now, Guard. In one minute.'

'That's okay. Don't pressure yourself.' He smiled at her.

Greasy Pole whispered, 'Over one hundred killers with rifles and bayonets. When I bounced the door open I fall right in their arms. I bawled, 'Oh God!' They hit me with the rifle and locked me arms behind me neck, and you should hear the language. They gave me a few slaps and handcuff me behind me back, then the one with the short white hair hit me with the helmet in me face.'

'That's why you eyeball so red.'

'And me face swollen. I could feel it.'

'Swollen, but not bad. At least they didn't kill you.'

'I don't think so.'

'Of course you ain't dead, stupid. Look, it's a pity you wouldn't be there Monday, but we'll make them pay for everything. We'll have to beat up a few policemen. I hope God will help us and we could cripple a few policemen.'

'No,' cried Greasy Pole, quietly. 'No, no. Eva, you crazy? They'll shoot. They have guns and they'll shoot us down like flies. I'll tell you something. Me name is Greasy Pole, and I'll slip out of here for Monday. The guard nice and when you going out talk to him nice. Perhaps he'll take a grease-hand, you have money? Eva, Oh Christ, Monday I have to be out of here, guard or no guard, grease-hand or no grease-hand. Trust me. I'll get out of here by the hook or the crook.'

'Keep you voice down. We want you bad, but take it easy. My advice to you is to stay behind bars. Don't do nothing. Edgar will get you out, maybe next week. Monday will have ruction but you – you listening? You don't try nothing. Maybe you'll come out when things quiet and it wouldn't have no soldiers in the Red House. This week we'll miss you. As Mzumbo not here to organise us we not so strong, but at least—'

'Mzumbo not here? Where Mzumbo?'

'In Mayaro. Some schoolmaster friend died—'

'Oh, that's what Mr Edgar was trying to tell me? But I didn't take that on because Rosetta said she saw him last night.'

'Where? Here in Port-of-Spain? Rosetta saw a spirit. Mzumbo not here. But please don't say nothing to nobody.'

He cursed. He said, 'All the more reason for me to be outa jail. Hell!' and he thumped his hand on the plank in front of him. It was the heavy wooden frame that held the iron bars. The guard, who was looking at Eva, saw the anger and just smiled.

Eva said, 'Look, I have to go now. I'll go and cook something for you, if I could make the time, but when I come back I can't stay. The guard nice but we can't impose. I'll just hand him the food and scram.'

She said it loud enough for the guard to hear, and then she took her leave. As she turned to go she walked near the guard and said, 'You called me Madam Holder when I was coming in?'

'Beg pardon. I made a slip. I know it's Madam Greasy Pole but as you see—'

She stood up, her eyes wide open: 'You know what?'

'I know once you was living with the sergeant.'

'That is true. Once upon a time.'

The guard laughed, 'Rosie too.'

'Who Rosie.'

'Rosetta. My lady.'

'Oh yes,' Eva said. Then she looked him in the eye. She couldn't tell him he was mad to call Rosetta a 'lady', but the main thing she wanted to ask him was how could he look at a woman like her and call her Madam Greasy Pole. He had already shut the heavy gates that separated the prisoners from a view of the road, and Greasy Pole could not see. She kept her voice low. 'Greasy Pole is just a friend and I feel so sorry for him. I guess you all know him well.'

The guard smiled. Greasy Pole was in the jail about every other week. It was as though the jail was his residence and he only went out occasionally on a little holiday. One thing he, the guard, could not understand was how nobody was able to keep Greasy Pole secure behind bars, and he was glad the jailbird was only Eva's friend, for behind the smile was a determination that Greasy Pole wasn't going to outsmart him this time.

He said to Eva, 'Your friend is a nice boy. Just a little slippery, but he's okay. I heard you tell him you coming back?'

She began to notice there was a certain light in his eyes. She was amused. She said, 'I really want to come back. But there's so much to do.' She meant it. There was really little time between now and Monday.

He said, 'You have to go far?'

'Not really. Just down the road.'

Of course she wasn't going to tell him where she lived. But since he liked her, a few sweet smiles could help Greasy Pole. She almost asked him if he'd be at the Red House on Monday, before she called to mind what he was and where he was working. In fact, he was nothing but the enemy.

She smiled sweetly. 'Look after my friend for me, please, Officer. I have to go now.'

'But you coming back later, not so? You only going to cook something for him.'

She laughed. This guard had been really paying attention. She wondered secretly if he had heard anything else.

She said, 'I hope to come back. But I might not be able to come.'

'Why?'

She could see the wolfishness in his eyes. She chuckled. 'Why? Because I'm staying too long now. But I have to ask why you are interested.'

He said, 'Why? You know why.'

'So if I was Mrs Greasy Pole?'

'You could never be Mrs Greasy Pole.'

'But while ago you yourself said you thought I was Mrs Greasy Pole. Anyway, I have to go.' Then she said, 'I believe I saw your face before. Maybe with Rosetta.'

'We ain't together again you know.'

'No? Since when? Since you saw me?' She laughed, and he had to laugh too. She said, 'Look, I just must go now.'

He said, 'What time you'll be back?'

'It's almost certain now that I can't come back. You know what caused that? Standing up here and talking to you. So no lunch for Greasy Pole. You see? And you said you like him? Anyway, tell him I say I can't come back today.'

She began to walk off. He decided to try everything. He had nothing to lose. He said, 'I could meet you later?'

As he said that a bright idea flashed to her head. But she was calm and calculated.

'If you could meet me later? Let me see! Perhaps. What time you finish here?'

'Ah scared to say it. Because you wouldn't come.'

'What time?'

'Twelve midnight.'

'Oh well, that's all right because that's about the time I should be coming back from San Juan tonight. I'll be back on the 11.17 p.m. train and I have to walk up here. Which will take twenty minutes. I should be here at about exactly twelve midnight. You'll be here? Don't make me walk up for nothing, you know.'

'I'll be waiting for you,' he said nervously.

'That's like a love-song, "I'll be waiting for you". By the way, I forgot to give Greasy Pole this Vicks for that chest of his. To rub in the night. I could run back quick?'

'Just don't give him no vaseline,' the guard laughed. 'He done slippery already.'

'No, it's just the wheezing. And I don't know how long he'll stay here, you see. The man talking to me and wheezing and wheezing.'

'That's one of his tricks!'

'Let me just run back now, because I can't come back with any lunch for him.'

'That's all right. I know he's your friend but he's a scamp.'

'But who doesn't know he's a scamp? You think everybody decent like you?' In her hand she had a bottle which just happened to be in her handbag. The guard opened the iron gate and then he went and called Greasy Pole again. When Greasy Pole saw her he said, 'Oh you come back?'

'It's that wheezing of yours,' she said, and she winked quickly. 'Let me give you directions for how you have to rub your chest.'

As the iron gate was closed back Eva informed Greasy Pole, very hastily, and softly, that she would be coming back at midnight to meet the guard. They would walk up past the Victoria Institute and they might cross Albert Terrace at the head of Frederick Street, and who knew, they might even take a ride on the belt tramline. She whispered, 'You get me? I can't stay long now. When I take the guard for a walk tonight we'll be away for at least half an hour. That means you'll have no guard for half-an-hour. So if you really slippery that's your business.'

'But you so trusting! You going in that dark area with the man? You know the man? Suppose—'

'Take it easy. I'll get Clement to shadow him.'

25

Major Rooks was standing right atop the Red House, keeping sharp sentry, looking down all around him. It was just past midnight on Sunday, in fact just the hour when the intruder had broken into the Red House on Wednesday night – or rather, Thursday morning – and he was taking no chances. He got out of the tower and, walking gingerly on the roof, gun in hand, peeped up and down St Vincent Street, and then he looked up and down Hart Street, although he could not see much of the near side of it; then he went back into the tower and turned to his normal position, which was facing Brunswick Square. And even though it was pitch black he looked well into the square and in the road between the Red House and the square.

That little strip of Abercromby Street was very important, because he was sure if any other intruder was trying to break in, it was to that big door he would come. Although he had two of his soldiers on sentry at the front he was taking no chances because the night was black and he did not know who could slip past his soldiers, especially passing close to the side of the Red House, by the hedge. His face was serious and he was somewhat tense. Although they had apprehended the scoundrel and had given him a good beating he couldn't help feeling a little embarrassed because the whole of Port-of-Spain probably knew by now that the Government had soldiers hiding in the Red House. However, he could easily have been more embarrassed because it was a real coincidence his men were in the Registrar's office at that time. For they were supposed to be hiding in the office above that, the Colonial Secretary's office, and had only been passing through from Police Headquarters to go to the balcony upstairs when it happened. Since last Thursday only half of the number of soldiers were going out on the balcony after midnight.

He listened for the men below him and he could not hear a sound. He looked towards the northern end of the square but there was absolutely nothing. Of course, this was deceptive. He knew that there were policemen there. Apart from the two standing guard at the entrance, there were three policemen at every corner of the Red House.

He was looking but still thinking of the intruder of early Thursday morning. What was this man's purpose? What had he come to do? Suppose he had met no one, what would he have taken? Did he just come to steal something the Registrar had, and the matter had nothing to do with the waterworks bill? He laughed to himself. No chance of that, he thought. Especially that particular intruder. He himself did not know the character but Holder had told him this was the notorious Greasy Pole.

He did not know what to think but he had a hunch it was the copy of the waterworks bill in the registry that Greasy Pole was after, and that it was Lazare who had sent him. But this did not make the slightest bit of sense because after all, the Ratepayers' Association had the bill, and in fact Alcazar had his personal copy. So Lazare did not need that.

He looked up and down and around the Red House, then he checked to see that his rifle was loaded, which he knew it was, then he looked on the other side, and as he turned back he jumped, but it was nothing. Just the wind shaking a bough in the trees below. His mind was focusing on Greasy Pole. Normally he would not have been doing this sort of sentry himself but he did not trust anybody else to do it. For something was up, and he could not afford to slip. He was sure it was something that Lazare and his mob wanted for Monday, but what it was, he did not know.

He looked at what seemed to be a shadow moving on Brunswick Square North, but he soon realised it was one of Inspector Norman's policemen. He came back to thinking on the security of the Red House and was determined that nothing should breach it. The men were sharp but Colonel Brake had given him the assignment and he was accountable. For instance, Colonel Brake did not like the fact that Greasy Pole had reached up to the front door and broken it open before being caught. He, Rooks, was going to make sure nobody approached.

He looked towards Trinity Cathedral and at the deanery, the white walls of which were barely visible in the darkness. He only fleetingly thought of Bishop Hayes, and tried to push him far from his mind. But moving his eyes round more to the north he could see there was a light in Darwent's house, just upstairs and back of the fire brigade station, and this brought him to attention. Was that light there all the time? He could not say. He felt concerned enough to think of going down and asking

Inspector Norman, but he could not leave this post. Not now. He did not know what Darwent was up to, and he really did not trust him. How could one trust a man who was going after one of the local girls? he asked himself. He put the rifle horizontally on the ledge of the tower and just shook his head pityingly. I mean, could you believe it? he asked himself. He himself had never seen anything but there were all the signs that Darwent was in league with the rabble. For he was the only Englishman – was Darwent born in England? He smiled. Anyway, Darwent was the only Englishman to find fault and argue against the waterworks bill. Incredible, that red-necked bas— He checked himself. He was really angry now. Just fancy Darwent saying 'We had no right.' And just fancy Superintending Sergeant Peake saw him chatting with Lazare! The traitor. And to cap it all were all these rumours about this little washerwoman. He was fuming now. He told himself, 'Have you ever heard of an Englishman fraternising with—' He stopped and then he said aloud, 'Let's get this straight, Walter Darwent is no Englishman. Inspector Norman and the Honourable Wrightson both told me this and I know. Even if—' And then he cried, 'Oh!'

The deputy inspector laughed. 'Looking all around for you. The men said you were upstairs. Couldn't believe you were in the tower.'

'Well, you could believe now,' Rooks said. He was still feeling annoyed that Alfred Owen should make him cry out 'Oh,' and make a fool of himself.

'Every man jack's on duty tonight. But why did you come up to the tower? You could have sent—'

'Yes, I could have sent lots of people. I could have sent my officer-in-charge. Listen, Inspector – I mean Deputy Inspector – do you know what could have happened on Wednesday night? Thursday morning, rather? And when Colonel Brake heard of the incident do you know what he said? In that high-pitched voice of his, he said, "You damn well have thirty-five armed men in the Red House and you let that beggar break the blasted place?" No, not me again. Not only because of Colonel Brake, but for, well, for England, why not? We Englishmen—'

The deputy inspector of police burst out laughing.

'What is it?'

'No, carry on. It's amusing me. Carry on. You were saying "We Englishmen".'

Major Rooks looked at the deputy inspector, puzzled. Then he said, 'How do you mean it's amusing to you? Don't we take a pride in ourselves as Englishmen? To fly the flag?'

'Yes. Of course. I'll fly the flag because I'm British. But I'm no Englishman. I was born here. That's why I'm laughing.'

'Oh,' Major Rooks said. He was trying to think of a way to pass it off but Owen was looking at him full in the face.

Owen said, 'Since you came, you are at St James's Barracks with the troops and so you don't know the constabulary officers.'

'That's right.'

'And you assume every white face is English. But there are two or three officers who were born here. Take Darwent for inst—'

Major Rooks put up his hand. 'You can take Darwent, not me. I want nothing to do with that traitor.'

The deputy inspector was put out of his stride. He said, 'No, well, I am not holding him up as an example. A model. I'm doing no such thing. All I'm saying is that he's British but he's like me. Born here.'

'Well, you can't blame anybody for that.'

The deputy inspector laughed heartily.

'Don't take it as anything personal.'

'Of course not.'

Major Rooks was talking but keeping a sharp lookout, and sometimes he just looked right around the Red House. He noticed a little greying in the skies and said, 'What time is it now?'

'Should be about three.'

'Three already?'

'Oh yes.'

'Well, this is the crucial day. We have to prepare for action.'

The deputy inspector said, 'You are all so scared. The mob won't do anything. What can they do? We've got the guns.'

'You don't know what could happen. We have the guns but we are only very few. We are only a couple of us, more or less. That's why we have to support each other. And this is precisely why I hate Walter Darwent. Just fancy, he's saying outright that we are wrong on the water bill. And just fancy keeping a distance from us. He is just like us. Let's stick together. Not look for a difference.'

Deputy Inspector Owen said in his mind, 'And you yourself are trying to

204

look for a difference? Whether one was born here or born in England. Isn't it you who's doing that?'

While he was thinking, Major Rooks was turning around to him and saying emphatically, 'And the worst thing is, and we could never forgive him for *that*.'

'You mean the washerwoman?'

'You saw them?'

'Saw what?'

'A few of my soldiers saw them together already.'

'Oh yes?'

'Not here, you know. In Santa Cruz. Where she washes clothes. You could believe that?

'No I can't.'

'Well it's true. And that sort of thing, Inspector – rather, Deputy Inspector – I was saying, it makes us ashamed in front of these people. And where is his self-respect?'

As Major Rooks turned towards the fire brigade station and Darwent's residence at the back of it he saw that the light, which was there before, had been extinguished. He put down his rifle and looked at Owen. 'Oh. Oh-h-h-h! I see. I now understand. You know what's happening now? She's over there. A light in his home was on all the time. That's for her to come. Now she's in, he turned the light off.'

'But are you sure? You are talking but are you sure? I know his wife and children were in England, but they are back. We can't always bother with gossip. I saw his wife last week, and I know they are there. And the ship's list mentioned their arrival. So how could the washerwoman be there? Come on!'

'She might be somewhere on the premises, you don't know. Downstairs.'

'That is hardly likely.'

'The only way of knowing is to raid the place.'

'What!' the deputy inspector shouted. He completely forgot the rank of the officer he was talking to. He said, 'Major Rooks, are you mad?'

26

After Captain Walter Darwent turned off the light he hurried downstairs excitedly. He was in his pyjamas and his heart was thumping. When he reached the foot of the stairs he made a grab for Eva but she pushed him off. Then as she turned round he grabbed her round the waist.

'What's wrong with you, Captain Darwent?'

He let her go. 'Come in quick and let's shut the door.'

'No, I'm not coming in.'

He was bitterly disappointed. He said, 'You know, Eva, I could never understand you?'

'Because you pretending you don't understand English.'

'What do you mean by that?'

'What I told you last week? In Santa Cruz. Didn't I say when everything is finished then I'll come inside?'

'Yes, but—'

'But what, Captain Walter?'

'It's about three o'clock in the morning. From the time you come and knock the knocker on the door like that, I knew it was you, and—'

'Of course you knew it was me. We didn't agree on that knock, Captain Walter? It's a good thing I didn't knock hard for that one upstairs to hear. Eh, Captain Walter?' He heard her giggle.

'Not *Captain* Walter. Call me Walter.'

She laughed mockingly in the dark. She said, 'Where you ever hear any Englishman telling a native to call him by his name? Without any handle. Where you ever hear that? Especially a servant, and a washerwoman. If they have to say anything about how to call them, they'll say "Call me Massa."' And when she laughed again her voice sounded to him like jingling bells.

This made him make another grab at her and she wrested herself away. He said, 'That laugh sounds so pretty.'

'Look, I going back home.'

'Eva, have some reason.'

'What you mean, reason?'

'You come here at quarter to three in the morning, and you wouldn't come inside!'

'So what? This is my house? Tonight I couldn't sleep and something on me mind. And we talk last week in Santa Cruz? I couldn't sleep and I want to ask you something.'

Glancing towards the square, he could see the beams of torchlights everywhere, and he knew that there were lots of policemen around.

He said to Eva, 'Where did you pass to get here?'

'I walked straight down Richmond—' She stopped. A beam of light went up into the trees and across by Trinity Cathedral, and funnily enough the instinct came to her to duck. Although in the darkness neither of them could see the other's face, Darwent said, 'Eva, for God's sake, step inside the door. Let me pull the door in. Aren't you afraid of those—'

'I was going to duck.'

'Duck? You could duck from these wicked so-and-so?'

'That's your own people you calling that. I'm glad you realise how they are.'

'Do you know you speak correct English?'

'That's not because of you.'

He was genuinely impressed. He liked how she had said 'how they are'. Although she had said her English was not because of him, he was certain that it was. Because she used to be distinctly different when she began working for him. He quickly forgot that and he said, 'Please step inside, Eva. There's a lot of scandal whirling around us. All that's left now is for them to see us together at three in the morning. Not three. A quarter past three.' He chuckled.

'And under the house,' she said. She gave the jingle bell laugh again.

He said, 'Oh God.'

'You see him here? Where he is?'

'Who?'

'God.'

Captain Darwent laughed dryly. 'Eva, please step in.'

She did not hesitate now. She went into the door and made two steps. She said, 'Thus far and no further.'

He said, 'I would respect that.'

207

'Good. I know that. Thank you.' Although she did not know why, she had got to like him very much for his gentlemanly ways. She knew when he said he wouldn't do something, he wouldn't. And it was also good to have a friend like him, who might very well be a friend in need. She said, 'Captain Walter, I couldn't sleep. All night I was wrestling with this. God alone knows what will happen on Monday.'

'Like what?'

'Well, we plan to make ruction. We have to make ruction. I only hope you don't go and sell us out now. I telling you because I say you is me friend. Or, rather, *you* are my friend – you say I talk like you,' she smiled. 'You know what happen to Greasy Pole?'

'I was hearing something...'

'And you know Mzumbo's not here.'

'Lazare? Where is he?'

'I only telling you because I say you are one of us.'

'You can confide in me. I'll never let you down.'

'I know. Well Mzumbo's in Mayaro. Some schoolmaster friend dying or died. But something has to give on Monday. Mzumbo likes law and order, well now it ain't having no law and order. In fact, we made him leave the scene, me and Clement. I'll tell you the truth. Please never let me down. I can confide in you?' Then she said: 'You know Lolotte Borde? The fat lady at Harriman corner who—'

'Do you mean the stone-thrower?'

Eva giggled in the dark. Her giggle, which sounded to Darwent like gurgling water, seemed to go down into his belly. His heart felt very soft towards her.

She said softly, 'Since Lolotte got three months for pelting stones everybody know her as a pelter. Anyway, I met with Lolotte. She told me she had a little meeting, and she'll be helping to run the show.' Eva deliberately did not mention the name of Maresse-Smith. She continued, 'Lolotte said she wants me by her side because something has to happen. It's brute force against brute force.'

'No,' said Captain Darwent, 'It's brute force against bullets.'

'Oh God I hope it's not so. It's a chance we have to take. Lolotte always have a basket of stones.'

'What is stones against bullets?'

He could only see her eyes, and she, his. She did not answer.

'Eva, it isn't worth it. I don't want you to die. If you get shot, what happens to me?'

'What happens to you? You'll live nicer.'

'Please don't. Don't talk like that. You please listen to me. I don't want you to die.'

'You crazy? You talking as if I want to die. I want to live, but we have to break this blasted prison house called Trinidad. Excuse me blasting. I don't mean the prison where Greasy Pole is. I mean this island. We have to do something to get your people to respect us. And force is the only thing. Force is the only thing they respect.'

'Eva, take my silly advice and take things easy. Because if you die you can't do a damn thing. And the country will remain just as it is. When's Mzumbo coming back?'

'I believe the round-island steamer is not due until next week Monday.'

'Who is the man who died?'

'Nobody died. We tried a trick on him.'

'Oh, Eva! Why do you do that kind of thing? That's terrible!'

'Forget that for now. You said you want me to live. But I already told you about Clement.'

'Good heavens!'

'It's not a matter of good heavens. You have your wife. If the worst comes to the worst you wouldn't leave her for me.'

'What? Girl, you don't know.'

'To live where? In Trinidad? That will be painful. We'll never make it. But let me just tell you this, quick. Saturday night a feller at the jail. A guard. Fell badly and suddenly in love. Wanted me to meet him at midnight. He would do anything for me. Long tears in his eyes, he love me. What? Why I went up to meet him? Okay, I know I'm evil, but listen. We went up to the Victoria Institute. Then I wanted to take a tram round the Savannah just to kill some time, but trams wasn't running. He said he felt so good being with me. He offered me money. When I saw about three quarters of an hour passed I told him I'm going. He said, "You don't really love me." I told him no, frankoment. But look, this is what I really want to tell you. He said, "You have somebody now?" I told him—'

She stopped and laughed. She said, 'Listen to this: Clement was in the background all the time. I had him trailing us, just in case, but he couldn't hear nothing. You know what I told this prison guard? I told him, I love two men: one is Clement and with the other one the name rhyming with Clement. You understand?' She laughed the jingle bell laugh again. He said, 'Oh God, Eva. Thank you so much for saying that.'

'Let's forget that for now. I came to ask you to do something for me but I didn't say this just to sweeten you. I was playing around with the guard to get something done in the meantime. Don't bother to ask me what. Tomorrow something's got to give. We suffering too much.'

'You want my advice?' Darwent said. 'Take things easy. Go to the Red House and make noise, that's all. All of you. Make a lot of noise so that they know you are there. But don't do anything crazy. Don't do anything to make them shoot.'

While she was reflecting on that, he said, 'And it's not tomorrow, it's today.'

'Oh yes.'

She was still reflecting. She was reflecting on what might happen, and that was exactly why she had come at this hour in the morning. It occurred to her that if the worst came to the worst, Walter Darwent could be of great help to them.

She said, 'All right, Captain, if—'

'Call me Walter.'

'Tomorrow – I mean today, when everything is over I'll call you Walter. If everything go good. But please listen to me now. If the worst come to the worst, I'll need you. *We'll* need you. Three of us. It might be two, but let's say three.'

'Who's that?'

'You know what happen to Greasy Pole?' Her voice sounded tense. She was so nervous that she did not even remember she had asked him the question already.

'I heard the talk.' He was going to say that was why the police were so nervous. Why torches were flashing all over the place.

She said, 'You know what he's famous for? You know why they call him Greasy Pole?'

Her voice sounded charged. She was nervous too.

'No. I don't think so.'

'Well they call him so because he's so slippery. No jail could really hold him if he wants to slip out. And he wants to slip out to do a job Monday. That's why I took the guard for a chat.'

210

'Eva! My goodness! Do I understand right? I mean, what's that? What are you up to?'

'What's what? I was telling you about Greasy Pole.'

'And you were up to helping him to slip out of jail!'

'Of course, Captain Walter. Because I want – I talking in parables now – I want to fight fire with fire. But mind you, this is Monday morning, what, about half-past three? And I don't know if he's out, but I only hoping. This man break jail so many times. Captain, I don't need any help from you in this.'

Darwent was relieved.

She suddenly straightened up. With the door shut she couldn't see outside, but she fancied she heard a noise. She imagined the torches in the trees and in the square and on the streets and she said to herself 'This place infested with police.' She knew what she would do when she was going back. She would ask Walter to take her right down the carriage drive to come out on Queen Street. She looked a little bewildered.

Captain Darwent said, 'What is it now? Something happened?'

'Nothing. It's nothing. It's about half-past three really?'

He couldn't tell and he did not want to go and watch the big clock up the stairs. Because he knew she wouldn't come up. Although Gwen was asleep in a room far on the other side. He himself did not want to go up and leave her alone down here, not even for a moment.

He said, 'I don't really know the time.'

'Just imagine, Captain Darwent ain't have his pocket watch.'

'Even if I had it I can't see in the dark. I don't want to scare you but it must be at least four-twenty. Judging from the time you are here.'

'I talking so long and I ain't say nothing yet! You know what –I'd better go and take a little rest.'

'Please don't go.' Captain Darwent put up his hands in the dark. In any case she couldn't see that.

She chuckled. 'No, I mustn't go. Hear Captain Darwent: *Please don't go*. And his wife's upstairs, you know. But I mustn't go. I mustn't go till morning. Till day clean. Till the police could see well enough to shoot me. Not so, Captain? Let me tell you this, I going to church first thing this morning.'

He had paused because it was as though he had heard a sound, but it was really nothing. The night was so still, he thought, anything could make one feel it is something. He said, 'As I told you in Santa Cruz—'

'Stay right there. Hold up there. I was to tell you this. Don't come back there again. Not that I don't want your company but anybody could see you. It's risky. It stand out. A white man on a big grey horse. Captain, you know you surprise me? Last week when you gone I just shook me head.'

She looked round again, forgetting the door was closed. She said, 'Look, is better for me to go. This is March and these days it getting light early. Let me tell you now what I really come to tell you. Today will be confusion. We coming, as you yourself said, and we making noise. Not because you said so but we coming in any case. We done plan that.'

Her voice was cracking up and she was getting nervous again. 'God alone know what going to happen. I could calm down some of them. On Saturday morning I was talking to Lodrick John, and he's a terror but I could keep him on me rein. I could boil him down like bajee. That's like spinach. How ah talking! Me English nice now? Ha, ha. Let me tell you: Lolotte, I don't know, she so hard to boil down. She's so calm but she could get so excited. But in any case Lolotte is a lot to boil down. You like me joke?

'Captain, serious now. I talking to you because I know you really care and I want to ask you something. A favour. Greasy Pole swearing to God he'll break jail and he have a job to do. Don't ask me what job. But what I want to ask you first of all is not to do nothing. It depending on you but I begging you, we don't want you to do nothing. Now don't ask me no question, because I think you know what it is. The second thing is, the police know us. Not me so much but Lolotte – what you called her? The "stone-thrower"? The police know Lolotte and when it come to Greasy Pole, well he's their regular guest. I think it was Edgar who told Lolotte that Greasy Pole has his own room in the queen's big house. Anyway it's not the queen again since Victoria died. He break jail about five thousand times, Greasy Pole. And Holder know me. As you know I used to live with Sergeant Holder, and when I left him, well he still wants to kill me. And he told me flat if he gets me in his rifle range I'm a dead duck. So I saying this, and you is me only bigtime friend. If the worse come to the worse today – because the people really vex – if the worst turn the very worst, you know what I mean. If the case is—'

She did not want to say blood. She was silent for a while, and then she said, 'If they shooting afterwards, we'll have to get out of town.'

'Eva, I talked to you already. You are determined. Take it easy. Don't be so determined.'

'Me? Not me. But you know how things could happen. At first when I came here tonight I was feeling for thunder and brimstone. Fire and brimstone. When I came here tonight I was in that mood. But listening to you, I think you right.'

'Thank you.'

'I liked it when you said if I die I can't do a damn thing.'

'That's true.'

'That's so true. But you yourself said, "Go to the Red House and make noise." And I think that's right, and even if you didn't say it nothing would stop that because if we don't do nothing they'll think we scared. But what I telling you now is, who know what could happen when we go there making noise? Sometimes the police could be so provoking. You know what I see them do already? That day when Lolotte was throwing stones and when it took six policemen to capture her and get her under control – that day Lolotte wasn't going to throw any stones—'

'Yes, but she walked with a bag of stones so what was her intention?'

'That was just in case, because she knows what the police is like.'

'Well if she walks with her basket of stones tomorrow, no, that is today—'

'Oh God. It must be after four now. Walter, I mean Captain Darwent, it's time for me to go.'

'That's right. Call me Walter again.'

'You feeling nice!' She gave her jingle bell laugh.

'I love you.'

She pretended she didn't hear but at the same time, although she had laughed, she was genuinely concerned. She said, 'Let me tell you quick and ah going. On Monday, some time, if they shooting, some time we'll have to get out of town. Me, Lolotte and Greasy Pole. That is, if Greasy Pole is out of that place and come and do the job. We don't want you to do *nothing*, although they paying you for that. But you is a man for justice, so don't do nothing. Then, as ah was saying, after that we might be depending on you because we have to get out of town—'

'But I can't— What do you want me to do, Eva?'

'I want you to meet us by St Joseph Road. You know by where Lolotte live?'

'How would I know where Lolotte lives? I hardly know Lolotte.'

'Wait for us by the toll gate. On the main road. That is if they shooting. We know your horse and carriage. Wait for us there and speed us out of town.'

'Where to?'

'To wherever you like.' And she thought, 'You may need to be out of town too.' But she did not say that. She said, 'How far Mayaro is? Clement told me it's the best place he ever know. You know how far Mayaro is?'

'Eva, you are crazy. Mayaro? It's Mayaro you are asking about? I am only now convinced you are as mad as a March hare!'

'That's okay, since we in March. But what about Mayaro? Why? Mayaro not in Trinidad?'

'This girl's mad as a hatter.'

'It's mad people who put the world straight. Mayaro not in Trinidad? I asking you.'

'It's in Trinidad but you can't get there overland. Didn't you say Mzumbo went there by boat? Look, I was born in Trinidad and I never even got near to Mayaro. It's so far it's about a thousand miles. Of course that's the sort of way one talks, but it's not far from a thousand miles.'

'But don't say you can't get there overland. Clement travelled there by horse-and-cart. Somebody was going somewhere and he went to visit Dick. The schoolmaster who's dead. Who's supposed to be dead.' She laughed and the captain laughed too, and shook his head. She said, 'We in the dry season and your carriage could go right through. Look, to cut a long story short, you'll take us there? Take us there because that place is nice and I'll get to like you there because you is a nice man.'

'What about Clement?'

'He'd come afterwards. Because Mzumbo will come back and he'll tell him we in Mayaro. I don't know what will happen then but right now I'm just thinking of you taking us to Mayaro. I heard Mzumbo use some words once, *The calm after the storm*, and that is just what Mayaro will be. You'll take us there. Right? Look, I have to go now because from the time we talking here, day must be getting ready to break. To show how long we here, I could almost see you now. Oh Christ, I hope no policeman's anywhere round. I gone. Bye-bye, as you always say.'

Captain Darwent stood on the stairs feeling confused and yet feeling glad. She said she would get to like him in Mayaro. He felt good but he was momentarily worried about her and when he stepped out of the door with her he could see how much the day was beginning to clear.

She said, 'Let me take the carriageway to get out to Queen Street.'

'Out here is shorter. Don't you want to go out this way to Abercromby Street?'

'Somebody might spot me. I feel safer to go out to Queen Street.'

'I think you are right. Okay, pass so.'

'I gone.'

'Bye-bye.'

27

As soon as the wharf officer spotted Mzumbo by the light of the cabin, he rushed to him. The sloop *Pioneer Rust* had just come in to the lighthouse jetty in Port-of-Spain and was still being tied up. The officer boarded the vessel by the plank and said, 'Mr Lazare, I have to speak with you right away.'

'Why? Is something wrong?'

'Yes, Mr Lazare. You stepping off the vessel now? I want to talk to you, urgent.'

Mzumbo went and thanked the captain, and a few of the crew, and he stepped out upon the lighthouse jetty. The wharf officer could hardly wait. He took him aside near the very plank, and whispered, 'Mr Lazare, it's a good thing I spotted you first, and it's a good thing it is dark. But they'll find you, so get out of town quick.'

Mzumbo Lazare was taken aback. The little kerosene light hanging from a pole at the tip of the jetty was not bright enough for him to see the officer's face, but he felt pretty certain the officer was out of his mind. He said, 'May I ask, Officer – who are you?'

'You don't know me, Mr Mzumbo Lazare. I attend almost every one of your meetings. I listened to you the other day on the Savannah. Could be two weeks ago. I remember you said something like, "When you go to the debate let them see you are discontented. Don't sit quiet. But do not play into their hands. Do not let them arrest you." Mr Lazare, please take your own advice now and do not play into their hands. Last week they grabbed Greasy Pole and put him in prison and—'

'Greasy Pole is in prison?'

'Yes.'

'What for?'

'Nobody knows, and believe me, nobody really cares. Greasy Pole is always in prison. But the lady who sells the cake, the hefty lady, she told me they want all the troublemakers behind bars by tonight. Because tomorrow is trouble. She said Emelda George told her Holder said that. And I – I personally know they are looking all over the town for you. They came down here.'

Mzumbo began to feel a tinge of fear. He said, 'And I know they regard me as a troublemaker.'

'For them you are the biggest troublemaker. Some nights ago they held Mr Edgar Maresse-Smith when—'

'They held Edgar?'

'Since Friday night. And they are scouring the town for you. If we lose you the whole fight is lost.'

Mzumbo was silent for a while, and then he said, 'Who else they held?'

'I don't know. The fat lady with the cassava cake told me they went to her house twice, looking for you. She said they broke down the door. She said she's glad you went to the funeral in Mayaro.'

Lazare mumbled, 'She's glad about death? In any case Dick did not die.' Then he shook his head and said, 'What will we do with these beasts!' He said: 'Officer, I was in Mayaro but I am here now. I am not afraid, and I will not run as a deer. This is the island in which I was born and I will not—'

The officer interrupted him in desperation. 'If they put you in jail that won't help nobody. People will lose courage. I know you is a brave man. You is a soldier and captain in the Light Horse regiment. But they'll clamp you in jail.'

'But what must I do? I cannot turn back. The *Pioneer Rust* is not returning to the petroleum well until next week.'

'Mr Mzumbo Lazare, I am not just speaking on behalf of me. I am speaking on behalf of the people. And I am not speaking in patois. I am speaking in your own language and in your own style. You yourself, or was it Mr Maresse-Smith?' He paused a little. 'No, it was Cyrus David. Mr Cyrus said when Napoleon was fighting and could not take it any more he retreated, saying: *He who fights and runs away, shall live to fight another day. But he who is in battle slain will never live to fight again.* We laughed, but it is good sense. Mr Mzumbo, what you have to do is to run. Or hide. It have a lot of police around. I'm surprised none's here now. Police like bush. They are all over the town. This water dispute will finish. But we want you to be here because it's a lot of fight ahead.'

217

Lazare said nothing. The officer could not see the anxiety in his face as he stared blankly towards the water.

The officer broke the silence. 'Mr Lazare, can you stay around here in the dark until I am off duty? It is past midnight but the last sloop isn't in yet. I will bring you something to eat, but I cannot take you to the office where anyone can see you. Because we cannot trust anybody, not even our own people. Maresse-Smith was picked up just like that, when he went to see a friend on Picton Street. There is another one, yes Papa Bodu. He was picked up on George Street for not parking his carriage straight – a really bogus charge imposed by Holder. When the crowd gathered and cried shame on Holder for the silly charge, Holder crossed it out and charged Bodu with inciting. Then there was a young man called Clement. Right over here this happened. This puzzled me because I don't think I know this person at all, but really I didn't see well, and I don't know if I know him.'

Mzumbo was looking into the wharf officer's eyes. The wharf officer continued: 'They say he is a young feller, about twenty-six. He was giving some pep talk to a little crowd round about eight o'clock, and he was saying tomorrow have to be really different. That is "today", of course. People were so excited they carried him to have a drink in Railway Bar. The police took him just over there on South Quay. They charged him with inciting too.'

Mzumbo ground his teeth. He cried, 'Oh God, how long?'

The wharf officer said, 'I happen to know these things but there might be a lot more that I do not know. Because it's all hush-hush. My girlfriend told me that Holder said when you playing a game you must play to win.'

Mzumbo was feeling downcast and dispirited and overwhelmed by hurt.

The officer said, 'I have to get back to the office, Mr Lazare. It was a good thing I spotted you. My house is at Laventille, way up on the hill. After work I'll try to get you there. Stay right here, or perhaps you can move a little more where it is darker.'

'All right. Thank you. What's your name?'

'Joel. Joel Asnel.'

'And what do you do here?'

'Well they call me wharf officer but it is really water police.'

'All right, I'll be staying right here. I am grateful to you, Mr Joel.'

'No, it's just Joel, Sir.'

◆

Mzumbo's heart was thumping, although now he was a little relieved. He had not slept many hours but he had woken up to a bright, nervous morning. He was sitting in the gallery and looking down on the town, and the wharf officer's grandmother was in the rocking chair not too far away. The young man was getting dressed to go to the Red House and Mzumbo was eager to go, but he knew he shouldn't and wouldn't. The old lady said, 'Well if they tell you the schoolmaster died and when you reach Mayaro he was alive – what you said again, alive and kicking? Then you shoulda come right back. Why you didn't come right back? What they did was wicked.'

Mzumbo looked at the furrowed brow, the head of white hair. He did not feel to talk. He was thinking of a lot of things and Mayaro was a little way back in his mind. Last night, after he reached up the hill safely, and he lay down, exhausted, he had relived the whole tiresome journey. The whole episode, in fact: when he had arrived at Mayaro, how shocked he was to find Dick hale and hearty, how he was so vexed and upset and wanted to rush back but how Ivy pressed him to stay; how yesterday he had got wind of the petroleum barge leaving for Port-of-Spain. And he thought of the long, uncomfortable journey back on the *Pioneer Rust* and especially what came at the end of it. Indeed, the big scare he had had on the lighthouse jetty could not completely go away. He was glad that within fifteen minutes the wharf officer came and they were ready to leave. Because the incident had truly shaken him. He had been standing there in the dark when he had heard footsteps and imagined it was the wharf officer's, and when he had walked towards the footsteps, the policeman had said, 'Who are you!' It was a good thing he was quick-thinking and it was also a good thing he knew how to change his voice. For he had replied, imperiously, 'Who are *you*? Do you know members of the public are not allowed here?' And the reply came, 'Save your breath, Sir, this is a police officer.' Thinking about it now, he found that although he was in no mood to laugh, it was hard to repress a chuckle. For he had then said: 'Oh, yes, a police officer, very nice. It's nice to see a police officer on the wharf when one is late and trying to wrap things up. If it was a damn thief or vagabond or a fugitive from justice standing up here in the dark there wouldn't have been any policeman for miles.' And then had come the scary part, for the policeman had replied: 'Right now, Sir, Colonel Brake hasn't got a single man to spare. He's right up to his neck because of the debate later on. I only on the wharf because we hunting down Lazare.'

'Which Lazare? You mean the—'

'It only have one Lazare. Mzumbo. The feller who's always agitating. We searching night and day for him. We done have the other one inside.'

And with his heart thumping he had said in a resolute voice, 'Well, you wouldn't find no Lazare on this wharf, but you could rest assured that if the culprit comes across here at all, we'll put a clinch on him and then send up the hill to call you.'

And full of gratitude the policeman had left.

It was not long afterwards that the wharf officer had come.

◆

Mzumbo suddenly raised his head and saw the old lady looking at him. He said, 'Did you speak?'

She chuckled. She said, 'He say, "Did you speak?" I speak so long now I almost forget what I ask him.'

He called to mind. 'You asked, I think, you asked why I could not come right back. It's hard to answer you. In any case I couldn't come right back. The steamer doesn't pass Mayaro except once a week. Sometimes twice.'

She said, 'Oh.'

'In fact I had to come on Rust's barge. You heard about the oilfield?'

'Oilfield?'

'Yes. Petroleum. Where they are drilling for petroleum. Not too far from where I was. It's in a place called Guayaguayare. Randolph Rust is my friend and so I happened to get a lift on his equipment barge. That's why I am here. Else I could not have come.'

The old woman nodded her head as though she had understood. She did not understand anything. She understood neither what exactly Rust was, nor what was petroleum, nor where was this place called Guayaguayare.

She said, 'But you enjoyed yourself. You say you spent two days?'

'No I did not enjoy myself. Because I was vexed how they fooled me.

And this is a crucial time – I don't have to tell you, you know what's happening at the Red House this morning. But they in Mayaro didn't know what's brewing because Mayaro's far and news travels to Mayaro very slowly. At least they claimed they did not know. They just wanted to see me, but they they didn't have to go to the extreme.'

'It's because they love you.'

'Especially Ivy. Especially the wife.'

He was looking over the town, over which the skies were gloomy and grey and then all of a sudden he saw sunshine engulf the whole place beneath him. He whispered, 'Into thine hands, O Lord!'

The old lady, who had still been looking at him, spoke again. She said, 'Mister, tell me: you is the real Mzumbo Lazare?'

Mzumbo looked at her and smiled.

She said, 'I have to ask, don't mind me asking, because Joel always talking so much about Mzumbo Lazare and when he bring you home last night he was so excited, although he was really frighten for you, you know. So when I heard him say "Mzumbo", I asked if it was the real Mzumbo! If it was the same man everybody always talking about. Because I didn't know. And he said the police out for you. I don't even know now. Because you came late, late. And in any case I didn't think the police will want to hold Mr Mzumbo Lazare. Unless to shake his hand.' Mzumbo laughed. She said, 'You really came late you know. I was sleeping orreday.'

'Sorry, Ma Asnel. Police was thick, especially around South Quay. Joel and me passed by Immaculate Conception, but we couldn't even risk going up Duncan Street. Not even George Street. We stayed a long time avoiding police in Marine Square and then King Street, and then we managed to slip up to Duke Street, using Henry Street. It wasn't very easy, Ma. At one point we had to slip into Rosary Church, and when I heard footsteps behind me, my heart gave voom! voom! and I put me hand over me face pretending I praying. But nothing happened. Afterwards we skipped across the bridge, and passed up by Mango Rose.'

The old lady listened to him. She was convinced that this could not be the real Mzumbo Lazare.

She said, 'I was worried about Joel because as a rule he ain't ever late.'

Joel heard, and came out of the bedroom. He said, 'I was later than usual because I don't usually have to contend with so much of the

221

constabulary. Of course if Mr Lazare wasn't there we wouldn't have had that development. It was frustrating. I think I am going to hear the debate.'

His grandmother looked at him. She said to herself: 'What's wrong with Joel this morning – he swallowed a dictionary? He trying to talk like the mister.'

Joel had put on his wharf officer's uniform although nobody in his department was going out to work. Everybody was taking a holiday in Port-of-Spain. He said, 'Grandma, do not look out for me, I will be back later, basically.' Then he turned to Mzumbo.

'Mr Mzumbo Lazare, I know you are dying to visit the Red House and hear the debate, but my advice to you is, basically, to keep far from it. I have left something on the bed, which you can put on, obviously if you insist on being there, but if I were you I would not approach nearer than about the middle of Prince Street. From there you would be able to see right across to the main entrance and it might soothe your mind to see the people will not riot. I am going. Mr Lazare, I would like you to remember those words of Napoleon which I basically quoted: *He that is in battle slain will never live to fight again.* The debate begins at nine, and I will be back home for lunch.'

He said all this with his grandmother still looking at him, and wondering what had come over him. As he stepped out to go down the hill she eyed him from head to foot. She said to herself, 'What do him!' She turned to Mzumbo, 'You think he all right? I mean, he okay in his head?' Mzumbo did not answer. She chuckled and shook her head. She said, 'Trying to talk like you.'

She gazed at Joel until he disappeared down the hill, among the houses.

222

28

Inside the Red House in the office of the Colonial Secretary, Major Rooks had his thirty-five men ready. They were ready and waiting, as the roar built up outside. There was only one person in the room that was not a soldier, and that was Walsh Wrightson. He had spent the night in the Red House because Brake did not want to risk his coming over like the rest of the members of the Legislative Council. He knew how much the rabble hated Walsh Wrightson, holding him chiefly responsible for all the troubles in Port-of-Spain, and he particularly did not want Wrightson to show himself outside this morning. For the mob was bigger and in a worse mood than he had ever seen, and more than that Holder had told him the crowd was planning to seize Wrightson.

Colonel Brake was outside. It was only twenty minutes to nine o'clock but although he had wanted to dash upstairs to see Rooks and Wrightson, he did not want to leave now. He wanted to see all the council members inside. He did not know why he was being like that, and in fact he chided himself. But it was his training. He was head of the constabulary and it was his duty to protect. He had a head and a heart and his heart was telling him to protect those who deserved protection, and to hell with the rest. To hell with the Alcazars and the Wainwrights, and to hell with the Wilsons, and the Cyrus Davids. Let them reap what they sowed. But then he had laughed at himself. The people who were against the waterworks bill were in no danger. Those were the stooges of the mob and no harm could come to them. It hurt him. As he looked around he said sharply to himself, 'And do you mean my police have to protect those villains?' His face got red.

He looked up and down, but he could not leave the door of the Legislative Council chamber. His clerk at the door was constantly turning back people who had no ticket, and there was a tremendous crowd building up by the door. He was trying to have some of Inspector Norman's policemen control this crowd and thin it out.

He glanced to the left and there he could see both Inspector Norman and Inspector Empson, with their policemen strewn out along Brunswick Square North, past Dr Pollonais's residence and on the other side of Pembroke Street in front of where the new library was. There were people in the square and he wanted to get them out of the square because you couldn't always see them properly owing to the foliage of the trees; and in case of a riot, who knew what missiles could fly through the leaves? But he could not attend to that matter now because here was like a Tower of Babel with people shouting and threatening. His men were keeping everybody away from the door, except those who were taking tickets, and those were a few of the respectable people. And there were lots of so-called respectable people like George Goodwille, Mr Mole, old Mr Conrad Stollmeyer, he saw them all there, but he was not going to argue with any of them. He would not even speak: if they happen to be stubborn and difficult, his policemen with their batons would speak for him. He looked around and he tried to see outside. His men still did not find Lazare, and he found that strange. Wherever Lazare was hiding was a good hiding place, because they had scoured the whole of Port-of-Spain, and even some areas outside of Port-of-Spain itself. Of course Lazare's wife had tried to throw them off the scent when his men went to Diego Martin for Lazare. She had told them he was in Mayaro. They had had a good laugh. But Lazare had already been in hiding for when they carried out a search at Lazdale he was not there. At any rate Lazare was not present to whip up this crowd. He would have made capital this morning with a crowd as big and as furious as this. Anyway, Lazare must still be found, even if it was after the debate. For since Maresse-Smith was grabbed and placed behind bars in the early hours of Saturday morning then if Lazare was left free he could easily claim he was untouchable. Not only that, but the Government had to show the people its power. Since Friday evening he had decided that jailing the two agitators was in the colony's best interest.

All of a sudden Lazare fled from his thoughts. He saw a breaking of ranks of the policemen near Dr Pollonais's residence and he knew Governor Maloney was here. Quickly he glanced at his pocket-watch, which was showing six minutes to nine, and he rushed out into the street, with a formation of policemen behind him, and another set of policemen spreading out and pushing the crowd back. Standing in the street and looking across to the Brunswick Square side he called out to Sergeant Holder, and Holder came running. Holder saluted and they talked, then he made some brief military steps and came back to the chamber door. The chamber door was already cleared for the Governor by Inspector Empson's men, who, on the sight of the Governor's carriage had rushed here. They now smartly lined the entrance to the chamber.

The Governor got out of the carriage in front of the entrance facing the chamber door. As Sir Alfred Maloney walked in there was a barrage of hooting from the crowd which greatly angered and shocked Colonel Brake. His face was red with shame when he saluted the Governor. He took it as a personal slur on him that this could be allowed to happen, and as the Governor walked into the chamber the colonel felt it difficult to control his rage. He wanted to call on the police to use their batons freely, but as inspector commandant could he do a thing like that and get off? There was bound to be a Royal Commission of Enquiry on his action. Stepping beside the Governor, he spotted Holder standing on the other side of Abercromby Street, and Holder was looking at him as though begging for that very signal. He remembered something and after escorting Sir Alfred to the Governor's chair he rushed back and signalled Holder to come. He whispered in his ear, 'Go and tell Inspector Charles Norman I have to go upstairs to fetch the Honourable Wrightson and escort him to the chamber, so please to send twenty of his men here on armed alert.' Holder nodded. Colonel Brake asked, 'Where is the parcel for Wrightson that Peake brought, just in case?'

'It's on the Registrar's desk.'

'All right. Go to the inspector now. Because the debate is soon to begin and I must get the Honourable Director of Public Works. The debate cannot begin without him.'

All the while the police chief was talking, Holder was glancing round at the crowd as if to suggest the conversation was about them. This was to give the impression that the police chief was ordering blows. He did not fail to convey that impression for a lot of people moved back. Lolotte Borde, for one, went right outside the building, for he could not see her. Holder went down the flight of steps and when he came back with the twenty extra policemen, the crowd moved even further back. And hastily. Lolotte looked towards the deanery hedge where she had placed her basket of stones. Colonel Brake came out, walked round, then went upstairs to get the Honourable Walsh Wrightson.

◆

Up in the Colonial Secretary's office Colonel Brake asked, 'Where's Wrightson?'

The soldiers, with their bayonets fixed on to their rifles, were looking tense. Major Rooks, looking even more tense, said, 'Colonel Brake, it's a little after nine now. When I did not see you I ordered ten of my soldiers to escort him.'

'Oh, he's in the chamber?'

'He's in the chamber.'

'Where did they pass?'

'At the front. There's a hell of a massive crowd on the St Vincent Street side. You should see the rabble.'

'I know.'

'Today will have trouble.'

'Hope to God not. Let's keep it tight. They got Walsh Wrightson in easily?'

'Well, without killing anybody.'

'I couldn't come up before. It's murder down there.'

'It might very well turn out to be exactly that.'

The men looked away. The close ones walked away.

Major Rooks said, 'Colonel, I didn't want the mob to know that soldiers were inside.'

'I know. Sorry about that. But I couldn't come up before.'

Major Rooks said nothing.

Colonel Brake said, 'I wanted to thank you for putting Maresse-Smith away.'

'Don't thank me, thank Holder. Holder saw the carriage with Lolotte Borde in it and he went straight to the address. By the time he got there he saw neither Borde nor the carriage. He said something told him to amble back and late that night he saw the carriage down the hill from her home. He said they conspired for more than two hours, and then when Maresse-Smith came down he just brought him in.'

'Holder is a godsend.'

226

'But it's the case of Bodu that's amusing.' The major was laughing. 'Bodu was arrested for not parking his carriage straight in Pembroke Street. A crowd gathered and when Bodu began to argue with him, the mob began to boo Holder, and Holder dropped the first charge and he said, "Papa Bodu, you inciting to riot?" And he charged him with inciting to riot. Look, I'm not in the mood to laugh. Holder called me and I had my gun and bayonet and I marched the old man up to jail.'

Colonel Brake, too, was not in the mood for laughing, but he and several of the soldiers laughed out loud.

But as they were laughing the roar of the crowd mounted, and now it was high, and rising and ebbing like the tide. Both men realised the debate had begun but they said nothing. Their faces became serious again. Then Brake said, 'I've got to go down.'

◆

Eva was now inside Brunswick Square. She had been by the chamber door since about seven o'clock, but from the moment Brake had brought Sergeant Holder to the chamber door and was whispering with him she had moved well back. But it was when she saw Holder looking round and his eyes fixed on her she decided not only to move back but to move well away from the Red House. For those eyes glared with hate and who knew what that wicked man could do to her? And the fact was, although she did not want to admit it, when she saw him and looked at his rifle, she felt a pang of fear.

So now she was well inside Brunswick Square and by the fountain. From early on she had seen Lolotte Borde, first on the greens of the Red House, then on the steps near the chamber door, then by Trinity Cathedral, and now when she was heading for the fountain she waved and hailed out to Lolotte to come over and stand with her.

The first thing Eva said to Lolotte now was, 'I feel something will happen this morning.'

'Something will have to happen. It will have to have some kinda riot. You see how the crowd booing? Wrightson want to pass that bill.'

'Yes, but Wrightson can't pass the bill alone. You didn't hear what Uncle say? That they have to put it to the vote? It's Maloney and the whole of that damn bunch. If the bill pass, don't blame Wrightson alone.'

'What happen to you voice? You hoarse already?'

'I didn't sleep last night. I was talking to somebody up to four this morning, you could believe that? Then I went home and I lay down on the bed but I was afraid to close me eyes in case I sleep. Then I yawned, tired, and at the same time a cock crow so mournful I jumped up. It was a good thing too because outside was daylight. I put on me clothes and I rushed right here. And I know why I really hoarse because when Maloney and those sufferers was going inside, those clowns—'

'I heard you. I heard some heavy words but I didn't know if they was yours because you so light. You heard me too? Oh, yes? That's good. Everybody was screaming. But one thing I have to tell you. You said, *when those sufferers was going inside*. Don't call them sufferers. It's not them who suffering, it's us.'

'You right.'

Something passed through Eva's mind. When she had said she did not sleep last night, it had occurred to her, but she had no intention of saying she had been talking to Walter Darwent. But as she thought of Darwent she remembered how she had arranged with him that if the worst came to the worst, and something terrible really happened, he would take herself, Lolotte, and Greasy Pole to Mayaro. And maybe Clement? She said to herself quickly, 'Oh God, you know I ain't even see Clement since Friday! She did not want to forget what had come to her mind because she wanted to let Lolotte know Walter would be waiting for them. And that he would be in his carriage at the toll gate on St Joseph Road. When she had asked him to wait for them and to take them to Mayaro she had been very emotional, although calm, and now as she listened to the roar of the crowd, with the noise getting louder and more intense and even hostile, she seriously began to feel that something would happen and that she would really need him there.

A chorus of voices breaking like a tidal wave interrupted her thoughts. She cried, 'Lolotte, things boiling up. We a little far.'

'I was just thinking of going and standing up by the hedge, by the deanery.'

'Why?'

'I have something in the hedge.'

Eva laughed nervously. 'The usual?' She remembered how Walter had said, 'The stone-thrower.'

Lolotte just looked at her and said, 'You moving? We can't stay far, because we all in it.'

Eva said, 'You know I ain't see Edgar at all this morning?'

'Nor me. But he's somewhere around because the carriage parked near to Police Headquarters.'

'Yes, but I ain't see him.'

'Nor me. That's odd. But he somewhere around. This is people like bush. People like fire, girl.'

As Lolotte said 'fire', for the first time Eva wondered if Greasy Pole had broken out of the Royal Jail. But there was a lot of noise coming from the Red House and there was going to be a fray. She wanted to move into it. She looked at Lolotte and couldn't understand why she was so well dressed – for the scrimmage. Lolotte was not in white today, but wearing a red dress with a red head-tie.

'What you wearing red for – I mean, a day like today?'

Lolotte, who was already breathing hard, turned to her, surprised. She said, 'Red is especially for a day like today. Red is for victory, girl. And as – Oh God you know what I just remember? You know who I saw when I was standing on the lawn over there?'

'No.'

'Good Christ! And I just remembered this. I was going to tell you but I forgot. But as you mention me red dress, he like to say red is to hide blood, and just in this split second, me mind go on him. I spotted him a while ago. Or somebody like him. But it's he!'

'Yes, but who? He is who?'

'Greasy Pole.'

'Good God!' Eva held her heart. 'Greasy Pole? You sure?'

'Yes, I spot him in the crowd in front the registry door. After Colonel Brake called Holder, and Brake was passing through the registry door the crowd had to heave back and I feel sure sure that at that time I spotted Greasy Pole.'

From the time Eva had heard the words 'Greasy Pole' her heart began pounding. She said silently, 'God be praised. The little half-an-hour he had look like he put it to use. He brake jail once again, for Colonel Brake. Thank God. Lord, he has a little job to do and help him to do the job good. And let this be glory day, Jesus. Amen.'

Eva's face was still full of wonder. She said, 'Look, I'll tell you honestly, this morning me head was so hot with this bacchanal here that I forgot Greasy Pole completely. But he told me he'd be here. He was saying so. He said he have a job to do and if he have to do a job he have to do it.'

'What job?'

Eva stuttered. 'Ah, um, I don't know. He was saying somebody paid him to do a job. I don't know. When I see him I'll ask him. That is, if they don't catch him before.'

She looked at Lolotte but Lolotte was hardly listening at this stage. In fact, she was on the point of advancing and at the same time her mind was on moving towards the deanery hedge. Ahead of them the roar of the people was awesome and beginning to sound like an angry storm, and now they could see scuffles with the police, and there was shouting and screaming and cursing. Eva stopped talking right away. The two women did not speak, and as they were watching and listening a barrage of stones hit the Red House. They both moved off, running towards the scene of the riot. Eva made for the middle gate by the concrete path that led directly from the fountain to the Red House, but Lolotte made for the gate which led to the corner by the deanery hedge. At this point people were running to and fro, scattering, and some were fleeing the scene. Stones pounded against the Red House and there was the sound of shattering glass, and then the crack of gunshots, and she could hear an English voice shouting: 'Fire in the air!'

Eva was panting. She said to herself, 'I knew something was going to happen today.' And then she thought, horrified: 'You know I didn't get to tell Lolotte that Walter would be waiting for us by the toll gate on St Joseph Road? I have to tell Lolotte and I have to see Greasy Pole.'

29

A woman was hurling abuse as two policemen chased the boy Stamford Lord in front of the Red House down Abercromby Street. As Lolotte came running to the western gate of Brunswick Square from the corner of the deanery she heard the uproar and saw the crowd scattering and when she spotted the young constables who were now close to Stamford Lord, with the same speed she threw herself right between Stamford and the two policemen and the two policemen came tumbling down in the street. A cry went up at the southern end near the fire brigade station, and from where Joel was he could see the crowd on the other side of the square rushing towards the spot. He wanted to go, too, but he could not do anything. He was almost pinned against the chamber door. A moment before, he did not know how or why, but looking towards where the woman's voice was coming from, he had spotted Eva running over to the Red House side of the street and his head went wild. He had screamed 'Eva,' so she could hear him, but he did not know if his voice came out or not or how it came out because he could not hear himself. The scrimmage was all around him, and he could do nothing because with fighting in front of him the crowd was tending to move back on the building and he couldn't rescue himself from that throng. But he heard someone saying soldiers were in the street now, although he could not see them.

There was a great heave which pushed him away from the building but he did not fall. He heard a voice from behind say, 'You'll beat us with you damn rifle butt? You ain't shame?' Then suddenly things seemed to go black before him, but when he caught himself again he was on his feet. He had only fallen over some bushes, some hedges, he did not know what or where. There were wild angry arms flinging about him. He saw something which looked like a policeman's uniform and he made a lunge for the policeman to pull him down in the stampede.

Not too far up from the chamber door – in fact, right in front of the Red House proper, by the big door to the registry, Inspector Norman was held by the throat and pressed against a concrete pillar. He was struggling to get away but he was held by a bigger man than himself. The man, Lodrick, was frantic with rage, and was butting him on his head repeatedly, and there was a punch which landed flush upon his jaw. He had dashed into the crowd to catch a stone-thrower when Big Lodrick slid out a leg to trip him, and as he had tumbled over, Big Lodrick had caught him and gave him a full-blooded elbow in the face. Blood came. It was after this that Big Lodrick held him against the concrete pillar and began butting him.

Big Lodrick kept on saying with every butt: 'Take this! Take this! Take this!' Two other people rushed to hold on to Inspector Norman but Lodrick screamed 'Leave him to me! Let me fix him up!' As the inspector struggled to get away he felt a hand gently pull his revolver from his side pocket. He did not say anything. He thought he was going to be shot instantly. But it did not mean he had given up the struggle with his attacker. As Lodrick released the inspector's arm in order to give him a heavy punch to the jaw, Inspector Norman frantically tried to grab him and spin him round and he succeeded in holding Lodrick's neck in a lock. But the grip was not good enough and the two men tumbled on to the ground.

The inspector had fallen on top of Big Lodrick and now he tried to choke him to death, but there was another heave, and as they both tumbled sideways, Lodrick held on to the inspector's khaki shirt to pull himself up, and with the same force gave Inspector Norman a heavy butt in the eye. The inspector screamed, but no assistance came to him because no policeman heard him. In fact the noise of the crowd was so loud that Lodrick could hardly hear his own voice, but he cried, 'You Inspector Norman you is a pig and I go burst you blasted mouth and slap you up. You English fellers mean to make us ketch hell. But it's time, it's time, it's time. I had this in for you in particular because you let Holder beat me up last week. It's Brake I wanted but you will do. Because I can't catch Holder without gun in hand. He have a gun today so you'll pay the cake. You bastard, take this, and this.' He punched and kicked and let fly a flurry of punches. But the worst of his blows was a butt to the mouth, for this shattered many of the inspector's teeth.

'Oh God,' the inspector cried.

'You calling on God? I thought you was God.'

Lodrick John was shouting angrily but nobody could hear. The roar was ear-splitting. As Inspector Norman and Lodrick John struggled on the ground other fist-fights had broken out on nearby Abercromby Street, and inside Brunswick Square; and on the northern side of the Red House there was a struggle between a part of the crowd and some of Inspector Empson's men, and here the policemen were using their batons wildly. Three people lay on the ground bleeding from baton blows. On the southern side of the square, near the entrance to Trinity Cathedral, the woman who had taken Inspector Norman's gun was asking a few people how to use it. Nobody knew how to use it. Joel, who found himself over on this side now, said, 'It's just like a gun. You know if it's loaded?' The woman did not know. Joel took the gun to see. A policeman was approaching, and Joel handed back the gun to the woman. The woman, seeing the policeman, said, 'Take it and run.' Joel could hardly bring himself to run. He felt it was too undignified. He had never run from the police in his life. But when the policeman drew near and made a lunge for him, Joel sprinted off towards Frederick Street and got lost in the crowd.

The policeman smiled. He said to himself, 'That is not Mr Joel, the wharf police? He even wearing the uniform. Tomorrow he'll tell me good what he was doing with a police revolver.'

◆

Big Lodrick John and Inspector Norman were still on the ground and the crowd which surrounded them was calling on Big Lodrick to beat Norman to death. But all of a sudden Norman got his boots under Big Lodrick's belly, and he suddenly and frantically kicked from the waist and he had Big Lodrick falling heavily beside him. Then he whipped out his whistle and blew, and although at the same instant he was hit by a big stone which knocked him over, about a dozen armed policemen rushed towards the place. The crowd broke and fled.

◆

In the street just in front of the Red House there was a fierce battle going on. The crowds were stoning the policemen and there were a few policemen throwing stones themselves. They were furiously pelting stones into the crowd.

233

Major Rooks was standing in the tower and the key man in the whole fight was standing not too far from him. He asked Major Rooks, 'Anybody find the JP yet? Bowen? Bowen the warden?'

Despite the gravity of the situation, every time Major Rooks looked at his companion he had to stifle a laugh. He said inside him, 'You are really looking like a bloody clown.' Aloud, he said, 'No, we can't find Bowen. I don't know why the hell they can't get somebody else to read the Riot Act!'

'They cannot. It must be a JP.'

Major Rooks was overwrought. He simply said to himself, 'Yes, Lady Wrightson.' Then he said, 'So if one can't find a JP and it's life and death – I mean I know it has to be a JP but it doesn't make sense!'

'But that's British law.'

'It's British law that has us in this bloody mess. And now outside over there it's the law of the jungle. I can't understand it but both Empson and Peake went looking for Sidney Bowen, and not one of them can find him. I wonder where the hell Inspector Norman's gone off to. Anyway, Colonel Brake is the man to decide.'

'We have to get out of this place.'

'Yes, but you know we can't move until the Riot Act is read. We can't shoot, we don't dare to shoot. I know you want to get out of here quick. I also. But remember it's you who have us in this situation. God forbid! You think you dare escape from here without the soldiers having to shoot to defend us? Try it! Even though you're dressed up as a woman and with all that powder and rouge, they'd recognise you and tear you to bits. In fact, you are the man they want! That's why we've got to get the Riot Act read.'

'Well then give me up to them and cut out the fuss.'

Rooks glared at the Director of Public Works, and then he screamed, 'Honourable Walsh Wrightson, will you shut up!'

◆

Inside Woodford Square, the mob wanted to lynch Holder. They were stalking him. He had five policemen with him but he was not afraid. Even if he had had none with him he would not have been afraid. He had his gun fully loaded, and the bayonet fitted to it was shining, but he didn't like to see the bayonet looking like that. He wanted to see it red. Red with blood. He had never really seen blood dripping from a bayonet, and the more the crowd stalked him and eased up on him it was the more he grew mad and wanted to stain the bayonet red.

As the crowd swelled in the square, Holder, who had moved back some distance from the fountain, became furious. He called one of the policemen. When the policeman went back he removed the blanks he had in his gun and replaced them with a live cartridge. The crowd saw this and realised what the situation was, and instead of continuing to move forward it suddenly began to ease back. The other policemen laughed. But Holder neither laughed nor looked back at them. All the time in his mind he was praying for the Riot Act to be read. Although it would be exciting to him to hear screams and to see people tumble and to hear people beg for their lives, the most exciting thing for him at that time would be to find that woman who had rejected him. He glanced towards the tower where Rooks was, and he opened out his palms and then he tried to act as though he was holding something like a newsheet in front of his face. What he was trying to say was: 'What is the matter – why can't you read the Riot Act?'

His mind was on Eva. He had spotted her once, earlier today. He did not know what happened since, he did not know where she had gone. He let two of his policemen continue moving back the people to the western gate – the gate facing the Red House, and he followed the little crowd that was backing off to the south-western gate. Here on one side was Trinity Cathedral, on the other was the southern end of the Red House, and in front, in a diagonal across the street, was the fire brigade station. This whole place seemed to be on the boil and indeed boiling over. There was a lot of fighting out there.

No sooner did Sergeant Holder emerge from the gate here than he had to duck. A big hunk of blue flagstone almost took off his head. He charged the crowd immediately, and as that part of the crowd scattered, there was a cry, 'Run, Eliza, run!' and a young girl dashed across to the footpath on the other side and made towards Trinity Cathedral. Sergeant Holder chased after her. As he was closing in she dodged him round a tree and swung back on to the pavement, but as she was going to plunge and disappear into the throng of people, someone cried, 'Why you don't go in Trinity Cathedral, the devil can't go there.'

There was uproar in the street. When Eliza had dodged the sergeant around the bayleaf tree, he had slipped and fallen, and although luckily the gun did not go off he had a twisted bayonet. The crowd had laughed and roared and he had got up, furious. Eliza, confused when she was told to run to the cathedral, turned to bolt up the street and another policeman chased her. She turned back and ran through the path again straining to reach the cathedral door. She did not know Sergeant Holder was still in the path. When he saw her coming he made a dash for her. There was nothing she could do. She could not turn back. As she stopped short to plead with him he ran the bayonet through her belly. The crowd cried, 'Oh God!'

A constable said, 'Sergeant, they didn't read the Riot Act yet.'

The sergeant said, 'And why she attacked me?'

◆

At the moment there was no side of the Red House that did not have violence. As the crowd saw most of the police drawn to the eastern and southern sides of the Red House there was a barrage of stone-throwing at the western end. But here was Police Headquarters and Colonel Brake, with a police escort, reached it and brought out the few remaining policemen who had been left to protect it. Nobody could tell what happened to Superintending Sergeant Taitt who was in charge of this side. As police and soldiers tried to arrest people there was a lot of fighting in the street and the police continued to fire shots into the air. The rioting had gone too far. Colonel Brake, with his hair flung about his face, and with the grimace of the devil, was about to cry, 'Shoot to kill,' when a stone knocked him over in the road.

Although there was pushing and scuffling too on the northern side of the Red House, this was the quietest part. But this was not the part for Greasy Pole. All the policemen knew him and as sure as the light of day he was going to be arrested and beaten up and shoved back into the Royal Jail. But he had a job to do and he was not taking the slightest risk of being shoved back there before he did this job. So the northern side was no side for him. Nor the western side where there was a lot of blood in the street and a lot of policemen, who, the way he looked at it, were forming the fool. The best side was the eastern side, not so much near the fire brigade station where the crowd was heaving back and forth, and where there was a lot of police attention, but in front of the eastern door, facing the square.

236

At the moment the biggest crowd was here, for there were many members of the Legislative Council who were still inside, especially those who knew they were not popular with the crowd.

Greasy Pole had no idea who was still inside the Red House, nor did he care. He might have been glad to know that the key man, Walsh Wrightson, was still inside. For although Wrightson was disguised as a woman he was in no hurry to risk his life, and without the Riot Act read, anything could happen. Greasy Pole also did not know that Governor Sir Alfred Maloney had not left yet, for Colonel Brake would not take the responsibility to let him go before the Riot Act was read. Greasy Pole was wildly thinking of one thing, doing the job. For the greatest noise was here and he knew that as sure as tallow grease and cartwheel here was the part which was going to have the hot action soon. But not before his action. He did not even need all his appliances this morning. He had his screwdriver and his pliers in his back pocket and as the sea of people raged around him he eased and pushed his way and he knew all he had to avoid was the grey and black police uniform.

He reached right up to the big door. There were two policemen whom he could see at the Brunswick Square gate before him and he felt the need to get them active so they would rush the crowd and have the wave of people hit the door and then heave back to the street. Amidst the cries and curses and shrieks of confusion, and amidst the hellish screams of the crowd came a swish. The stone Greasy Pole pelted across the street was so well directed that it nearly knocked off one of the policemen's helmet, but it hit a man on the head. Nothing like a cry of pain could be heard in that din, but as the man fell and the police tried to clear the crowd, with the crowd rushing back then heaving forward, Greasy Pole deftly opened the door and slipped in. As the door opened dozens of people rushed into the Red House but Greasy Pole went straight to the Registrar's desk. The Registrar's desk was full of books and papers and he struck a match. He lit paper in several sections and made sure it was well ablaze, for he knew he would now be in the full embrace of the law. He could hear the police already in the next room. He got out of the Registrar's office, and crept on the floor behind a desk and then he saw the full light of day. It was the open front door with even more people rushing in. He unbuttoned his shirt and as he rushed out and a policeman, taken unawares, made a grab at him, he left his shirt in the policeman's hands, and he was outside and in the crowd.

He was happy, and there was a great grin of satisfaction on his face. Not so much because he had escaped the police but because he had finally done that which he had been aching to do. He wondered where Eva was. Wherever she was she would soon be seeing. He felt relieved and fulfilled but the moment he truly felt ecstasy was when somebody cried, 'Smoke!' And shortly afterwards, amidst the confusion, there was a distinct crackling. Then there was the cry of 'Fire!' from the police. Greasy Pole, bare-backed, was by now across the road. There was a stampede and people on that side were running for the square. Greasy Pole was already in the square.

30

As soon as the Red House was set alight Major Rooks got his soldiers out. Justice of the Peace Alfred Sydney Bowen, seeing the smoke, frantically searched for Colonel Brake. Within five minutes they found each other and Bowen read the Riot Act. He had been reluctant all the time, and hiding, but now he was glad to read it, and when he had read it, Colonel Brake got a loudspeaker and cried to the policemen to shoot to kill. As the crowd fled, the colonel sent Inspector Norman and Superintending Sergeant Peake with their armed soldiers to protect the fire brigade because he was sure the crowd was keeping the fire brigade away. Because it was passing strange that the Red House was alight for what seemed ten minutes now and Darwent had not brought out the fire brigade yet. When the companies of the inspector and the superintending sergeant came to the fire brigade station there was a huge crowd, and as the policemen fired their rifles and soon had three people lying on the street, the crowd fled, and the fire brigade was free and without hindrance. But there was nobody there to command the fire brigade men, who were ready. There was nobody there. The crowd of people were cheering when they saw this.

Flames were beginning to burst through the roof at the middle and northern sides of the building. The police were furious and people were running everywhere, and every now and then there were the cracks of rifles. There was nobody now on St Vincent Street. The boy, Stamford Lord, who had returned, all bruised and swollen, threw a few stones and had run up St Vincent Street when the Riot Act was read. And now he had the courage to come down the street to watch the Red House on fire. He came down just a little below Duke Street, from where he could see the column of smoke billowing up and sometimes a flicker of red inside the black smoke. Then he eased down to the solicitor-general's office which was just before Knox Street. He was definitely going no further because with the Red House in flames the police would shoot just for wickedness. He leaned up against the wall with a big smile on his face. Suddenly he saw

239

a policeman walking up the street and his blood ran cold. The policeman stopped then cocked his rifle and aimed. Stamford Lord began to beg for his life. The policeman pulled the trigger, and when Stamford Lord fell, the policeman looked for a stone and put it into his hand.

As soon as the Riot Act was read an armed escort led Sir Alfred Maloney out of the building, as well as someone else behind him who the crowd thought was his wife, although they did not see his wife come to the debate. Inspector Empson, who headed the escort, could not help stifling a laugh every time he glanced at Walsh Wrightson.

Because of the police shooting, in little time there was no crowd to be seen around the Red House, although there was quite a group of people who sought refuge in the square. Brake had given the order not to shoot anyone in the square, and in fact not to shoot at anyone that wasn't attacking the Red House. People were afraid and trembling because a few were lying dead on Abercromby Street, and there was one on Knox Street, and there were two near Brunswick Square, lying fairly close to the cathedral. One of these two corpses was the young girl Eliza Bunting, and the other was a burly man who people hardly called anything else but Big Lodrick. So the people who were in Brunswick Square were trembling, although Colonel Brake had gone there himself with a loudspeaker and told them they would not be attacked and they had nothing to fear once they left the Red House alone and let the police do their work. He warned them it was beyond his powers to ensure their safety if they attacked the Red House.

Colonel Brake did not stay in Brunswick Square more than two minutes because he was frantic to find Walter Darwent. He did not know if Darwent was kidnapped and beaten and even killed by the crowd. Or abducted and taken away, or was in the Red House and overcome by smoke, or perished in the fire. For he could not believe it was possible the fire brigade chief would refuse to put the fire out. Despite the problems with him Darwent was not a man like that. As the colonel crossed the street towards the fire brigade station it occurred to him that he had heard of some plot to take Darwent, but he was confused and he was not sure now what exactly he had heard, whether it was in respect of Darwent or whether it was not about Wrightson. It must have been about Wrightson, he told himself, because nobody knew there would be fire in the Red

House. As he reached the fire brigade station and saw the blank faces he knew that nobody had seen Darwent.

He asked Major Rooks, 'Did you have your men search his room?'

'We went to his compound. His wife and two children are there but she said she does not know where he is. When they woke they did not see him. She is sure he was kidnapped.'

Colonel Brake said, 'You said his family is there?'

'Yes. His wife is in tears.'

The sound of the flames roaring in the wind drowned everything. Colonel Brake was confused and did not know what to do. He realised now that as much as he had been planning for Lazare and Maresse-Smith and the rest of the agitators, they had been planning for him. For they got someone to set fire to the Red House while kidnapping the fire brigade chief. The more the colonel stood up there and wondered, it was the more helpless he felt and the more desperate he became. Because with every second that went by, flames were devouring the Red House. He turned to the group of fire brigade volunteers that had collected and asked the head volunteer, 'And you fellows have no keys whatsoever to the equipment?'

They had told him at least six times that they had none. They did not even have the key to the fire-engine.

He looked desperately at the Red House. The flames had practically engulfed the whole building. There in front of the fire brigade station the heat was unbearable. It was a good thing they had not waited but had got Wrightson and Governor Maloney out. God, what to do? What to do now? thought Brake. He held on to his hair. It was as if he was going insane. He turned to Major Rooks and Inspector Norman and pleaded with them to say what to do. He turned to the superintending sergeant and again to the major and the inspector and all he saw were blank faces. He collapsed in tears.

241

31

Eva Carvalho was inside the square, running around and looking frantically, and from the time Sergeant Holder spotted her, he stopped in his tracks. He had been on the Frederick Street side of Brunswick Square South, just between the Grell corner and Trinity Cathedral, and he had been elated because right here he had already killed five people trying to escape into Frederick Street. He felt he was a great strategist to stand here, possibly the greatest strategist in Trinidad, and as raging flames consumed the Red House he did not want any other policeman here but himself. He had looked at the Red House and had felt a searing pain, as if the flames were aimed at him, and were destroying the inside of him. He had wondered where was Darwent, what was keeping Darwent. He had run to the fire brigade station only to hear that Darwent was not there, that he had been kidnapped. Although he had hated Darwent he felt bewildered. There was nothing to save the Red House – at least not now! How could they possibly have tricked him and taken Darwent and his carriage away while all the policemen and the soldiers were engaged in trying to keep the mob in check? They must have kidnapped the traitor by way of the southern gate of the compound, the gate that opened out on Queen Street. It was at the point when he thought this, that he had come – with tears welling up in his eyes – to take up duty here. And he had since realised this was the greatest spot for revenge. He had taken one glance at the mob and the Red House in flames and decided if he was the only true British, as Colonel Brake often said, he would avenge British honour and British glory. For never in the history of Trinidad was there was so much shame, so much injury done to the British flag. And he was going to avenge Queen Victoria, and all that was noble, and all that was best in Britain. And he would avenge the dead queen's son, Edward the Seventh by the Grace of God.

Despite the fact that Colonel Brake himself had run around with loudspeaker asking policemen not to attack people in the square, that the square was sanctuary and that they were British, he, Holder, had nothing to do with that. When Colonel Brake had declared that it was not a massacre, and that it was just to preserve law and order that he had given the command to shoot to kill, he was speaking only for himself. He, Tom Holder, was for once going to take his own sanction, he was going to be his own judge, and carry out his own death penalty.

The colonel had acted so wildly, weakly, and nervously, just because he, Holder, had shot Emelda by the fountain. Emelda George, a girl who had hurled sharp words at him earlier on. He did not know what had happened directly after the shooting, but when he had rushed to the fire brigade station to find out what was keeping the fire brigade from coming out, he had heard that after they had dragged the dead woman from the square, there was a big hullabaloo, and Alcazar had gone crazy, complaining to Colonel Brake that it was British law and that if people were rioting, yes, shoot, but that the people in the square were not rioting.

Holder had ground his teeth. He had only wished he had found Alcazar alone and with nobody to see. And it was around this time that he had thought of Queen Victoria and had locked the north-eastern gate and had come and stood here. For the people now remaining in the square did not have a chance. If they came out, trying to escape down Frederick Street, they'd better say their prayers first. To come out at all now, there were only four gates open to them, for he had caused Inspector Empson to block the north-western and western gates, saying Colonel Brake had ordered this to control snipers. Both the northern and north-eastern gates had been closed to prevent access to Pembroke Street. To escape, they, the rioters remaining in the square, would have to either go down Abercromby Street from the south-western gate, or Frederick Street through the eastern or south-eastern, or flee across into Trinity Cathedral from the southern. And it was because he was standing in this position that he had managed to shoot down five people as they tried to leave the square. Because if people were not rioting when they were inside the square, and if the square was sanctuary, then when anyone emerged from the square there was no sanctuary any more, and that person was a rioter.

Sergeant Holder had been trying to keep his eyes on both sides, for since Trinity was between, there was no need to keep a special watch. And there was enough time to fell anyone crossing from the square into the cathedral.

It was while thinking this that he had spotted Eva. She looked so wonderful in the black bodice and the white skirt. He had chuckled to himself, madly. The right colours, darling, he had said to himself. Yes, the right colours.

The constant roar of the flames seemed to get him more crazed, and now as Holder wheeled around with his gun he felt he wanted to shoot to kill everybody. He was keeping his eyes on Eva all the time. Now as he walked towards the Trinity Cathedral gap, wheeling round every now and then, and continuing walking, he noticed that she was talking agitatedly with a fat woman in red, and then when he recognised the fat person he said to himself, 'Oh, is you? I like you paymie and you pone, girl. And especially you benay sugar cake. You could make them as good as you could throw stones. I don't know what I'll do with you today, girl. You in flaming red. Red for fire. But red for lucky, and red for glory, and even red for victory, but red for blood, too. I don't know what I'll do with you today. But you partner wearing the right colours.'

He shifted a little to the western side, to a point where the leaves of the trees obscured him from the square. When he raised his head a little to the left he saw the raging flames of the Red House. The heat was terrible and he was sweating. He stood up there on the alert. Then a thought came to his mind and he laughed as a madman. It was a sentence that came to his mind. He said to himself, 'Line, boy. You know poetry!' Then he said the line again, aloud: 'Somebody have to pay for the heat of this day.' Then he realised this had come from no poem, this was his own line. Sergeant Holder laughed again and ground his teeth.

◆

On the northern side of the square, almost obliquely facing Trinity Cathedral, was Dr Pollonais's office. It was just beside Pembroke Street, which in fact was directly opposite the cathedral. Dr Pollonais, whom the police thought was brave, was in the veranda looking up and down the street. The police had not too long ago shot a boy at the street corner, and it appeared the boy had been trying to flee to Dr Pollonais's house. Dr Pollonais was furious the police had done that. He and the man visiting had just come out to the veranda after a lull in the shooting, and it was just at this precise time that the body of the boy was being removed. Inspector

Norman saw the two men and tried to order them both back inside and they both defied him. Norman had stood there in wonderment.

Inspector Norman stood staring in amazement not only because these were two exceptionally brave men standing there, men who were not afraid to be shot, but mainly because of the man in the white, frilly shirt, and the black cravat, whose face was lined with fury.

Inspector Norman came through the gate and up to the veranda. Looking towards Dr Pollonais's friend, he said, 'Am I seeing right? I understood you were not in town.'

There was silence and a cold hard stare. Dr Pollonais was so angry he just turned his back and walked back inside.

Inspector Norman said, 'I am glad if you were out of town, for it is better than where they would have put you. You know they were scouring Port-of-Spain for you?'

The man did not answer.

The inspector said, 'I personally was not looking for you. I know you are a man of peace.' Then seeing the man he was talking to looking bitterly at the flames, he said, 'You will not speak, but don't be angry with me, I am just keeping law and order. I did not destroy the Red House. It was your mob.'

From the veranda of Dr Pollonais's house there was an unrestricted view of the flames at the northern end of the Red House. Inspector Norman looked and saw them billowing. He said, 'Since you will not speak, I will say no more. You see how my face is bruised and my teeth are shattered? This came from the scuffling I had. I took a lot of blows. But don't think I am glad of what happened. This is a terrible situation. The worst thing now is that the Red House is allowed to burn like this because Darwent cannot be found.'

'Darwent can't be found?' The man in the frilly shirt seemed to have suddenly come to life.

'No, Mr Lazare.'

There was silence.

Inspector Norman said, 'Someone said they kidnapped him. At first someone joked and said he ran away with his – he ran away with his friend.' He had been going to say he heard Darwent had run away with his washerwoman.

'He ran away with which friend?'

'I just heard that. I don't know, Mr Mzumbo Lazare. But that is gossip. They kidnapped him.'

Inspector Norman was looking all around while talking. The whole of the northern side was blocked off and the police had orders to shoot on sight. His heart was racing. He did not know what to think. He was afraid that another policeman would see Lazare and seize him. All the time he was thinking this, and now he said, 'Mr Lazare, even if you are not afraid of bullets will you go back inside from the heat?'

Lazare looked at him, and Inspector Norman could see the face soften. The Inspector felt thrilled, but he did not show it. He said to himself, 'Lazare is the only one of the natives I can stand. Because he really does not hate white people.' Then forgetting Lazare, he thought, 'Come, attention now, Inspector. Be on the alert. You have to be on the alert to save lives and you have to watch out for snipers.' Then he went out of the gate.

◆

When Lazare went inside Dr Pollonais said, 'What he told you? He told you they kidnapped Darwent, I suppose?'

'Yes.'

'I'm sure that is a job they cooked up. I'm sure it's a conspiracy. They never liked him. Because of the washerwoman they must have—'

Lazare said in anguish, 'I do not know. Oh God I do not know!'

'And they letting the damn Red House burn. I know he didn't run away with his washerwoman although they bound to put that in front. He didn't run away with her because I'm sure sure I saw her in the square.'

'You saw Eva?'

'Right there in the square.'

Lazare did not say anything, but he was happy and grateful that she was safe. The Red House was burning and it tore at his heartstrings. Since the fire broke out he was of the opinion they had kidnapped Darwent, for he knew Darwent would not let the Red House burn. Now he was sure that this was what had happened, and Darwent had not run away with Eva. At the moment the place looked dark. Everywhere thick black smoke obscured the sky completely. One could hardly breathe, and the two men coughed all the time. Every now and again came the crack of rifles.

246

32

Eva spotted the red dress far to the other side of the square and she ran towards her friend. When she reached she was out of breath. She said, 'Oh God, at last I meet you. I was looking for you all the time. I can't find Greasy Pole at all and we have to go because I don't want them to find Walter by the turnpike.'

Lolotte Borde was overjoyed to see Eva in this moment of confusion, but she was also taken aback. Things were very serious and bewildering and maybe it was only to be expected if Eva was now out of her mind. But she was extremely worried about her friend. She listened but she could make no sense at all of what Eva was saying. She said, 'Eva, take you time. What you telling me?'

'Oh, I see. You don't know. Yes, that's right. I so excited.' She looked round and whispered, 'Look, I'll explain when we going in the carriage—'

'Which carriage? Girl, you right in your head?'

Lolotte Borde was uneasy. There was so much heat in the air but it seemed she was trapped in the square. She had already made an attempt to get into Trinity Cathedral, and a shot just grazed her. She did not even see the policeman. She just heard the crack of the gun and she ran back and it was only afterwards she had seen that a man had fallen. And her forearm had begun to bleed. She asked Eva again, 'You all right? I know this sort of day could make the blood fly in your head. And we can't even see Edgar for comfort and Mzumbo's in Mayaro. You all right, girl? Take your time and talk now.'

Eva said, 'Lolotte, just listen to me. I now realise I didn't tell you before.' She began whispering now: 'Walter – Walter Darwent. Keep your voice right down, eh? Walter taking us to Mayaro. He waiting for us by the turnpike. I told him if Greasy Pole do the job they bound to get crazy and they'd be shooting in the street and when I escape I will be bringing you and Greasy Pole and I want him, Walter, to get us the hell out of here to Mayaro even if Mayaro is a thousand miles; and he said he'd be waiting for us at the turnpike on St Joseph Road. I was looking for you to tell you it's time to get out, because Walter taking us to Mayaro and that place so far it bound to be safe from these killers. And Walter already agreed and he said he'd be waiting for us at the turnpike on St Joseph Road. I was looking for you for half-an-hour and now we mustn't wait no more, because Greasy Pole, I don't know if they arrest him or where he is or if they shoot him for setting the fire. Clement would be in Mayaro by the next round-island steamer and I ain't see him for about three days, but when we was chatting last week he said if the worst come to the worst today and police on the loose let's get to Mayaro right away because Mayaro is far and Mayaro is the most wonderful place. But we ain't talking no more till we get in the carriage. I don't want them to find Walter waiting there. Let's go.'

She moved off running. Lolotte didn't quite understand. She had several questions to ask. But the main thing Eva was trying to say was that Walter Darwent was waiting for them by the St Joseph turnpike and would be taking them to Mayaro. That did not make much sense but then nothing was making sense today. At least she could see that Darwent was not at the fire brigade station and the Red House was left as a pillar of flames in the heat of this day. So where was Darwent, then? So it was either Eva was off her head or there was some little bit of sense in what she was trying to say. She did not know. If Eva was going to the St Joseph turnpike she, Lolotte Borde, was going too. For with the slaughter she had seen on the street today she wasn't going to remain anywhere near Port-of-Spain.

She was already blowing hard. As she looked, the light, skin-and-bone frame of Eva Carvalho, was already at the gate and, now setting out to reach her she felt as if she was rolling and tumbling and stumbling and panting. But when she lifted her head to see where Eva had reached she stopped in panic and terror. A policeman with a rifle was confronting Eva. Lolotte screamed.

◆

Sergeant Holder looked at Eva trembling in front of him. He said, 'Oh, it's you? Where you going?'

He had the gun lifted and pointing at her.

She said, 'Tom, please don't kill me.'

He said, 'Why you stay in the square so long? I was waiting for you here all the time.'

'Oh God, Tom, please. I know you was waiting for me. I'll come back to you anytime.'

He heard a shout and looked towards the corner and saw that it was Colonel Brake on the pavement opposite to the fire brigade station. The colonel was frantic, shouting and putting up his hand, meaning for Holder to wait, not to shoot. Holder looked towards Colonel Brake. He was going to wait. Yes. He wanted to wave back and say he was going to wait, just give him half a second and then he would wait. Then he turned the gun to Eva again and pulled the trigger.

When Lolotte Borde saw Eva fall she shrieked and she took off running again, and she ran with the same speed towards the south-west gate which opened on Frederick Street. And, as though she herself was going out of her mind, she kept saying, turnpike, turnpike, turnpike; and when, with the crowd scattering, she reached the crossing with King Street, she turned left and made for St Joseph Road. She ran frantically, bumping and panting, although she wasn't sure she would be travelling anywhere or doing anything, she just came here because Eva had said turnpike, and her own mind was in something of a trance. She wasn't sure if it was real and if Eva had really said this but she thought Eva had told her that Walter Darwent, the fire brigade chief, would be at the St Joseph Road turnpike waiting to take them to Mayaro. To take Eva and to take herself and Greasy Pole. It must be all a dream. She put up her hands to feel for the tray on her head, but there was no tray. She cried in anguish, 'Edgar, oh God what happening, boy? If you was only here to tell me what is what!' When she was nearing the turnpike she knew there would be nothing there, but she felt she had to get there just for Eva's sake. She was sure there would be nothing there, but as she turned the corner and came up on the turnpike itself she nearly crashed against the carriage.

◆

Walter Darwent looked down. He was furious. 'It's only now you all could have made it? Only now? I was scared stiff they found me here. Suppose they had found me? It's a good hour that fire's burning. Good heavens! Look at the black smoke. I can't see, Eva's with you or is she still behind? I take it that you are Lolotte Borde? Good Christ, if you are all here please jump inside and let us go. Wasn't Greasy Pole to be here too? He's here or not? And you mean Eva's still behind? Lord, put a hand! Tell me, I still have to wait? It's almost two o'clock and we have to go. Mayaro is about a thousand miles. Well, jump in, Lolotte. You ran so fast you left Eva and Greasy Pole behind? And they are so thin. Look, if you could see them just signal and tell them to hurry up. But please don't call. God, I don't want these people to catch me here. You could see them at all? Hurry them up and let's go. Mayaro is at least one thousand miles.'

He looked at Lolotte with frantic eyes. Lolotte could not say anything.